DUSTER

DUSTER

Andrew Howell

Rev. date: 06/13/2018

To order additional copies of this book, contact:
Xlibris
1-800-455-039
www.Xlibris.com.au
Orders@Xlibris.com.au
697670

Saturday night I was downtown,
working for the FBI

—The Hollies, "Long Cool Woman (In a Black Dress)"

To my father, Kenneth William Howell, US Navy Seabee, retired.

Thanks, Pop, for all you did for our country. Thanks for not letting me spend the night in jail when I was 15. Thanks for taking me around the world, and thanks for everything you did for me and for all of us.

I have one question for you, sir. Why, for most of my young life, were your instructions, words of wisdom, direction, discipline, ideas, and reasoning so ridiculous and frustrating to me as I was running around the world? But then, sir, when I hit the age of 35, you suddenly became a brilliant man. It's a pondering question indeed in the mystery of my life...

By the way, in Florida, when you tore my butt up one day at the tender age of 11 for not mowing the lawn, I was a bit miffed, so I was mowing the grass like a madman and not paying much attention to the task at hand when I hit a big fat Florida yard toad. The toad got the worse end of the deal as I sort of made a huge bloody mess of toad gore everywhere when the Lion lawn mower started blowing toad blood and offal in a six-foot circle all over the side of the yellow house. It took me twice as long to clean the blood and guts off as it would have to just mow the lawn properly. Maybe you knew; maybe you didn't, although there was not much you missed in those days.

Thanks for the work ethic, the patience, and the time, Pop. You never missed one of my football, baseball, or basketball games. I never paid much attention back then. I get it now. Love you, Dad.

Also noted in this dedication are James Houghton and Sandy. Gents, you have given me the idea to create this story at the rugby sevens in 2016 after a discussion about guns, the Ghoul Bridge, Skeleton Creek, Oklahoma girls, and the Six-Mile Bar in Logan County, Oklahoma. It's taken a little over a year to finish it up, but here it is.

A special dedication to Gerd Ortloff and honorable mention to Nick Cooper, for you two gentlemen gave me the feedback and pushed me to write and complete this book instead of *Children of the Night* as my mate Dave Raye suggested. Thanks, gents, for all the times you read my stories and gave me honest feedback on which ones were good and, well, not so good. And as original members of the THE AD FIVE, you certainly deserve some billing.

Gerd has spent time in Oklahoma, and he gets it. Plus, the Union Carbide connection has surprised even him, which doesn't happen often. My dad has worked for Union Carbide in the uranium mines after he had gotten out of the Navy, and the story has just come together.

None of my books can truly go out without a mention to Davy Cairns, and The Grand Conqueror, Grant Vincent. You have seen it all begin, gents. Let's see where it all goes.

Ian Brown, you deserve a shout-out also, buddy. I appreciate your time and effort. You always provided a detailed critique of everything I have sent you. A few of those critiques I would rather forget as I am sure you would also rather forget a few of my stories.

Paul Bayley, sir, nothing else needs to be said except thank you.

Oh yeah, shout-out to my "little" brother, Josh, who stands 6'4", currently lives in Oklahoma, and drives an oil field service truck. He will understand the story. He has also seen the remnants and remains what is left . . . and what is coming.

INTRODUCTION

Another continued conversation.

I had three choices for this next book, so shall we have a discussion about why I picked *Duster*?

Since I am the aspiring writer, it is—in the end—my choice to choose what I write. You, as the reader, have your choice to choose what you read; and by the way, if you are reading this, I truly thank you and appreciate your time to read my humble book. Davy Raye has said *Children of the Night* is the story I should really focus on and publish, but I have gotten motivated with *Duster*. As I am usually working on several stories at once, maybe *Children of the Night* is coming out next. The Grand Conqueror agrees. He has said it's the right move for now to do with *Duster*.

Many of you told me my introductions and conversations are too long and tedious and that I should reduce the rhetoric and just introduce the story. I obviously have not listened. You see, it's my prerogative as a writer to set the tone and capture the moment in history that this book and story is about and the moment in time that I *have written* the story. I choose to exercise that prerogative with this introduction.

"Saturday night I was downtown, working for the FBI." The line, of course, is from the song "Long Cool Woman (In a Black Dress)" by the Hollies. Since the FBI plays a major part in the story and I love the song, I think it is the most appropriate opening line for the book.

Duster is a story about life in the oil field boomtowns during the late '70s and mid-'80s. It brings to life the construction crews, roughnecks, roustabouts, geotechs, and drillers who go along with the industry. It also takes a dive into the dark side of that day and age and includes racketeering, gambling, guns, girls, and the wild life that many of these people have led. They are mainly good old boys and girls who are hardworking, hard-partying, and loyal to one another.

The story covers the United States from Wyoming, Montana, Colorado, Utah, Texas, all the way down to Mexico and is focused mainly in Oklahoma, where most of my oil field production and safety career experience really began. Much more occurred in Oklahoma during the time *Duster* is about, so very much more than just oil production, racketeering, and gun battles. I have tried to capture a bit of the "so much more" in the tale.

In the story, I often spend lots of time describing the clothes the ladies and gents are wearing because it was the cowboy-cowgirl 1985 period, and the clothes during that period were really amazing. Often, the outfits the characters are wearing add to the tale when the scene of the story is happening. There is a reason for this, just like there is a reason my introductions are so lengthy. The details tell a story, and in this story, a lot of the clothes make the scene. The country bars in Oklahoma, along with the ladies who wear them, really are stunning. My dad's wife, Sherry Howell, still wears many of the same type of Western outfits that I write about in the story. You're looking good in them, Sherry.

So to set the tone for the Oklahoma cowgirls a bit, let me introduce you to a music group called Sweethearts of the Rodeo that were hot from about 1984 to 1991. They actually got the name of their group from an old Byrds song. Christine and Janis Oliver were the twosome and the bandleaders. Janis was once married to a punk named Vince Gill. In the late '70s, they had a band called Pure Prairie League, which had some notoriety around small colleges in those days. Vince was the lead singer and got most of the attention, but Janis and Christine were the real talents and wrote most of the songs and music. Vince made a grave error by hooking up with Amy Grant, and the girls said, "You know what? Who needs him?" They dumped his butt and the band, went out on their own, and tore the world of country music apart. Pure Prairie League lasted less than six months after they left.

OK, to be fair with Vince and Amy, they did some great things for a lot of organizations and people. It's just my personal opinion that he boned it up. No one compares to Christine and Janis in this music genre.

Sweethearts of the Rodeo—just go on YouTube, and watch six of their videos, preferably in this order: "Satisfy You," "Since I Found You," "Midnight Girl in a Sunset Town," "Chains of Gold," "Gotta Get Away," "Como Se Dice." Look at the clothes that they are wearing, and then you might understand why I spend so much time describing the clothes in the story. The Oklahoma ladies in *Duster* wear the same style of clothes. You can't help but stare and appreciate them—well, I couldn't anyway.

BTW, everything the Sweethearts of the Rodeo sing is brilliant. Their look, their style, their lyrics, and their music are incredible.

Now about the story, While it is written in the first person, it's fiction based; and of course, I have *not* done the things I write about in the book—well, not most of them anyway. It's written to entertain, and while I have used a lot of the local history and what has occurred in the area and the time to add to my fictional tale, it is just predominantly fiction.

The writing style switches from Western philosophic to redneck hick, depending on the scene and what I am trying to say. In the end, it is—as all my work—meant to entertain and possibly enlighten just a bit.

Several of the scenes in the story are total fiction, as I have mentioned, but three of them are pretty much the gospel truth. I lived them; I own them. It's up to you, as the readers, to decide which ones those three are. Those of you who know me as a safety guy will realize how it all started and recognize at least one of the scenes.

Another bit of truth, I was two days away from being indicted or at least detained and interviewed by the FBI in Oklahoma, and I never even had a clue it was coming. I found out six months after I left. I just got lucky. It was a classic case of the wrong place at the right time. The feds were just rounding anybody and everybody up, and I was an anybody. It made for a great addition to the story line though.

While I introduce several colorful players into this tale of intrigue and good-old-boys network, one of my favorite characters in the book is Yona, a very attractive half-Cherokee bartender who works at Tumbleweeds in Stillwater, Oklahoma. To truly appreciate and understand Yona, you should watch two videos that are both available on YouTube. I have added the links out of habit. The first is the song "Indian Reservation" by Paul Revere and the Raiders (https://www.youtube.com/watch?v=SraaOCwRnbA&list=RDMMSraaOCwRnbA). The female singer, the Indian goddess who is dancing, *is* Yona and the inspiration for the character. The second one is going back a year or two and is the song "Half Breed" by Cher (https://www.youtube.com/watch?v=Z6E98ZRaU1s).

Another great character is the elderly rancher Dave Raymond. Dave is a compilation of about three different people I know or have known for a long time, and he's quite a clever character.

Then of course, we have the "Long Cool Woman (In a Black Dress)" (https://www.youtube.com/watch?v=CUdhVQSbsvc). You're going to have to read to find out who she is. It doesn't take long though, as I give you plenty of clues.

Add to this Mary Chapin Carpenter's video "Down at the Twist and Shout," and that pretty much sets the scene for the day and age of the times in Oklahoma that the story is set in (https://www.youtube.com/watch?v=SuapCENFM2U).

Also, when you read the epilogue of *Duster*, you might be able to appreciate the bonus short story a wee bit more. "The Ad Five"—this was the story I wrote in two weeks, being inspired by several elements. It all started with the five guys, including myself, who lived at the hotel in nearby apartments and hung out at the local pub. During one of our conversations, we took a deep dive into the realm of possibilities.

I have been paddling that canoe for a while now and have decided to give the story a go. It captures David Icke's theory of alien reptilians and touches on the Illuminati (or whatever you wish to call them). It begins and ends. Interesting. And again, it is *all fiction*, even the scenes in the bar. Just good crack.

Well, it looks like this may be my shortest introduction ever. So I will leave it at this and wait to hear your thoughts, dear readers, on this latest yarn I have spun.

In the words of Three Dog Night *"Well I never been to Heaven… But I been to Oklahoma"*

Thank you for reading the book.

PS: Possible other books coming up next—*Children of the Night* (thanks, Davy Raye), *Black Dove* (thank you, Davy Cairns), *The Night Rider* (that's just me), *Armageddon with a Six Iron* (thank you, Vince, Billy, Davy for tales of Turkey), *Die Einflüsse* (thanks, Gerd), *Grandpa's Tall Tales* (thank you, Billy and Jacob Greer), *The Realm of Possibilities* (for this one, I have to thank all of you), *Victories' Secret Realm and Other Tales* (thank you, Ziva, Valeria, and Veronica).

I also have eighteen short stories that might need to be put into publication in the near future. But as you know, Paul Bayley, Ian Brown, Grand Conqueror, and Davy Cairns—well some of them— just may not need to be published.

As a reminder, I recalled what my son Jarod said when I published *Get Out of Denver*, and I was concerned I might somehow offend my children or family members with something I had written. His response was, which his brothers Morgan and Logan concurred with, "Dad, don't worry about your stories embarrassing us. No one is going to buy them anyway."

Well, angel boy, shall we see?

1

The headline in the *Oklahoma City Herald* read TWO KILLED IN SOUTH KINGFISHER COUNTY AS THEY FLEE FROM FEDERAL AGENTS. The story line read:

> Early Friday morning two Oklahoma men were killed by State Police and FBI agents after a lengthy vehicle chase leading through multiple counties. The men were wanted for questioning in the hijacking of several crude oil tankers in the Chickasaw oil fields East of Cimarron and the Elk City area. The chase began when State troopers attempted to pull over a crude oil tanker that had been reported as stolen. The men sped away in an effort to escape and were pursued by law enforcement for over an hour. The chase ended when the driver of the stolen tanker was shot dead causing the truck to tip over on an oil field lease road in South Kingfisherisher County near Skeleton Creek Bridge. The passenger tried to continue on foot and fired at the police repeatedly. The Police then returned fire also killing the second man. The men are believed to be part of a large crude oil theft organization that has been operating in Oklahoma, Texas, & Mexico for the past several years . . . names not yet released . . . Ongoing investigation . . . FBI involved . . . local officials . . . potential cases worth over $18 million . . . several indictments have already been served . . . connected to the recent local FBI Raid leaving twenty-seven dead.

The oil field would get in your blood. Well, it did in mine anyway. The summer I turned 16, I started working for a core-drilling company called Connors Drilling in southwest Colorado and Utah. It was killing hard work, but the money was good, and I liked the money. I was a tall, lanky kid hanging out with drillers and roustabouts, and everyone always thought I was older. In between listening to Molly Hatchet, Bob Seger, Sweet, ZZ Top, Foghat, Stevie Ray Vaughan, the Eagles, and Bad Company on cassette tapes, I learned a lot about oil field drilling and construction. I also learned about setting up and tearing down drill rigs and basic roughneck work. I was hooked. Good money for hard work was a fair deal, I thought, and I really covered a lot of ground over the next three summers.

One of my favorite things about working for Connors Drilling was picking up my paycheck every Friday. Connors had a couple of very attractive young ladies who worked in the payroll department at the main office. Lavonne Clifford and Angie Lucero were in their early twenties, and I was smitten by the lassies. They always looked good, always smelled good, and always smiled at me. From that time onward in my life, it seemed like I was in constant search of the ladies' smile, wayward glance, simple eye contact, occasional touch, and other lovely attributes. I became a sucker for a pretty face and was a downright dumbass if there was half a chance that sex might somehow materialize.

Being born in southwestern Colorado, I guess you could say I was a cowboy. I worked on ranches and farms from the time I was 12, and it formed the basis of my work ethic. My folks didn't have a big spread or lots of cattle, but most of my friends did. I didn't have a horse or a pickup truck, but most of my friends did. I did, however, have a god-awful desire to make money, and while hard work was the focus in the beginning, I was soon introduced to several "acceptable" ways to make extra money in the oil field, which would eventually turn into a pattern of making money any way I could. While I was always willing to work hard, I kept my eyes open for possible opportunities, legit or otherwise, to make some extra bank. It was a slippery slope indeed, but I was pretty sharp, and it took several years before I slipped down the muddy banks of damnation into a quagmire of unescapable muck and mire.

Each summer during my early college years, I returned to working in the oil field. As mentioned, I had developed a strong work ethic; but by this time, I wasn't above dropping off a few company hand tools at the pawnshop on a Friday to get drinking and gas money for the weekend. Seldom did I ever pick the tools back up when the weekend was over, and seldom did anyone ever notice the missing tools. The company just bought new ones. Such was the day and age of the booming oil biz back then. Everybody got a wee bit; some got a whole lot more.

Blatant thievery was never really my thing. Some guys would steal generators, welders, cutting torches—hell, I even knew one rig hand who got pissed off, stole a company truck, and sold it down in Mexico. No, wasn't really into the blatant thievery aspect, but I did practice the "borrowing without intent to return" now and again. I was easily affected by the actions of my older peers, and if I liked the blokes and they did it, well, how bad could it be, right?

During those summers of working on rigs, roughnecking, working worm's corner, and constructing pipelines, I would drive the roads between boomtowns like Green River and Rawlins, Wyoming, either as part of a job or searching for a job. I could often hit a rig setup or construction site at 7 a.m., show my driver's license, tell them what I could do, and be working by 10 a.m. That was how it was in the oil boomtown areas during these times. You could be on the run from about anything, have a couple of warrants out for you, and still make some good bank for a few weeks before the company got wind of it and you had to split, or you did some other dumbass stunt and the local LEOs (law enforcement officers) picked you up.

As I started college, I often found myself listening to the deeply dark music tracks of Jim Morrison and the Doors, pondering their jagged intent and the meaning of their music. I learned many of my early lessons in life from the construction guys, drillers, and roughnecks I ran with. Like I said, if I liked the blokes and they did it . . . Well, I could never see myself as a real thug—I mean, like a murderer, drug dealer, or bank robber. I liked to party too much and was too fun of a guy to get into anything that heavy. But I was young and naive, and it took years before I realized I had been rubbing shoulders each day with men who did not have near the moral conviction against those things that I had.

As my work experience grew, the money got better, the women got friendlier in direct proportion to my increasing salary, and my life experience accelerated exponentially until I dropped out of college altogether. At each of my jobs, I would seek out the leaders of each crew to find the ones I could most identify with. These were often hardworking, hard-playing, and very clever men. They lived the real tales of the oil boom days of guns and drugs, prepaid prostitutes, local girl love stories, shootings, gambling, racketeering, and other colorful, often dark slices of life. In many ways, it was a lot like a modern-day Old West to me, and I couldn't get enough. I never saw myself as part of the really bad stuff. In my mind, I was always on the outside of an impenetrable ring, a sort of protective circle that would let me in just enough but never expose me to the true darkness that can come into a man's heart. I always felt sort of shielded for some reason, and I was comfortable with that.

My first introduction to the Federal Bureau of Investigation was outside Green River, Wyoming. I was working for an outfit named Sundown Construction, and the boys on the crew and I became quite fond of the Gordon Lightfoot song of the same name ("Sundown"). In the local bars at night, you would often see us chatting with one another, eyeing up local ladies or rowdies, and we would wink and sing softly to the words of old Gordon. "Sundown, you better take care if I find you been creeping round my back stair."

On this particular night, I was playing poker on a weekend and actually winning for a change. The setup was in the back room of a bar called Rattlesnakes in north Green River. The bar was packed with wild men and women who were kicking up their heels and living for the weekend. Most everyone had cash as we were paid weekly, so money was flowing pretty loose. You could find just about anything you wanted here and often several things you did not want.

The game was fairly high stakes, with invitation-only players in attendance. There were about $10,000 showing round the table, and I was getting good cards. I had caught the eye of a sweet brunette called Brandi (and yes, she was a fine girl), and I knew it was going to be a good night.

What I did not know was that three of the other six people sitting at the table were high on the FBI's Wyoming most wanted list. I mean, seriously, how would I know this? I never went to the post office and never saw the wanted posters. FBI's most wanted? C'mon, really? That was Hollywood crap.

In those days, I never thought about carrying a gun. I always wore boots, and I had a pristine double-edged Arkansas toothpick with a six-inch blade tucked very nicely in a slight sheath attached to my right boot. It was mainly for show, but the ladies liked it. It became one of my best lines for late evening conversations, and I met more than one lovely with the line "Hey, my name is Drew. Would you like to see my shiv?"

It was rare that I was involved in one-on-one disputes or fisticuffs. I was just a popular guy and usually talked my way around issues. Most of my troubles came in big chunks when ten to twenty guys would go at it, and I just happened to be in the vicinity. In these cases, I would usually grab the drunkest guy I could find and swing him around in front of me until the cops came, or the fight otherwise broke up. I learned that this was not an uncommon way to get a solid reputation as a brawling badass without ever really having to brawl or be a badass.

Had I known how my attendance at this card game with the FBI's most wanted lads would eventually affect my life, I truly believed I might have just walked away. However, to do that would mean I would have missed out on Ms. Brandi, and she was really something. Even now looking back, knowing what I now knew—well, life is full of hard choices, so I guess it's often better we don't know what the future holds.

Just after midnight, the mood at the table became a bit serious as the game drew to a close. I had just won a pot of about $1,800 and, by doing so, really pissed off a guy with a ponytail who was wearing John Lennon specs, boots, and a bright blue button-up shirt. He was giving me the bad eye when the place suddenly exploded. Two doors were kicked open, and the place was raided by half a dozen feds. The agent-in-charge (AIC) lead guy was wearing shades, even though it was midnight, when he busted in. They were joined by some Bureau of Alcohol, Tobacco, and Firearms (ATF) guys and some local LEOs.

As the chaos ensued around the room, the AIC shades man started grabbing guys and slamming them around. I was able to grab most of my cash and shove it over to Brandi, who had suddenly materialized next to me. She stuffed it in her shirt and was gone like a ghost. Several fights broke out, and I grabbed a really drunk guy from Cheyenne and started my brawler dance, keeping him between me and the feds.

Then all hell broke loose. The drunk Cheyenne guy pulled out a .45 Colt automatic from his waistband and slammed me upside the head, gashing my temple something fierce. Then he leveled his piece at one of the players from the table and pumped three rounds into him. The FBI shades AIC shot the Cheyenne guy, and I heard reports from at least three other guns, including one booming blast from the firearm of Randall Pederson, a big lean Wyoming state trooper who was blazing away with a .44 Mag.

I dropped to the ground and tried to find some kind of cover. I was in good company as there were several guys and gals trying to do the same thing. There must have been at least a dozen shots fired, and it was, without question, the most intense life scene I had ever been involved in. When the shooting stopped, I saw at least six bodies on the ground oozing blood and not moving.

One of the bodies wore an Absaroka County deputy sheriff's uniform. Another body was the guy sitting across from me at the table, and then there was the drunk Cheyenne guy, also dead as a road-killed cat. I could smell the acrid copper odor of blood and see pools of red mixed up in the sawdust on the floor. Gun smoke hung heavily in the air, and my ears were ringing like a brass band from all the shooting.

After the ER teams hauled away the dead and wounded, the feds carted about ten of us off to the local jail for sorting. I was given the third degree by the AIC shades guy and a couple of his cronies, but I could tell their hearts just weren't in it. I didn't have a clue what was going on and no idea what they were after, and they knew it. They did their best, though, to try to not show me that they knew I did not know. I was beginning to think I was being used as some kind of interrogation training tactical dummy for some junior agents to practice on. After an hour, I was taken back into the holding cell with the rest of them.

After three hours, I was bailed out by my soon-to-be-favorite Wyoming cowgirl, Ms. Brandi. I stayed the night at her place and had rarely been with anyone who rocked my world like the fine woman

Brandi. Like the words from the Looking Glass song "Brandy," I was sure that, along with being a fine girl, she would indeed make a good wife, but my lady was the sea . . . of oil.

After breakfast with Brandi the next day, I stopped by the company field office to see how this was all going to play out. It seemed they chose discretion as the better part, and they gave me my final week's check, and that was that. I was once again just another unemployed oil field drifter. I stayed with Brandi for over a month until most of my money was gone. We went to Cheyenne Frontier Days and spent some time in West Yellowstone at the Montana State eight-ball pool championships. It was four of the best weeks I had ever spent. Not a month would pass for the rest of my life where I would not, at some point, think of the fine Brandi and her smile. As the years passed, she faded a bit; but as the Kid Rock song "All Summer Long" said, I still often find myself thinking, "Man, I'd love to see that girl again."

2

The word got out that the feds wanted to have another chat with me and a couple of the others based on some new intel they had gathered. I just did not see any sense in sticking around to talk with them at all as I had, by now, acquired just enough shade to my past that they might be able to railroad me into a state-sponsored institution should they be so inclined. I got a tip from a friend, and I hitched a ride south with Recco Engineering and Construction Company. They had a contract with Wesco Productions and would be installing 4" to 10" oil and gas transmission lines throughout Colorado and Utah. These lines all brought in feedstock to the small local refineries and process facilities established on the Colorado side, and there may be a solid year's worth of work there.

We worked seven days a week, and the company paid us a $35 per diem, which was high back then. We also got salary, OT, plus completion bonus. Now this was some very good money. After the first month, I had $6,000 in cash, and I decided to join the twentieth century and open a bank account at the Dove Creek State Bank in the one-horse town of Dove Creek, Colorado. After the third month, I bought a three-quarter-ton 1979 Chevy pickup and a new rifle. It was a sweet-shooting .223 Savage Model 110 with a 4 × 12 Leopold dot reticle scope mounted for optics. I also had my .357 Colt Python pistol and figured, for now, that would be a sufficient arsenal to have with me in my wanderings.

We rolled in about a 120-mile radius most weeks as we laid pipelines throughout the high desert mountains and would often change towns every week. Most of the local towns had at least half a dozen bars, and they all liked our business, even if we were a bit rowdy. We usually did the weekends in the western town of Cortez, and we became regulars in Dolores and Durango as well. Drinking booze and smoking dope in the oil field was a common practice in those days, and nobody really paid any attention. If you didn't get busted, wreck some equipment, or hurt anybody, it was no big deal.

The Recco crew consisted of about seventy men and ten women. Seven out of the ten ladies spent a whole lot of time driving around in trucks for the bosses and very little time doing any actual work. Welders would come and go as the work scope increased. Most of them were prima donnas showing up in slick rigs and did nothing but burn rod.

Sometimes a man-and-woman team would show up and work for a month or so, moving with the crews. Just because they came in together, though, was no guarantee whatsoever that they would leave together. It was a rough, rugged, and sometimes ruthless life, and it only appealed to people of a similar vein.

Although I liked the tight jeans and toughness of some of the field ladies, I never really got tangled up with any of them. Most of them had a company man sugar daddy, and it would have been a quick way to wind up jobless. By this time, I was firmly entrenched in the Jimmy Buffett philosophy of "occupational hazard being [when] occupation's just not around," and I was keen on staying employed as long as possible. Besides, the local girls at the bars loved us, so I had options.

Most of the men on our crews treated the ladies well and spent a ton of cash on them. We were good for that renegade streak the farm and ranch girls had in them. We were fit, and almost every night of the week, we were out at the bars for a drink and distraction. Everyone usually had a good time along with some memories, and then we moved on. The local girls went back to their lives, colleges, or boyfriends, and we went to the next job location.

It was not so smooth with some of the married local ladies though. They wanted adventure, often seeking affairs to replace long-lost romance and forgotten dreams. The construction boys were big on both, and few had the moral fortitude to say nay when a smoking hot lady was putting her sexy on them, even if she was married. The silence of many a weekend night at the local hotels was shattered by gunshots when an irate husband kicked open a door to find his wife shacked up with some oil field construction hand . . . or two.

One of the key elements of the work for installing the pipelines was drilling and blasting mountain bedrock to open a trench for the pipe. We had four big pneumatic rock drills that we used to drill into bedrock and then load the holes up with blasting charges. The blast was usually more like a muffled whoof and a cloud of dust, just enough to loosen the rock so it could be removed by the long-armed track hoe excavators. Once the rock was out, we would put sandbags in the trench for bedding and lower the pipe in, tape it, pad it solid, and then backfill the trench.

One Sunday we had a small crew finishing up the blasting in a long run of Rocky Mountain bedrock just on the Colorado-Utah state line. A middle-aged construction foreman named Jack was left in charge of the six of us doing the drilling and blasting work. Jack had his little nipper Amy along for the shift, and we were all working on OT. Amy was a plump twentysomething whom none of us looked twice at, but she sure did it for old Jackie Boy.

We were halfway through with the job by 10 a.m., only having about seventy yards of rock left to drill and load charges in, when Jack called a coffee break to have a chat with us. He pulled out a pint of Jack Daniel's Old Number 7 and passed it around. As I said before, if you didn't get busted, wreck some equipment, or hurt somebody . . . He looked at us like an old soldier would to his mates in a prebattle conference and said, "Now, boys, it's been a good job here in Monticello County, and we just need to finish up this little stretch of blasting and be ready for the rest of the crew to come in tomorrow and place the pipe. This here land belongs to some highfalutin Mormon named J. D. Crowley. Those are his bean fields right next to us here." He jerked his thumb toward 1,800 acres of pristine pinto bean ground as he took a sip and passed the bottle again.

"I, er, uhm . . . I gotta run into town for some stuff, so I am going to leave WeJo [*WeJo* meant Wesley Johns, and his brother was called *Mojo* for Morris Johns] in charge. You guys finish loading the holes, and don't get stupid with the blast as we don't want to mess up ole Crowley's field. I'll be back in a couple of hours to light the charge off. Remember, none of you are licensed blasters, so we all go to the pokey if one of you morons decides to get cute and set the blast off." What he meant was if anybody lit the fuse, *he* would have his middle-aged ass in the hoosegow for some time as he was not supposed to leave us unsupervised while we loaded explosive charges.

Jack took off for town with Amy riding shotgun. The boys were laughing and betting they would be able to see her head bobbing up and down before the pickup went out of sight. Ole Jackie Boy was cruising nice and slow, and sure enough, about 100 yards up the road, Amy's head disappeared like a prairie dog heading for a hole.

Mojo slipped over to his backpack and grabbed a liter of tequila, took a sip, and passed it around while we planned out the rest of the work. In those days, serious job planning usually included alcohol. Normally, we would drill each hole about six feet down and then carefully load the holes with half a cup of Prell (beaded explosives that looked like little white nitrogen fertilizer) and half a stick of dynamite and then repeat—half a cup of Prell, half a stick of dynamite for a six-foot hole—and then plug the hole and cap it off. We used a ten-inch plastic Tupperware cup to measure out the Prell. Any of us could load the Prell or cut the dynamite sticks in half, but only Wejo or Mojo could thread the primer cord through the sticks or mess with the blasting caps themselves. That was the critical part of the operation and also the most dangerous.

We finished the tequila—it didn't take that long as there were six of us drinking—and jumped back on the rock drills to finish out the holes. We completed the drilling in a couple or hours, about fifty holes in all. As the tequila kicked in, we may have drilled a few of them a bit deeper than six feet. I remember bottoming out my ten-foot drill steel more than once.

We found a cedar tree for another break, and Scotty (from Scotland) broke out a joint of Colombian, and we then passed that around. As we started loading the explosives into the holes, the more enlightened of us began to discuss what would happen if we loaded a wee bit more Prell and maybe added an occasional extra half stick of TNT to some of the holes. I really wasn't paying too much attention to the conversation. I was checking out the box of dynamite which said in black block letters "Property of Union Carbide." Down below that in smaller print was written the slogan "Union is the name. Uranium is our game." I thought this was a cool slogan, and it was fire-burned into the wood, so I put a piece of wood with the slogan on it in my backpack as some sort of ridiculous backwoods souvenir. It was an innocent gesture and would turn out to be one of the dumbest moves I would ever make in my life.

Our little experiment started out like this: half a cup of Prell, half a stick of dynamite as normal. Then we went to an additional half a cup, half a stick, another half a cup of Prell, etc. By the time we were on the last hole, it was up to about three full cups of Prell and three full sticks of TNT per hole… Perhaps *enlightened* was not the best word to describe our thinking at the time.

Wejo inserted the blasting caps in each stick and ran an adequate length of primer cord through each hole in preparation for blowing the charges. He then tied in all the perimeter cords to a main feeder, and we were good to go for the blast. We cleared the rock drills, heavy equipment, and other tools from the area and retired under the shade of our friends, the cedar trees, to wait for Foreman Jack to return and set off the blast.

At 4 p.m., we saw Jackie Boy's truck coming up the easement road with Amy at the wheel and Jack riding shotgun with his head leaned back like he was sleeping. Amy parked the truck 150 yards away from the loaded holes which would normally have been out of the blast zone for a properly charged load. Jackie Boy staggered out of the truck, backslapped us all for doing such a great job, and promised to buy the first round of drinks at the bar. I doubted Jack would even make it to the bar as he was about to pass out where he stood.

Wejo must have felt the same way. He put his arm around Jack's shoulder and led him over to the blast ignition fuse. The rest of us took our places behind the big Caterpillar D8s and track hoes as we awaited the blast. After three failed attempts at lighting the primer cord, Jack handed the Zippo to Wejo. WeJo pulled out a Marlboro Red, clicked the Zippo, lit the fag, and then used the glowing cherry to ignite the fuse. The law required that you have a ten-minute burn length minimum on any lit fuse charge, and Wejo certainly did not want to break the law. His fuse was near perfect, and the ignited blast went off right at ten minutes.

The normal whoof and dust cloud that usually followed our blasts was replaced by an earth-shattering kaboom that blew bedrock chunks the size of Volkswagens a hundred feet into the air and all over the pristine pinto bean field of Mr. Crowley, the highfalutin Mormon. The shock wave blew out the windows of Jack's Ford pickup as rocks and debris rained down like hellfire for nearly a full minute while we all watched the display with childlike awe.

The growing dust cloud crept outward from the blast area along the ground like a fast-moving fog from Baskerville Manor and was soon covering the crew. Jack stood up in the thick dust, and he appeared to be stone-cold sober at this point. Wejo and Mojo stared at each other wide eyed, while Scotty grinned like a drunken sailor at all the carnage. I figured we would all be fired or, worse, sent to the hoosegow since a blasting violation of this magnitude would most surely be reported somewhere.

We worked until midnight dragging boulders clear and repairing Mr. Crowley's bean field. Jack paid us all overtime rates and a decent bonus despite our attempt to recreate Hiroshima. I added another $6,000 to the bank account that month and enjoyed a great weekend learning to country-swing-dance in Cortez with Teresa Medal and Tori Fatcher, two local ladies from Dolores County.

Needless to say, we were pretty much spot on the standard with our hole charge loading for the rest of our drill and blasting operations in Monticello County. We continued to build the pipelines, terminating all of them at some type or another of hydrocarbon or oil-processing plant in Colorado.

Inside these process facilities, they had operators, mechanics, and foremen wearing company clothes and all driving company trucks and were company men—steady, good-paying, smooth, and easy jobs. Being an operator looked like the job to have, so I set my sights on achieving that lofty perch. After a lot of smiling, shaking hands, buying drinks, attending church, and basically getting lucky, I landed a job as a process operator for a small plant in Colorado owned by Gulf Energy out of San Antonio, Texas. It was going well for the first year. I picked up operations easily, and with my overall knowledge of the oil field, I got on well with the senior staff.

Right before my twenty-first birthday, I met Laverna Schultz, a sweet, stunningly attractive little blond girl from Dolores. She was very tidy looking, and I was smitten. It was summer, and she was working at a local restaurant and bar called the Bear Cave. Look, I was not totally dense; the bar served alcohol, so I sort of assumed she had to be 18 to work in there. I just never got around to confirming it. She was a wild tiger in my truck every night, and she really liked having sex, so it made sense she was older. She certainly taught me a thing or three.

We dated all summer, and I liked her. I did not intend to stop seeing her until, one day, I dropped into the Bear Cave, and I saw a poster of the candidates for Dolores High School Homecoming Queen hung up at the bar next to money collection jars for each candidate. Right there in the center, looking like a million-dollar baby, was sweet little under-legal-age Laverna... Discretion being the better part of valor and me wanting to seriously avoid jail, I stopped seeing her. She was really pissed about being dumped. I tried to work it out as smoothly as possible, but it didn't matter. She was an underage woman scorned, and she went after my oil field ass like the voodoo queen from New Orleans, Marie Laveaux.

Things turned really sour for me right after that. Laverna started dating the high school football quarterback, and she ended up getting pregnant and blamed it on me out of spite when her folks found out. I knew I could not be the father as too much time had passed since our last, er, intimate encounter, which I, of course, tried to explain to her parents in my most honorable way. Somewhere in this discussion, it did, however, become clear that I had been intimate with their little girl at some time, who was underage, and they had the sheriff start preparing a warrant for my arrest. I was somewhat trying to do the right thing, but that didn't seem to matter here in southwest Colorado anymore as Dolores County had just about had all they wanted of construction and oil field trash. Even though I was now technically in operations, I was still part of the oil field stigma as I was not a local.

A couple of days later, the Cortez press released a story about a double fatality during a blasting operation for my old pipeline company Recco, stating this was the third interstate blasting incident for the construction group. The FBI was investigating the possibility they were also using and selling unauthorized explosives, and this might possibly involve missing ordnance and contraband from the local uranium mines in the area. The FBI was to serve warrants in the southwest area related to the blasting incidents on sixteen people. This was just what I needed after our little Hiroshima incident. I wondered if my name would somehow wind up on one of those FBI warrants, and I would see a few of my old FBI buddies from Green River. It would be nearly two years, though, before I got my answer.

I dipped and dodged around for about a week, trying to figure a way out of this mess, but was getting nowhere. Just when I thought I was at the end of my rope and ready to turn myself in for the baby doll warrant, the Gulf Energy plant superintendent called me into his office. He told me the company had been bought out by Gary-Williams Energy and that they were cutting my position. The good news was, however, that I could transfer to their facilities in Oklahoma if I wanted. This sounded great to me. FBI coming in, a warrant out for me in Colorado, FBI in the news again—yes, sir, at this time, Oklahoma looked mighty inviting. So I packed my trash, including my knives and gun arsenal, and hauled it out to the new frontier of Guthrie, Oklahoma.

The company merger included three organizations: my little bunch called Gulf Energy, another group which had four large plants in Oklahoma named Buckeye Natural Gas, and the parent company Gary-Williams Energy. The main facilities in Oklahoma were the east and west plants, the Buckeye facility, and Pauls Valley. They were all much bigger and more complex units than anything I had operated before, and it would be quite a task to learn the next level of oil field operations. I was, however, out of Colorado, off any FBI radar for the moment and looking forward to the new challenge.

I reported to the company main office in Edmond, Oklahoma, about twenty-five miles north of Oklahoma City, eager to get started on the job. I checked in and was immediately reminded of my Friday paycheck days at Connors Drilling. The office had two floors and was loaded with gorgeous Oklahoma girls in tight jeans who all seemed curious about the new kid in town.

Kimberly Gibson, the HR manager, introduced me around to the area managers and plant superintendents who were in the office. They all seemed to be part of a good-ole-boy network that would be giving me a thorough evaluation before I would even possibly be invited in.

Kimberly ran me through the company orientation and policies and then told me I would be reporting to Tony Williams at the west Guthrie site, the company's largest process facility. I would have company accommodations for thirty days until I found my own place. She told me I would be able to pick up my company truck from Tony when I reported to the west Guthrie plant and that my raise would be reflected in the coming month's salary. *Company truck? Raise? Perhaps things have taken a turn for the better here in Oklahoma.*

One of the things that had always appealed to me about my previous oil field experience was that, after a day or two of working together, everybody seemed to get along and make it work. Oh, sure, there was always the occasional ass hat on every crew; but for the most part, it had been easy for me to get to know people and make quick friends.

Up until this point in my career, I had mainly worked with construction crews and new operating facilities. I would soon realize that I had walked into an old-world part of the oil field that had been around for a long while, was well established, and was loaded with secrets.

3

I headed out to the west Guthrie (WG) plant bright and early the next morning, eager to get started on the next step in my career with this move to the Sooner State. Kimberly had told me there were thirteen people working out of the WG office, so I expected a crowd this morning. Driving in, I saw three shiny new company trucks parked in the laydown storage area, but there was only one truck in front of the office when I arrived. I turned off Bruce Springsteen's "Born in the USA" and headed to the office door. I was all pomp and professional when I opened the door, something which was wasted on the man sitting at the operator's desk.

Oklahoma native John Lordell sat in a swivel chair with his head back and his dirty Red Wing work boots propped up on the desk, sawing logs and snoring like a tornado. He was a skinny runt of a man with acne scars that would have made the craters on the moon pale in comparison. I shut the office door, and he jumped up like he had been shocked with a cattle prod. He wore big Coke-bottle-bottom glasses over beady little pig eyes and a squint nose. He reminded me of a rat or a weasel, and I swore I could smell a hint of eau de cannabis in the air.

"Who the fuck are you?" John snorted as he straightened his Coke-bottle glasses on his rat nose and pulled his boots off the desk.

I looked at him. Any doubt of him being anything other than a piece of human excrement and a confirmed dumbass had been removed when he spoke. "Drew Hall. I transferred in from the Papoose Canyon plant in Colorado. Main office told me to report to Tony Williams here at the west Guthrie plant," I answered dryly. "And you are?"

He jumped up from the chair, all aggressive like some kind of psycho banty rooster off his meds and got right up next to me as if he was going to get physical with me. As I mentioned, I was a pretty fair-sized guy, and I was standing nearly 6'4" in my work boots, looking down at a moron of a man who—now that he was closer to me—definitely smelled of some high-grade cannabis.

"I'm John Lordell, senior operator, and this here is Buckeye Natural Gas. That's right, fucking Buckeye, and we ain't changing a damn thing. I don't give a shit fuck who bought who or sold what. We are Buckeye, and that's the way it is," Acne Man spouted off as he staggered in front of me in a lame attempt at a swagger.

I saw no point in extending a hand in the way of introduction. A gentlemanly gesture of this nature would obviously be lost on such a redneck punk ass. There was a freshly brewed pot of coffee in the back and ignoring Coke-bottle-glasses John, I went over and poured myself a cup. John watched me through his Coke-bottle lenses and semi-drunken stupor, not really sure what to make of me. He plopped his skinny butt down into the operator's chair again and proceeded to light up a Marlboro Red, blowing smoke in my direction, which permeated all over the office.

I pointed toward the No Smoking sign hanging on the safety bulletin board, and Johnny Boy just grinned like a drunken opossum and took another big drag from his fag. He had just placed his dirty boots back on the desk and was in mid-exhale when the office door opened again. A rough-looking big man entered the office, and I got my first look at Tony Williams.

He was big, taller than me, at least fifty pounds heavier, and he filled the doorway when he walked in. He was solid, had huge shoulders with obvious strength—not pretty-boy strong, not all-toned-biceps or six-pack-abs strength but tough-ass, working-man, Hoot Gibson–type strength. He had long, shoulder-length wavy brown hair that was combed neatly back. He wore jeans and a Western shirt with clean, polished Red Wing work boots on his feet. His face was rough looking, scarred, pitted, and tough, while his eyes were dark brown, serious as death. Johnny Boy started gagging and choking when Tony walked in, and he quickly tried to extinguish his fag.

"Lordell, what the fuck have I told you about smoking in this office, you dumb sumbitch?" Tony bellowed. His voice had a strong, commanding presence that suggested he would not lightly suffer fools. I had seen my share of tough characters in the Western oil fields, and I knew right away this guy was nothing to mess with.

"I . . . was just telling this guy . . . this is Buckeye and not Gulf Energy," John stammered.

Tony seemed to notice me for the first time and sized me up with a cold stare. "You the guy from Colorado?" he asked and then, without waiting for my answer, said, "You check in with the company office in the city?"

"Yes and yes. I arrived yesterday and did all the paperwork." I handed him a copy of my assignment letter.

He read it, eyed me up again, and then stuck out his massive hand. "Tony Williams," he said quietly.

"Drew Hall. Good to meet you," I replied, shaking his hand. His grip was firm, but I could tell he had a lot more pressure to apply to that viselike grip if he was so inclined.

"Likewise. Have you ever worked in Oklahoma before?" Tony asked.

"No, mostly Colorado, Utah, Wyoming," I replied.

"Wyoming? You ever work in Rawlins?" he asked, eyeing me again.

"Some but mostly Green River," I answered.

Tony walked over to the coffeepot and poured himself a cup. "You ever run into a guy named Tim Smith? Or Ray Stafford?" he asked, turning toward me.

"Ray Stafford? A pumper for South Oil Company? Hippie kind of guy, wears two pair of glasses, one prescription and then a pair of cheap sunglasses over those. That Ray Stafford?"

Tony chuckled dryly. "Yeah, that's the one. His brother runs a pipe supply business over in Kingfisher. They are both about the same." I wondered why Tony had asked about Ray. The guy was a real thug up in Rawlins. Maybe they had heard some rumors down in Oklahoma also.

Coke-bottle-glasses John felt the need to get involved in the discussion and spouted off, "Well, this here is Buckeye Natural Gas, and we do things the Buckeye way, and we ain't changing shit."

While I was wondering what exactly that had to do with the hippie Ray Stafford conversation, Tony looked over at the idiot man. He eyed John now with those dark eyes and said, "John, go wash off the three north White Gas Turbine model LA GTLA compressors, and change the filters in the propane compressor—"

"What? I been working all night. I got called out when the refrigeration unit went down, put this work horse plant back online. Ain't had no food, no sleep, and you want me to wash off those fucking compressors?" John saw Tony's dark eyes turn to death eyes, and he slowly rose from the operator's chair and headed for the door, muttering and cussing under his breath, "Work a man to fucking death. Gonna call HR. This is bullshit." John mumbled under his breath as he stumbled from the Plant office.

Tony invited me back to his office, and we continued to talk about Wyoming, Colorado, and the Oklahoma oil field operations. After about thirty minutes, I offered to go help John wash off the GTLA units. "Let John do it. It's good for him now and then to do some actual work. He is pretty much a dumbass when it comes to anything other than this plant, no tact or couth at all as I am sure you noticed," Tony said.

I smiled.

"Yeah, John's a confirmed dumbass, but he does know this plant inside and out. He has been here for ten years and knows the landowners and pipelines well also. You can learn a lot from him. Give him a few days to get past this company merger, and then see if he settles down a bit. Clay Haynes will be here in about twenty minutes. He's around your age, and I think you two will get on well. He works over at the east Guthrie plant and helps us out here several times a week. Clay can show you around for the next couple of days," said Tony.

"Roger that," I replied.

"Roger?" Tony asked quizzically. "Were you in the military or something?"

I smiled again. "No, my dad retired from the Navy. We always had military guys hanging around the house. I sort of picked it up."

About this time, the office door opened again, and a good-looking stocky guy about my age with blond hair and a devilish grin walked in. He greeted Tony, asking, "Is this the guy from Colorado?" He jerked his thumb in my direction.

"Yeah, he has already met John. He got called out last night and is in rare form this morning," Tony said, rolling his eyes.

"Clay Haynes from Crescent," said the blond guy with a Robert Redford smile as he extended his hand.

"Drew Hall . . . er, from Telluride, Colorado, originally." I shook his hand.

Clay and Tony talked a bit about some of the day's assignments, and then we turned to go. "Drew," Tony asked absently as I was at the door, "what kind of beer do you drink?"

Not "Do you drink beer? What kind of beer do you drink?" like it's expected? "Coors Light," I replied curiously.

Tony smiled a bit. "That's my brand." He pointed to a large fridge in his office. "We all bring a case of beer a week in here. Put it in the fridge. No drinking in the office before five. Got it?"

I paused for a minute as I had never had a beer in any company office at any time in my life and then said, "Got it, Tony."

"Give him the three-quarter-ton Chevy, unit no. 13, for his company rig," Tony told Clay.

Clay showed me around the west plant for the rest of the morning, and it was quite a facility. Four GTL and four GTLA clean-burn compressors powered the large natural gas process facility and pushed the gas through several large stripping towers. The plant was capable of producing 350 MCF of natural gas per day, and it was a fairly large operation.

We headed out to the west side field units, and I noticed three 20,000-gallon condensate tanks just inside the plant security fence. Next to them were a dozen or so pull-behind trailer tanks. Half of these were trashed out from hauling paraffin, water, and non-desirable crap from tie-lines, meter runs, or other pipelines. Four of the 1,000-gallon tanks were in pristine condition and well maintained.

When we finished covering the west plant, west field, and pipelines, Clay gave me the keys to a brand-new midnight blue Chevy pickup, company unit no. 13, and we went on a tour of the east side pipelines and meter stations. We must have passed fifty pickups all pulling 500- or 1,000-gallon pull-behind trailer tanks.

Some were trashed and dirty like the first few I had seen at the west plant. Others were in good condition like the last four I had seen. Clay waved at several of the pumpers and ranchers who were pulling the trailers, and they waved back at him. He was personable enough to me, if not just a bit standoffish at first.

As the day wore on, we both relaxed and found some common ground. He showed me the best rock and roll and country music stations on the radio and pointed out several local hangouts that had good food and good folks and "took" the company credit cards.

We stopped for gas in the late afternoon, and Clay showed me the mileage logbook system and how to use the company credit card to pay for items. We went inside the Crossroads Country Store to pay for the gas, and he grabbed a case each of Bud Light and Coors Light and placed them on the counter.

The checkout lady behind the counter was a real sweetheart wearing skintight jeans and a snug halter top. I tried to be polite, but I could not help but stare, a fact which was not lost on her. "Hey, Clay, who's the new guy?" she asked as she checked me out in return.

"Name's Drew. He is from Colorado," Clay replied.

"Hi, Drew, I am Bonnie Love. So how do you like Oklahoma?" she said with a fetching smile. She was very cute and tall with an athletic, tough, rancher-girl look about her, and her smile—well, her smile would melt an iceberg.

"I like it more and more every day," I replied with a smile of my own.

She grinned and turned to Clay. "Oil?" she asked, pointing to the beer.

"Yep, that darned ole mechanic truck we have drinks up the stuff," Clay said with a wink.

Clay signed the ticket and handed me the receipt. It showed ten gallons of gas, two cases of Pennzoil, and $20 for services. Bonnie rang up the sale and handed Clay $20 cash. I grabbed both cases of beer and headed to the truck matter-of-factly, but this was all new to me. In the back of my mind, I tried to decipher what had just occurred with this transaction and how accepted was this practice of buying "oil" with a company card. I learned later that, at the proper establishments, you could buy damn near anything you wanted on a company card as long as they wrote it up as something that would pass the accountant audits at the end of the month.

"Bonnie is great and knows the score. Her brother, Carl, is kind of a dick, so I usually don't buy 'Pennzoil' or get 'services' when he is there. You can do what you want, but I never get more than $20 worth of services a day. If you get more, it flags up on the monthly finance audits," Clay said in way of education and explanation. "That dumbass John pulled out over $2,700 of 'services' on the card one month to cover Brenda's coke habit, and it nearly cost him his job. Tony had to sign off on it all the way to San Antonio."

"Who's Brenda?" I asked as I turned onto the I-35.

"John's skank of a wife. She's a stripper at the Wellingtons Way Dance Club. She does guys in the VIP for cash also. John is such an idiot he thinks she is the club manager no matter what you tell him."

"That idiot has a stripper for a wife?" I asked incredulously.

Clay chuckled. "I said she was a skank. She is a real slut bitch too. She is over 40, skinny, and bony with big, 38DD fake tits that are so old they are like concrete. She has bleach blond hair and has been dancing at Wellingtons for almost ten years. She has probably banged half the local cops in the VIP rooms and honestly has probably had more pipe up her ass than is buried in Logan County. She is a cokehead to the max and often goes missing for days at a time. John will find her down in the city or in Dallas and drag her back home. In the dark corners of Wellingtons, she looks like a pretty good dancer. But when you get up close, she is gag ya city. And when she talks, hell, she makes John look like a Harvard professor."

"You make her sound so appealing. I just want to run over now and get a lap dance." I smirked.

"Dating material, she is definitely not. John swears they are in love. He calls her from the office, like, six times a day. Half the time, he ends up screaming at her in a huge fight. Watch for it. It will crack your ass up for sure," he replied with a chuckle.

"What's his story anyway? He really seems like a moron, and why would Tony cover for him on the $2,700? Why not just run him off? Tony doesn't seem to like him from what I can tell," I asked.

Clay's demeanor changed a bit from comical to semiserious. "Don't be fooled. Tony and John are major-league tight. Tony rips his ass all day long at the plant, and then the two of them go out drinking and clubbing almost every night. They have been hooked up together for years. John's pretty smart in some ways but a real dumbass in others, like when it comes to drinking or his wife. Plus, he's shady, has been for years. They got some stuff going on."

"Shady? What do you mean?" I asked. "In what way?"

"Travelin Man" by Bob Seger came on the radio, and Clay turned up the volume, suggestinging he may have already said too much and wanted to change the subject. "You like Bob Seger?" Clay asked.

"Yep, 'Hollywood Nights,' 'Get Out of Denver,' and 'Night Moves' are some of my favorites," I responded.

"Cool, I am a big Bob Seger fan. Most of the guys I hang out with are also," Clay added. "Do you have any guns?"

Well, sir, that was my opening right there. I told Clay about my .357 Python and my .223 Savage, and we talked about guns and hunting for the rest of the afternoon. He offered up that he had a .22-caliber bull-barrel semiauto Ruger pistol and a .30-06 Winchester rifle.

I had three beers at five thirty that night at the west plant office, and I met half a dozen other folks there. Some worked for the company, some were suppliers, some were local ranchers who were just stopping by to have a beer and talk about rain, hail, and tornadoes. Even John got tolerable after a few beers.

I saw Tony watching me several times during the evening as if he was keeping an eye on me. I did not think much of it. It had been a full day and a good day, just about everything I could ask for from a first day at a new job.

4

Over the next few weeks, I spent the days working in the plants and running the pipelines and the evenings drinking beer with the boys at the west Guthrie office. I met people every day out in the field and, for the most part, got along with all of them, especially the ladies. It seemed like every local lady I met, single or married, was interested in the new kid in town, and I dug the attention. It didn't matter where I went; the girls were very friendly, very attractive, and very curious.

I was full-on 21 now and rearing to kick up my heels at one of the local hoedowns, maybe catch a real strip club in the city or something equally exciting. I dropped several hints to Clay, Tony, and a couple of the other guys at work that I would be keen on a night out with them but had no takers. They just seemed to politely ignore me and dodge the issue.

It was late September, and the weather had turned from that killer central Oklahoma August heat to a pleasant cooler climate that was most refreshing. It was Friday, and I had the next two days off. It was the first time I was off two days in a row since I had moved to Oklahoma, and I was not on call. I was determined to go out somewhere, even if it was by myself. I pulled into the Crossroads Country Store, filled the midnight blue Chevy three-quarter ton up with gas, and went inside to pay the bill.

Bonnie was looking gorgeous as always in boots and faded jeans, and I began to daydream watching her as she helped the guy in front of me pay his bill. "Hey, Drew, how's your week?" she asked, flashing her smile and rocking her hip just a wee bit as she talked.

"Fine, how about yours?" I replied.

"Same, glad it's Friday. No oil today?" she asked sweetly. "The weekend's coming up. I figured you would be stocking up?" I nodded absently and went to the beer coolers, pulled out a case of Coors Light, and walked back to the cash counter.

"Do you have any plans for the weekend? You doing anything?" Bonnie asked, her eyes twinkling.

"Yes and no," I responded. She raised an eyebrow and looked at me curiously. "Yes, I am doing something this weekend, and no, I do not know what it is yet." I went on moderately.

She cocked her head a bit to the side and crossed her legs in a sexy cowgirl move that made me turn red. "That sounds a bit cryptic. Are you OK?" she asked, leaning closer.

"Yeah, I am cool. It's just I have been here for nearly a month now and have yet to go out to any of the bars or hangouts," I answered with a pout. "I am going to do something this weekend for sure though."

She laughed and said, "You're a dork. Do you like bar bands? The Logan County Line Band is playing at Trips tonight. Want to meet me there about eight, and I will show you around?" She was looking about as sexy as anything I had ever seen at this point, and I could feel the red in my face deepening, and the blood flow didn't stop there.

"Er, yeah, I love a good bar band. That sounds rad—I mean, cool . . . uh, yeah, sure, I would like to meet you," I stammered. "Where is Trips?"

"You know where Highway 7 connects to County Road 59, just outside of Crescent?" I nodded, trying to keep my eyes from drifting over her body, but I failed miserably. "At the T intersection, turn right. It's about five miles ahead on the right-hand side. You can't miss it. It's a big Road House–type bar with a huge parking lot and nothing else nearby," Bonnie explained.

"Got it, Bonnie. Sounds like a great time. Thanks for the invite," I said, face now a deep shade of crimson.

She smiled a serious smile and met my eyes. "Can you swing dance by any chance?" she asked.

"Like a fireman, cool 'em down, so I can burn 'em up," I replied in my best George Strait imitation.

Now it was her turn to blush.

5

I was in high spirits when I pulled into the west plant office that afternoon. It was only four fifteen, but there were at least ten cars already parked out front, and I could hear Creedence Clearwater Revival blasting through the office window. I went inside, and Clay tossed me a Coors Light. I said hey to the crew and made the rounds. I said hi to the folks I knew and introduced myself to the folks I did not know. John Boy staggered over my way and tried to say something clever, but he was already three sheets to the wind and could barely talk. Apparently, the "no drinking in the office before five o'clock" rule must have shifted to New York time tonight.

I chatted with Tony about the week in general, and I told him I was meeting Bonnie at Trips tonight. "You will like the Logan County Line Band. They are good and always bring in a nice crowd. I have some business over that way later tonight. Maybe I will stop in and buy you a beer," Tony said almost friendly-like.

"Sounds great. Hope to see you there. I am looking forward to getting out. I haven't gone anywhere yet," I mumbled.

"You haven't been out and around yet? You have been here over a month now," Tony stated. "I will talk to Clay and Mark. They can show you a few places here, some in Edmond, and even down in the city."

Everyone continued to loosen up, and Tony started pouring shots of Jack Daniel's into coffee cups while Mark and Clay poured a near-passed-out John into the cab of his truck. I had a great time and was feeling no pain when I left the office.

It was already nearly seven, so I was hauling ass down Highway 101 to get to my place and spruce myself up before I headed out to meet Bonnie. It just would not do at all if I was late for our first rendezvous at Trips.

I had just stepped harder on the gas pedal and turned up the volume on the Eagles' "One of These Nights" when I saw the lights of an Oklahoma state police cruiser kick on in my rearview mirror and heard the solo siren whoop-whoop. I pulled the pickup over and got my driver's license, truck registration, and proof of insurance ready for the trooper to inspect without giving a second thought to the amount of alcohol I had consumed in the last two hours.

State Trooper Leon Spencer approached the pickup as I rolled the window down, and tipping his hat to me, he said "Evening, son. You have a hot date tonight or something?"

Not expecting that frank of an opening, I decided to respond in kind as I handed Trooper Spencer my license and registration. "Er, yes, sir, I actually do. It's my first date in Oklahoma," I muttered sheepishly, and I immediately felt like a teenager.

"Colorado? Nice country up there. Which part are you from?" Leon asked as he looked at my license.

"Telluride, western slope. Delta, Montrose area mostly," I replied.

"You ever hunt elk or muleys? I was on a hunt two years ago up in Collbran. It was pretty crowded though. I saw a lot of small muleys but no elk. I did a hunt a few years back in Pagosa Springs. That was much better. I shot a four-point bull, my first elk," Trooper Spencer reflected proudly.

"I grew up hunting all over the western slope. Pagosa is great elk country," I responded.

We talked about hunting, rifle calibers, calling coyotes, big mule deer that got away, and the conversation ate up nearly twenty minutes before Trooper Spencer went back to his cruiser. It was about then that I realized I was probably pushing the legal limit on the BAC (blood alcohol concentration) count and still behind the wheel of a vehicle. Trooper Spencer returned five minutes later and handed me a warning for speeding, which was quite gracious of him considering I was doing eighty-two in a fifty-five. "I know there isn't much traffic on the roads out here this time of night, but it's best you keep it within ten miles an hour of the speed limit for safety's sake." He winked.

I shook his hand, thanked him for the warning, and sped off toward my place, very conscious of the clock ticking away. I had no idea at the time, but this was just the beginning of a long relationship with Oklahoma State Trooper Leon Spencer. Over the coming months, our chance meetings increased in severity, often with me doing dumbass shit; however, at each and every turn, my encounters with Trooper Leon Spencer ended to my benefit no matter how precarious they became. He inadvertently became one of my biggest supporters and was key to my selection as an asset to the FBI during the sting operation Black Gold.

6

It was 8.15 p.m., and I was driving exactly ten miles over the speed limit down Highway 7, trying to make up some time so as not to be too late for my rendezvous with Bonnie. I came to the T intersection at County Road 59, and I saw a broken-up barnwood sign that read "bar" with an arrow pointing to the left. I did a California stop and turned left, accelerating into the night, not realizing I was going the wrong way on County Road 59. I was fully confident that I would be able to soothe Ms. Bonnie for my tardiness with a few dances, and I turned up the volume on Molly Hatchet's *The Deed Is Done* as I rocketed into the night.

Exactly six miles down the road, on the right-hand side, I saw a large butler building with a neon sign that said "Six-Mile Bar." *Strange*, I thought as I parked the Chevy, *Bonnie said the place was called Trips*. I could hear the Judds' "Why Not Me" blasting loudly from inside as I entered the bar, and I immediately noticed the clientele was definitely local Okie yokels.

I had been acquiring a humble collection of cowboy boots for a couple of years now, and in an effort to impress Bonnie, I had chosen a pair of exotic Tony Lama El Rey back-cut boas in a stained night blue color to adorn my dogs for the evening. I topped this off with a new pair of Levi's and a turquoise brushpopper shirt. This look had been all the rage the last time I passed through Denver, and the Colorado cowgirls liked it. I would soon learn that while the girls in Oklahoma City and Stillwater could appreciate this level of fashion, many of the locals in Kingfisher and Logan County did not.

I found an open spot at the bar, ordered a Coors Light, and scanned the room thoroughly for Bonnie. I did not see her, so I assumed she was using the woman's prerogative of being fashionably late, and I began to relax. I took a drink of my beer and another look around the bar, slower this time, checking the place out.

There were two ladies working behind the bar, both attractive in a tough-redneck sort of way, but neither held a candle to Bonnie. The bar was lively and spacious, not too crowded this early in the eve, with maybe thirty people inside. There were a few couples sitting at tables, but the bar had mostly rough-looking oil field guys playing pool or standing at the bar in twos and threes. A state-of-the-art jukebox blasted out more of the Judds' jams, and most of the folks were in tune with Wynonna and Naomi. A big bouncer who would go 300 pounds stood in between the jukebox and the toilets. He gave me the once-over and decided apparently that, no matter what my reputation may have been in Green River, Wyoming, I was of little or no concern to him in his Oklahoma bar.

I noticed a guy with a ponytail wearing boots and a blue button-down staring at me from across the bar. He looked vaguely familiar, but I could not place him. *Must be from the oil field around here*, I thought.

I was ordering a second beer from the wild brunette in a miniskirt behind the bar and wondering why I could not see a stage for the band when two local boys came up to the bar and stood next to me. I politely moved a bit to give them space to order their drinks. I mean, why else would they be approaching the bar next to me, right? They ordered two Budweiser beers and stood next to me talking among themselves and looking in my direction.

Okie number one was tall, as tall as me but slimmer with no waist or legs at all. He had a narrow hawk face with punky-looking offset eyes that darted this way and that when he talked. He wore a local co-op ball cap with the bill meticulously shaped in a narrow smooth bend. His mate was pretty much a brute—shorter, uglier but all muscle and squirrelly hair. I noticed them noticing me but did not let on that I noticed.

Okie Hawk Nose had a pool cue in his hand, and he was spinning it around back and forth like he knew it had other uses than just shooting pool. His oafish mate kept smiling like a Charles Manson wannabe and looking in my direction. Hawk Nose with the cue moved in closer and said not exactly in the way of welcome, "Where did you get those boots from, boy?"

I looked at him, took a sip of my beer, and said, "Denver at Deb's Western Wear. I can give you the street address if you want a pair."

This caught him a bit off guard, and he paused but only for a brief second before continuing with his juvenile rhetoric. "Buy a pair? Hell, you couldn't pay me to wear those boots. They are fag boots for sure," Hawk Nose said smugly as Oafish Brute laughed and edged him on. I semi-ignored them and took a sip of beer, expecting them to go back to their pool game once their curiosity was satisfied.

"You hear me, boy? I said I don't like them fag boots you're wearing," Hawk Nose said louder than he needed to.

As mentioned, I had been 21 for over six months now and was never going to feel like more of a bulletproof man than I was right then. I could feel my blood begin to heat up, and I looked at the two morons in front of me, and the aggression switch flipped. "You would like them a lot less if they were shoved up your ass," I replied just loud enough.

It was now their turn to pause, and regardless of what they chose as their next move, I was more than prepared to follow their lead. It was the moment of truth. Put up or shut up, and I honestly had no idea what these two idiots were going to do.

Hawk Nose narrowed his eyes and looked me over again, sizing me up in his wee mind. Gripping his pool cue tight, he uttered the proverbial backwoods phrase that usually led to an inevitable physical encounter of some kind or another no matter where you were. "You ain't from around here, are you, boy?"

I sipped my beer, which was now halfway gone, and considered my options. Before I could reply, I heard his mate Beast Breath Boy blather for the first time. He said in a piggy high-pitched squeal, "Well, if you ain't from Oklahoma, then you ain't shit!" He slapped a lame high five with Hawk Nose, and they were so busy hooting and yee-hawing that they almost missed my classic response, almost but not quite.

"So does that mean that if you are from Oklahoma, you are shit?" I answered quietly.

Hawk Nose screamed at me in an effort to rouse the bar on his side. "You saying people from Oklahoma are shit?"

He had gotten some people's attention, and I saw movement to my left as several men started easing toward me at the bar, one guy picking up a cue ball with his hand as he approached. This guy was going to be trouble. Hawk Nose might be an issue with the pool cue stick, but I learned some years back the cue ball was much deadlier. I noticed Ponytail Man stand up in the back, but it was more so he could observe what was going on than it was to get involved. A quick count showed seven men either in range or approaching, and I was about to take my best shot—possibly my only shot—at Beast Boy, when, out of the corner of my eye, a large shadow flashed near the door, and I saw someone enter the bar.

The crowd around me paused in recognition of the newcomer, and I tried to get a good look at him. "He's with me. Now y'all go on back to your pool game or whatever you were doing and leave it be," I heard a booming voice say. I recognized the voice but couldn't quite make out to whom it belonged. I watched the crowd slowly shuffle away and turned to see Tony Williams bigger than life standing next to me at the bar. Maybe it was just the adrenaline, or maybe it was his attire, but damn, he looked big.

Tony was wearing a black-and-silver button-down shirt with a John Mellencamp style silver bolo tie, and he had changed out his Red Wing work boots for a pair of custom-made Lucchese black ostrich-skin boots with silver heel and toe protectors. "Two Coors Lights, doll face," Tony said to the sexy brunette behind the bar. She smiled at us and brought the beers out, giving one to Tony and one to me. I drank deep of the cold beer, trying to ease the adrenaline out of my system.

"I thought you were going to Trips, Drew. What the hell are you doing over here?" Tony asked with a twinkle in his eye.

"This isn't Trips? What? I thought—I mean . . . I turned at the County Road 59 intersection like Bonnie said. She told me . . . the bar will be about five miles ahead on the right . . . only thing around," I said questioningly, shrugging.

"You turned the wrong way, dumbass. This here is Six-Mile Bar and not a place I would recommend you come too alone or often. Trips is about twelve miles north of here up Highway 59," Tony explained, his eyes twinkling.

My heart dropped as I now realized why there was no stage for the band . . . and no Bonnie. She was going to kick my ass for sure. Making conversation while I finished my beer, I asked Tony, "So how did your business go? You tie everything up?"

"It's going down now. This is where I do business," Tony said dryly, looking me straight in the eyes. "And Bonnie won't give you a second chance if you stand her up, so you'd best be getting on out of here and head up to Trips. Bonnie is class, and you're lucky she gave you the time of day, let alone a night out."

I slammed the beer down and said, "Thanks, Tony, really great timing on your arrival by the way, and I appreciate the beer." I tipped both bartenders a ten and was heading out when I watched Tony walk over to the table where Ponytail Man was sitting.

Something caught my attention, and as Tony sat down at the table with Ponytail Man, I saw it again. There was no mistaking it. Tucked in the back of his belt was a .45 automatic pistol. I thought about this on the drive up to Trips and wondered exactly what kind of business Tony was conducting at the Six-Mile Bar that required a .45 Colt.

7

It was 9.30 p.m., and the parking lot was overflowing when I finally made it to Trips. There must have been a hundred vehicles packed into the main lot and another fifty or so parked around the edges. I found a dirt patch, parked the Chevy, and hurried toward the main door, running several apologies through my head to see which one would be the best to throw out at Bonnie when I met her.

As I turned the final corner, I saw a silver pickup truck rocking from side to side and heard a girl moaning loudly in the throes of obvious redneck ecstasy. She had one naked leg sticking out of the driver's side window and was heading toward a climaxing crescendo with her partner who, I gathered from her passion, had to be named Bobby. I caught a good look at the couple as I passed by while trying not to look like I was looking, and they were enjoying the moment to the extreme. *Damn*, I thought, *and it's only nine thirty. I might like this place.*

The band was playing "Is This the Way to Amarillo" by Tony Christie and doing a fine job with it when I walked through the main doors. The dance floor was huge and packed with people dancing and rocking out. I found my way through the crowd and moved to the back bar and ordered a beer.

I saw Bonnie looking at me about halfway around the dance floor and figured she must have been watching the door. Her face turned from concerned to defiant when she caught my eye, and she immediately began to chat up two cowboys standing next to her. I moved slowly down the bar, talking to a few people, until I was about five patrons away from where Bonnie was standing, talking to her new gentlemen friends. I waited patiently, hoping she would simmer down and mosey on over my way, but nothing doing. She just drank her Bud light from a bottle and continued to ignore me while catching my eye just enough to make sure I knew that she was ignoring me.

Determined to enjoy myself, I began chatting it up with the barmaid behind the bar, a lovely lady named Susan from Chandler, Oklahoma. She was dazzling and had an ass that would wake the dead, so it was not exactly a total loss for me. I caught Bonnie staring at me a couple of times, and I could tell she was getting frustrated. Bonnie looked like a million bucks, and I really wanted to be with her; I was just not sure how to go about it without blowing the night. Finally, in desperation, I ordered four shots of Patron tequila, sent three over to Bonnie and friends, and raised my shot to them when they turned my way, and we all slammed the tequila.

After about five minutes, Bonnie sauntered over with her sexy stride and slid in next to me at the bar. "OK, Drew, let's hear it. What's the excuse cowboy?" She sighed.

I stared at her for a moment, just drinking in the look of her, the allure of her, the sweetness, the smell. She was wearing skintight white Rocky Mountain jeans and white ostrich-skin boots with a baby blue lady tie-up shirt that had an open back, and she looked just absolutely amazing. "Six-Mile Bar happened, sugah. I turned the wrong way and wound up over there." I shrugged sheepishly.

"What? The Six-Mile Bar? Did you go in?" she asked concernedly. I nodded, again sheepishly, with my head down just a bit. "Oh my god. Drew, that's not a good place, especially for you . . . I mean, not being a local. Oh my god, are you all right? What happened?" She asked, obviously concerned. She had moved in closer and latched on to my arm with both of hers, pressing in close to me as she met my eyes.

I told her the whole story and then ordered us both another shot of tequila as she held on to me. "That was pretty ballsy. You sure as hell don't know anything about Six-Mile. Jeez, you're a dork, ya know, Drew." She laughed as she held me a bit tighter. "Once a month, somebody gets stabbed in there. And at least a couple of times a year, someone gets shot."

The band played "The Fireman" by George Strait, and I grabbed her hand and nodded toward the dance floor. She smiled, and away we went. I knew the country swing moves but was no urban cowboy à la John Travolta. Bonnie, however, was great on her feet, and she made me look good—so good that, more than once, I caught several girls looking my way, something which was not lost on Bonnie as well. We stayed out on the dance floor for the next four songs, and I was in heaven. The more we danced, the sexier she became and the harder my blood pounded.

We returned to our spot at the bar, and Bonnie began to introduce me around to a few of her friends. They all seemed to like hearing about Colorado, Wyoming, and all things Western, so I obliged by turning on the charm and buying drinks. A couple of her lady friends held my arm a little bit too long, leaned in a little bit too close when they talked, and tossed their hair back a bit too much—something about this new-kid-in-town thing in Oklahoma.

After about thirty minutes of this, Bonnie started to get this look on her face, and I eased over to her and pulled her to the dance floor when they started playing "Amarillo by Morning," another George Strait song, and I showed her my best attempt at a two-step. She brought my leg tight in between hers at every corner turn on the dance floor. Our eyes met as we danced, and I wanted her.

I had been noticing people going in and out all night and many of them hanging out in the parking lot, so I suggested we go outside for some fresh air. Bonnie looked at me, smiled, and agreed. We found a shadowy, quiet spot about fifty feet from the door and talked while we kissed and held each other. After about ten minutes, there was very little conversation, and we were both on fire and nearly dry-humping each other right there in the parking lot.

Bonnie suddenly pulled me very close and held me tight with her head on my shoulder. "Drew, I like you. I really do. You don't dance that great, but you're sexy, and your mouth is driving me insane," she said, trying to make light of the situation, but I could tell she was really nervous about something. Her eyes met mine. "Please understand . . . not on our first date. I mean, I really am having fun, but I just want to let . . . you know." Her eyes pleaded for understanding, and my heart melted.

I placed my hands on both sides of her face and kissed her long, soft, and deep. "C'mon, I can hear them playing Sweethearts of the

Rodeo now, sugah. Let's go give it a whirl," I told her in my best Marshall Dillon imitation.

After we danced a few more songs, we saw Clay and his girlfriend, Ann, at a table off the dance floor, and they waved us over. Clay was doing pretty well, but Ann had reached her limit and possibly exceeded it a wee bit. She was a fun girl, though, and a real looker, every bit as hot as Bonnie but more of a bubblehead, blonde, and not near the same quality. Clay bought drinks, and we began to chat while Bonnie and Ann talked.

Just after one, Tony Williams strolled in sin .45 and with the wild brunette from the Six-Mile Bar on his arm while trying to look like she was not on his arm. He saw us at the table, and Clay waved him over. They sat with us, and Tony bought us a couple of rounds of drinks, and it all seemed quite social. Tony and Clay headed for the men's room together, which I thought was a bit odd, but that left me at the table with the three ladies, and I quickly got over it.

Bonnie had slid up close to me and was holding my arm, and I realized she had pretty much gone quiet since Tony had arrived. I looked at her, and her eyes were trying to say something—what, I wasn't quite sure. When Tony and Clay returned, she squeezed my hand, and I asked her if she wanted to go, to which she quickly nodded. We finished our drinks, and despite both Tony and Clay starting with "The night is young" and "Have one more stuff," I knew Bonnie wanted to go, and well, at just six months over 21 in age and having the best night to date in Oklahoma, I wanted whatever Bonnie wanted.

We said good night to everyone on the way out and headed to the parking lot. Bonnie instantly relaxed, and we began to talk. "What did you think of Trips?" she asked.

"Loved it. Loved dancing with you more, but I loved the place," I drawled, not yet quite ready to totally give up on the idea that it just wasn't going to happen with Bonnie tonight. "I thought it was great."

"Did you ever go to any of the big dance bars in Cheyenne or Denver when you were out West?" Bonnie asked as we were walking to what I thought was her car.

I thought this was a strange question until I suddenly realized Bonnie had no idea I had only recently turned 21. At the bars in the oil boomtowns, nobody gave a shit how old you were or weren't. As long as you worked in the oil field, had cash, and paid your bills, you could get in most bars at 18; but in the cities and college towns, everyone got carded until you were like 30 something so even though I was quite the partier, I had never actually been in any official need to be 21 or show my ID in a dance hall, bar, or anything similar.

I didn't see anything at all to be gained by telling her that, so I replied with "Er, yes, I have been to the Grizzly Rose in Denver. It's bigger than Trips, but the people aren't as fun, and the girls aren't as pretty."

She punched me in the arm, and I pulled her close. We wandered around the parking lot and talked some more when she said, "What's the matter, cowboy? You lose your horse?"

"My horse. No, sugah, I was just walking you to your car," I replied.

"My car? You dork, I caught a ride here with a friend. I knew you would be taking me home tonight. Where's your truck?"

8

Unfortunately, Bonnie was true to her word. Driving her home and a few more good teasing kisses were all that went on that night, but I had a great time and was looking forward to seeing her again soon. She seemed to like me also, and I did not have to wait long.

Before the following week was over, we had entangled naked in bed twice—once at her place and once at mine. It went on this way for the next two months, and I was sort of falling for her, and for all practical appearances, she seemed to be right in step with this on her side. Each time we made love, it was better than the last; and every weekend, we went out together. She took me to Oklahoma City bars and dance halls, and I was having the best of times. She was so easy to be with and fun as hell, and you got the idea about the sex. Everything started changing for me after that first night out with Bonnie, and I certainly was no longer in search of companions for a beer.

I quickly got into the habit of having "one or two" with Clay and several others after we had our evening closeout session at the west Guthrie plant. There were five or six local watering holes that we went to regularly, and while I had not yet been back to the Six-Mile Bar, there were a few places nearly as shady that we did frequent. As I was becoming part of the local circle, coming in with the good old boys and not by myself, everything seemed OK, at least on the surface. I was mainly running with Clay and Mark Charter and their friends. Tony would come in on occasion but usually just had one or two with us and then moved on.

We even made a trip to Wellingtons Way, the dancers' club where John's wife, Brenda, worked. Clay was right. Like most of the dancers in there, she didn't look half bad in the shadows but just a total wreck when she came into the light. And sure enough, she took two guys up into the VIP for obvious sexual favors. I guess that was why they always had the local strip clubs pretty dark. There were a few younger ladies dancing on the stages who were pretty hot, but it looked like most of them were strung out on cocaine for the most part.

I noticed that the same guy with the ponytailed hair whom I had seen in the Six-Mile Bar was also in Wellingtons that night. He was tossing around to all the dancers $100 bills like they were nothing, and he was pretty blasted. Hell, Clay and Mark were tossing their share of twenties around as well. I must have seen them change out a $100 for twenties at least three times each. Don't get me wrong. I was no choirboy; Bonnie or not, it was simply a cash thing for me— cash which I did not have. I still could not place where I had seen the ponytailed dude before, though, and I was now more curious than ever.

It was at one of these "shadier joints" called Jack's Bar that I would first start noticing some interesting things about my new colleagues. As was typical in the Western areas, this turn of events would involve horses, guns, boots, women, and money.

9

As mentioned previously, I fancied myself in tune with fashion and did what I could to look good for the ladies. I had some nice boots and would get a couple of new jeans and shirts every month or so. Clay, on the other hand, was the Oklahoma version of a *GQ* model when it came to clothes and primping. I would change boots after work if we were going for one or two at a local place but usually only changed into a pair of cheap Justin lizard skins that cost me $150. Clay had a ton of boots, and none of them, not one pair, were Justins.

Everybody had a gun or two in their vehicles; we just did. It was as natural as drinking beer at the plant office after work each day. We would often end the night out on the river or in some backwoods area shooting at road signs, opossums, or whatever struck our fancy. We got along pretty well together and were all good with our guns. I had one gun in the truck most of the time. The Colt Python .357 and I had the shooting edge over both the Okies when it really counted. More than once, Clay or Mark would show up with a new gun, and I really didn't think much of it. None of their weapons were off-the-shelf Walmart models either. They always came up with top-quality firearms. They let me shoot the new guns along with them, and it was great fun. As I said, I didn't think much about it at first.

Clay bought a new Chevy Silverado during the week, and it was one tricked-out truck. It had a custom-installed stereo system, and he bought new custom wheels and rims the next weekend to go with it that cost $1,800 . It was a sweet ride, and the three of us would often jump in Clay's new rig if we were cruising around or heading to a bar that might have babes in it.

Tony was unusually sharp with Clay and John several times in the plant that week, constantly up their ass for one thing or another. He would send me out to the east and west fields to gauge the eight 20,000-gallon tanks, and when I came back, he had Clay and John washing off compressors and scrubbing down the plant. I got to cruise the back roads, listen to music, and wave at the pumpers and ranchers pulling their little 1,000-gallon tank trailers around while they worked their butts off. I noticed that many of the pumpers in their trucks were waving back at me by now. Yes, sir, I had a much better week than the other two did.

Each of the big 20,000-gallon tanks were supposed to be gauged every day. You would drive out to the tank, climb the tank ladder or steps depending on design, take your line gauge up, and drop it down to the bottom of the tank, sort of like sounding for the bottom of the sea from a ship. The gauge tapes all had number measures on them, and the tanks were twenty feet tall. So if your tape was wet or colored at 8.5 feet, that was the level of liquid in the tanks. Then you would mark the level in the logbook. When the tanks were close to full, usually around 17 feet, you called for a couple of big 10,000-gallon pump trucks to come and empty them.

Some of the richer oil fields added two feet of good-grade crude a day into the big tanks, while others would only add five to six inches. The tanks contained a combination of condensate drip gasoline or light crude oil, depending on which wells were tied into the tank. Some of the condensate drip was clear, clean, and high enough in octane that you could actually run it in your car if you mixed it half and half with gasoline.

If it was light crude, the company got paid about 65¢ a gallon. For the clear condensate, they would get almost 60¢ a gallon. This was all bonus cash. Overflow from the production wells, and they did not have to pay a thing for it. It was free profit. All they had to do was report it to the IRS as taxable income. Many of the smaller companies kept double sets of books, one for the company and one for the IRS, and only reported about half the total.

On Thursday, Tony had both John and Clay in his office, screaming at them when I came in from gauging the tanks. I didn't catch it all, but I heard enough. "And you dumb fucking pricks, if you think I am stupid, if I ever—now get the fuck out." He really was up their ass.

I talked to them about it when we went to the local BBQ for lunch the next day. "Tony is sure up your asses this week." I asked, "What's up with that?"

"Dunno, I heard his wife found out he has been banging Mandy from the Six-Mile Bar. Maybe he thinks I told her or something?" Clay replied as he jammed a slice of BBQ pork into his mouth. "He'll get over it. He always does."

"Because he's a fucking asshole sumbitch, that's why," growled John as he kicked a chair and went outside to smoke.

Mark Charter was the main operator for the company measurement teams, and he was married to a local girl from Edmond named Lori. They lived on a little ranch outside Crescent. She was big time into horses, and from what I could gather from listening to the banter at the bars, she was very attractive and a pro rodeo caliber barrel racer. She had a few barrel racers and quarter horses worth over $10,000 each, three of them courtesy of her loving husband, Mark.

Mark bought a new Chevy one-ton dual-wheel truck for his ranch shortly after Mr. Haynes bought his. While not as much of a chick magnet as Clint's Silverado, it was a ranch workhorse for sure. It had a six-liter diesel engine and a fully customized fifth-wheel towing package and was loaded to the hilt. He also bought a new five-horse trailer to go with the big dual-wheeled beast. *Good for him*, I thought. *His wife must be doing great at barrel racing to cover those kinds of costs.*

We were at Jack's Bar one evening during the next week, having beers. It seemed like a normal day, nothing really different about it in the beginning. Clay had a pair of boots on that I had not seen before. *Ostrich or emu*, I thought when I saw them, but I never asked. We were joined by Sandy Anderson, Mike Johnson, and Jack Lambert—all pretty good old boys—and I had no issue with any of them.

Sandy also noticed Clay's boots. "Are those the new Luccheses you been talking about?" Sandy asked, pointing out Clay's boots.

"Yeah, pretty nice, eh?" Clay said smugly, giving us all a view.

"Ostrich Luccheses?" Mike said, whistling low. "How much did they set you back?"

"Twenty-two hundred dollars, but man, they are sweet, aren't they?" Clay replied, once again flashing his boots for all of us.

"Yeah, man, they are sweet," Sandy said, and then he turned back to chatting with Jack.

I was stunned. *Twenty-two hundred dollars for a pair of boots? I don't care how nice they look or make your feet feel. I just couldn't fathom it.*

"My brother, Jeb, has a pair of custom Luccheses, cost him $4,000. I guess it's all about what you want to spend your money on," Jack told Sandy as he sipped his beer.

Jack was a local rancher who raised horses and no relation to the bar owner. He also had several high-producing oil wells and was doing pretty well for himself. Mark and Jack had been going at each other for weeks about the price of a horse for Mark's wife, Lori. The price had started at $17,000, and Jack was holding firm at $15,000. I had heard him make an offer of $14,000 to Mark a week ago, and Mark had countered with $12,000 and held solid. I liked them both and enjoyed watching the negotiations.

After several rounds and a few shots, they started back at it again. It went something like this. "Look, Jack, I have bought two horses from you already, and we go back a few years. I promised Lori I would be able to get her this horse, so why are you being such an asshat about the price?" Mark whined.

Jack's eyes lit up with a twinkle, and he said, "Because I can. Lori told Katie you promised to buy her the horse, and if you don't come through pretty quickly, you will be humping your fist." Jack hooted with laughter as he waved a bill of sale for the horse at Mark. "I have been keeping this in my pocket for two weeks, knowing you're going to have to give in soon."

Clay busted out laughing, and I followed suit. The whole table was soon laughing. Mark was not exactly happy, but he was a good sport about it. He leaned over to me and asked me real quiet, "How much cash do you have on you, Drew?"

I checked my wallet. I was pretty flush today. "Looks like $280," I said smugly.

He stared at me blankly and then said in earnest, "No, really, how much cash do you have on you in total? Or in your truck?"

I looked back at him just as earnestly but a bit confused. I counted the money in my wallet again and said, "Total on me is exactly $287?"

Mark rolled his eyes at me and turned to speak quietly to Clay while Sandy ordered us another round. After a moment, Mark leaned in real close toward Jack and said, "OK, buddy, you got me. You had your fun. You know I gotta buy the horse. Now let's get serious. I have a one-time-only offer for the horse, $12,000 tonight . . . in *cash*." I waited for the punch line that never came. It was a real offer.

"Twelve thousand dollars tonight . . . *cash*?" Jack confirmed, and Mark nodded. Jack paused for a moment, and then they shook hands. Mark elbowed Clay, who reached into his wallet and then down to his boot, handing Mark a wad of bills totaling $5,000. Mark pulled a bunch of bills out of his own wallet and counted out $12,000 on the table in Jack's Bar in Crescent, Oklahoma. Then he handed it to Jack like he did this every day. Jack made a quick count, signed the bill of sale, and handed it to Mark.

My jaw dropped as I just stared at them. Nobody else at the table seemed to be paying any attention. Clay and Sandy were chatting about boots and guns. A couple of local ladies popped over to say hello while Jack and Mark continued to talk.

Don't get me wrong. We were making pretty good money, and both Mark and Clay had the edge on me in plant experience so were making a dollar an hour more than I was. But even with the pay bump and OT, I knew what it was costing me to live each month, and this didn't leave me with a whole lot of money to be buying guns and boots and tossing twenties at strippers, and I was damn sure not ready to fork over the kind of cash money it would take for a new pickup or a horse like the one Mark just bought.

"Looks like you got yourself a horse," said Jack.

"Yeah, now you might start getting laid again," Mike chimed in, and the whole table turned jubilant again.

Mark bought the next six rounds as he was quite pleased with the deal. In his Okie mind, he had saved $3,000, so why not spend some of it on buying drinks? Plus, as mentioned, his wife, Lori, was supposedly very hot, and he was about to start getting laid again. No reason for him not to be happy.

My mind was preoccupied for the rest of the night—well, preoccupied and a wee bit on the drunk side as we were now in double digits on the drink rounds and no end in sight. The scenes kept running through my head—the boots, the guns, the horse, the trucks, and the cash. I mean, how in the hell did they have that much cash on them?

Right then, I made two decisions. First, I was going to the next rodeo that Lori Charter was barrel racing in and see how good she was—in all respects. Second, I was going to ask Clay and Mark why they carried that much freaking cash around and where they got it from.

I got the opportunity to act on my second decision just after midnight. Everyone had called it a night, and as the three of us rode together most nights, we would often relieve ourselves outside in the parking lot prior to departure. This was a bit of a drunkenly ritual, and it was during this ritual that I chose to inquire. "Hey, shit for brains," I asked Clay, trying not to sway too much and spray piss on his truck or, for god's sake, his boots, "do you *always* carry $5000 around in cash?"

Clay was also very concerned about any back splash catching his boots or his truck, so he was being doubly cautious. "What? Oh . . . no . . . the $5000 . . . today was . . . a bit of an unusual day." He slurred a bit.

"Unusual in what way?" I asked curiously.

Clay answered with a twinkle in his eye and slur in his speech. "Well, unusual because . . . I am a little short this week . . . I normally carry twice that much."

With the ritual over, Mark now joined the conversation. "What the fuck are you two doing to be able to have $5,000 plus in cash in your pocket every damn day?" I asked incredulously. I honestly thought if we had not been so drunk, the conversation would never have gotten to this point; but as we were drunk, it did.

"How much weight can your 79¾-ton Chevy pull?" Clay asked me, almost cackling.

For some reason, which at the time I could not quite fathom, this set Mark off on a hooting-and-hollering laughing jag, and Clay quickly followed him. They were backslapping and doing lame drunk Oklahoma white-boy high fives, while I watch puzzled at what was so comical.

"Tell you what," said Clay, "you get a 1¼-inch trailer ball hitch and a bracer welded onto your Chevy, and then we'll talk about it."

"We gotta check with Tony and Duster first, Clay," Mark said, no longer laughing.

"Who's Duster?" I asked curiously. It was a question to which there was no immediate reply, and now looking back, I might have been perfectly happy to never have found out.

10

Friday night, I picked Bonnie up at seven. She was wearing skintight Levi's 501 jeans, a wine-and-white women's Wrangler button-down with silver bangles sewn in, and scarlet roper boots. She was gorgeous, and I would have been perfectly happy to have just spent the night right there at her place, but I could tell she was feeling frisky and in the mood to go out. We headed out to Trips, and she was all over me in the pickup, hands roaming, kissing me, licking and sucking my ear; it was fantastic, and I damn near went off the road twice.

An Oklahoma state patrol cruiser suddenly appeared behind me and flashed its lights. Bonnie couldn't stop giggling and kept reaching for my crotch as I pulled over with an increasingly red face. I rolled my window down as State Trooper Leon Spencer appeared at my door. "License and—hey, Colorado? Is that you?" Trooper Spencer asked me with just a hint of a smile.

"Yes, sir, how are you tonight, sir?" I answered humbly.

"Good, well, maybe not as good as you," he replied, tipping his hat at Bonnie. "Have you been drinking, Colorado?"

"No, sir, not a beer at all," I answered honestly.

"Then why were you swerving all over the road? Ah . . . uhm . . . oh," Trooper Spencer said as if he had just answered his own question. He lowered his head, and I heard him chuckle while trying not to. He looked at Bonnie again with an appreciating eye, and this time, he grinned openly.

Turning to me, he said in his best state trooper voice, "Well, at least you were not speeding this time. Eyes on the road from now on, son, understand?"

"Yes, sir, thank you, sir," I replied meekly. I shook his hand, and he returned to his cruiser.

I carefully signaled and pulled out, accelerating to exactly the speed limit. Bonnie eased back over to me and started in on my ear again as her hand went back to my crotch.

"Yes, sir, thank you, sir. Can I bend over for you, sir? Please, sir, can I have another? God, that made me so hot," she whispered in my ear. She started working it even more, and I was totally on fire by the time we parked in the back lot of Trips.

She kissed me as I parked the Chevy—a long deep kiss, sliding her tongue in and out of my mouth and flicking my lips, a majorly erotic kiss. "You ever had sex in your pickup before, Drew?" she asked me, eyes smoldering.

"No," I lied, eager in anticipation of what was to come.

We were on fire, and Bonnie tore off my clothes and climbed on top of me, sliding me deep inside her in an instant. She was excited and started riding me like a wild mustang. The feeling was incredible. We were both so hot that we climaxed quickly but stayed together for a few minutes in the afterglow. It was amazing. I was really into her, literally and figuratively, and on the verge of falling in love . . . again.

We had a few shots of tequila in my Chevy as we relaxed and then walked hand in hand to Trips. The normal crowd was there. We joined Clay and Ann along with Sandy and Angie at a table and began to drink and dance. Ann was once again well on her way, but she looked hot as always. She was really a lot of fun, and Clay liked her.

I was happy, on a great high, and after an hour of dancing and nuzzling with Bonnie, I was ready to get out of there and take Bonnie home for the night. Hell, actually, I was ready for round two in the pickup parking lot. Watching her move when we danced and the way she was hanging on to me—sheer heaven. We left, went back to her place, and made love until almost sunup.

Around eleven the next morning, I was up making coffee, and Bonnie came out wearing white Victoria's Secret panties and my button-down from the night before. She kissed me good morning with an emotionally passionate long lingering kiss and then went over to check the messages on her phone. Her kiss had the same effect on me that it always did, and I could feel my blood rushing to the right parts.

I poured two cups of joe and started to whip up some eggs when I heard Bonnie in the other room say, "No, no . . . no fucking way. Goddamn bastard . . . bullshit . . . not now . . . not now."

Bonnie was obviously very upset about something, so I went to check it out and found her sitting on the floor with her knees drawn up, head in her hands, and tears starting to flow. I knelt down beside her and held her close to comfort her, which she accepted for a few moments, and then she gently pushed me away and went into the bathroom, where I could really hear her start crying. After about fifteen minutes, I knocked on the door quietly. "Hey, sugah, are you OK?"

"Not now, Drew, please, leave me alone for now, OK?" Bonnie said through her sobbing.

"Babe, just tell me what it is. And whatever it is, we got this, OK?" I said soothingly.

Her reply was volatile. "Goddamn it, I said not now. Leave me the fuck alone."

My options at this point were limited, so I returned to the kitchen and finished making breakfast, wondering what had Bonnie so upset.

She came out from the bathroom about thirty minutes later just as I was cleaning up the kitchen. She gave me a big hug, took my hand, and led me back to the bedroom, where she began kissing and fondling me with heavy passion. I wanted to console her, of course, so I did my best to support her and responded accordingly . . . for her sake. The sex was incredibly electric, and when we were finished, we lay in the bed holding each other close.

There are several phrases that a man hears in his life that usually bear ominous consequences. I had heard a few in my young but experienced life and was about to hear another. Bonnie pulled away a bit and propped up on her elbow so she could see me better. Even as an emotional wreck, she was gorgeous. Then she uttered that phrase that makes every man cringe when he hears it. "Drew, we need to talk."

Well, my gut began to wrench right then as whatever was coming could not be good, but I kept it all in check, simply held her hand, and nodded for her to continue.

"Dwayne . . . he . . . he gets out of prison tomorrow on some bullshit early release because of overcrowded prisons. He had a seven-year sentence, and he has only been in there for two. This is such bullshit, Drew. I am so sorry to dump all this on you, but I really like you, and I think you should know. I had no idea this was even a possibility."

Well, this doesn't sound so bad, I thought.

"What was he in prison for?" I asked, trying to be concerned.

"Racketeering, drug dealing, and manslaughter. He was selling coke for a big dealer out of Dallas, and he also got caught stealing oil out in Weatherford," she explained.

"And the manslaughter?" I asked as this was the one I was most curious about.

"He killed a guy in bar fight with a knife in the Six-Mile Bar over a bad coke deal. Three other guys were involved, but Dwayne went down for it. By this time, he was a real piece of shit anyway, so nobody really cared. I certainly did not."

I nodded sympathetically and then asked the only thing I could think of to ask. "Uhm, who's Dwayne?"

"My husband," Bonnie replied as tears formed in her eyes.

11

Bonnie went on to explain that she had filed for divorce nearly two years earlier and served the papers on Dwayne twice in prison, but he refused to sign, so technically, they were still married. We talked about a lot of things, and it went pretty well. I asked if she wanted me to move in for a while to make sure everything would be OK if Dwayne started coming around, and she said no; that would be a very bad idea right now. She told me Dwayne would stay with his family and not visit her. One of his brothers was a dirtbag attorney and had probably been responsible for getting his early release. He would be on parole and would have to be on good behavior as the local LEOs would be all over him. He would not give Bonnie any trouble, at least for a while. She said she had to take care of some things, kissed me goodbye, and pretty much sent me on my way.

I took a long slow drive through the Oklahoma backwoods areas as I left Bonnie's place. I ran the events of the last few days through my head and felt like I was diving into a deep pool in a part of the world I barely knew. While driving, I passed the usual locals driving their pickups and pulling their 500- and 1,000-gallon tanks behind them. I waved at them. Some waved back, and as usual, some just stared at me.

At dusk, I pulled out onto Highway 20 near Cimarron, about thirty miles north of my place, and realized I was famished. Clay had showed me a great local BBQ joint near there, so I decided to pull in for a meal. The restaurant was laid out for families, couples, and locals, although you could also buy beer. The food smelled great, and I loaded up a plate of sliced beef, pulled pork, Oklahoma sausages, fried okra, tomatoes, onions, and peppers. I grabbed a glass of beer and headed for a table.

I saw my favorite Oklahoma state trooper, Leon Spencer, with a BBQ plate of his own, sitting at an outside table by himself. I nodded to him, and he waved me over to join him. Not exactly sure what the best move was, I decided to give it a go and slid in next to him. "Evening, Colorado. How is your day? I am sure your night must have been pretty fair," he said with a slight grin.

I could feel the blush rising on my face as I responded, "Yes, sir, my night went very well."

"Good for you, son. I have known Bonnie since she was knee-high to a grasshopper. She is a good girl and doesn't really go out too much. She looked like she was enjoying herself as well," he said in between mouthfuls of pulled pork and coffee.

The conversation flowed smoothly, and I felt very comfortable with State Trooper Leon Spencer, so I went out on a limb and asked him, "What can you tell me about her husband, Dwayne Robinett?"

"Dusty? You mean her ex-husband. He has been in prison for the last two years or so," State Trooper Spencer said as he drank more coffee.

Dusty? What the fuck?

"Er, yeah, ex-husband, I guess. What can you tell me about him?" I asked.

"Well, he started off as a pretty decent kid—played tight end on the high school football team, did a bit of rodeo roping with his cousin Stoney Lambert, married Bonnie. He worked as a pumper for Anadarko for a couple of years, and then he got into drugs. He started stealing condensate at first to cover his drug habit. Hell, you can't really hold that against him. Half the people in Logan and Kingfisher Counties have 500-gallon pull-behind trailers, and then he hooked up with a crew out of Weatherford and got into it in a bad way. They got busted stealing crude oil tankers. Bonnie left him a couple of times, but they got back together until he got tied up with a major cocaine dealer out of Dallas. She moved out permanent after that." State Trooper Spencer paused and asked for more coffee.

"I heard there was a manslaughter charge against him also?"

"Yeah, Six-Mile Bar, our local shithole bar. Drugs, racketeering, gambling, prostitution, oil theft, you name it. A few of the local ranchers are fine in there as it's close to their places, but for the most part, it's the Kingfisher and Logan County organized bar," replied the state trooper.

"Organized bar?" I asked.

"Yeah, organized . . . crime, Okie mafia, whatever you want to call it. Why the sudden interest in Dusty Robinett anyway?" asked the state trooper.

"Well, Bonnie found out today he is getting out of prison in two days, and I hear he is a pretty bad dude. I just want to make sure she doesn't have any trouble, that's all."

"Dusty Robinett? A bad dude, around here?" State Trooper Leon Spencer chuckled, almost choking on his coffee. "Look, Colorado, he is more like a dumb kid gone bad. There were three other guys implicated in the manslaughter charge, and the prosecutor cut some kind of deal with them and left Dusty hanging out. He might be a total moron who got into drugs, but bad dude? Around here? Colorado, you got a lot to learn about who the bad dudes are in Oklahoma."

The checks came, and I offered to pay for his meal, but he refused. "On duty, conflict of interest," he said. He told me he would stop for a drink or two on Thursday, his off day, at the Bluebird Bar in Kingfisher and that, if I was up that way, I could buy him a drink there.

It was about eight in the evening, but my mind was way too switched on after the last two days' events to call it a night. I pulled into the Crossroads Country Store, even though I knew that Bonnie was not working, and grabbed a twelve-pack Coors Light. Linda, behind the counter, smiled and flirted some, but she knew I had been dating Bonnie, and when I did not bite, she backed off.

I popped a top on a beer and headed for the back roads to drink my beers and sort out my head. This was the first time I had driven the Oklahoma country dirt back roads at night, drinking, by myself. My thoughts spun. *Dusty? Could this be the Duster that Mark Charter had mentioned? Almost had to be. But State Trooper Leon said he was little more than a punk.*

Six-Mile Bar . . . organized Okie mafia hangout . . . what the hell would Tony be doing in there . . . and packing a .45 Colt?

Half the people in Logan and Kingfisher Counties have 500-gallon pull-behind trailers. That's what Trooper Leon said.

Twenty-two hundred dollars custom-made Lucchese boots, $10,000 cash, who the hell carries that kind of cash around, and how are they getting it?

Tony eating John and Clint's ass out for a week?

Ponytailed guy, why did he bug me so much? Obviously, I had seen him somewhere out here before I saw him at Six-Mile Bar or Wellingtons.

After my seventh beer, I turned onto Skeleton Creek Road and headed for the Ghoul Bridge, which was a way out in the boondocks area that used to be a booze transfer station in the Prohibition days. I was starting to connect the dots, but I still had way too many questions, and the reality of what *could* be happening around me had yet to sink in. The red dirt road was narrow and windy, and I was just chilling anyway, so I was only driving about ten miles an hour.

I turned a corner a bit too sharp, and Clay's Ray-Ban sunglasses fell off the dash. I picked them up and laughed, remembering why they were in my truck. Ann had been watching his Silverado like a hawk, trying to catch him going out. So we went out in my truck one day last week so she would not know he was going out to drink. It was comical. He liked her enough to not want her to *know* he was out running around all the time. He apparently did not like her enough to commit to her and *stop* running around.

Smiling inwardly, I returned to my thoughts. *Bonnie's husband getting released out of jail right now when things were going pretty good for me.*

State Trooper Leon Spencer's comments about the Six-Mile Bar flooded my mind again. *Organized, crime, racketeering, prostitution, gambling. Gambling . . . Ray-Bans! Ray-Ban Man, FBI AIC, that was it. I knew Ponytail Guy from the FBI shoot-out at Rattlesnakes in Green River, Wyoming. Son of a bitch, he was in the poker game.*

When I reached the Ghoul Bridge, I saw two sets of headlights on the other side of Skeleton Creek about a hundred yards away. Curious, I parked my Chevy and killed the lights. I have carried binoculars in my truck since I was old enough to drive, so I pulled out my Zeiss 8 × 32 minis to see who was parked on the other side. I saw a guy I thought I knew from Jack's Bar talking with Tony Williams and two other guys I did not know. I sipped my beer and chuckled softly to myself. *Well, I guess that answers why Tony hangs out at Six-Mile Bar. He is up to something, and obviously, since they met at Six-Mile Bar, Ponytail Dude is probably in on it as well.*

After a minute or two, I eased my pickup out of there but thought it best not to turn on my lights until I had driven a couple of hundred yards away. I just did not want to give any of those good old boys the wrong idea in any way, shape, or form. I opened another beer. I had the windows down, the night was cool, it had been one hell of a few days, and I was feeling good in spite of it all. *Probably because of my ninth beer,* I figured.

I was just about to flip on the lights when I heard gunshots coming from the Ghoul Bridge—three quick rounds, an automatic, 9 mm I would guess, and then two quick but booming rounds. Those would be from a .45 auto. I chugged my beer and drove another hundred yards, hit the lights, and hauled ass out to Interstate 35 as fast as I could. *They are probably shooting at possums,* I told myself, but my guts had started to crawl with the possibilities. In five minutes, I was so full of adrenaline that I thought I would have a heart attack, and I was shaking like a dog shitting a log chain waiting for the hook—and it wasn't from drinking nine beers.

12

Despite the last two days' events, the workweek was rolling along as normal. I had to admit that, when I would gauge the tanks now or I was looking at all the pickups driving up and down the lease roads with their 500- and 1,000-gallon pull-behind trailers, I saw things a bit differently these days, sort of with a coveted eye.

I had called Bonnie twice but got no answer, and she had not called me back. I figured I would give her some space and see how it went down. On Tuesday, I finally caught up with her at the Crossroads Country Store. She kissed me in the back room but seemed a bit standoffish. She said Dwayne had called her, but it was all OK. She just needed some time to sort things and asked me to be patient. On Thursday, I called Bonnie to confirm our normal Friday date, and she said she would get back with me, but she might be busy. *Might be busy? Well, crap, this week is turning to shit.*

By Friday at eight, I got nothing from Bonnie, so I went to her place, and she was not there. I left her a note, asking her to meet me at Trips. The usual crowd was there, Clay and Ann and also Mark and Lori Charter. This was the first time I got to meet Lori, and she was everything I had expected. It was easy to see why Mark would do anything for her. Nobody asked about Bonnie as word traveled fast, and they all just put it together. Lori asked me to dance a couple of times because, for all the things Mark would do for Lori, dancing was just not one of them. Lori was brilliant on the dance floor, and it was nice of her to show me some attention.

I was really not in the best of moods anyway, so I said good night at around eleven. I drove around for a while and then went to Bonnie's place. My note was still there and no Bonnie.

I went back to my place and found a message on my machine from one of the old ranchers I had met at Jack's Bar, a fella by the name of Dave Raymond. I had been looking for a cheaper place to live for a couple of months, more out in the country and away from town. He said his son had moved to Stillwater for college and that he had two-bedroom A-frame log house four miles south of Crescent now available if I wanted to see it.

I called him the next morning and went to meet him at nine on Saturday morning. The place was great, really quality, and fully furnished with upscale wood furniture, big homemade feather bed, great TV reception, and two fishing ponds right on the place. The rancher offered to rent it to me for 30 percent less than what I was now paying, and I gave him a $200 deposit and signed the lease right there. He gave me the keys, and the deal was done.

When I returned to my place, I found a note from Bonnie.

Hi Drew,

Sorry I missed you last night. Can you please meet me tonight at Randall's Bar at seven? I really need to see you. Don't call because I won't be home.

Really? "Need to see you"? Is that like "We need to talk"? I started to get that gut-wrenching feeling going on in my stomach again, and I had to swallow hard to get through it.

I focused on packing and moving my stuff to my new A-frame cabin-style home and, by five thirty, was all moved into the new place and ready to try out the shower for the first time. It was fantastic. Old Dave Raymond had installed a six-dial showerhead with two massage nozzles. He had also put in a high-pressure water tank and installed two water softeners. The shower was like a health spa, and I loved it. I spent thirty minutes in that first shower, and when I finished, I was mentally focused to deal with whatever Bonnie was bringing to Randall's Bar.

I saw her car outside when I pulled up and swallowed hard, trying to keep my gut in check. She was at the bar looking like Venus incarnate as usual. She gave me a great, big hug and kissed me twice, so I was thinking this might turn out OK after all. We chatted for a bit, and she reached for my hand.

"Drew, I am going to Tulsa for a while. Dwayne has filed his own papers for divorce, claiming half my property and 25 percent of my income for the last two years. My mom's place also has some nice oil rights, and he wants half of those also. He's a fucking bastard, and I am sure his brother, Richard, is behind it. They have named you in the divorce papers also, me committing adultery, all kinds of crap, which means I can't see you anymore. In the end, it's all so much bullshit, but I still have to defend against it, which is why I am going to Tulsa. My stepuncle is a lawyer, and I can stay with my aunt in Tulsa until all this crap is done." She lit a cigarette and exhaled deeply, the first time I had ever seen her smoke. She must be over-the-top stressed.

"No worries, I can come to Tulsa on the weekends?" I said meekly and reached to hold her.

She exhaled again. Looking down, not meeting my eyes, she said, "No, Drew. We can't see each other while all this is going on, not here, not in Tulsa, not anywhere."

My gut wrenching turned up a notch, and I said, "So we . . . are . . . on a break then?"

She crushed out her cigarette, slid a ten on the bar, and gave me a huge hug as tears started to fill her eyes. "No, Drew, we are broken up. I'm sorry, it's over. Good luck to you," she said through tear-filled eyes, and she walked out of the bar.

I watched her walk out of my life, and considering my options, I ordered a double bourbon at the bar.

13

Sunday, I woke up with a bit of a hangover; but after a couple of cuppas and some breakfast, I was feeling fine and started checking out my new place. There were about a hundred books on wooden shelves around the cabin, ranging from some real classics—Nathaniel Hawthorne, Jack London, Herman Melville, Henry David Thoreau, Dostoevsky, Edgar Allan Poe, Leo Tolstoy, Marcus Aurelius, Louis L'Amour, Edward Gibbon—to almost all the Tom Clancy novels. Quite an interesting little library indeed.

There was a shed in the back that had all the lawn equipment— mower, rakes, shovels, clippers, and some good fishing gear. It even had a nice Trek mountain bike hanging on one wall. The weather was cool as it was October, but the sun was out, and I could see fish rising in both the fishing ponds. I dug up some night crawlers from the yard and a fishing rod from the shed, put a six-pack in a small cooler, and decided to grab a copy of Edward Gibbon's *The History of the Decline and Fall of the Roman Empire* and head down to the ole fishing hole.

Dave Raymond had just pulled up in his 1969 Ford pickup to check on how I was doing. He stayed at the main place about fifty yards away from the A frame. He saw me with the fishing kit, showed me where he had stashed a couple of small lawn chairs for the ponds, and said, "C'mon, I'll introduce you to Joshua, Luke, and the boys. By the way, we only catch and eat the fish in the west lake." He grabbed a five-pound bag of dog food, I grabbed my kit, and we headed for the east lake.

He tossed out a handful of the dog food into the water, and five of the biggest channel catfish I had ever seen in my life came bobbing up to the surface to munch on the doggy treats. One monster had to be at least thirty pounds. In the next ten minutes, there must have been a dozen of them, several easily over twenty pounds.

"That there monster is Goliath," Dave said, pointing at the big thirty-pounder. "This one here is Luke. There's Joshua there. He is also a monster-sized fish. Judas, Mathew . . . I call this one Uriah the Hittite. You know the story of David and Bathsheba?" he asked.

I nodded. "Yes, I do. I am a student of the books of Samuel and Chronicles of the kings. Uriah pretty much got screwed and not in a good way," I replied.

"Well, I'll be darned," Dave said and shook my hand. "Some of these here cats have been around as long as I have. Before that, my dad had 'em in here. We feed 'em but don't think they really need it. It's a sort of family tradition and good meditation for me."

He tossed a few more handfuls of dog munchies, and then we walked over to the west pond. It was longer and wider but not near as deep as the east pond. "Now this here pond is loaded with blue cats, not real big, average about two to three pounds each, but really good eating. I seldom leave this pond without at least two for the pan. There is also some nice bigmouth bass in here. I usually try over here, right in line with that big pine tree for the blues, and if you're looking to catch a bass, I work the lake around the edges," Dave explained.

"I think I will drop a line out toward the pine tree. Was mainly coming to relax and have an afternoon beer anyway. You're welcome to join me if you like. Got a sixer here of Coors Light on ice," I offered.

"Well, that's mighty kind of you, Drew. Don't mind if I do. Don't mind at all," Dave replied as he sat up his lawn chair, and he pulled two cans from the cooler, offering one to me.

I rigged up the fishing pole, stuck a big fat Oklahoma night crawler on a hook, tossed a cast straight at the tall pine tree, and watched the bait plop exactly where Dave had suggested. I sat down in my lawn chair, snugged the line up on my pole, and opened my cold beer.

Dave took a gander at my book. "*The History of the Decline and Fall of the Roman Empire*, eh? Not a bad choice. I used to read *Walden Pond* often in my younger days when we were building the A-frame cabin, and I would bring it here to these ponds for an afternoon read, sort of in way of meditative reflection. In its day, it was supposed to be humorous, profound, and thought provoking. Plain boring, dull, and a waste of time is what I found it to be," Dave said emphatically as he sipped his beer.

I chuckled. "Yep, I got stuck reading it my freshman year at college in English literature class. I found it exactly the same. If I wanted to find out how much nails and boards cost, I could just go to a hardware store."

Dave guffawed in laughter so hard that he almost choked on his beer. He reached over and slapped me on the back. "You're all right, Drew. You're all right."

We talked of politics, blond and redhead chicks, and habits we ain't kicking until well into the afternoon. I caught two blue cats that weighed a couple of pounds each, just like Dave said, and fried them up that night for dinner. Afterward, I had a bourbon and continued reading the Edward Gibbon book. It wasn't until I climbed into that huge feather bed that I realized I had not thought about Bonnie all day.

14

Monday was a real strange day. I even skipped beers at the west Guthrie plant. I just didn't feel like it. I thought about Bonnie occasionally now. I realized the only contact number I had for her was for her place in Crescent. I stopped by the Crossroads Country Store and asked Linda if she had a contact number for Bonnie.

She said real sweetly as only an Oklahoma girl can, "Yes, honey, I do have a contact number for her. She asked me not to give it to anyone, but I will give it to you if you really want." Linda was a sweetheart, and she was getting more attractive by the minute; however, I declined, thinking that if Bonnie did not want me to be in contact with her, it was better to let it be. Linda was looking real tidy anyway, and soon I was distracted by her flirtatious banter. I talked to her for a good twenty minutes and ended up going home with two cases of beer and her phone number.

Tuesday was a bit better. When I drove into work, I noticed a brand-spanking-new 5,000-gallon pull-behind trailer tank parked with the rest of the pull-behind tanks at the west Plant gate entrance and wondered what that was going to be for. We did not have any truck in our fleet that could pull something like that with any liquid in it.

This was also the day of our monthly company "safety meeting." All the field guys from the east and west plants, the measurement teams, and the stray pumpers would attend a thirty-minute safety meeting each month. The meeting was followed by a BBQ, and this was usually followed by a social hour or two of beer drinking.

Every other month, we would be joined by Joe Dugan, Ryan Mathews, and a few others from the Pauls Valley plant, which was a three-hour drive south. Joe Reed, one of our senior mechanics who traveled between all the plants, came as well. The Pauls Valley plant was not as big as the west Guthrie plant and was much farther out in the boondocks, but it had plenty of oil and gas coming in. It was supposed to be way overcapacity with the current volume through the plant at 110 percent. There was some kind of county commissioning zoning red tape that prevented the company from expanding the operation at this time, so they were just biding their time until a ruling went their way.

Joe Dugan was the Pauls Valley plant foreman, and while not as big as Tony, he had that same kind of no-bullshit, borderline-renegade attitude. He never said much to me at all, even after a few beers. Joe Reed, on the other hand, was 6'7" tall and was about as friendly of a guy as you could ever find. He was long, lanky, and strong as hell for some odd reason. He had a rich Texas accent, and I liked him. We seemed to get on quite well. Tony and Joe Dugan always found a way to slip out together after a few beers, and I never thought much about it.

I was feeling restless after the safety meeting but really did not want to hang out with the "crew" at the moment, so I left early. More out of boredom than anything else, I stopped by the Crossroads Country Store to see if Linda was working. She was. She also seemed to totally ignore me. I mean, she was a little busy with a few customers, but that never stopped her from saying hey and flirting before. She seemed kind of nervous about something.

I noticed one guy in the back of the store staring at me; glaring was more like it. He was older than me, kind of rough looking but nothing really ominous—I mean, not like Tony Williams or the bouncer at the Six-Mile Bar; he didn't even look as bad as Hawk Nose, just a rough oil patch worker. He seemed fit enough, and I noticed a tattoo on his right forearm.

I moved around the store; grabbed a twelve-pack of beer, some buffalo jerky, and flashlight batteries; and then looked back. Yep, sure as hell, he was glaring at me the entire time. So I just stared back at him for almost a full minute. He finally grabbed some antifreeze and went to the counter to pay. I innocently slid next in line right behind him, carrying my stuff. I saw his neck turn beet red, and I knew it really burned him up that I was right behind him.

When he got to the counter, he said gruffly to Linda, "Where's Bonnie?"

"Don't know, Dusty. She hasn't been in here for a week now," Linda replied.

Dusty? Bonnie's husband? No wonder he was giving me the bad eye.

"Where did she go then?" he asked, turning up the tone in his voice.

"I don't know, and if I did, I wouldn't tell you, Dusty. If she wants you to know, she will tell you," Linda snapped back, not intimidated at all. "It's $8.75 for the antifreeze."

Dusty Robinett growled under his breath, tossed a ten on the counter, grabbed his antifreeze, and turned sharply to leave. See, the thing was I had moved in rather close behind him, and there wasn't much room to maneuver. He was pissed and had gained momentum when he turned quickly. He bumped into me pretty hard. I never moved. My feet were planted solid, and he didn't expect me to be so close, so he was caught off-balance and bounced back away. I saw fire in his eyes as his hand tightened on the gallon of antifreeze, and I knew it was coming.

The front door to the Crossroads Country Store opened, and in walked my favorite Oklahoma state trooper, Leon Spencer. He was quick to assess the situation and knew the score right away. "Well, I see you two boys have finally met. It was bound to happen eventually," he said evenly.

He stepped between us, pulled a package of Doublemint chewing gum off the shelf, tossed Linda a dollar, and tipped his hat to her. She actually blushed bright red. Perhaps young Linda had a thing for my favorite state trooper. "How's it going, Drew?" he asked me casually.

"Going well, sir, except I had no idea it gets this freaking cold in Oklahoma in the wintertime. It's unnatural to be so god-awful hot in the summer and still get this cold in the winter," I said profoundly. Linda laughed, State Trooper Leon chuckled, and Dusty Robinett stared blankly as if totally confused.

"Wait until you see one of our ice storms. They should start up after Christmas," Leon said.

"And then we got twisters and major hailstorms in the late spring. You'll love it, Drew," Linda said, smiling.

State Trooper Leon Spencer raised his hand toward the front door, pointing outside. "Dusty, can I have a word?" The two of them walked out.

I paid for my stuff and admired Linda's lovely figure as she worked the counter. "He's an asshole, Drew, but if he stays off drugs, he probably won't be a problem. He is just jealous someone finally had a thing with Bonnie," Linda said.

"Someone?" I asked, raising my eyebrow a bit.

"You dumbass, you were the only guy she's been serious with since he went to prison and Bonnie filed for divorce," Linda said, rolling her eyes.

Like somehow that's supposed to make me feel better? Tell it to this lump building up in my throat.

I headed out to my company truck and saw State Trooper Leon Spencer talking with Dusty Robinett out by his patrol cruiser. The conversation seemed paternal, and Dusty had his eyes on his boots and was nodding every now and again. I had to admire the state trooper; he was a class act. I even sort of felt bad for Dusty—I mean, to have someone like Bonnie and then ruin it . . . *Now who's the dumbass? Here comes the throat lump again.*

By Thursday night, Clay and Mark had just about had enough of me moping around and decided I needed to go meet some "birds," so we chose to go out for "one" at Pink-E's, a sort of yuppie college bar in Edmond. According to Mr. *GQ* Clay, it was supposed to have a ton of birds, mostly from Central State College in Edmond. The place did not disappoint at all, and Clay had some hot blond debutante bent over the seat in the Silverado, banging her brains out, within an hour of our arrival.

I was drinking Long Island ice teas for the first time and was soon blasted out of my gourd. I met a dozen lovely ladies from all over and even picked up a phone number by surprise. It would have been grand if she had written her name on it as well since as I was too pissed up to remember who she was. We closed the place down, and it was a night for the books. Yes, sir, I thought that Edmond, Oklahoma, was the place to be for lovely Oklahoma party girls for the next few months. That was before I knew about Tumbleweeds in Stillwater.

On the ride home, we had Bob Seger on the radio and were having our normal banter when I chose to discuss a thought path I had been following in my head of late. The realization that Ponytail Man was the same guy from the FBI raid in Green River and finding him here in central Oklahoma told me he was into some shit. Maybe racketeering, maybe drugs, maybe oil theft, maybe all three. The fact that Tony met him at Six-Mile Bar meant Tony was also involved in something similar. Then there was the cash my Okie boys packed around. It just made sense they also had to be involved. And who knew how many others I had met casually were running around stealing a bit of oil here and condensate there? I mean, for piss' sake, I passed fifty trucks a day or more on the road hauling pull-behind tank trailers.

So where do they sell the stuff? I mean, so many people? Is there like a mom-and-pop sell-your-illegal-petroleum-products way station somewhere? And what about those five shots I heard fired out on Skeleton Creek the other night? Tony was there, obviously involved in whatever happened. Seriously doubt they shot opossums. Then there is the Dwayne "Dusty" Robinett thing. He just got out of prison. How can he be a major player?

We continued to drive away from Edmond, and in a moment of inspiration, I piped up. "So what's the big deal about this Dusty guy anyway? I met him at Crossroads, and he doesn't seem like so much."

"You met who?" Clay asked questioningly. Mark's eyes got wide, and he went eerily silent.

"Duster . . . Dusty Robinett—you know, the guy you said you had to talk to before I put the trailer hitch on my three-quarter-ton Chevy for whatever horse shit you were talking that night. That guy," I said, reminding them.

"You mean Duster?" they both said in unison.

"Yeah Dusty, Duster, whatever, that's the guy," I replied.

Clay stared at the windshield and contemplated his response. Mark spoke up seriously. "Drew, there is as much difference between Duster and Dusty Robinett as there is between night and day."

"How so?" I inquired.

There was a brief pause, and then Clay said, "For starters, Dusty Robinett has only killed one man."

15

As the weather turned even colder, we started coon hunting at night and coyote hunting on the weekends, so guns became a big part of all our plans. My .223 Savage earned a solid reputation as a coyote getter. I had learned to skin and prep fur in Colorado and Wyoming, so I was soon popular with the coyote crowd. I had always been very interested in ranch furs—fox, mink, sable—and now that I had Dave's A-frame place out in the country, I thought about getting a pair of ranch fox to raise.

I started checking fur magazines and fox ranches and found a guy in Sand Springs, Oklahoma, who raised ranch fox. I built two cages on Dave's place and headed up to Sand Springs to see what kind of quality and type of fox he had there. His name was David Melton, and he was a great guy. He had eighteen breeding pairs and fourteen yearlings for sale. The fox were all superb.

He invited me to stay for a BBQ dinner, beers, and a chat. I accepted. His wife's name was Mary, and they were salt-of-the-earth people. We had a great evening, and I learned a ton about the history of the Oklahoma oil field, who the most powerful oil barons were, which families started out where, and which companies had a history of being "involved."

David mentioned Angus Williams, who turned out to be Tony's dad, as one of the big "heavies" in the racketeering and oil theft organizations that started up in central Oklahoma. Angus was just an oil field roustabout in the beginning but sharp as a blade and, according to the lore, was one mean SOB.

I drank as much beer as I dared and bid them adieu. I came back with a pair of silvers and a pair of amber fox and joined the ranks of fur ranching as a hobby.

Bonnie was long gone and rapidly becoming a fading memory. I was getting plenty of attention from the Oklahoma girls elsewhere, so I was not really in any hurry to jump into anything. I was dangerously close to asking Linda out but thought it would be sort of, well, tacky for some reason.

Clay and Mark had picked up a routine where, for three to four nights a week, neither of them was available to run around with. They always had some excuse or another, so I was only catching them on the weekends mostly. So I concentrated on hunting coyotes and raising my ranch fox.

There were five of us who were regularly hunting coyotes, and we had collected twenty-two prime coyote pelts, eight red fox, three bobcats, and another twenty-five coon pelts by January. We decided it was time to sell them and see what kind of money we could get. Being from the Western US with the most experience, I was elected the guy to find the best fur buyers.

While driving through Edmond one afternoon, I saw a well-tailored sign outside an upscale establishment with the words "Bob's House of Fur." The front gallery window had several very high-quality full-length fur coats and nice jackets on display. I went inside, where I was greeted by a very tall, very attractive, very fit, and well-spoken lady of about 35 wearing a tight black dress. She was well educated and spoke with a northeastern accent. I asked her if I could have a chat with "Bob." She introduced herself as Myra Breittlinger, Bob's sister, and asked me what I wished to discuss with him. I told her—with the adequate amount of pride and confidence—about our twenty-two coyote pelts and the fox, cat, and coon pelts we had for sale and that I was also raising a pair of silvers and a pair of amber fox. Myra seemed surprised I knew a little about fur, and she added that Bob would be back at seven that evening and that I could meet him then.

I noticed several flyers and pamphlets on a table in the store, and Myra told me to help myself. I scooped up copies of "Bob's Fur Buyers Price Guide," "Proper Fur Handling by Bob Breittlinger," a Hudson's Bay Company catalogue, and a copy of "Fur Fashion

Today," which was a pamphlet about furs in New York with a picture of Myra on the cover, modeling a full-length Kamchatka red fox coat. She was very attractive indeed. I thanked Myra and confirmed that I would meet with Bob at seven that evening.

Bob was wearing a nice Western suit with a bolo tie under his jacket when I met him later that night. He spoke with a rich Oklahoma accent and told me he was a native born in Tulsa. We discussed the ranch fox and fur business at length. It turned out he was very well informed about the entire industry, far more than I ever was. He told me he also bought wild furs, and we discussed some current prices on coyotes, coons, and bobcats. He took me on a tour of the fur house, pelting sheds, and the tannery. It was quite a facility, and had to say I was impressed.

After trying to return the favor and impress him with my self-professed fur-handling expertise, we both agreed that I would bring any more coons I got to him "in the round" (unskinned), and he would handle them from there. "What do you do with all of the coon carcasses after skinning?" I asked, thinking I may have found a possible bait supply for coyotes.

"BBQ," Bob said without hesitation. I guess I had a blank stare on my face as he went on to explain. "I have a couple of great family sauces, and we cook it up just right. You ever had any BBQ coon before, Rocky Mountains?" Bob asked.

"Er, no," I responded, quite sure I was being taken for a ride.

"C'mon then," he said, motioning for me to follow him. We went around to the very back, where he had a small eating area laid out. A large black man was cooking beef and pork ribs on a homemade closed-top grill in front of him. He waved at us.

"Hey, Tyrese, do we still have any coon left on the grill?" Bob asked the man.

The big man pointed to another grill to the left. "We got some legs still. They should be pretty good. Just finished 'em up for a crew from Logan County a half hour back. I can whip some fresh ones up really quick, if you like."

Bob and I walked over to the smaller grill. I had to admit the smell of BBQ meat was lingering everywhere, and whether it was beef, pig, or coon, it all smelled really good to me. He opened the lid, and right there smoking nicely on the grill in front of me, neat as you please, were four coon legs. It looked like two front shoulders and two back haunches, and it did smell very good. I could tell they were real coon legs because, even though the hide was off, they still had their little finger coon hands at the bottom of the bone.

"Go ahead, Rocky Mountains, give it a try. It's pretty fair, if I do say so myself," Bob announced.

Next to the coon legs was a small roast of rich dark-looking meat that also smelled delicious. Next to that on a small table were several BBQ sauces. I started to reach for a scrumptious coon leg and then hesitated. All those years of memories of being the butt of practical jokes and humor at my expense flooded in. I turned to Bob and said, "You first."

He shrugged, pulled out an old-timer pocketknife, and stuck it in one of the smaller legs. He dabbed a tad of sauce on it, brought it up to his mouth, and started eating it. That was enough for me. I picked up a paper plate, plucked the other small leg off the grill and did the same.

It was delicious. I ate not only my wee coon leg but one of the big ones as well. The meat was dark and rich and tasted fantastic. Although it was a smidge greasy, reminded me of duck, it still had a very nice flavor.

"What's the roast there, the small one next to the coon leg?" I asked, pointing to the rich-looking darker meat.

"Muskrat, it's even better than coon," he replied, slicing me off three big pieces of the muskrat roast and plopping them onto my plate. The meat was to die for, and it was indeed much better than the coon.

Tyrese brought us out a couple of red solo cups (long before anybody even heard of Toby Keith) filled to the brim with Bud Light from a tapped keg. It was a feast fit for kings. While we dined on wild meat and Anheuser-Busch beer, Bob talked about his family history of trapping and hunting furbearers over four generations, covering the entire history of the American fur industry. He confessed that beaver, grilled or roasted, was his favorite meat, with nutria from Louisiana a close second. Wild meat recipes for coon, opossum, beaver, muskrat, rattlesnake, nutria, bullfrog, alligator, venison, buffalo, bear, cougar, and others had been passed down his family line for generations, and Bob had added a little bit here and there to most of them.

When all the meat in the small grill was finished and I was on my third red solo cup of beer, I asked Bob what he would pay for opossums as we often caught several of them incidentally as well. "Uhm, well, you bring me all your coons on the round, along with your other pelts, and as a favor, I will pay you a dollar for each opossum, maybe $1.50 for the extra big ones—in the round though. You have to freeze 'em quick and bring 'em in, on the round," said Bob.

"A dollar? Heck, that's really nothing. OK, so what if I skin 'em, flesh 'em, stretch the pelts myself? How much will you give me then?" I asked, calculating potential profits.

He thought for a minute and then said, "Fifty cents."

"Fifty cents more? For all that work, that's not hardly worth it," I grumbled.

"No, not 50¢ more," Bob corrected, "I mean 50¢ total."

"What? You're going to pay a dollar on the round for frozen, dead, grinning opossum and yet only 50¢ if I skin and handle the hides?" I asked, confused.

"Yep." Bob chuckled. "C'mon, let me show you something that may clear it up." We went into an insulated building that had several large industrial freezers inside. He moved to the last one and opened the lid. The freezer was chock-full of three- to five-pound packages of opossum, coon, and other wild meat.

I looked at him curiously, still not quite grasping it all. "I pay you a dollar for an opossum. I get four pounds of meat off the same critter and sell it for 55¢ a pound. That's $2.20. I get another $1.50 for the skin, total of $3.70. That's $2.70-plus profit per opossum. I get about 4,000 opossums each season, just over $11,000 for the work. Plus, I keep people employed." He intentionally did not call the opossum hide a pelt. "I can pay all my folks here for two months and still pocket $4,000. That makes me grin," he said, flashing a big old Oklahoma smile.

"Besides, I consider it my civic duty to give something back to the community," he added smugly.

I must have still looked puzzled about his last comment. "Look, with hamburger at $2.89 a pound and climbing, somebody has to feed all these hillbilly rednecks and locals. Most of them have way too many kids to feed, and if it wasn't for the coon and possum, many of the kids would not get much meat. It's my civic duty to help out," he said with a second grin. I laughed and sipped my beer.

"Where did you say you worked at, Rocky Mountain?" Bob asked inquisitively.

I don't believe I did say where I worked at. What are you up to with that comment there, raccoon Bob? "For Gulf Energy at the west Guthrie plant mostly, but I cover the east plant and the field tanks as well," I replied.

"The old Buckeye plants?" Bob asked, eyeing me curiously.

"Yeah." I chuckled, remembering the animated conversation when I first met John at the west plant about the Buckeye–Gulf Energy–Gary-Williams merger.

Bob's eyes sort of went a bit sly for a moment and then brightened quickly again. "Hey, you said you are a bourbon guy, right? Have a seat, and I'll grab a bottle of Buffalo Trace, and we can have a shot."

I don't exactly recall saying that I am a bourbon guy either. Buffalo Trace was, however, grand stuff, so I said, "Sure, sounds great."

Bob returned with the bourbon and a slinky, absolutely gorgeous tall Myra by his side. She was stunning in her black dress and the way she walked in heels, definitely a model. She joined us at the table, and Bob poured three drinks. Myra was a brilliant conversationalist, and over the next thirty minutes, she had me babbling out my entire life history, including the early days as a roustabout; the FBI raid in Green River; my work with Recco, including the Hiroshima episode; how I became an operator; how I arrived in Oklahoma; and how, when, and with whom I lost my virginity.

"So, you work at the west Guthrie plant now?" she asked me, her eyes twinkling seductively. "Do you know Tony Williams or John Lordell?"

The bourbon had warmed me up considerably, and I was quite relaxed by this time. "Sure, I actually work for Tony. He is the area superintendent, and John is an operator at west Guthrie."

She crossed her legs, appearing casual, but it was an incredibly sexy move. She sipped her bourbon and asked, "So how long have you been there?" I told her nine months and looked at her sexy legs while trying hard not to look like I was looking.

Maybe it was Myra, maybe it was the bourbon, maybe it was because Bob and I were eating coon legs together earlier, or maybe I really was just a dumbass; but for whatever reason, it never dawned on me to ask why she was so interested in my life and work history. Her questions were intricately woven like a fine tapestry, and she pulled information out of me as natural as me exhaling a breath. She was beautiful and smooth as silk and had this attractive way of moving her body that kept the sexual energy flowing regardless of the conversation topic. Her laugh was intoxicating, and she laughed at just the right time to get you to expand more detail on whatever you were spilling your guts about at the moment. She was amazing to talk with.

In one brief intuitive flash of reason in between staring at her legs and listening to her laugh, I thought, *If she is Bob's sister, then why does she speak with a northeastern, almost New Yorker, Brooklyn accent and he is pure, unadulterated Okie?* The moment was fleeting and passed quickly as I continued to watch the high-cut slit in her black dress ride up and down her thighs. Little did I know that, just like the Hollies song, this long cool woman in a black dress would weave her spell and have me deeply entangled with the FBI in less than a year.

16

It was after 9 p.m., and I was feeling pretty good, so I stopped by the Crossroads Country Store halfway, hoping to see Linda, but I knew she was off work. I grabbed a twelve-pack and headed out to the dirt roads by the old east Guthrie plant. Around beer number three, I saw some lights back in the woods at the end of what I always thought was an abandoned four-inch pipeline. Curious—yeah, I completely forgot the old adage about what killed the cat—I turned off my truck lights and eased a little closer until I noticed Mark Charter's big, one-ton dual-wheeled, six-liter diesel truck hooked up to the new 5,000-gallon pull-behind tank. Then I saw Mark talking to Tony Williams, so I figured they were doing some late work or something. I saw a twenty-foot-tall red-colored tank battery near the truck. Funny, I never even knew it was there until now. *I guess it's part of the abandoned system.*

I was just buzzed enough to miss what was actually going on and thought I would go see if they needed me to lend a hand. I grabbed six beers by the plastic ring tie holder and walked over to them. They were in deep conversation. About the time I got there, I saw a three-inch hose hooked up to the top valve on the tank, and it was jumping; obviously, gravity was feeding liquid to the big 5,000-gallon pull-behind tank hooked to Mark's truck. *Why are they loading a pull-behind tank in the middle of the night?*

"Hey, guys," I called out in the most naive way possible, holding out the beers, "need a hand?"

Tony spun around quick as lightning, and I was staring at his cold, dark eyes and the barrel of his Colt .45 auto. I heard the hammer cock. "Tony, stop!" Mark yelled.

Just about then, the tank filled up and started gurgling liquids over the top. Mark ran to the large tank to close the valve. Not sure if I was going to get shot or not, I set the six beers on the bumper of his truck and helped Mark drain and unhook the three-inch red hose, coil it, and put it in the bed of his truck. Tony still had his .45 on me, but it was no longer cocked, and the barrel was pointed more at the ground than at me. I grabbed a towel from the rag box and cleaned off my hands. Then I picked up my six beers, handed one to Tony, handed one to Mark, and opened one for myself. Other than the fact that I downed my beer in about two gulps, you really couldn't tell I was so full of adrenaline from almost being shot that I thought I was going to have brain aneurism.

"What in the fuck are you doing out here?" Tony demanded.

"Drinking beer," I replied. It came out way more sarcastically than I intended.

Mark stifled a laugh, and I quickly added, "I mean, drinking beer, driving around. I saw Mark's truck, thought you guys might need a hand. Sorry, Tony, did not mean to cause a problem at all."

Tony stared at me for a minute and then said, "Well, you have seen too much now. Even a dumbass like you can figure this out. So either you're in or you're out. If you're in, then you meet Mark tomorrow, and he can explain. If you're out, then you get your ass home, pack your trash, and be out of here by sunup. And if I ever see you in Oklahoma again, I'll make sure you're shot on sight. So what's it gonna be, Drew?"

There it was, either in or out. I considered my options carefully for a full minute and then said, "Well, I guess I better get my three-quarter Chevy to Joe's all-night truck stop and see if he can put a trailer hitch and a 1¼ ball on it by daybreak."

17

Joe had my trailer hitch and bracers welded on and ready to go by seven the next morning, and I met Mark for breakfast at the Waffle House in Guthrie. He ordered pancakes and ham steak, while I ordered country fried steak, eggs, and hash browns. Mark was a real friendly guy, and it didn't take much to get him going on about the various operations they had working. He told me about the several company condensate tanks that they were pulling from as well as several lease tanks on private property. Then he explained the lower crude grades from other tanks they pulled from that were located over three counties.

I knew about half the places that he mentioned and had the general location of all the rest of them in my head. From what I picked up at that first breakfast, I could see this could have huge potential. I did some quick numbers in my head while Mark rambled on. It appeared that Clay and Mark were both getting an average of 3,500 gallons of either condensate or crude oil per day, three to four days per week, roughly 10,000 gallons a week, 40,000 gallons a month apiece. Even at 35¢ a gallon, that would be around $14,000 a month. They probably had to give Tony a cut, say, 35 percent, I was guessing; but still, they had to be pocketing between $9,000 and $10,000 a month in cash.

They had tanks and lines you could pull from during the day, and they had tanks and lines you could only pull from during the night. Tony pretty much ran the show but did little of the actual oil-procuring work. He would just pop in for ride-alongs to make sure that most of the stolen product was making it to his drop-offs and not "getting lost" in between. They operated their oil thievery scam year-round, but the summer heat caused a lot of issues, so they ran light in the summer but really kicked it up in the fall, winter, and spring.

"You will pull from these four tanks here," Mark said, pointing to the locations marked on a handwritten paper map. "They are all low-grade crude and can get nasty, so I would wear coveralls and get some elbow-length rubber gloves. You will start using a 500-gallon trailer at first. Use trailer number 3 or 6 if you can as they have new tires. You will have to pull at least two loads a week from all those locations and three loads each from these three here. That's a minimum of eleven loads total. If you take any less, the tanks may fill up too much, and the pumpers will get suspicious. If you take too much more, same issue. When the pumpers or operators gauge the tanks, it may look suspicious."

I looked the map over. I knew each of the locations. Three were very old company tanks, and one was on a property next to the east plant, close to where I had seen Tony and Mark the previous night. On all the oil field production maps, the older tank was listed as abandoned, which meant you could take unlimited loads. "Where do I haul the oil to?" I asked.

Mark pointed on the map. "There will be three empty 15,000-gallon tanker trailers parked here in a storage yard," he said. "Each trailer has a gauge to indicate how full they are, so check to make sure you have room in the trailer before you start pumping into it. Your smaller 500-gallon trailer and pump won't be able to buck 12,000-gallon head pressure in the trailers, so you won't be able to pump off if they have more than 12,000 gallons loaded already." I nodded and studied the map.

"The storage yard the trailers are in is locked by company lock 20112. You should already have a key for that one," Mark said. I nodded again.

"In the compartment in front of each trailer, you will find a lined notebook to mark your loads. Your call sign is DC. You will put the date, DC, and the code for the tank or line you pulled the load from. These are the tank codes for your four tanks," Mark explained.

Call sign? Tank codes? Logbook? This is beginning to look very organized indeed.

"You don't want to go inside the yard with a load if there is someone else already in there that you don't know. I doubt if you will see anybody other than Clay or me, maybe Joe Reed. He drives the trailers out when they get full." Mark added, "If it's anybody else, just park way off to the side, and let whoever it is do their thing before you go in. People don't need to know who you are, and you don't need to know who they are. It's better that way, believe me, especially in your case."

"What about Tony?" I asked.

"Specifically, Tony," Mark said emphatically. "Trust me, Drew, he has a lot going on, and the less you run into Tony, the better. If you see him out anywhere doing anything, always let him approach you first, and never go up to him. Got it?"

"Roger that, buddy," I replied sincerely. Staring down the barrel of Tony's .45 Colt last night was not something I ever wanted to do again.

"Any questions?" Mark asked.

"What does DC mean?" I asked curiously.

"Drew Colorado," Mark said as he got up from the table.

Mark paid for the breakfast and headed out to do his measurement duties while I reported for work at the west plant, deep in thought over what I was about to get myself into.

18

I made four runs that first night, one to each of the tank locations. I pumped my four trailers full of stolen black gold into the big tanker trailer without any incident other than a family of grinners (opossums) running away from me when I pulled into the big tanker yard.

Everything was business as usual the next day at the west plant. Nobody mentioned anything to me, so I did not mention anything to them. I did the same thing the next night, four loads from the same locations. This time, I saw Clay inside the tanker yard, so I went in and chatted with him a bit. Something was really heavy on his mind. We had a beer, he told me his route and what times he usually got to the tanker area, and I told him what I was doing.

He was hauling the high-dollar condensate, and he had a different call sign and codes for the logbook, even though we pumped it into the same tanker. Curious, I asked him about this. "So where do they take the tankers? I mean, they have to separate the high ends from the condensate and the low-grade crude, so it obviously has to go to a process plant somewhere. Where is it?" I asked curiously.

"The less you know, the better, Drew. But I will tell you this. Nearly every night in the spring, winter, and fall, those three tankers leave here with 14,000-plus gallons of product in each one. And if you start playing with the numbers, then you can realize how big this is and maybe will just keep your mouth shut and not ask so many questions. There are more tanker stations as well. This is just the one we use."

"Uhm, when and how do I get paid then? That's a normal enough question," I countered.

"End of every month. Tony will pass you an envelope around the first. Maybe in the office, maybe in the bar, maybe at Crossroads, maybe inside the plant. When he does hand it to you, just take it, and don't say shit," Clay said firmly. "If you have any questions, then check with me or Mark, and we will try to explain. Remember, Drew, questions make everybody nervous, and you don't want these guys nervous, trust me."

Other than having to replace the head and turbo on one of the big eight-cylinder GTL-A8 natural gas compressors, the following day was also pretty much routine. Clay was really on the rag again, so John worked side by side with me, and I had to admit the man was one sharp mechanic. He showed me several tricks and tips on the best way to manage the mechanic work, and I learned a lot from him that day.

I went home to my A frame, took care of the fox, and thought about what Clay had told me the night before. I jumped into my super spa shower and reflected on the events of the last three days. I poured a double of Maker's Mark bourbon, grabbed a pencil and paper, and started working on some numbers. I had worked about three and a half hours a night for ten nights and had made my eleven minimum loads for the week. Just doing two more a night for the next two nights would give me fifteen loads of 450 gallons each for a total of about 6,500 gallons per week. I didn't think this would upset the applecart and give the pumpers anything to squawk about. I figured I could make four weeks for a total of fifteen loads, totaling 26,000 gallons, which when multiplied by 35¢—the minimum price I had come up with in my head—was equal to $9,100. Even giving Tony 30 or 40 percent, I should clear at least $5K at the end of the month—hard cash money.

I poured another double shot of bourbon and played with the numbers some more. *Three trucks at 14,000 gallons times, let's say, twenty-five days a month equals . . . jeez, that's over a million gallons a month. At .35¢, that's $47,000 per month after we get our cut. There are more tanker stations than these, Drew. Isn't that what Clay had said? Holy crap.* I continued to calculate several more factors as the bourbon flowed. Nowhere in any of my calculations did the equation have a factor quotient that led to the possibility that I might get caught or wind up in jail.

My head was reeling with the numbers and possibly a bit from the bourbon as well, so I decided to go for a drive. I knew Clay would hit the tanker yard in about an hour, so I hauled ass to the west plant, hooked up ole number 6, grabbed a quick load from the closest tank battery, and headed for the tanker yard. He was unloading and kicking rocks and cans around like a schoolkid while sipping on a beer. He was still in a foul mood, but I wanted to chat with him anyway.

"'Sup, Clay?" I asked, grabbing a beer from his cooler, even though it was a Bud Light.

"Same shit, different day," he said, throwing a rock hard at a barrel in the yard. "Same stinking shit. Are you done for the night?"

"I was going to make another short run but not critical. What's up?" I answered.

Clay threw another rock and said, "You feel like a beer at Randall's?"

"Sure, I am up for it," I replied.

"OK, meet you there in an hour," Clay said.

That left me enough time, so I made my second tank run and arrived at Randall's an hour later. The place was buzzing with people, and it was a good crowd. Clay was already there and shooting on the pool table. It looked like he had been winning for a while, which was normal. He was a fair player and decent shooter. I put my quarters up for the next game and ordered a Coors Light from a cute waitress named Cindy. She brought the beer, flirted with me just enough time to ensure she was going to get a tip, and then went back to serving.

I was up next, and Clay beat me rather soundly, with me leaving four balls on the table. The pool games seemed to have calmed him down quite a bit, so I let him continue playing. I stood at the bar and talked with Cindy and a few others, enjoying the night.

Dave Raymond came in, and I bought him a beer. We chatted for a bit. I gave him an update on his catfish, and he gave me the latest local news. He told me they were going to reopen two wells on the back of his property that had been capped for almost ten years. A new company bought the lease and had brought in workover rigs on the wellheads with surprisingly good results. "Heck, Drew, I was drawing $6,000 a month ten years ago. If those wells come in at the same production level, I should get nearly twice that now," Dave said.

"Damn, you're going to be like Jed Clampett from *The Beverly Hillbillies*. I'll have to start calling you Black Gold Dave. What are you going to do with all that bank?" I asked with a smile.

"Don't need much these days. Probably just save it up for my son and future grands. I have been checking out your silver fox though. I may just buy me a pair or two also. They are quite the animals," he replied.

We talked about the fur industry and his old days of trapping coons, mink, and muskrat; and as usual, the conversation drifted to blondes, brunettes, and redhead chicks. I liked Dave and was becoming quite fond of him.

Clay had finally lost a game and was at the bar ordering shooters of tequila, so I wished Dave all the best and wandered over to Clay's side of the bar. I signaled to Cindy for a second shot for me. She gave me a wink and brought it over as only a sexy bartender can do. As she walked away, I, of course, was staring at her ass when I heard Clay say under his breath, "Bitch."

"Who? Cindy? Don't be a dumbass. She's a sweetheart. What's up your ass anyway? You been a shithead for the last week. What's bugging you?" I asked.

"They're all bitches, except when they are worse," he muttered and then slammed another tequila. He was getting drunk, and the anger was coming out.

Well, looks like whatever is bugging him, it's some kind of woman trouble.

I nursed my beer, and Clay turned to me unsolicited and said, "She caged me, Drew. The little bitch caged me."

"Caged you? Who caged you?" I asked.

"Ann, she's pregnant, planned it too. She caged me, trapped me," he muttered as he ordered us two more tequilas.

"Caged you, how? Like what? Like locked-you-in-a-cage-and-forced-your-dick-into-her caged you? Tied you to a cage and raped you? C'mon, Clay, you have been going out with her for as long as I have been here. It takes two, ya know," I offered.

"Nope, the bitch planned it, started pushing me to get married, and I backed off, so she got prego on purpose. Damn, that bitch, I really liked her too." He went on.

I sipped my beer and raised the tequila shot. Clay sighed and did the same. We downed the shooters, and I spoke up. "And besides, if you really like her, then why are you so angry? She seems like a real catch to me."

Clay sighed again. "Yeah, she is that. She is a real catch, real sweet, cute as hell, fantastic in bed. We have a lot of fun. It's just that my life is going to change forever now. Hell, Drew, I am going to have a kid. Do you know what that means?"

I thought about it for just a minute and felt a pang in my stomach for Clay. I mean, I liked kids, but I sure as hell never considered having any. I mean, with our lifestyles—running hard, running wild, maybe with the right woman, maybe someday, but running like renegades the way we were—it was not exactly the best environment to meet the "right" woman in to settle down with and certainly not the right environment to raise a kid in. Everything would be changing for him one way or another now, that was for sure. "So what are you going to do?" I asked, trying to be supportive but obviously failing.

He sipped his beer. "I dunno, Drew. I thought about several things. Abortion, give it up for adoption, but it's my kid. I can't really do that, can I? Hell, I am even thinking about marrying the bitch. I just don't know," he said as he hung his head sheepishly. "What do you think, Drew? I mean, what would you do?"

"Well, there are three key points I would advise for you to ponder on right now," I offered most sincerely.

"Yeah, like what?" he asked with red and misty eyes.

"First, for the next week or so, I would take it one day at a time until you get your head sorted. Second, if you are considering marrying Ann, then I suggest you stop calling her bitch in every other sentence. That will probably not go over so great on the honeymoon," I said a bit sarcastically.

"And the third one?" Clay asked.

"The last one, that's easy mate. Let's have another tequila."

19

Clay calmed down over the next week, and I even saw him out with Ann at Trips the following Friday. She was not drinking but was still smiling, dancing, looking as cute as ever in her tight jeans, and she seemed happy. Clay was doing OK, but he looked to be on a mission to drink the extra alcohol she wasn't drinking.

I saw Myra Breittlinger at the bar with a couple of other ladies, and she looked smoking hot. I passed by to say hello, and she was very friendly. We bought each other drinks and had a good conversation. She was an amazing woman who could really get you talking. She looked much younger in the bar lights, with her blond hair feathered slightly. Dressed sharply in tight black leather jeans, black boots, and a dark blue shirt, she looked the vision of a sexy midnight siren incarnate. I was about to ask her to dance when she excused herself with her friends and told me to pass by the fur house some time. I danced with a couple of other ladies, but after the conversation with Midnight Myra, I was just not into them.

I left around eleven, went home, changed from my dancing duds, and made three oil tank runs. I was in the mood for my first cash payout in the next two days or so and was counting my chickens. *Surely, I would get at least $5,000, right?*

The big news at the plant that next week was that Brian Dugan, Joe's brother, was being transferred up from Pauls Valley to the west Guthrie plant. The inside scoop was that he got into some trouble with the local LEOs there and had to get out of Dodge.

I was out in the plant changing some compressor lubricators with Clay when John came stomping around, all pissed off, to tell us what went down. John loved to gossip, and he was pretty savvy on catching just about everything that went on. We stopped working to watch his ranting and raving and listen to the news. "Damn, sumbitch fucker will probably get a raise too. Why the fuck do they have to send him here? Fried-faced fucker he is. That bastard will just screw things up around here. You mark my words: something bad is going to happen when that sumbitch gets here," John ranted on and was still ranting to himself when he walked away. He stumbled on a conduit line and nearly fell over, and I laughed at his idiocy.

I had no idea who Brian Dugan was, but I was chuckling at John's antics and shaking my head until I saw Clay's face. It was pale, and despite John's comical display, there was no humor in Clay's face at all. We finished up the changeout and went into the shop to clean up and put away all the tools. "Who is Brian Dugan?" I asked.

Clay washed off his hands and looked at me. His face was dead serious when he spoke. "He's Joe Dugan's brother from Pauls Valley. He's bad news, Drew, really bad news. You met him once about four months ago. He came up with the Pauls Valley gang for one of our safety meetings. A kind of weird-looking guy, stocky, looks a little like his brother, Joe, but wears glasses."

"Yeah, I recall now. I was hanging out with the big, tall guy, the other Joe—Joe Reed—and never paid much attention to that Brian guy," I replied.

"Joe Reed is cool, but Brian Dugan . . . bad news, man, just nothing but bad news," Clay said softly.

"He didn't look like much. But like I said, I never paid much attention to him," I added.

"He's not a badass like Tony or his brother, Joe, not a tough-guy type. He's worse." Clint went on. "He's a sneaky coward and just plain mean. I think he is some kind of psycho. No shit, the guy is a psychopath. When he was in high school, he wanted to date some girl from Elk City, and her dad said no, so Brian burned down one of his wheat granaries. The farmer almost died trying to put it out. Brian was seventeen, so he went to juvy for about three months. He started a fire in there as well. Story is he also killed two guys in Dallas a few years ago over a girl down there, cut their throats when they came out of a bar all drunk and not paying attention. Nobody could ever prove anything, though, no evidence, no witness. He has been in Pauls Valley ever since, and there are a ton of stories about him down there. I am surprised Tony let him come up here."

Clay finished drying his hands and then added absently, "But there is a whole helluva lot that I don't know. Maybe Joe Dugan has more stroke with Tony than I realize. Watch this guy Brian for sure, Drew. I mean, if he is around, always keep one eye on him. He's that bad." Clay was serious as death, and he was a tough Okie bastard in his own right. Despite his *GQ* approach and Robert Redford smile, Clay was a real scrapper for sure; and if he was concerned about this Brian dude, I would be foolish not to heed his words.

I was unloading my first tank load on the thirtieth of the month when I noticed that there was a new logbook in the compartment. I caught up with Mark a couple of hours later on one of the lease roads and asked him about it. He smiled a big Oklahoma grin and said, "That means its payday. Tony will give you an envelope in the next day or so. I don't know how, and I don't know where. Just take it, and no matter what is in it, don't bitch. If you have any questions, just talk to Clay or me, OK?"

"Roger that," I replied and headed on to my next tank. *Isn't that almost verbatim what Clay told me? Weird.*

We all had radios in our company trucks so we could communicate with one another during working hours. Tony had a real nice Chevy Blazer as a company ride, and he drove it pretty much 24/7. A couple of days after I spoke with Mark, I got a call from Tony on the radio. He asked me to pick up two hydraulic jacks from the west plant shop and meet him at the big auto junkyard on Highway 59. I found Tony in the back of the yard pulling the transmission out of a 1968 Camaro. "Did you bring the jacks, Drew?" he asked.

"Yeah, I got them both right here." I climbed under the Camaro with Tony and helped him set the jacks. He pulled the last two bolts from the transmission and told me to lower the jacks. "What? That thing has to weigh 350 pounds. How are you going to deal with that?" I questioned.

"You let me worry about that. Just drop the jacks, and move out from under the car," Tony replied.

I dropped the jacks, and Tony deftly maneuvered the heavy transmission free like it was a Tinker toy. The man was incredibly strong, and he handled the heavy transmission with ease. I helped him load it in the back of the Blazer, more as a gesture than anything else as he certainly did not need the help.

He handed me a rag to wipe the grease off my hands, and tucked neatly inside the rag was an envelope. I was rather new to this level of criminal subterfuge, and this surprised me a bit. I was just standing there looking sort of stupid while Tony began to wipe down the transmission and finish up. "From now on, Drew, do everything as if someone is watching you because they probably are. If you screw up, then it might come back to me, and that is something we can't allow to happen," Tony said softly. He was looking at the transmission while he spoke, but his words floated easily to my ear, and their meaning was clear.

"Roger that, Tony, 100 percent," I replied just as softly.

Tony went to the back seat, opened a cooler, and grabbed two beers. We chatted about the west plant and Oklahoma in general and drank the beers. Apparently, this was a seal-the-deal-type tradition with Tony. He mentioned Clay's buying the new Silverado and always flashing his boots and cash around as dumbass moves that might bring unwanted attention to him. I got the point straight away. *That explains why he was so pissed at Clay that week when he bought the truck. I wonder what John did that pissed Tony off.*

He was pleasant enough and a sharp character, so the conversation flowed smoothly. Despite my best efforts, however, my mind kept drifting back to the way he manhandled the transmission and the night I heard the gunshots near the Ghoul Bridge. This was a dangerous man, and I was determined to stay on his good side.

After another beer, Tony started packing up, and I did the same. He opened his door, and just before he got in his Blazer, he said, "One more thing. Buy yourself an automatic. That big ass .357 revolver you carry around won't fit in your back belt, worth a shit, and it only has six shots. You might find yourself in a spot in the near future where you need a better level of protection."

"I like the Python, and I doubt if it will take me more than two shots to hit somebody, let alone six," I replied defiantly.

"What if there are two or three somebodies? You don't want to wind up like those morons down in Miami last April who were using revolvers, do you? No revolvers. Automatics, Drew. That's the way to go. More shots and faster, easier to reload. Now I like the Colt .45

government caliber, but you can get a 9 mm or even a pussy .380, whatever suits you. Just get an auto." He headed out, and I drove back to the west plant thinking about his order to get an automatic.

I was pulling into the main plant gate when I remembered the envelope. I parked my truck by the shop so I could return the jacks. I pulled the envelope out of the rag and opened it slowly. Sure as heck, there was a stack of bills inside that appeared to be all hundreds. I counted the cash—$8,500 in total. I had never held that much cash in my hands at one time before in my life. I closed the envelope, carefully wrapping the rag back around it, and placed it in the glove compartment.

I put the jacks away and was cleaning up the shop, thinking about the $8,500 and all the possibilities. My first mission was to buy an automatic pistol, and same as Tony, I was a fan of the .45 Colt. I mean, what's not to like—230-grain bullets with a huge muzzle blast and enough impact energy to stop a rhino? Yep, a .45 was for me. I decided as I thought about the cash again.

For some reason I can't fathom, it still had not sunk into my brain that I was doing something illegal and taking some huge risks. I guessed the comment from State Trooper Leon Spencer—"Heck, half the farmers in Logan County have pull-behind tanks"—sort of made it an accepted practice, but then there was the whole automatic-pistol thing.

A big shadow filled the doorway as Tony walked into the shop. He went to the inventory shelf and started pulling some compressor-valve parts down. "You good?" he asked me while looking at the valves.

I nodded. "Yes, sir, I am peachy," I said with maybe a little too much enthusiasm.

Tony grunted in a half-hearted smile. "You got any questions?"

"Yeah. When can I start pulling the 1,000-gallon tank?"

20

The 1,000-gallon tank had some pros and cons. I only needed to pull half the number of loads, so I could get more loads faster during the week, but since I was only able to pull so much out of my tank batteries, all this really did for the moment was complete my weekly tank runs quicker and left me with more time on my hands. Plus, there was one tank that I still had to use, a 500-gallon pull-behind tank, because the road was just too rough. I was whining about all this to Clay and Mark at Jack's Bar one night, and with their usual level of support, they both just busted out laughing.

"Gets in your blood, doesn't it, Drew? The oil field, the sidelines, the extra cash," Clay said matter-of-factly.

"I'll tell Tony you have some free time in the evenings and see if he will give you another tank or two to pull loads from. Otherwise, you can go out bootlegging, but that shit gets real dangerous really quick," Mark added.

"Bootlegging?" I inquired curiously.

"This is a big state, and there are several groups that all have their own territories. All do their own thing. The big dogs sort it out at the top and agree who gets what. Duster runs most of southeastern Oklahoma but is rumored to control a hell of a lot more than that. The quadrant from 170 miles north of Guthrie, all west of I-35, it includes Elk City and Pauls Valley. This includes the ranchers and farm lease tanks and wells also. If it produces oil or gas, it's in someone's territory," Clay said as he sipped his beer in retrospect. "Most of the production companies have been around long enough that they have an inspector or county commissioner in their pocket, so everybody gets a cut. The only thing everyone has to watch out for is the company financial or production audits. They all have to be done by a third party, and more than once, these fucking audits have taken folks down."

"Folks, hell, they have taken whole companies down and put people in jail," Mark added spitefully.

Jail? Is that even a possibility for what I am doing? Having no interest to discuss people going to jail, I returned the conversation to the previous subject. "Bootlegging?" I inquired again patiently.

"Every now and then, some dumbass or dickhead will get greedy and try to grab a load or two out of somebody else's territory. It's not hard at all really, and it does happen, but it's hellfire and brimstone if you get caught. One of the worst things that can happen to you is to get caught or even get accused of bootlegging some crude out of someone else's territory. They don't always kill you, but you're pretty much run out of the state on a rail, unless there's a war going on," Mark added.

War? What the heck, a war? You mean like war? *Huh, what is it good for war? Absolutely nothing. Say it again. That kind of war?*

"A war? Like, c'mon, what kind of war?" I asked, now really curious.

"Some shit will go down between a couple of crews, and then everybody just starts going batshit crazy for a couple of weeks, stealing oil right and left, starting fires, shooting shit up," Mark commented.

"Including each other. It gets real Wild West 'cause just about anything goes. As long as you don't hurt women or kids, it's fair game out there," Clay added.

"You guys ever been involved in anything like that?" I asked, now extra curious.

"The three-day condensate war between Caddo and Grady Counties a few years back, just south of here about seventy miles. It lasted nearly ten days. Don't know why they called it the three-day war. I was only eighteen and was running with my cousin Quincy from Elk City at the time. We were just going for the rush, but we still pulled several loads out of Caddo County, made some cash, and drew fire a couple of times," Clay spouted off a bit cocky as if he were a veteran soldier relaying an account from a battle on the front lines.

"Yeah, it was great until you got caught pounding that Anadarko foreman's wife outside Grady. They chased your ass back to the city and shot your pull-behind trailer so full of holes it was spewing oil out like a sieve all the way down Highway 41." Mark hooted. "That spewing-oil, leaking tank covered Highway 41 in oil and caused three accidents on the road. It was so slick."

"Piss off, dickhead," Clay responded, flipping Mark off.

"You guys are so full of crap, mildly entertaining but as full of shit as a Christmas goose," I chimed in.

"Did Tony tell you to buy an automatic?" Mark asked. "You think he would do that if we are totally full of crap?" Mark slugged me in the shoulder.

"Shootings happen around here, Drew. They happen way more than you think, and most of them never even make the papers unless its high profile. Full of crap or not, you can't deny that it happens after your introduction to the Six-Mile Bar," Clay added.

I thought about telling them about the night I heard the gunshots out on the Ghoul Bridge, but something switched on inside my head, and I decided to keep that to myself at least for now, so I changed the subject. "Why can't I just ask Tony myself for some more trailer loads?" I asked, sounding a bit like a 5-year-old.

"It's Mark's job. He coordinates for all of us. That way, if there is a mix-up, Tony only has to go to one guy to get his answers," Clay said.

"How many of us 'guys' are out there helping manage the crude and condensate tank inventories?" I asked.

"There you go with the questions again, Drew. Just keep your eyes open, listen, and don't ask questions," Clay responded dryly.

Again, changing the subject, I asked about the best place to buy an automatic pistol. After a lengthy and entertaining discussion about who had the largest weapon selection, best-looking girls, and lowest prices, both Clay and Mark agreed the best place to buy a gun was the Rifleman in Oklahoma City. "The place is huge, like the size of two high school gymnasiums, and they have indoor shooting ranges in the basement for firearms and archery. They have everything you can think of in there. It's definitely the place to go, Drew."

"Do they have all the equipment and supplies for handloading? I used to reload all my rounds with my dad, and it's a great way to get precision ammo. If you know what you're doing, you can load up some hot-ass hollow-point rounds that can outperform any factory load. And get this, they almost always cost less than factory rounds," I said knowingly.

Clay and Mark looked at each other wide eyed. "Handloading?" Mark said questioningly. Thus began an hour-long conversation on the virtues and benefits of loading your own ammo. I explained the reloading press system, the dies for each caliber, and the difference in handloading pistol rounds, rifle rounds, and shotgun rounds. I further explained the increase in foot-pound impact energy and the incredible damage you can do with proper bullet selection for your rounds.

I was on the way to becoming a minor weapons legend in central Oklahoma, and this would be confirmed when I returned from the Rifleman later in the week. It was something added to my soon-to-be racketeering résumé that would haunt me in the coming months.

21

On my next day off, I put in some Bachman-Turner Overdrive and headed into the city with $5,000 cash, burning a hole in my pocket. My first destination was, of course, the Rifleman, but I thought I might check out the Boot Warehouse as well. *No sense in Clay having all the fun with new boots.*

When I arrived at the Rifleman, it was exactly as the boys had described—huge, incredibly high-tech with all the latest and greatest. I spent nearly an hour wandering through the store, checking out compound bows, rifles, knives, shooting optics, and just about anything you could imagine involving hunting or shooting. In the optics section, they had some brand-new Starlight scopes that would collect enough light at night to be able to shoot without a spotlight. The scopes were amazing, and at a cost of $2,800 each, they damn sure better be.

Remembering my primary mission, I wandered over to the far west wall, where they had twenty yards of shelved, glass-covered pistol showcases. The shelves behind the counter were eight feet high and also stacked with pistols. They easily had over 500 models on display and probably another thousand in their inventory. I had always fancied myself as somewhat of a gun buff and was generally ahead of the crowd during bar conversations regarding guns, rifles, or pistols, especially here in Oklahoma.

I moved over to the automatic pistol section and was blown away by the amazing selection of firearms they had. There were several brand names I did not even recognize and new pistol models everywhere. I was worse than a kid at Christmas who was about to get everything he had asked for. I just stood there staring at each gun, looking back and forth.

"Hey there. How you doing? Can I help you with anything?" I heard a sweet female voice say in a smooth semi-southern accent.

I looked up at a very attractive blue-eyed blonde about 5'7" tall who was as fit as a bodybuilder. Her blond hair was cut short and tucked under—very cute—while her blues flashed like azure pools. She was gorgeous, built like an athlete with her toned arms and abdomen easily seen through her snug-fitting T-shirt. I could tell through her skintight jeans that her thighs were strong and muscular but still feminine and attractive. Her name tag said "Amy," so I took a leap of faith and said boldly, "Hi, Amy, my name is Drew. I am interested in buying a .45 ACP, maybe a Colt or a Beretta."

"Why?" Amy answered just as boldly, her blue eyes staring straight into mine—not seductively but certainly to get my attention.

Why? What does she mean why? That's a sort of crazy response. I want to buy a gun. I can't tell her I want a .45 because Tony has one.

Amy smiled and said, "I mean, why the .45 ACP when there are so many better options available today?"

"Uhm, OK, stopping power, I guess, and I sort of like the big muzzle flash," I murmured, again not wanting to say I liked the .45 because Tony had one.

"Have you shot the .45 much? And where did you get the idea about their muzzle flash and stopping power, from Hollywood?" She was smiling but obviously, in her cute and professional way, was telling me I was an uninformed moron.

"Er, uhm, a friend has one. Just thought it had good stopping power, is all," I replied, trying to find some way to save at least a little face. Suddenly, I felt inspired. "I notice there are several pistol models here I have not seen before or even heard of. Are these new brands?" I pointing to a few of the models on display.

This was Amy's cue, and away she went. "These models here are state-of-the-art firearms designed by Gaston Glock. This is the Model 17 in 9 mm caliber."

She dropped the magazine, quickly double-checked the chamber expertly, and handed me the Glock Model 17. It was amazingly light and not even made of metal. It was a type of textured material I had never felt before. I looked at Amy, puzzled. "Is this a form of new metal? Aluminum or something? It's so lightweight."

"Good catch. It's actually a high-strength nylon-based polymer material invented by Gaston Glock, a Swiss engineer. It was developed in 1980 and immediately became available to law enforcement, specifically the FBI, in 1982. It has only been on the market to the public since 1984. It's one of the hottest-selling automatics for law enforcement agencies around the world right now. Check out the sights," Amy offered, pointing to a target behind the counter.

The sights were square on square, highlighted with a bright white square "U" on the rear sight, and the sight picture lined up incredibly. "Impressive," I replied sincerely, truly impressed.

"The most impressive thing about the G17 model is it carries seventeen 9 mm rounds in its standard clip. Your Model, 1911s, .45 ACP only carry seven to ten." She continued.

I had started staring at her body, and she knew it. I was a bit embarrassed as the lady obviously knew her stuff, and here I was once again reducing the experience to the fact that she was sexy and attractive like the piggy boy I was. Determined to overcome the moment, I moved on. "That's awesome. What about this model here?" I asked, pointing to a new design I had also never seen before.

Amy smiled, selected another model from the middle shelf, and performed the same exercise, expertly dropping the clip and double-checking the chamber before handing me another stellar firearm. "Nice one. You do have a good eye. This is the SIG Arms P225 that just came out in 1984. It's literally brand new. They are the American branch of SIG Sauer, a Swiss German company who set up a design, build, and test firearms factory in Virginia. It's designed for close carry and protection. While it shares similarities with the Glock, it is not on the same level of firearm as the G17 for range. It's slimmer, carries twelve rounds in the standard clip, and is known for its accuracy even with the compact-carry design. It's big with the FBI, Secret Service, and American military intel groups at the moment."

The SIG was fine, but she pretty much had me at "the standard G17 magazine holds seventeen rounds," so that was my focus. I sighted the SIG at the target behind the counter to be polite, and again, similar to the Glock, the sights lined up quickly and impeccably.

"Here's the Colt Stainless 1911-A1, basically the high-tech version of the .45 ACP," Amy said, handing me another gun. It was a classic .45 and everything I had envisioned I wanted before coming into the Rifleman and my firearms-awareness session with athletic blue-eyed Amy. While it still looked good, the Colt felt like a Mack truck in my hand compared with the Glock.

I gave the SIG back to Amy, picked up the Glock again, and looked it over thoroughly. I returned it to its box and asked, "Can I see the magazine?"

Amy handed me the magazine, and the design was amazing. She showed me how to load the rounds and pointed out several technological advancements on the G17 that were brilliant. When she finished, I looked down at the three weapons on the counter. I rolled my eyes at the $2,800 price tag on the SIG, the Colt was $765, and they were pretty damn proud of the Glock also at $1,880.

"Does the Glock come in the .45 ACP?" I asked for no good reason.

Amy raised her eyebrow and then reached down to a lower shelf and brought out a new Glock. "Yes, the G19 is also chambered for the .45."

"How many rounds in the standard magazine?" I inquired.

"Nine, plus one in the chamber for a total of ten," Amy replied and then added curiously, "What is it exactly about the .45 that you like?"

Not sure where to go with this, I said and as mentioned having already embarrassed myself "Well, energy foot-pounds, I guess, for starters. You can handload a 230-grain hollow-point and get about 500 foot-pounds of energy from the .45, which ought to stop a rhino. It's got a big muzzle flash so scares the hell out of people if you miss them. And what's the standard factory load for the 9 mm 117-grain or 125-grain bullets? How can that compete with 500 foot-pounds of energy on impact?"

"You a handloader?" Amy asked, raising an eyebrow. I nodded.

She turned around and stood up on her tiptoes, flexing and accenting all the muscles in her athletic legs and ass, totally causing me to lose focus again. I caught the butterscotch-colored, tanned skin tone on her luscious lower back area as she reached up high for a Sierra reloading manual. She returned to me at the counter and said,

"Well, not too bad on your data, but you're a bit off on your ballistics there, Drew."

She flipped the pages to the 9 mm section and pointed to the 117-grain handload data. "Since the 9 mm is going 350 to 400 fps faster than the ACP, the 117-grain round actually has more energy on impact," she said sweetly. I looked to where she was pointing and was amazed. Sure as heck, the 9 mm with the smaller bullet was 545 foot-pounds of energy on impact. "And if you're a handloader, you can load up to 180-grain bullets in the 9 mm." She flipped the page and pointed to some new data. "I would go with the 154-grain Teflon and copper Sierra hollow point. It's got precision accuracy and puts out just about 700 foot-pounds of energy on impact."

I looked at the information in the manual and was again amazed. *A 9 mm at nearly 700 foot-pounds of energy on impact? With seventeen rounds. I gotta get me one of those.*

"Want to try the guns out?" she asked me, eyes twinkling.

How can I say no? I nodded again, and Amy went into action.

She loaded up a store basket with the three guns and three boxes of ammo. She called for someone to replace her at the counter and then went into the employee locker room. She returned with a Glock in a shoulder holster and some customized Smith & Wesson (S&W) shooting glasses. "Personal weapon," she said, grinning. "I like to squeeze off a few rounds when the customers are trying out their guns."

The firearms shooting range in the basement was easily the most advanced range I had ever seen, and while we were signing the release paperwork and getting set up in a shooting alley at waist-up targets, I learned a bit about Amy. Along with being tidy, athletically fit, and attractive, she was a fascinating person.

Her father was a retired US marshal and had taught her to shoot at an early age. She took to it like a duck to water (her words) and had been shooting competitively since the age of 14. She had graduated from Oklahoma State University in Stillwater with a BS degree in law enforcement and a minor in criminal justice. She had just been accepted at the FBI Training Center in Quantico and would be leaving for Virginia next September. She had worked part time at the Rifleman for the last five years because she loved firearms, and they gave her great discounts on guns and ammo.

They called my number, and Amy lined me up in the shooting slot and gave me some last-minute guidance on the G17. The gun was flawless, and I was shooting four-inch groups of three at the head and heart at a distance of fifty feet. Recoil was nearly nonexistent, and there was almost no deflection from the front and rear sights after each shot. I dropped the clip, double-checked the chamber on the G17, and traded her for the SIG. It was also a stellar weapon—light, trim, fast, amazing. Ten rounds in the standard clip, though, and one hefty price tag.

I noticed an attractive tall blond woman with her long hair pulled back into a ponytail shooting in a slot about five lanes away. She seemed to be shooting quite well, and she had a digital timer above her shooting lane. She was wearing skintight blue jeans and a tight-fitting T-shirt, similar to Amy's outfit. Even with shooting glasses and double earmuffs on, she was looking incredibly sexy, something I always seemed to notice. And somehow she looked vaguely familiar.

I noticed Amy noticing me noticing the tall blond woman with the ponytail, so I quickly stepped back and motioned for Amy to have a go at a couple of targets. She smiled like the Cheshire cat and introduced me to her weapon. "It's a Glock 19 modified with an adjusted featherweight trigger pull and one-quarter-inch longer barrel than the G17," she said with pride.

She signaled to move the targets to 100 feet and moved into shooting position. She adjusted her shoulder holster and donned the S&W shooting glasses. She had a two-target setup, and I noticed the electric timer was now lit up in her shooting lane as well. What happened next was almost like a blur. Amy drew her Glock and began to fire in quick groups of three. Head and then body, head and then body as she changed targets.

Her shooting was superb. She had drawn the pistol and put three shots in four-inch groups in the head and heart of both targets at 100 feet away. She had fired twelve rounds. The timer read 5.2 seconds.

I was standing there with my mouth open, catching flies and staring at Amy, when I realized I was still holding the SIG Arms 9 mm. I dumped the magazine and cleared the gun. I had almost forgot about the Colt when Amy handed me the stainless .45 and a magazine. I popped the magazine in, chambered a round, took my shooting position, fired two quick rounds, and promptly missed both shots at the head. The recoil was almost double that of the Glock and the SIG. I lined up again and hit the target in the body area with the last six rounds, but the shooting was not at all impressive.

I dropped the magazine, double-cleared the chamber, and handed the Colt back to Amy, who was smiling like a striped-ass baboon. "So? You still want a .45, Drew?"

22

I ended up spending $2,600 at the Rifleman in total, but Amy cut me some great deals. I chose the Glock 17, and she knocked $200 off the price of the gun, so I only paid $1,680 for the pistol. I bought a Super Rock Chucker reloading press, a set of 9 mm dies, powder measure, brass polisher, a current Sierra reloading manual with the latest ballistics and loading data, and two cans of IMR 4350 gunpowder that matched the Sierra reloading data. On Amy's advice, I also bought four boxes of bullets, all 150 to 154 grain. I bought 100 premium copper-coated Speers, 100 cross copper Sierras, and 200 Teflon, copper-coated Sierra hollow points.

I added to that a set of those smart-looking S&W shooting glasses, a shoulder holster, and 300 rounds of premium completed 125-grain federal ammo. Amy said they were great brass for reloading after you fire form them in your gun. It would add up to 400 rounds of high-quality ammo in the coming weeks.

On the way out to my truck, I saw the tall blond woman from the shooting range in the parking lot. She had the trunk open on a new Crown Victoria LTD parked just one car away from me. She was organizing some gear in the trunk, and I was, of course, standing there staring when she turned and looked at me directly in the eyes. It was Myra Breittlinger. When she noticed me, she also stared for a moment, and then she walked straight over to me. "Hey, Drew, how are you? What's in the box?" she asked with her incredible smile.

She was standing there with her hands on her hips and her tight jeans, looking incredible like a feline ponytailed tigress, and it took all I had just to speak and not continue to stare. "Gun . . . er, I mean, I bought a gun . . . and some other stuff," I stammered.

"Really, what did you get? I saw you shooting the 1911, but if Amy had anything to say about it, I am sure she talked you into something of more precision," Myra said, again with that smile.

She had moved in closer and was considering the box I had placed on the tailgate of my truck. She made a low whistling sound. "And some other stuff. Looks like you're setting up for handloading rounds for half a county. I take it you know how to load your own ammo?" she asked me as she cocked her head inquisitively to one side.

"Yeah, I started reloading with my dad when I was 12. It's a great hobby, and I enjoy it. Plus, you can really develop some great rounds once you learn the data," I replied.

She noticed the gun case in the box and said with appreciation, "A Glock, very nice. The 17?"

I nodded and reached for the case. I pulled out the Glock 17, dropped the magazine, and double-checked the chamber just like Amy had showed me before I handed it to Myra, who was watching me with one eyebrow raised in appreciation. "So you grew up around guns then. How long have you been shooting?" she asked as she admired the Glock.

I couldn't help myself and just admired her while she admired the gun. I was glad I had my sunglasses on, but I got the feeling Myra knew where my eyes were looking anyway. "Uhm, probably about fifteen years, give or take. It's in my blood for sure," I answered.

"Kind of like the oil field," she said very softly as she targeted several things with the Glock. "Very nice weapon, Drew. I like the Glocks."

"What do you shoot? I saw you on the range and noticed you had the timer going in your lane. You practicing to join the FBI or something like Amy is?" I joked.

She handed me back the G17 and said quietly but rather profoundly, "Well, I don't really need to practice for them. Here, let me show you my weapon." I followed her over to the LTD and again was glad I had on my sunglasses on as she bent down into the trunk.

She pulled out a SIG Arms leather gun case and opened the box, revealing a very nice handgun. It was not like any of the SIGs that I had seen inside and certainly not like the one Amy had shown me. Myra ejected the magazine and double-checked the chamber twice before handing me her weapon. I glanced at the gun, looked at her questioningly, and said, "This is a SIG? I mean, it looks a lot different than the ones I saw inside."

She laughed her intoxicating laugh. "Yes, it's a SIG Arms, just a different model and caliber. It's a prototype, the SIG E6 PR in a .40 S&W caliber. It has four customized trigger options and several other features that may become available next year on the production SIGs."

The gun was impressive, and it had a different sighting setup than the SIG E225 I had shot inside. She saw me looking at the sights and commented, "Again, it's a prototype. This model has the day/night sight design. It is great for shooting at night or in low or bad light conditions."

I checked the sights again. Very impressive. ".40caliber S&W? I never heard of it before," I said and pulled out the Sierra reloading manual from my box of newly purchased accessories.

"You won't find any data in the reloading manual, Drew. Like I said, it's a prototype, which means it's a sort of test gun to see how it performs, and then it may go into production. The .40 S&W caliber is the same. It's a new caliber designed to support law enforcement based off the Miami FBI fiasco that happened last April, leaving four people dead. It has more penetration and stopping power than a 9 mm," Myra said matter-of-factly as she put her SIG in the back and closed the trunk.

*What the hell did she just say? Miami what? FBI fiasco in April? Who? Didn't Tony say something the other day about April in Miami? Automatics?*Myra laughed at the look on my face.

"I, er, sort of thought you were a model—I mean, the fur coats and all that. I like this look also by the way. It's just the two don't often connect. How did you learn so much about shooting? Prototype weapons? I mean, jeez, Myra, you just schooled me on handguns like I was . . . er, a schoolboy," I stammered.

She looked at me in a sort of tigress-licking-her-fur way and then opened the door to her car. "It's a long story, Drew, longer than I usually like to take the time to tell it."

"How about lunch then? I have time. I'm buying," I asked hopefully.

"Thanks, Drew, nice of you. But I really have some place to be. Tell you what, I will take a rain check on that, though, OK?" she said as her dazzling smile returned.

"Roger that, Myra. It's a deal I said. She waved and flashed that smile again as she drove away.

Clay and Mark had told me about a BBQ place, Wayne's, off I-35 south, close to the Boot Warehouse, so I pulled in for some lunch at Wayne's BBQ. I was hungry, so I ordered pork ribs, sausage, sliced pork BBQ, peppers, onions, and fried okra. The food was really good as are most of the BBQ places in Oklahoma. In between bites of dead pig, my mind drifted back to the encounter with Myra the Tigra. *Just like the oil field? We were talking about shooting. Where did that come from?*

Having seen her now in a snug-fitting T and tight blue jeans with her long blond hair up in a ponytail, I was more enthralled with her than ever. *She's out of my league. Just too cool, too experienced, too sophisticated, but I like her. Can't help that.*

Prototype SIG? If it's not available to the public, how does a model like her get a hold of one of those, and who exactly is it available to then?

What did she say when I made the crack about the FBI? "Well, I don't really need to practice for them"? What is up with that?

Why did she make the point about the sights being good for shooting at night? It's a pistol, not a hunting rifle. I doubt she is out shooting opossums on Skeleton Creek. When is she going to be shooting at night? And at what?

I went back to the food, and I focused on my last few bites of sausage and okra as I checked out the rest of the crowd at Wayne's. There were suits and ties, farmers in overalls, families, local LEOs, hot soccer moms, and oil field workers. Oklahoma was indeed an interesting mix of folks, and I found myself feeling a sort of distant part of it all.

I left a $5 tip on the table and headed out to my Chevy and the Boot Warehouse. I plugged in some Lita Ford, "Kiss Me Deadly," and turned onto I-35. About three miles later, I saw the Boot Warehouse sign on my right and was taking the off-ramp when I was suddenly slammed by a wild thought. *If the .40 S&W caliber is also a prototype, then where the hell does she get her ammo?*

23

With that thought ricocheting off the wall of my brain I pulled into the Boot Warehouse which was also a huge store with wall-to-wall boots, jeans, hats, and assorted men's and women's Western wear. Several attractive girls seemed to be helping the customers, and I knew this was going to be my kind of place. There were so many things about Oklahoma that I truly loved, and the Oklahoma girls were at the top of that list. It just seemed like everywhere I went, there they were—attractive, smart, fun ladies—and the Boot Warehouse was no exception.

I met Samantha while I was checking out the Tony Lama El Rey boot section. She told me to call her "Sami" and showed me several pairs of the El Reys. I tried on a couple of them, and they were nice. Then she asked me if I wanted a beer. *A beer in a Western wear store? I am so loving Oklahoma.*

I said sure, and she went to the back and brought me a red solo cup (again, years before Toby Keith made them famous) filled with Bud Light. It seemed they kept a keg in the back for their customers, and I found it to be a nice touch. Sami took me over to the Lucchese boot section, and I had never seen such fine-quality boot wear in my life.

"Have you ever worn a pair of Lucchese boots before?" Sami asked.

"No, but my friend Clay has a couple of pairs. They look great, and he raves about them," I replied.

"Clay Haynes? From Crescent?" she asked.

"Yeah, the one and only. Do you know him?" I inquired.

"Oh yeah, he is one of our customers. We sell boots to many of the guys from up in that area," said Sami.

We were perusing the boots as we walked, and I checked out a pair of coal black ostrich-skin boots. I liked them, but they looked too much like the pair I had seen Tony wearing at Trips and figured that somehow it would backfire on me if I bought them. Sami was explaining that the high quality of Lucchese boots was because of the top-grade materials they used, and each pair was handmade. We stopped in front of a natural-colored pair of full-quill ostrich boots. They looked nice, really nice. I looked at Sami questionably. "Want to try these on?" she asked with a wink.

I was nearly drooling over the natural ostrich-skin boots, so I just nodded.

"Luccheses are made a little smaller than the El Reys, so I will bring you a size twelve for starters instead of your eleven and a half," she added. Sami brought the boots out and knelt down in front of me in a totally professional manner. She was describing the stitching technique and explaining again why the fit and feel of the boot would be much different than other boots I had worn, while all I could do was stare at her nether region and imagine the fit and feel of what was under her jeans.

I snapped out of my daydream as Sami tapped the back of my heel, suggesting I needed to stand up to press my foot into the boot. As I stepped down firmly, sliding the ostrich-skin Lucchese over my foot, this put Sami's head at just the right height, and her hair brushed against me, causing the blood to begin to flow to the wrong places and a tightening in my jeans. When she looked up to ask me how it felt, my face started to turn a bright red. She looked at me curiously, stared at my crotch, and stifled a short laugh. She did, however, maintain her professionalism and helped me into the other boot.

The fit of the boots was indeed amazing. I had never had anything quite like them on my feet before, and the feel was fantastic. "What do you think?" Sami asked me with a smile.

"Wow! These are a great fit. I love them," I replied as I began to stroll around the store, enjoying the amazing feel of the handmade boots.

I did not see a price tag hanging from the boots, so I went to check the box, still no price, so I turned to Sami and asked, "I really like them. These are a fantastic feel. How much are they?" I asked as I continued to stroll.

"Gives you happy feet, doesn't it? Just like the movie," she said, smiling. "These are top-of-the-line Luccheses and cost $2,600." She looked very sexy and was smiling at me with her best "I come with the boots" sales pitch.

As good as Sami looked, that price sort of felt like a sucker punch, and my head was already spinning from watching Sami move around for the last thirty minutes. Instead of playing it cool, I just told the truth. "Uhmm, I really like the boots, but I only have $2,400 cash on me, and I need to pick up a couple of shirts also. A bit limited on funds today."

Sami knelt in front of me again and adjusted my jeans around the boot to reveal the best look for the boots. I could feel her breath on my manhood, and my face started to turn red again. She stood up and said, "Tell you what, let me get you another beer, and we can talk about it."

"Sounds good," I mumbled as Sami took my red solo cup and headed for the back of the store.

Talk about what? I can't pull $200 out of my ass, and I am not going to drive all the way back home to grab another $500. And I need the new shirts. Still, Sami was hot, I loved the ostrich-skin Luccheses, and I was getting a second free beer.

Sami returned a moment later with the red solo cup brimming with Bud Light. "I just talked with Linda. Why don't you take a look at the new brushpopper shirts we have over here? She will be out in a few minutes to talk with you."

"Linda?" I asked

"The store manager," Sami replied, handing me the red solo cup. I watched her walk away to help another customer, and she turned to catch me staring at her ass. She did smile though.

I wandered over to the brightly colored new brushpopper Western shirts that were becoming so popular. The new collection they had was very good. There was at least a dozen or so shirts in my size on the rack that all looked cool. They were running in price from $45 to $110. That might have seemed high to the uninitiated, but the brushpoppers lasted two to three years easy, even though the colors sometimes faded a bit.

Brushpopper shirts were made by Wrangler and Lucchese, and each shirt model had a name. They only made that particular shirt for about two months, and then they would bring in new colored shirts in a new collection. It was a great sales pitch and add to that the fact the shirts felt great, looked good, and lasted forever. Plus, chicks dug them, and they had become a gold mine in men's Western wear.

I was checking out a Tequila Sunrise shirt that started with a sunset yellow color on the lower section, changing to a light orange in the midsection area and then a bright narrow band of sunset orange with a band of darker orange near the upper chest with just the smallest hint of red near the top. The shoulders, collar, and one arm were black, and I just thought it was one cool-looking popper. It reminded me of one that Kix Brooks of the band Brooks and Dunn liked to wear.

I had my hands on the Sunrise and another shirt when I was approached by another gorgeous Oklahoma lady. "Those are both good choices," she said, talking about the shirts I had my hands on. "Although the Tequila Sunrise is selling fast, so if you like it, you might want to jump on it."

She was about 10 years older than Sami but no less attractive, no less fit, and as she stood there in painted-on jeans, my jaw dropped; and without intending to, I quickly ran my eyes up and down her body, appreciating it from every angle. "Uh, yeah, it's a nice shirt for sure," I finally stammered.

She smiled and held her hand out. "I'm Linda." She looked down at the new ostrich Luccheses I still had on my feet. "You must be, Drew. Nice to meet you."

"And you also," I said, taking her hand. She had a strong but feminine grip, and it was like Bonnie electricity all over again.

"So which shirts do you like?" she asked.

I showed her the Tequila Sunrise and another dark blue model shirt with some silver stars falling from around the collar down each shoulder. It also had shiny silver pearl buttons and was called Night Rider. "Both nice," she said. She showed me a couple of more models until I had four really nice shirts in my hands.

"So, Drew, what do you think?" she asked. She was close enough that I could smell her subtle perfume, and it was very enticing.

I looked at her again, and at that exact moment, I was thinking whoever invented the term *camel toe* was a genius, but what I said was "Uhm, which ones do you recommend? I was thinking of buying two."

"As I mentioned, the Sunrise is selling hot right now. I also think you will look good in the Night Rider with your blue eyes and height." She looked at the other two shirts in my hand and then began to search the rack, pausing on occasion to look at me and then back to the search. Whether it was real or for effect, she certainly had my attention.

She stopped her search, looked at me a final time, and pulled a soft pink popper off the rack. The shirt was made with barely visible, alternating, textured pink diamond shapes all over the material, and you could only see them if the light struck them just right. It had small, thin fine white lines that really made the diamonds stand out. It was not a hot pink color, not a satin pink color but a very cool-looking "strong soft pink" as Linda said.

Normally, I would have scoffed at the idea of buying a pink shirt, especially in Oklahoma after my Six-Mile Bar experience, but I had to admit this shirt looked good, and the diamonds-in-the-sky thing when the light hit them just right was pretty cool. The material was extremely refined, and it was the softest brushpopper I had ever touched. I really wanted to try it on. "What's it called?" I asked Linda.

"Tequila Rose," she said, eyes gleaming like those of a succubus.

"You mean like the drink?" I asked. She nodded.

I took the three shirts to the dressing room to give them a try. The Tequila Sunrise was a definite buy at $65, and I looked good in it. The Night Rider also was good, a bit higher at $75 but very nice. Then I got to the Rose. The feel of the shirt against my skin was unbelievable as I slid the shirt on. It was still a tough popper, but it felt like pure silk. I tucked it in and buttoned it up. I had to admit it did look good. I checked the price—$145—and almost choked. Still, the shirt looked really good on me.

"How's it going, Drew? You want to try on anything else?" Linda said, standing outside my dressing room door.

I boldly opened the door and said, "I'm fine, but be totally honest with me. If a guy shows up at a dance hall wearing this shirt and asked you for a two-step, would you dance with him?"

Linda checked the shirt out a bit, looked me in the eye, and in her best Oklahoma southern drawl said, "Sugah, if a man has the confidence to wear this shirt in a bar and comes over to me, I guarantee you I would do a whole lot more than dance with him."

Standing there speechless and staring at her, I think Linda realized that she had just overwhelmed me a bit. She picked up my red solo cup, which was on the bench, and said, "Let me grab you another beer while you decide which ones you want."

When I exited the dressing room, I saw Sami talking with Linda about the pricing of the Lucchese. "Do you like the boots, Drew?" Linda asked, pointing to the Luccheses.

"Well, yeah, I really do. I mean, I have had them on for thirty minutes, and they are amazing. I figured you're going to start charging me rent on them any minute now," I replied. They both laughed at that, and as the third beer was kicking in, so was the realization that I was chatting it up with two very attractive, intelligent, fun, and sexy ladies. *Man, I really like Oklahoma.*

Sami and Linda talked a bit more, and then Sami went to the counter to get a calculator. "Which shirts do you like?" Linda asked as she punched numbers into the calculator.

"The Sunrise for sure, and I think I will also take the Night Rider, although I must say I really like the Tequila Rose also. Just not sure if I am man enough to wear it at Trips yet or not," I said with a sheepish grin. Again, they both laughed.

"Well, Trips, yeah, maybe, but if you wear it at the Oxblood Dance Hall here in the city or Tumbleweeds up in Stillwater, you would rock the place. I like the shirt, Drew, and one thing is guaranteed: you would be the only guy in the bar wearing a shirt like that, something a girl might notice," Sami said with plenty of eye contact thrown in.

I'll bet she sells a thousand shirts a month with her style.

"How much cash do you have on you exactly, Drew?" Linda said, now all business but still no less attractive.

"Twenty-four hundred dollars today, Linda, but that's my total shopping spree for the week, I am afraid," I replied.

"OK, so I'll discount the boots," Linda said, still working the figures and sort of thinking out loud. "And for the Sunrise and the Night Rider poppers . . . and I don't want to leave you without any cash at all, so for the boots and the two shirts, uhm, let's see, OK, today only . . . $2,250. That leaves you beer money for the next week. How does that work for you, Drew?" She winked after that last bit, and we all laughed.

The third beer was nearly gone now but even in my feeble, starting-to-buzz oil field mind, I quickly counted close to a $500 savings. Plus, I get to walk out with a pair of ostrich Lucchese boots on my dogs, so all things considered, I said in my best imitation southern manner, "Damn straight that works for me. Thank you, ma'am. I'll drink to that."

The store was not overcrowded, and I spent another fifteen minutes talking to the two of them as I checked out. Linda shook my hand, and Sami gave me a bouncy hug that had the usual results. I thanked them both for the beer, and I promised to be back soon to look at some more shirts.

24

On the way home, I was feeling a bit reflective, so I played some Paul Simon music, which of course included some of the Simon & Garfunkel stuff. I bounced back and forth between them and Three Dog Night for the next hour. *I am probably the only person in Oklahoma that understands how Three Dog Night got the name for their band.*

I thought about Amy, her luscious thighs, and her shooting skills. She was highly intelligent and had a great chance at becoming an FBI field agent or even a special agent/investigator. My thoughts went into this daydream about dating Amy and studying law enforcement myself. Although the whole servant-of-the-people concept was really not that appealing, I liked Amy and liked what she liked.

I was mentally shocked out of my daydream by another profound thought. *Two stunning girls with guns in the same day? Both mentioned the FBI? And both outstanding marksmen . . . er, markswomen. If there is no such thing as coincidence, then what the hell just happened to me?* Amy, I got. Her dad was a US marshal, she grew up around law enforcement, and it came together. But what was Myra's story? Strange hobby for a model, and she was way ahead of me on weapon technology, which was also strange.

When I reached the A frame, I noticed Dave's truck was leaving his place and heading out to check on the progress of his newly worked-over wells about a half mile away. I parked and unloaded all my new toys. I set up my reloading press and equipment on a workbench in the laundry room and organized all the kit in the proper order. I was pumped up as a kid on this third cotton candy. I put the Lucchese boots back in their box and tucked them under the bed. *Too much direct sunlight is not good for high-quality processed animal skin products. I was sure I had read that somewhere.*

I took the Glock 17 out of its case, and 1 loaded the clip with seventeen rounds and then placed the clip into the magazine. I was putting the gun in the shoulder holster to hang on the wall when the phone rang. It was Tony. "Where the fuck you been all day? I called you twice," he said, annoyed.

I noticed my messages, and I had three missed calls. "I went into the city to buy an automatic," I answered.

"Good, did you buy anything else?" he grumbled.

Not sure where this was going, if he was angry, drunk, or just in a bad mood, I said, "Er, yeah, I bought a pair of boots."

This seemed to lighten his mood up a bit for some reason. "Really, what kind did you buy?"

"Lucchese, natural ostrich, full quill," I replied choppily, again not sure where this was going.

"Those are damn nice boots, Drew. I have a set of customized Lucchese black ostrich. I really like mine." Tony went on, seeming more relaxed now.

Yeah, no shit, I almost bought the same pair a couple of hours ago but didn't want you to shove a .45 up my ass. "Yeah, I saw them at Trips. Those are great boots, Tony, really nice," I mumbled softly.

There was a short pause, and he said, "They cost me $3,300, customized, but worth every penny."

"Wow!" I added, beginning to wonder what he had called for.

Tony went on. "So, I ran into Mark last night. He says you have some 'free time' in the evenings. Want to meet me at Trips tonight at eight to talk about it?"

"Uh, sure. That will be great, Tony," I replied.

"See you there." Click.

I checked the three messages: two from Tony—the second one was pretty agitated—and the third one was from Clay asking me if I was doing anything tonight. I called Clay back and told him I was meeting Tony at Trips at eight, and he agreed to meet me there about nine.

I heard a knock-knock-knock softly on my door as I hung up the phone. Checking the window, I saw that it was Dave Raymond. "Hey, Davy Boy," I said with a big grin, "come on in, and sit a spell."

It was my best mock hick Oklahoma hillbilly accent, but Dave didn't mind and just grinned back. I went to the fridge and pulled out two ice-cold bottles of Coors Light, opened them, and gave one to Dave as he took a seat at the kitchen table.

"How's the well retrofit going?" I asked him.

"It's going really good, Drew. They got this new company up from Austin, Texas, called A. H. Beck. They have a couple of young A&M engineers that tried this spiral downhole treatment, and it is kicking donkey butt. Both wells are on schedule to be in production next week. It's amazing what these boys are doing these days," Dave said, taking a big drink of the ice-cold beer.

He continued to talk about the workover rig techniques and the A&M engineers for the first two beers before he stopped to take a breath. Until then, I had not realized that Dave had graduated from Texas A&M University out at College Station and had a degree in mechanical engineering and a seeming soft spot for his fellow Aggies.

Opening the fridge for his second beer, he asked, "Where you been? I thought it was your day off. Haven't seen you around all day."

I opened my second beer at the house, fifth one for the day. "I went into the city to do some shopping. I wanted to buy an automatic pistol and a couple of those new brushpopper shirts. You ever been to the Boot Warehouse in the city?" I asked.

"Oh yeah, I drop by there every time I am in the city. They have a keg in the back for their good customers," Dave said with a grin.

"Oh yeah," I said, again in mock response, "love those red solo cups. You ever meet Linda?"

"Linda? Oh yeah, you betcha. She's a beauty, always has been, very good lady. Her husband was killed in Caddo County a few years back, but she has made a huge success of the Warehouse on her own. The free keg beer was her idea. Yep, she's a fireball for sure. 'Course she is a lot younger than me, but that don't keep me from looking, and I would kick her back doors in if I ever got the chance." He hooted.

And so it went for the rest of the afternoon. We talked of politics, blond and redhead chicks, and habits we ain't kicking. I was becoming fonder of Dave each time I had a beer with him.

We talked about my purchases in Oklahoma City, and when he saw the Glock, he insisted on firing such a "precision firearm."

So we jumped in his pickup, drove out to the dump site at the far back of his place, and blasted through three clips of ammo. "Son, I carried a Colt 1911 .45 ACP in Korea, and I have shot several 9 mm's, Smith & Wesson, the Beretta, the Bernardelli and a few others, but I have never fired a weapon as precise as this one. It's just amazing what they can do with technology today. How did they design it so lightweight?" he said, shaking his head.

"Amy at the Rifleman told me it's only been available to the general public for, like, two years. Look, see here, it's made of some kind of nylon polymer, not a metal at all," I pointed out.

Dave checked out the Glock again, but being an old dog with a heart just like mine, he turned to me questioningly as his eyes twinkled. "Amy?" he asked.

I shared the entire tale about the absolutely stunning Oklahoma State graduate Amy, including her outstanding shooting prowess and her acceptance at Quantico with Dave. Then I had a thought. "I also saw Myra Breittlinger at the shooting range in the Rifleman. I think she is smoking hot, and she shoots damn well. I thought she was like a model or something. What the hell is she doing shooting like that? Do you know her, Dave?" I asked curiously.

"Myra, oh yeah, she is another good-looker but with style, and something about her seems like she gets you talking and just sucks your life story right out of you," Dave replied with a grin. "You know Bob is her brother, right, the guy you sell all your furs to?"

"Yeah, I have met Myra a couple of times at the fur house, and she is always dressed to kill, and now I guess it's shoot to thrill with her. It just boggles my mind, Dave, how someone that is such a stunning model can shoot like that. I mean, why? And, Dave, there is another thing," I said, pausing to take a drink of beer.

He gave me his total focus, and I said, "She had a prototype automatic pistol, a SIG Arms E6 PR or something like that, I think. I have never seen anything like it. It was made of similar material to the Glock but a different weapon altogether, more . . . advanced."

"More advanced than that auto we just shot?" Dave asked, eyes wide. "That's . . . hard to believe."

"Yes, I did not shoot it, but she said it was a prototype SIG and had several new features, yada, yada, yada, that it *might* be available to the public in two years. So who the hell do you think is it available to now? And why would beautiful silver-fox-fur-wearing Myra the Tigra be shooting one at a public range?" I said, a bit exasperated.

"Myra the Tigra?" Dave asked, raising an eyebrow.

I just smiled and sipped my beer for a moment and then continued. "Dave."

"Yeah, Drew," he replied.

"And there's another thing," I said.

"Another . . . another thing?" he said with a twinkle in his eye as he sipped his own beer.

I couldn't help but laugh a bit, and I said, "Yes, another thing. She said the E6 PR or whatever was chambered for a .40 caliber S&W cartridge. Have you ever heard of that caliber?"

"Uhm, no, can't say that I have, but things are moving pretty quickly with guns and technology these days, especially after that event in Miami last April. That really caused law enforcement to take a new look at their entire program, and the weapons manufacturers have responded with a flood of new equipment and technology."

Again with the Miami in April thing? Am I the only one who doesn't know what's going on? "Miami in April?" I asked, totally confused.

"The FBI shoot-out with the bank robbers? You didn't hear about it? Drew, it was all over the news and followed up in the papers for nearly a year." He sipped his beer and looked dead at me. I just sort of shrugged, a bit embarrassed.

Dave sipped his beer and then continued. "Eight FBI agents tracked down two ex-Army bank robbers just south of Miami who were wanted for murder. One of the robbers was an ex–Army Ranger, they forced them off the road, and all hell broke loose. The robbers opened fire on the feds, and the feds returned fire on the crooks. Two of the FBI guys had revolvers, hit the robbers a couple of times but basically with no effect. While trying to reload, one of the feds was killed and the other wounded. Both went down while reloading their revolvers. The guy that was killed was even wearing a bulletproof vest, but it was only good for small pistol rounds. The ranger had a Ruger Mini-14 .223 ranch rifle with custom ammo and a fifteen-round banana clip, plus two spares, and he was tearing the feds up with that .223. He basically had them pinned down, even though six of them were returning fire. In the end, they killed them both, but it was a game changer for law enforcement in a ton of ways.

"There are a dozen versions of the event, but what I got out of it was that the investigation opened the eyes of law enforcement on weapons and tactics. The federal agencies, especially the FBI, were told to go to automatic pistols and tougher vests. The guys with revolvers were shooting .38 special caliber and hit the crooks like two or three times but no bullet penetration, which allowed them to continue fighting and wounding or killing several feds. It was a huge deal. You never heard anything about this?"

"Er, no, buddy, I had no idea. It sounds pretty wild," I said, which was about all I could think of to say, even though my mind was racing a mile a minute. We sat in silence and sipped beers for a moment.

"There have been some articles in *Guns & Ammo* magazine about the new caliber bullets and advances in weapon technology, so maybe the .40 caliber S&W has been mentioned there," Dave said with a sigh. "Ya know, Drew, this is a problem with your generation. You're sharp guys, but you're all too busy chasing tail and buying new boots and doing god knows what, all to keep up on national news, hell, let alone international news. This event rocked things all the way to the Israeli Mossad."

"The Israeli who?" I asked innocently.

Now it was Dave's turn to laugh. "Never mind, Drew, it's a story for another day. Besides, there is something else pretty damn big that happened today that I don't think you're getting."

What the hell could be bigger than this conversation? Not to be outdone and with my BAC (Blood Alcohol Content) rising by the beer, I said, "Well, enlighten me, oh wise one."

Dave's eyes twinkled with a devilish gleam. "Biohythms, Drew, biorhythms, and yours today have every planet in the solar system in alignment, let alone Jupiter and Mars."

I just stared at him, obviously lost. He chuckled and shook his head. "Amy and Myra at the Rifleman, Samantha and Linda at the Boot Warehouse, have you ever met this many lovely, sexy ladies that paid you this kind of attention in one day, heck, in your life?"

I thought about it for a moment and said, "Now that you mention it, I don't think I have. But what the hell are biorhythms? And what does that have to do with me meeting these beautiful ladies? I mean, it's Oklahoma, Dave. I meet nice ladies all the time."

"But never this nice and never this many and never in the same day. Eh, Drew?" Dave went on to explain the concept of biorhythms and how each of us are basically reduced down through our souls and spirits into energy, and when the universal energy lines up with our individual energy, this increases our biorhythms, and amazing things can happen. Of course , then he countered with that when everything goes to shit, our biorhythms are out of whack with the universe.

I pondered his point and said, "Davy Boy, are you a bit drunk?"

He laughed, slapped his knee, and said, "Yes, of course, but that does not change the concept of biorhythms, Drew. Doesn't change it one bit."

We carried on chatting about biorhythms, Amy and Myra, and Dave's favorite, Ms. Linda, until I realized it was after seven, and I needed to haul ass to get ready to meet Tony at eight. Dave gave me a big hug and left the A frame shaking his head about blond college girls with guns, the naivety of today's youth, and nylon polymer precision technology. I jumped into the super spa shower, trying to decide what combination of my new clothes I was going to wear tonight. There would be no question, however, about what would be on my feet.

25

I was wearing my Tequila Sunrise popper button-down and my most faded Dwight Yoakam–style blue jeans, topped off with my Lucchese boots, when I pulled out of the driveway of the A frame. *Topped off? I guess bottomed off might be more appropriate as they are boots on my feet.*

To keep the mood, I was listening to Dwight Yoakam's "Fast as You" as I turned right onto County Road 59 and accelerated toward Trips. It was 7.50 p.m., and I would be just parking and walking for a beer at the bar by eight.

There were plenty of people inside when I arrived, but it was not crowded at all. People were hanging together in small groups of three or four. I saw an open spot at the bar near one of my favorite bartenders Susan, so I went over and ordered a beer. "Hey, Susan, how's your night?" I asked.

"Hey yourself, nice-looking shirt, Drew. Looks new," she said admiringly.

"Yeah, I just picked it up today at the Boot Warehouse in the city," I replied, sipping my beer.

"You're stylish tonight for sure, cowboy," Susan said, checking out the shirt. "Got any plans for later?"

"Not really. I am going to meet Clay later, probably just hang here for a while, maybe a dance or two if the mood suits."

Susan caught sight of the Luccheses. "Damn it, boy, and new boots too? You get a big bonus or what?" Susan asked.

"Something like that," I replied with a slight smile. "Have you seen Tony tonight?"

"Tony Williams? No, not yet. Why?" she asked, seeming a bit concerned.

"Nothing, he just said he may pass by, is all," I replied, trying for nonchalance but achieving schoolboy anxiousness.

"He makes me nervous, Drew. He has a real rough reputation," she said with a half smile. "Why do you want to hang out with him?"

"He's my boss, Susan. Yeah, he's tough, all right, but he has always done right by me. As long as I do my job, we seem to get on OK. And we don't exactly hang out. He just said he might pass by and asked if I was going to be here," I replied maybe a bit defensively.

"Well, here he is now. Just walked in the door," Susan said, nodding to the side entrance.

Whenever Tony walked through a door, you realized just how big he really was. With his boots on, he was easily over 6'5" and weighed about 280. Tonight he had traded his black shirt for a white button-down with red Native American arrows crisscrossed in the back. He made his way in my direction, never really acting like he had seen me but obviously heading my way. He chatted to a couple of guys and smiled at all the ladies he knew until he was eventually next to me.

I beat him to the punch this time and turned to Susan. "Two Coors Lights, please, Susan."

"Coming up, Drew. Hi, Tony," she said as she scurried after the beers. Of course, I was watching her walk away. She had such a sweet walk, and it was even sweeter when she was hurrying.

"Those are nice boots," Tony said, checking out my Luccheses. "I like the natural color or a dark color, nothing in between. These are one of a kind." He flashed his black ostrich-skin boots with the silver toe and heel covers. I was struck by the thought that George Michael wore a very similar pair of boots in his new MTV music video "Faith," which had just been released, but didn't really see any need to point this out to Tony.

Tony raised his beer and slammed half of it in the first drink. He certainly seemed in a mood of some sorts. We talked a little about the west plant and what was going on in Pauls Valley. Tony always spoke with his mouth pointed sort of downward in a way that you heard everything he said, but nobody else around did. *The guy does this a lot. That's why he is good at it, lots of clandestine conversations.*

Susan brought two more Coors Lights before either of us said anything, and Tony smiled at her. Tony dropped his tone a bit. "You got your first payday, and you're already asking for more territory. You're a greedy little bastard," he said with a half smile. I sort of shrugged and smiled back. "I let you in because there is a lot going on, and I needed to recruit a couple more . . . that I can trust." He seemed like he wanted to say more but just let it set. So I just stood there and drank my beer.

Two ladies whom Tony knew came over and began to chat him up, so he was all about the ladies then. He must have bought three rounds at least before he had his hands all over the brunette. I recognized her from the Six-Mile Bar, the bartender Mandy. She was certainly hot enough, that was for sure. There was just something really rough about her. *I guess that's the way he likes them . . . whiskey girls. He likes 'em rough.*

The other lady she was with put a couple of moves on me, but she really wasn't into me, and I was damn sure not into her. The two girls went to the bathroom, and Tony ordered the two of us a shot of Jack Daniel's. The man could drink, and he drank fast. I was well on my way, and he seemed to be just fine. "Talk to Mark tomorrow. He has some 'tasks' for your spare time. You know about this guy that just came up from Pauls Valley, Brian Dugan?" Tony asked.

"Not much. Clay mentioned he may be bad news," I replied.

"No *might* about it, Drew. Keep your eyes out. He's a sneaky piece of shit for sure. He should never be anywhere near your territory for any reason. He runs southeast of Guthrie and much more south than east. If you see him around the tankers or your tanks, tell me right away. You got that? This guy is going to be trouble. Don't know how and don't know when. I just gotta deal with it and can't do much until it comes." Tony's eyes flashed, and I could tell he was pretty pissed.

That sounds real close to what John said. So why don't you just tell Joe Dugan to back the hell off and keep Brian in Pauls Valley?

"You remember that tall drink of water from Pauls Valley, the Texan Joe Reed?" Tony asked.

"Yeah, I remember Joe well. I thought he was OK," I replied.

"Yeah, Joe is a straight shooter and not part of that old Pauls Valley clan. You might see him around driving some of the big tankers you're hauling too. Don't worry. He is cool, and he knows your area. He is a solid guy you can count on if anybody ever starts some shit," Tony said more matter-of-factly than I would have liked.

What does he know that he is not telling me?

The brunette came back by herself and started getting all up and over Tony. I saw Clay come in, so I raised my glass to Tony, threw Susan a $10 tip, and moseyed over to catch up with Clay. He saw my boots from about twenty feet away. "Hey, Drew, nice boots. Man, and Luccheses too. Damn," he said admiringly. He was wearing his African tan elephant-skin Lucchese boots tonight, and the conversation flowed around dead animal skins, guns, who the cutest ladies in Trips were, and the events of the week.

"Where's Ann?" I asked.

"Prego shit. She has been sick for a couple of days. It's getting kind of old really," he whined.

"Jeez, you're such a great, sympathetic boyfriend. No wonder she loves you," I said sarcastically.

Clay didn't respond; he just ordered another round of drinks. I watched the ladies on the dance floor and was enjoying the music when Clay gave me a hard shot in the arm with his elbow and nodded toward the door. I noticed the three men come in together. I was surprised to see Brian Dugan and Hawk Nose from the Six-Mile Bar together, but it was the third guy they were with who really got my attention. It was the long-haired, ponytailed guy with the John Lennon specs, the one from the big FBI bar fight in Green River.

"Oh, man, this is so going to piss Tony off really bad," Clay whispered. "That's Jay Randall, one of Tony's biggest rivals. He runs rackets, drugs, oil, you name it, from Mexico to Montana, and he is trying to move into some more stuff around here. So far, Duster won't let him in, but him hanging around here like this is not good, not good at all." Clay's eyes darted back and forth between Tony and ponytailed Jay, awaiting the moment when Tony would become aware of the three men and the fact that they were sitting together.

Again with the Duster thing? Who is this guy?

"I saw Tony meeting that Jay guy the night I was at the Six-Mile Bar. They seemed to get along OK. I mean, they sat at the same table, and it looked like they were having a drink and civil conversation. I did not get the impression they were in competition," I told Clay.

"Six-Mile Bar is famous for being a sort of neutral place for the big dogs. This area is also Tony's home turf. Plus, Tony was probably packing his .45, so I am sure that Jay was on his best behavior. He always will be good in public. Jay is a pretty sharp operator to cover as much ground as he does. It's the fact that Brian Dugan is with him. That's what's really going to piss Tony off," Clint replied.

Tony was totally involved with his sexy Six-Mile brunette, Mandy, and didn't really seem to notice much at the moment other than her, so I just sort of followed Clay's lead, edged over to the bar, and watched. The place was filling up quick, and there were several packs of pretty cowgirls and coeds strolling slowly past the bar, looking to meet guys who were looking to meet girls.

Clay was more than willing to oblige and started a conversation with two really cute ones. Rhonda was an attractive blonde from Iowa and going to Oklahoma State (OSU) up in Stillwater. Lorena was a tidy tight-bodied Latina from San Antonio, also going to OSU. Both were gorgeous and were staying with some friends in Edmond for the weekend. I forgot all about Brian and ponytailed Jay, and soon the illustrious Mr. Haynes had the four of us drinking tequila shots and having a big time. Lorena was grabbing my arm every time I said something even halfway funny, and I was suddenly interested in someone in a way I had not been interested in anyone for a long time.

Susan noticed I had found my way back to the bar, so she came down to chat and check on our drinks. Clay ordered four more shots, and everything was going great. Then for some reason, I could not understand why Susan got a bit cold toward me and started giving me the bad eye. I tried a shrug and a silent "What's wrong?" to her over the bar, but she pretty much ignored me. *Is it because I am hanging with Lorena? I just met her.*

The band started playing "Satisfy You" by Sweethearts of the Rodeo, so I asked Lorena if she wanted to dance, and we headed out on the dance floor. She was really sweet, and I thoroughly enjoyed dancing with her. When the song was over, my initial interest had turned into full-blown desire, and I wanted some of this. I noticed Clay and Rhonda heading out the side door, and I figured they were getting some fresh air. I suggested to Lorena that we do the same, and she agreed it was a good idea.

While we walked around the big parking lot outside, Lorena told me she was a senior at OSU planning to major in business and also studying economics. I was studying her something fierce while trying to look like I wasn't studying her. She caught me anyway, and we both laughed. It seemed like I was always getting busted looking at women. Not sure I ever even wanted that to change. The timing was perfect, so I kissed her softly, fully on the mouth. She responded, pressing herself against me and returning the kiss passionately.

It was really starting to get heated up with Lorena when we heard a bunch of noise over by the Trips side doors. Five or six guys were outside shouting and shoving one another. I recognized Brian Dugan and Hawk Nose but did not see any sign of ponytailed Jay. The shoving turned into hard punching and kicking. Suddenly, I heard two gunshots, and I saw a muzzle flash from the group of men. They were too far away, and I could not see who pulled the trigger or who shot whom. They all took off, and I could clearly see a body on the ground. It was not moving.

Lorena stifled a scream, and we ran toward Clay's Silverado. We arrived at the pickup just in time to see Clay and Rhonda hurriedly throwing their clothes back on. I was close enough to the truck window to see plenty of Ms. Rhonda from Iowa, and what I saw was very nice. I slowed down a bit, trying to give them a few more seconds to don their garb, but Lorena was having none of it. She charged toward the truck like she had seen Rhonda naked in a parking lot plenty of times before. *What am I thinking of giving them some space? There's a bloody damn shooting going on thirty yards away.*

Clay unlocked the doors, I put Lorena next to Rhonda, and I climbed in at the shotgun slot. I had barely closed the door when a big white Ford truck with huge tires and a lift kit went zooming by us. Brian Dugan was driving with a wild-eyed look on his face. I saw him, and he saw me. Hawk Nose turned around from the shotgun seat and stared straight at me. I did not know if they recognized Clay's truck or not, but they sure as hell recognized me.

26

Clay had Bob Seger playing on the stereo and was talking ninety miles a minute, trying to distract us as we drove so Rhonda could finish putting her clothes back on. Lorena squeezed my leg and was nearly sitting in my lap, which I, being the aspiring southern gentleman, did not mind at all. "Did you see who fired the shots, Drew?" Clay asked excitedly.

"No, but there were five or six guys going at it when I heard the gunshots," I replied, easing my arm around Lorena.

"Tony?" Clay asked, semi-concerned.

"Nope, never saw him, only Brian Dugan and the hawk-nosed punk from Six-Mile," I replied dryly. Lorena smiled a bit at this and squeezed my hand as she tossed one of her legs over mine in the pickup cab. Rhonda was now pretty much fully dressed, so Clay suggested we all go to breakfast at the 76 Truck Stop on I-35 just outside Edmond.

During breakfast, the girls talked about Oklahoma State University, the various party elements of Stillwater, Oklahoma, and what a great time they were having there. Clay asked them if they had ever been to Tumbleweeds in Stillwater, and they both looked at each other and busted out laughing. *I'll take that as a yes.*

It was nearly three when we finished breakfast, and as the girls were staying with some friends, they asked us to take them home. They invited us to meet them in Stillwater the next weekend, which we, of course, accepted.

Apparently, Tumbleweeds was like a drug to Clay as his eyes glazed over at the mere mention of the place. I took twenty minutes kissing Lorena good night, and the moon wasn't the only thing rising. I knew there was no way I would get to sleep this night. *Biorhythms. Thank you, Dave.*

I was wrong on the sleep. I did catch about three hours and rolled off the bed groggy at about seven thirty. I headed out to the field to change charts, already about thirty minutes late. I hauled ass and was caught up with all the charts in an hour.

I met Mark for lunch at Uncle Bob's BBQ, and he showed me four more tanks I could add to my route. They were all near paved roads and some of them close to Gulf Energy production lines, so I asked him about this. "Hey, these tanks, they are all right next to main roads, and it looks like they are real close to the Gulf Energy plant systems. Are they ours?" I asked questioningly.

Mark laughed, nearly choking on his beef brisket. "No shit, Sherlock. They *are* part of the Gulf Energy plant system, dumbass." He shoveled more beef into his mouth and continued. "Look, Clay gauges those tanks. I run the charts. You can take 1,000 gallons a week from each, and we cover it. Hell, you moron, Clay and I are already pulling 3,000 gallons a week out of them."

So he's telling me we are stealing 10,000 gallons of crude a freaking week? Just from these company tanks? I had paused mid-bite on my pulled pork and must have had a stunned look on my face.

"That's how it works. The measurement guys in the field, like me, doctor up the charts by 25 percent or so, and the operators, like you and Clay—well, mostly Clay, Sandy, and Robby—gauge the tanks and mark them lower than actual. The company still makes plenty of money, everybody gets a cut, and I buy the wife a new horse and get laid whenever I want." He winked.

"I always mark the tanks exactly what the tape says. I mean, this is the first time anyone said anything," I stammered, feeling like I had somehow screwed up.

Mark laughed while chewing on fried okra. "Relax, Drew. Of course, you do, and until you get more experienced with this stuff or I tell you different, just keep doing that. That's why you only gauge certain tanks. We don't want you boning things up or saying something to an auditor. If you only tell them what you're actually doing on the job and nothing else, they can't trip you up, right?"

"Yeah, that makes sense, I guess. So what do we do when the auditors show up? Stop making tank runs?"

Now Mark really damn near choked; he was laughing so hard. "No, dumbass, it's business as usual. Think about it. If production suddenly jumps up 30 percent every time an auditor comes around, don't you think somebody will catch on that things are not quite jake? We do, however, do a few less night runs and are damn careful. Clay and I will usually go out in pairs just to make sure no one is following us. We grab the portable Nextel radios and stay in contact in case anything comes up."

"Why don't we just do that all the time? That sounds like a great idea and a good way to stay in touch and ahead of the game," I said as if I had just had an epiphany.

Mark shook his head and laughed. "We all do. You're the only one who doesn't carry a portable radio, Drew."

Well, we can change that shit.

When I stopped by the west plant office the next day, there were two brand-new Nextel radios and additional chargers in Tony's office. "Hey, Tony, how goes it?" I asked, eyeing the Nextels.

He just sort of shrugged and nodded toward the new radios. "Are you going to be busy enough in the evenings now?" he asked me with one eyebrow raised.

"Damn straight. I doubt if I'll even make the bar hangouts or strip clubs for the first few weeks," I said, trying to be funny.

Tony snorted. "I doubt that. The more you take on extra work, the more you want to play. Pretty soon you'll be acting like you own grown-up Toys 'R' Us and buying a new truck like the rest of the dumbasses."

"Good point. Don't want to be too conspicuous. What do you do with all your extra cash?" I asked innocently.

Tony's eyes narrowed, and I felt like I was staring death in the face. "Compressors number 5 through 8 need to be steam-washed and scrubbed clean. I suggest you get right on that," he said coldly.

Right. Rule no. 1: don't ask too many questions. Damn it. I scrubbed the compressors down until they were, as Madonna would say, "bright, shiny, and new." I figured I needed to get away from Tony for the rest of the day, so I headed out to ole unit no. 13 and drove toward the east plant. I was cranking up Stevie Ray Vaughan's "Love Struck Baby" when Clay called me on the radio.

"Hey, Clay, go ahead," I replied in radio-speak.

"Go to channel 2.7," he said. He sounded agitated.

We had access to eighty-seven radio channels on our Nextels, and there were about thirty-five guys working around the area who could pick up on any of those channels. There were four main operations channels for work that you stayed on until someone called you. If it was work related, they would just tell you what the issue was. If it was a maintenance task or irregular task, you went to one of three other channels. If it was, well, something other than work, they would tell you go to one of the "off" channels.

The first thing you did whenever you heard anyone tell someone to go to an off channel was turn the radio knob to the off channel with them to see what was going on. People were basically nosy bastards, especially with all the clowns we had working on the area and all the "tasks" everyone was doing. Clay, Mark, Sandy, Robby, and I had a code we sorted every couple of days to make sure no one followed us to our off channel. For the private chat channel, we would agree on a plus or minus number that only the four of us knew. Today was plus thirteen, so that meant "go to channel 15.7."

I switched to channel 15.7 and checked in. "Go ahead, Fred." Once you were on an off channel, it was OK to get stupid with your response.

"If you see Ann or she calls you at the plant, tell her we were working until ten the other night and then went out on one last coon hunt Friday since the weather is starting to get warmer. I told her that is what we did. Got it?" Clay blurted out, panicky.

"What the hell did you tell her that for? Don't drag me into your shit," I said defiantly.

"Just do it, Drew. She likes you and trusts you, and someone told her I was banging a chick from OSU in my truck last Friday," he whined.

"You *were* banging a chick from OSU in your truck last Friday. Rhonda was her name, if I recall," I said sarcastically.

"C'mon, Drew, she really trusts you, so if you tell her we were out late coon hunting, she will go for that," he said, exasperated.

Wonder how long she will trust me if he keeps this crap up and I keep covering for him. "Roger that, dumbass. I gotcher back," I replied. *Maybe shit for brains has learned his lesson.*

It was funny in a weird, ludicrous sort of way. I had been in Oklahoma for almost a year now and had seen people get shot, get shot at, almost got the living shit beat out of me at the Six-Mile Bar, was stealing crude oil and condensate at a federal crime-level rate, and was being slowly introduced to an even more intricate level of racketeering thievery weekly, and my biggest concern at the time was that I would hurt Ann's feelings if she found out I had been lying to her. *Nothing wrong with caring about how a woman feels. I mean, I like women, wouldn't want to be on this planet without them.*

27

I spent the rest of the week hauling from my new tanks and working on my handloading. Dave passed by several times a week now, and we had a couple of beers while we worked on handloading together and talked of politics and blond, brunet, and redhead chicks as two ole boys would do—well, at least these two ole boys. I believe I had mentioned those were some of our favorite topics.

"Looks like they are pulling about three tanker loads a week off each production well, Drew. Damn, that's a lot of crude. I never imagined they would produce like that again," Dave said as he measured a load of IMR 4350 gunpowder for a 9 mm round. Between the two of us, we had worked up quite a precision handloading system; and our ammo rounds were always superb, carried maximum foot-pounds of energy and knockdown power, and were 35 percent less costly than factory ammo.

"Must be your Aggie engineers, Dave. They are doing amazing things with technology these days as you have said," I replied with a wink as I pulled the handle of the reloading press seating a 154-grain Sierra Teflon bullet into the loaded brass completing the handloaded 9 mm round.

"Mechanical side, Drew. Mechies, not Aggies," Dave grumbled.

"Don't be so sensitive, Davy Boy. The whole country calls them Aggies. Thought it was a handle you A&M grads were proud of," I commented.

Dave chuckled. "Yeah, we are. There was a lot of competition among the Aggies and the mechanical bunch back in my day. It's different now with the twelfth-man concept and all."

"Twelfth-man concept?" I asked.

Dave went on to explain about how Texas A&M football coach Jackie Sherrill had come up with an idea about seven years ago to have a twelfth man from the normal student body join the team each year and play at least a couple of plays each game. One year it was an Aggie. Next year it was a Mechie. The move was huge among the college football crowd, and several of the twelfth men went on to become permanent members of the team, even starters, the following season.

Dave Raymond was an icon of education and information, and I always enjoyed our chats. Dave was almost always usually headed for bed by just after nine thirty unless he was out, so at about nine, we packed up the reloading kit and said good night.

I called Lorena up in Stillwater, and she seemed happy to hear from me. We started talking about Tumbleweeds Dance Hall, some of her antics over her four years in Stillwater, and her group of friends majoring in political science, accounting, law, and medicine. We talked about some of the country bands she had seen there and how she was looking forward to me coming up the following weekend. Somewhere in the conversation, it came out that she was 26, but that did not matter to me in the least. She made a big point to me to be sure to wear something "cowboy" when I came up to see her on Friday. I was pretty sure I could comply with her request.

I learned later that Clay had been calling Rhonda, and apparently, he had not learned a thing since the encounter with Ann, and we were going to ride up together while he fed Ann some BS story. At least it did not include me this time.

28

Friday, I skipped the west plant crew evening beers and headed straight to the A frame with my thoughts full of the lovely Lorena from San Antonio and my expectations of the weekend. I hit the super spa shower and was running my wardrobe through my mind, trying to figure out what would be the best "cowboy" attire to impress my brunette from San Antonio. In the end, I went rogue and selected a new pair of black Levi's 501 straight legs, my Night Rider brushpopper shirt, and my Tony Lama El Rey blue back-cut boa boots of the Six-Mile Bar fame. *Dressed to kill, shoot to thrill. Why am I thinking of Midnight Myra the Tigra now? She could not be more different from Lorena than night is to day.*

I met Clay at Randall's, and we had a beer and a couple of shots before we took off to Stillwater in his Silverado. All he could talk about was Rhonda from Iowa, and I refrained from mentioning Ann as I was pretty sure I knew where my night was going and did not want any negative energy to spoil the mood. Biohythms.

It was about an hour to Stillwater, and we listened to Bob Seger all the way. "Hollywood Nights" and "Night Moves" were my favorites, while Clay pushed "Travelin' Man"—"Everyone trying to cage me"—and "Turn the Page," both from a similar vein about men being played by women. It was his to sort things out, and I was not contributing to his situation. I did, however, get into "Sunspot Baby" when it came on. Like I said, I knew where my night was going, and I saw Lorena's face and body in my mind for the entire hour we drove.

Tumbleweeds, or Weeds as everyone in Stillwater called it, was unbelievable. Based off the Gilley's Bar concept from the movie *Urban Cowboy*, it was huge. The dance floor was maybe half a football

---

133

field long with seven bars lined up around it. There were six pool tables and accessories in a large room off to the side, plus a dozen of the hottest barmaids I had ever seen assembled in one place working the crowd. They had a kitchen on the far north end and a dozen picnic-style tables for drinking, eating, or gathering. Even though there were only about a hundred people in here now in small groups, the place could easily hold a thousand or more.

Clay headed to his favorite bar on the opposite side from the main entrance. His eyes had started to glaze over with that "I'm in Weeds daze," and he was mumbling about Melanie, Stacey, Charlotte, and Yona, whom I took to be barmaids or bartenders. The drool was practically running out of his mouth. When I met Melanie behind the bar, I saw why.

Nothing I had met in Oklahoma to date had quite prepared me for Ms. Melanie Himmel. She was 5'7" with brown hair and brown eyes and a body that had *Playboy* written all over it. *Attractive* just did not do enough to describe Ms. Melanie. In the words of Bob Seger that we had just heard on the drive up here, "She had been born with a face that would let her get her way." Her features were feminine and lovely, just an incredibly beautiful face.

Since Clay was halfway over the bar chatting Melanie up, I moved down a bit and ordered a beer from Stacey, who was also gorgeous. Clay had apparently forgot we were there to meet a couple of ladies because if anyone coming to meet him saw him slobbering over Melanie, they would have been enraged. Not that it would matter to him. He was the proverbial hound dog, always on the hunt.

Stacey was sweet, and even though I knew she was angling for a tip, she asked all the right questions, made all the right moves, and touched my arm just enough while she laughed at the dumb stuff I was saying, so I dropped her a $5 tip for the beer. She gave me a killer smile and moved on to the next guy down the bar line, and she did move intentionally well, looking back to see if I was checking her out as she walked away, and indeed I was. *It's appreciation, no disrespect. I just gave her a $5 tip for the beer.*

I could hear a lot of the conversation between Clay and Melanie, and although, as I said, she could have posed for *Playboy* and actually may in the future, there was something about her that made a big red blip come up on my radar screen. Her words and her antics were sexy as hell, but there was something dark there also—something, well, maybe not so much sinister but like a dark flaw.

It was just a strange feeling. It was just there, and it sent a bit of a shiver down my spine all the same. I could stare at her face and body all night, but I had no desire at all to be with her or even speak to her. She had a dark aura, which probably suggested a darker heart. *The words of that old Cher song. What was it? Dark Lady? Yeah, that was it. "Dark Lady laughed and danced and lit the candles one by one." That is Ms. Melanie Himmel, indeed the Dark Lady.*

I left Clay at the bar with *Playboy* Dark Melanie and went over to check out the pool tables. They had some great music playing, and there were several pool games going on. I watched a couple of guys shooting and asked if they would mind if I joined in. They were both Oklahoma locals and were pretty cool guys. We talked about what guys talk about and played a few games, and then I went back to the bar looking for Clay.

The only change in the last thirty minutes was he had two empty beer bottles beside him, and Melanie was now leaning in just a bit toward his side of the bar so she could get closer to his ear. This also provided Clay a deeper look down her shirt. Clay was oblivious, but Melanie saw me watching them, and she returned my stare. She smiled seductively at me, tossing her hair sexily to get my attention, but her brown eyes turned almost black when she watched me walk farther away down the bar, away from them instead of coming over to vie for her attentions with Clay. *That's her game. She seeks the attention of men like a vampire seeks blood, and shit for brains is giving her a ton. Dark Lady, darker heart.*

The pace was picking up now as the band started coming in. Three of the guys wore cowboy hats. The bandleader was a short, stocky young cowboy everyone was calling Garth, an OSU student who did the band on the side. The two lady backup singers were all about their tight black Dittos jeans and button-up tops with sequins and bangles and were smoking hot cowgirls.

The crowd had nearly doubled since we arrived, and I was enjoying the atmosphere. There was one main entrance, with three smaller side doors you could exit from. OSU Football Linemen managing the doors. I found a spot on the opposite side of the dance floor from Clay and Dark Lady Melanie where I could see all the exits and watch Clay and the main entrance, in case Lorena walked in. I noticed that almost all the bouncers were watching Clay and Melanie. Did they know her game? Had she played it with them? It would fit after all. She was that kind of woman.

The band played their first song, and they were pretty good—damn good actually. The short, stocky cowboy named Garth had tons of energy.

"Hey, cowboy, you ready for another beer?" I heard someone say from behind me. I turned to see an amazing woman standing behind the bar. She was dressed in a Native American style with a soft, smooth, fringed white doeskin vest that had jade and silver bangles hanging by jade-colored leather and an Indian choker that said volumes, but most of all it said, "I am Native American." She was absolutely beautiful. Yeah, yeah, yeah, that was what I said about all the Oklahoma ladies, but she was, as they were, gorgeous, truth be told. Her skin was tan; she had dark eyes, dark black hair, and a face of a legend. Her angular face and eyes, with her high cheekbones, made for a one-of-a-kind, amazing look. Not the *Playboy* face of Dark Melanie but a more exotic beauty, truly rare. She was tall, at least 5'9", and with her boots on, she was staring me nearly dead in the eyes. She was thin but fit and very attractive.

I was awestruck. *Thank you, Dave. Biorhythms must be in sync.* "Uhm, yeah, sure, thank you. Yes, another beer please." Then in a bold moment, I made a move. "Name is Drew, and your name is?"

She looked at me with laughing eyes and said, "Yona. You look like you have never seen an American Indian before, cowboy."

"Not at all, Yona. I am from Colorado, girlfriend. I went to school with members of the Navajo, Ute Mountain, and Jicarilla Apache nations. I also worked side by side in Wyoming with members of the Sioux, Blackfoot, and Cheyenne nations. Yeah, I know my tribes. Sorry if I stare. It's not because you are an Indian, love. It's because you are one drop-dead, stunning, gorgeous Indian." *Fuck me, did I just say that out loud?*

Yona looked at me long and hard, and then her eyes softened, and she hit me with a dazzling smile as she gave me a beer. "Where in Colorado?"

"Durango, Cortez, and the western slope. Sorry, sugar, did not mean anything with my comment, just that . . . well, you're really gorgeous, and that's that. Where are you from?" I asked, trying not to be awkward.

"Oklahoma, Chickasaw," she replied with a smile.

"Cherokee? Makes sense. Doesn't matter to me. All that matters is you're sweet, stunning, and you serve great beer," I said with a wink.

That broke the ice, and she laughed an honest laugh. "Yes, Drew, I am half Cherokee and very proud of my heritage."

"As you should be, but apologies, it's not your heritage I am interested in as much as it is you. I think you are absolutely gorgeous." *Shit, did I just say that out loud again? And after only two beers? I have been hanging around Clay too long. Oh yeah, we did start at Randall's, I guess.*

Yona smiled an honest, open smile, making her even more attractive. "OK, cowboy, three compliments in less than a minute is the limit. This your first time in Weeds? Are you meeting someone or on your own?"

"Yeah, first time here. Yes, meeting someone. Well, I hope anyway. I work in Guthrie, and my friend over there, the dumbass hitting on Melanie the Dark Lady, brought me here, but I am supposed to meet a friend here and hoping it works out."

Yona laughed heartily out loud. "So you get her, do you?" she asked, pointing out Melanie with a nod. "She is one major player, and most guys get sucked in by the face and body."

"Well, she does have that. Maybe Hugh Hefner at *Playboy* is interested, but I am not. The eyes are the pathway to the soul, and her eyes—well, that's one hell of a precarious path that I would never choose to walk," I said, impressed with my own philosophy. "She just doesn't do it for me at all, Yona. I am all about the true heart." *Shit, did I just say this crap out loud again?*

"You're a cornball," Yona said, flashing that smile a second time. "Why do you call her the Dark Lady?"

"Just something that came into my head after I heard her talking to Clay for a bit. Her actions reminded me of a song. You know who Cher is?" Yona's eyes opened wide, narrowed, and then softened, and she nodded while she was cleaning a glass.

"That song she came out with a few years ago. I guess it was over ten years ago by now, 'Dark Lady.' You ever hear the song?"

I asked, wondering what it was about my Cher question that was bothering her.

"Oh yeah, the one about the gypsy fortune-teller who was having an affair with the girl's boyfriend, and she kills them both. I know the song. Not a bad song really for '70s pop," Yona said, now seeming relaxed again.

"There was a couple of music videos that portrayed the fortune-teller as a darkly, selfish, greedy woman, Dark Lady. That's what I thought of after being around Melanie for about five minutes," I added.

Yona laughed. "Yeah, that's pretty much her. She will play with any guy that is dumb enough to let her play him. She even got one of the bouncers to buy her a car last year, brand-new Trans Am. It's parked right outside, a white one with a black-and-pink firebird. It's a really nice ride."

"Yeah but driven by a dark driver," I said sheepishly. We both laughed.

Staying on a roll, I asked, "I dig your choker. The small pieces of turquoise are a nice color. It matches the jade leather strips on your vest. Did you get it around here?"

"Wow! You know what turquoise is?" she said, pleasantly surprised. "Nobody in this place has a clue."

"I told you I grew up in the Four Corners area of Colorado. They have big tribal trading posts all over out there. They make some great turquoise jewelry. My grandmother used to collect them. She had some really nice pieces," I said proudly.

Yona put the glass down and said with a half smile. "You're for real. You seem to be anyway. I hope you are."

"Why do you say that?" I asked, confused. "I guess I am for real. I mean, I try to minimize the head games. I probably do pass on compliments to attractive ladies a bit too much, but they are sincere compliments, and I won't risk embarrassing myself unless the lady is truly deserving, such as yourself, Yona." I winked at her, and she laughed.

"It was the Cher thing. I thought you might be an asshat going somewhere ugly with that one," she said seriously.

"You lost me on that. What could go ugly about me talking about an old Cher song? I think she is pretty hot herself, and she has a great voice. You have to give her that," I replied, still lost on the point.

"It wasn't the song, Drew. It was the fact that you mentioned Cher," Yona explained.

I looked at her with a blank stare and shrugged. I still didn't get it. "Are you serious? She is part Cherokee," Yona said, exasperated.

"Sorry, I still don't get it, unless you're saying you're both hot, which I would have to agree with," I said with another wink.

Yona laughed a rich, sexy laugh and said, "Cornball, you may be real, but you're still a cornball."

We talked for another fifteen minutes or so, and I was becoming infatuated with Yona. The more we talked, the more I wanted to talk. The conversation rolled back around to Melanie when she walked right past us with her ass moving in a way that would wake the dead. Yona laughed. "Wow, you really got her attention."

"Why do you say that?" I asked curiously. "Didn't you see that dagger look she tossed at me?"

"She is going on break, probably going outside for a smoke. She could have exited at either of the other two side doors, but she went out of her way and walked all the way to this side of the floor just to make sure you noticed. And you sure did, cowboy. You had your eyes glued to her walk and never missed a twitch of that sashay," Yona joked.

"Yeah, I can look at it her for a while, kind of like a dark porn starlet, but that's it. She just doesn't do it for me at all," I said to Yona.

Yona laughed, leaned in close to the bar, and looked deep into my eyes for a long time. She was so gorgeous. Then she said, "Well, Colorado cowboy, what does do it for you?"

The moment was there. My head started spinning as I looked at this amazing woman. She was like nothing I had seen before, and that said a lot because you knew how I felt about Oklahoma girls. I was about to go ballistic. Yeah, yeah, yeah, this was the problem in Oklahoma. It just kept getting better and better.

Just then, I saw a group of people coming through the main entrance, and Lorena was with them. There were six girls: Lorena, two tall blond debutante types, Rhonda, and two others. There were three guys who appeared to be in the pack as well. They were all dressed to the hilt in the latest Western wear outfits. The tall blonde in front seemed to be the leader of the pack, and everyone was following her around like little baby ducks.

Lorena looked good, really good, in black jeans and a white top with white roper boots. The outfit really offset her Latina beauty, and she was looking good tonight . . . but nowhere close to Yona, not even in the same league. But I had made a commitment.

I looked at Yona, and I was sure she could see the disappointment on my face, and I nodded toward the main entrance. "Lorena. I met her last week in Edmond. We had a great time, and she invited me up here. Plus, as mentioned, my friend Clay, the punk ass currently caught in the black widow's web over there at the bar, has been raving about this place for weeks. I am really glad I came, and so nice to meet you, sweet Yona. You're incredible. I . . . I . . . I got it to do," I stammered like a schoolboy as I pointed out Lorena.

Yona squeezed my hands and said, "A date's a date, cowboy. Now it's all about you and what kind of person you want to be. By the way, which one is Lorena? I don't know her."

"She is the cute one in black jeans and white shirt, brunette, Latina from San Antonio," I said, feeling conflicted.

"Ooh, Latina. Look at you with your cultured South American self. Everyone around here would just say Mexican." She winked as she leaned in a bit closer, acting like she was checking Lorena out but getting her face really close to mine. I could smell her subtle perfume. She was killing me. "She's cute, Drew. You're a lucky guy."

"Yeah, lucky, that's me. My biohythms must be on overload this month," I said sheepishly as I stared at Lorena.

I paid Yona for the drinks, plus a $10 tip, and turned to go meet Lorena when suddenly I felt this steel grip on my arm. It was Yona. "Drew, how well do you know her?" She relaxed her grip and continued, "Sorry, cowboy, not my business. Sorry . . . I mean . . . I really don't know Lorena at all, but that crowd she is with . . . they are really uncool. You know what I mean?" Her eyes were full of compassion, and her touch on my arm had softened from steel death to genuine concern.

"Yona, what? I don't understand. Lorena seemed really down to earth," I blatted.

"That blonde in the yellow shirt, the one in front, she is bad news. You called Melanie Dark Lady. Melanie plays men and uses them. That blond bitch plays everyone and seems to get off by leaving a trail of emotional refuse in her wake each night. And the other blonde in purple, just as bad but a follower. The three guys, two of them are trust fund babies from the East Coast just out here playing cowboy and spending Daddy's money. You see the guy in the blue with the turned-up collar?" Yona asked sincerely.

I watched them meandering around. *All have new high-fashion Western outfits, probably never even rode a horse.* "Yeah, I see him," I replied quietly.

"He was banned in here for, like, six months because he was accused of slipping girls roofies and raping them in the parking lot while they were passed out," Yona said angrily as her eyes blazed. "They flash money around like water, the girls get drunk, he takes advantage. And the story is the tall blonde, they call her Gwen—the word is she orchestrated the rapes, picked the girls, coached the guys on, and watched the show. Nothing was ever proven, and he got a lawyer from the city to file a liability suit, so it all went away. I knew a friend of one of the girls involved, and she said she was out cold and could not remember a thing but that when she woke up, she knew that someone had definitely had sex with her without her consent. No question, she had been raped, even if she did not remember anything. My friend said she was pretty messed up over the whole thing. They are just uncool, Drew, nothing good about those three anyway. I don't know the others."

She saw my eyes, and I could tell she was disappointed. "Just watch yourself, Drew. I have good instincts and think you're OK. I have worked here three years, and those girls your friend Lorena is with, they are just bad news. That's all. Watch yourself, OK?"

I was blown away by the concern and compassion in her touch and her eyes. I felt like I was about to walk into a pit of vipers. "Thanks, Yona. I trust you. You're quality, the best there is, but like you said, sugah, a date's a date. I have to at least check in with Lorena," I said, looking at the floor.

"Drew, nobody I know actually saw anything, but where there's this much smoke . . ." she said, her eyes misty.

"Yeah, I got it, Yona. There is usually fire." I squeezed her hand softly, gave her another $20 tip just because, and headed over to join Lorena and her crew.

I glanced in Clay's direction to see if Rhonda was going to bust him, but Melanie had gone on break, with her wake the dead ass as had three of the big linemen bouncers. He was always a lucky SOB—on the edge but seldom got caught. I doubted if he even noticed the bouncers who followed Dark Melanie outside, but true to form, he caught Rhonda and Lorena's crew coming in and swooped in before I was halfway across the floor. Like a true hound dog, he had cut her from the herd, and those two went to the bar, while the rest of them grabbed a big table.

I took my time going over to the group, not really sure what I was walking into. Lorena saw me when I approached, and she leaped up, gave me a huge full-body sexy hug, and led me to the table to sit next to her. I looked back at Yona; she gave me a thumbs-up that broke my heart. She was indeed a class act.

Lorena introduced me to the others at the table. Gwen was the tall blond debutante. She was from Houston, and it was fairly obvious right from the start she was controlling and synthetic. Her body and face had been augmented surgically in several ways, so she appeared to have the perfect top-heavy Barbie figure and face, but her eyes—her eyes were a shallow pitted blue, cold as ice. She looked almost 30 or at least way too old to still be in college, but what did I know? I was just an operator at a gas plant.

Next to her in purple was Kathy, another blonde; her eyes were always darting this way and that as if seeking some hapless victim to target. She was sucking onto Gwen's every movement like a blond leech.

Lorena had her hand on my leg under the table, so I figured things were all right, and the night would not be so bad. I barely caught the names of the other two girls, even though they were cute enough; they just seemed ditzy. Lorena came to the three guys next. The guy with a turned-up dark blue shirt collar was named Ted, and his mate in a red brushpopper shirt was Chip. *Ted and Chip, there's a couple of reject Ivy League names, if I have ever heard any.*

My first impression was they seemed like a great match for Gwen and Kathy, and I pictured the four of them on some future road trip in a convertible leaving a trail of broken bodies behind them. I filed the rest away as tagalongs or just lost spirits. I could not figure out how Lorena fit in with them at all. It made no sense. Rhonda had vanished to the bar with Clay, and maybe Lorena just happened to be here with them but wasn't really with them. They called the last guy Stew, and while he was from back East, I did not get any big negative-aura vibe from him. He seemed like a guy just out to enjoy a cowboy bar.

Ted and Chip ordered drinks and shots for the table. They did not ask what anyone preferred; they just bought what they wanted. They flashed the cash just as Yona described and tipped the barmaid way too much, but she was happy. She smiled and gave them solid eye contact as she went into her stride to the next table.

Gwen and Kathy started whispering about some girl who had just walked in as if she was one of their playthings. I drank my shot without thinking and started sipping on the Long Island ice tea that Turned-Up-Collar Ted had bought. The drink wasn't half bad, even if he was an asshat. "Which university did you go to, Drew?" Chip asked me pleasantly enough.

"I went to Western State in Gunnison, Colorado," I replied in like fashion, and it was totally true, even if it was for less than a year.

"Never heard of it. What did you major in?" Ted said, slamming his shooter. He was not a big guy but big enough, and he sure as hell seemed to have an attitude.

"I did not graduate. I had a chance to get into the oil field work early on, so I decided to make some real cash instead. I can finish my degree up later if I choose," I responded with confidence.

Ted was raising the Long Island tea to his lips; he paused unusually long and raised one eyebrow as he stared at me. Chip responded likewise, and the two blond witches shared quick snippets and looked at each other aghast as if I had just committed six of the seven deadly sins in one go. "So you're in oil then?" Ted asked as he took a big swallow of his drink.

"Not really in oil. I am an operator at a large gas-processing facility in Guthrie." I continued and also drank a large swallow of my own drink.

"Wait, you actually work . . . at . . . a . . . facility?" Kathy said, holding her hand against her chest in mock horror.

Gwen looked at Lorena, rolled her eyes, and said to me with obvious disdain, "Do you live on a ranch also by any chance or have a horse?" Kathy giggled, and Ted guffawed at this last part.

What the hell kind of people do they think come to a cowboy dance hall place like this? I am so going to go with this now. "Why, yes, ma'am. I can ride and rope, hammer and paint, do things with my hands that most men cain't. Girls want to dance, but they have to get in line, but I ain't nothing but business, y'all, from nine to five," I responded with my best Ronnie Dunn Okie drawl, which really was not very good, and it sounded more like hillbilly than anything else, but it made the point that I was willing to give as good as I got. Stew got it, and he chuckled a bit but not to the point of anyone else seeing him.

"I went to Syracuse for three years and am only here to maintain my GPA for graduation before law school," Kathy bragged.

"Sorry, did you say maintain or attain your GPA?" I said with no accent whatsoever.

Stew laughed out loud this time, and Gwen gave me a piercing, dagger look, her blue eyes now squinty and the cosmetic augmentation lines turning red around her face and nose. Kathy was inhaling deeply like she was about to pass out.

I drained my glass and noticed Tornado Ted looking at me. It was not a pleasant look. His eyes were in a wild, nearly out-of-control realm as he stared unblinking at me. I had to say there was something about those eyes that disturbed me. "Time for another round, don't you think?" Ted said dryly and waved the barmaid over. He ordered the same drinks as before, and Lorena politely declined the shot as did the other two girls across the table.

Ted insisted the barmaid bring a full set. "Bring them all. We will find some party girls somewhere that will drink them," he said rudely. He flashed the cash again and tipped the barmaid another $20. I noticed several young ladies noticing Turned-Up-Collar Ted and whispering to one another.

The band played "Hooked on an Eight-Second Ride" by Chris Ledoux, so I asked Lorena to dance. We took off spinning and twirling around the dance floor, and I was having a blast. I noticed, however, that while she was dancing, well and smiling, it seemed that Ms. Lorena was semi-preoccupied and not having the same level of a good time that I was. *Did I step on her toes or what?*

We danced a second song, and then Lorena took my hand and led me back to the table. Chip was telling a disgusting joke about a ten-inch donkey penis, and Kathy was egging him on. Turned-Up-Collar Ted was trying to rub his hand between the legs of one of the other girls at the table who was quite uncomfortable with this. I found out later her name was Lori Ann. She was very cute with feathered brown hair and a nice pair of bright blue Tony Lama boots, and she was wearing a very classy blue Wrangler button-up that had a similar diamond set look as the Tequila Rose that lovely Linda had shown me at the warehouse. She was forcing a smile but obviously not happy with where Ted kept trying to put his hand.

Ted waved to a couple of girls standing at the bar, and they came over to join us. They were, as a lot of college girls are, plenty cute enough but a bit drunk and therefore lacking in class. Turned-Up-Collar Teddy bought them some shots and then stood up between them and started hanging on to them.

Gwen turned to Kathy, tapped her nose, and said, "Time to take this party outside for a pick-me-up, y'all."

Chip and Ted did a lame-ass white-boy high five and said, "Yeah, that's what I am talking about."

Gwen and Kathy led the way outside as Teddy Boy and Chipper slammed the rest of the drinks. Teddy latched on to Lori Ann, again making her uncomfortable, and I walked out last with Lorena. Gwen took her baby ducks out to the side of the parking lot to a shiny new silver Ford pickup that was decked to the nines. Gwen opened the truck passenger door, and Kathy pulled a small purple case from the glove box, began to draw lines of cocaine on the lid of the box, and passed them around. These were not your recreational social lines either. These were big-ass LA gangsta lines. When it came to Stew, he declined, but he did fire up a joint. Lori Ann also declined, but after some egging from Teddy, she took one. I declined also.

Lorena shook her head no, and Gwen looked at her questioningly and said "Lorena?" as if she was a dog on a leash, and Lorena took about half her line; it was obvious she did not want to. This, of course, pissed me off, so I took Lorena's hand and tried to ease her away from the group so we could have a walk and leave the rest to whatever they were doing. As we walked away, Gwen called out again. "Lorena, the party is over here."

Now I was really pissed off, and before I could tear into Gwen for being such a bitch, Lorena grabbed my arm and shook her head. *This is such bullshit.* So I stood there steaming for about twenty minutes, holding Lorena's hand, listening to Gwen and Kathy mock the fact that I was holding her hand.

Eventually, they had enough, and we all headed back inside. It was now after midnight, so they were checking IDs at the door. When I handed the bouncer my ID, he said in full complimentary fashion, "Colorado, eh? Cool place, man, love those mountains."

Gwen snatched my driver's license from the hand of the bouncer. "Colorado, I have never seen a Colorado driver's license before. Oh my god, Kathy, look at this. You won't believe it," Gwen said more mockingly than ever, pointing out something on my license. She showed it to Kathy and made some point I could not understand. And Kathy did the whole oh-my-god thing all over again as they both acted like I had the plague.

I took my license back from Gwen, a bit puzzled about what they were going on about. Gwen went up to Lorena and said, "Do you realize he is *only* 21? Oh my god, that is too funny. You're dating a kid. You're a pedophile."

This kid is about to tear you a new one, bitch, if you don't shut the fuck up.

Teddy, Chippy, and Kathy all guffawed in hysterical, holier-than-thou laughter; and with that, they all strolled back inside and were followed by all the baby ducks. I figured that would be enough for Lorena, and we could now have our night, but she strolled in right along with the rest of them. When I went to reach for her hand, she pulled it slowly away and said, "You're nice, Drew, but this isn't going to work out."

What the hell just happened here? Did an asteroid strike a planet and destroy my biorhythms?

Lorena said something to Kathy about not feeling good, went to the big bouncer at the main door, and asked him to call a cab. I followed her out and tried to talk to her, but she pretty much just ignored me.

So there I was, just standing there, watching Lorena talk with the bouncer, and trying to figure out if I was heartbroken, fucking pissed off, or both. I noticed Clay coming back in the side door with

Rhonda. It didn't take much to figure out what they had been up to. I meandered around for a minute and then found an open spot where I could listen to the band and bought a beer and a shot. *I sure as hell did not expect this, but I am out, so I am going to make the best of it.*

The band was good, and after my second shot, I started talking to a sweet girl who popped up next to me at the bar. She asked me if I could two-step. I said sure, and we had a couple of dances. I bought her a drink, and she moved on while I settled in at the bar to just drink and enjoy the band and not give in to my emotions.

I hadn't really noticed the bartenders would change every hour or so, and I was listening to the band play another Chris Ledoux song called "Hairtrigger Colt's .44" when I heard a sultry familiar voice from behind me say, "The night didn't quite turn out like you expected then, I take it, cowboy?"

I turned to see Yona looking at me with twinkling eyes. She was wearing a thin white leather headband now to match her doeskin vest, which really set off her exotic beauty. "Hi, Yona, not exactly. It looks like an asteroid hit a moon that knocked two planets into the sun, causing a galactic supernova," I said dryly.

Yona turned her head slightly to one side as if she did not understand the point, but she did understand the frustration. She handed me a shot of Jack Daniel's. "It's on the house, Drew."

Between the band, the drinks, and chatting with Yona, I had almost forgotten the earlier part of the evening. A new bartender came up, a blonde named Charlotte, and talked with Yona, who then turned to me and said, "C'mon, Drew, I am going on break. Let's take a walk outside."

Yona was a great conversationalist, and I began to think maybe the asteroid that fell wasn't so big after all, and maybe it only hit one planet. Perhaps the supernova was really just a dwarf star that did not do all that much damage to my biorhythms.

Yona took my arm as we walked around the parking lot. She moved gracefully and was getting more attractive by the minute. The late-night stars were out, and I was glad Yona was on my arm and also for the fresh air. I had not realized how much I had drunk, and the alcohol was kicking in now with full effect. Yona put her head on my shoulder as she laughed sweetly to some stupid thing that I said. The night was turning out for the better, or so I thought. This was all about to change.

We turned the corner of the bar toward the parking lot and were about to head back inside when I noticed what looked to be like a couple having sex with the passenger side door open in a new silver Ford pickup. Then I recognized Gwen and Kathy on the driver's side, their eyes wild and crazy, and they were both talking to someone inside the cab. I couldn't see the man, but it was obvious he was banging some girl on the seat. Then I recognized the light blue Tony Lama boots sticking out of the passenger door. It was Lori Ann.

Yona saw Gwen and put it all together about the same time I did, but I was already on the move. When I made it to the Ford, I saw Gwen and Kathy holding Lori Ann's arms back while Chip was on top of her with her shirt off, and Turned-Up-Collar Ted had a camera, taking pictures. It really wasn't necessary to hold her arms as it looked like Lori Ann was out of it. Gwen just had to have some control and involvement, and she seemed obsessed with it as she was telling Chip what to do to Lori Ann.

I saw red and went crazy. I ran to the pickup and slammed Ted's head hard into the side of the Ford twice, opening a gash that split his forehead and began to spew blood. I yanked Chip off Lori Ann and began to beat the shit out of him. I must have hit him a dozen times before I felt Yona pulling on me and screaming for me to back off. Gwen and Kathy were yelling to the bouncers inside the bar, "Help! The guy is crazy! He's killing them! He's a psycho! He's killing them!"

I'm the psycho here? What the fuck?

Yona finally pulled me away from Chip, who looked like a pound of raw hamburger by now. "Go, Drew! Go now! Get the hell out of here. I will take care of Lori Ann and tell the bouncers what happened. Just go *now!*"

The red fog was clearing some in my head, and I saw several big bouncers leaving the bar, heading our way. I squeezed Yona's hand, ducked out between two large pickups, and slid into the shadows. I went around the back, looking for Clay's truck. When I found the spot where he had parked, the truck was gone. *Where the hell is shit for brains now?*

I could see several bouncers searching the parking lot, slowly moving in my direction, and I could hear the wail of police sirens in the distance. I thought of Lori Ann, her blue boots, Yona. I had no idea what to do next and was at a real loss. *I know I may have hurt Teddy Boy, and I damn near killed Chipper. Shit.*

Suddenly, a souped-up older model blue Chevy truck pulled up next to me and revved the engine. I looked inside and saw a familiar face, telling me to climb inside. The police cars were starting to pull into the parking lot, and without a whole lot of options at this point, I quickly opened the door and jumped inside. The blue Chevy drove nice and easy right by the cops and out onto the road. The driver never said a word. He accelerated to five miles over the speed limit, and we headed toward Guthrie. I looked over at the man next to me and realized it would be a slow and possibly quite interesting drive home.

I was sitting in the front of a pickup driven by John Lennon–spec-wearing, ponytailed racketeering mogul Jay Randall.

29

I woke up Saturday morning with swollen hands and a swollen head. I soaked my right hand in peroxide and iced it down. Dave came over at around ten for coffee, and I told him the whole story from beginning to end. He was very concerned. "Drew, you need to call Leon Spencer. You can't let something like this lay, and you can't run away. You have to turn yourself in. Today call him. He will make sure that you get to the right cops in Stillwater. You did a good thing by helping that girl. Now don't go getting yourself in trouble by doing a stupid thing by running away now," Dave said caringly but firmly.

So that was what I did. I called Leon, not sure how he was going to respond. He agreed to take me to Stillwater at one that afternoon as soon as he got off his shift. In less than ten hours since this whole thing went down, I was back on the road to Stillwater, chaperoned by Oklahoma State Highway Patrol's finest. I told Leon all the details on the hour-long drive. We talked a lot about Yona and the band that was playing there with cowboy Garth. Leon seemed to be in an unusually pleasant mood about something despite the fact that I may be on my way to being incarcerated.

We pulled up to the Stillwater Central Police Station and went inside. Leon talked with a couple of the officers on deck and motioned for me to have a seat. I plopped down on a chair and tried to hear what they were talking about, but they were out of earshot.

The main doors opened, and in walked two men wearing cowboy hats, boots, and sport coats. They didn't really look like cops, but they damn sure looked important. I heard Leon and one of the other cops call the smaller of the two men "Judge." *Judge? This can't be good. Is this how they do it here in Oklahoma? Just drag the judge in on a Saturday and string me up right then and there?*

Another officer from the back came out, and they all shook hands. The man called Judge pointed over toward me and said, "Is he the one?" Leon nodded affirmative. The two guys in cowboy hats started my way. I looked down a long hallway beyond them and could see an interview room, and I figured that would be my next stop. I stood up slowly to prepare to meet my fate.

Destiny, however, had other plans this day, and what I did meet was a county commissioner/judge and the chief detective for Stillwater County. The judge looked me over, and it seemed like he had a bit of a twinkle in his eye when he said, "I understand you got in a scrap with a couple of fools last night, son. Story is they attacked you, and you responded in self-defense, responded pretty damn good from what I hear."

The larger second man said, "That's right, Judge. He acted in self-defense. I have a written statement to that effect right here, ready for him to sign, and we just close this out."

Self-defense? What the fuck? They already have a statement for me to sign?

The judge reached his hand out in the way of introduction. "Ronny Macklemore, county commissioner and county judge."

I shook his hand firmly and said, "Drew Hall, uhm, operator at a gas process plant in Guthrie."

The judge smiled at that, and the second man said while also extending his hand, "Dave Allen, chief detective. It's nice to meet you, son, a pleasure."

One of the officers suggested that I should go into a large office with him. The judge and Detective Dave followed. They showed me a very simple statement neatly typed on a paper with a police letterhead which stated, "I _____ agree that I acted in self-defense to protect the life and limb of myself and others in the event that occurred at 2.45 a.m. on March 7, 1985, in the south parking area outside the Tumbleweeds Club in Stillwater, Oklahoma."

I looked up at both men, and the judge had a real twinkle in his eye for sure now. "Is that what happened, son?" he asked, almost smiling.

"Er, if that's what the paper says," I replied and then reached for a pen to sign the statement.

"I think that wraps it up here, Judge. How about grabbing a late lunch and early beer out at DJ's with me?" Detective Dave asked the judge and then turned to me. "Mighty fine to meet you, Drew Hall." They both stood up, and I shook their hands again and shuffled on out the office door, still confused about what had just occurred. I noticed Leon over by the front door with the two officers, and I headed that way. I shook the hands of both the officers. Leon opened the door, we bid them both a good day, and we headed out to his car.

As we drove back to Guthrie, I was trying to get my head around it all. I sort of turned to Leon questioningly, and he winked at me and said, "Lori Ann is the judge's niece. She is real lucky you stepped in when you did. No real damage was done, and she can't remember a thing. There's a lot of grateful folks in that family today."

"What happened to the two guys that attacked her? Are they hurt?" I asked quietly.

"Two guys and two girls. The girls were as bad as the guys were or worse. Both boys overnighted at the hospital while a couple of Dave's guys interrogated the girls. They executed search warrants on all four of their rooms, and they are in some real trouble with what the detectives found. The only reason they are not in jail right now is the boys are rich kids, real rich kids, and a team of lawyers came out from the city and got the four of them released on bail for now, $50,000 bonds each. Hell of a night, huh, Drew?"

I nodded and went back to staring out the window. Leon put on some Waylon Jennings, and it was a pleasant return ride to the A frame.

Dave Raymond was outside when we pulled in, and he suggested we all go to his place for a beer and a chat. I really wasn't in the mood, but they pretty much insisted on it, and I knew that, however things had gone down, both these men had helped me out in a big way, so I obliged. Dave opened up the conversation, talking about his well production rates, and Leon chimed in with the price of crude oil continuing to go down. I drank a beer and just felt better being part of the group.

Three beers later, we were talking politics; blond, brunet, and redhead chicks; old dogs and new tricks; and habits we ain't kicking as good old boys would do.

30

I kept a pretty low profile the next week, even passed on the west plant 5 p.m. happy hour beers a couple of times. I made my tank runs and chatted with Dave at the A frame often but mainly just kept my head down and absorbed all the experiences that were going on around me. Clay and Mark Charter invited me back up to Tumbleweeds the next weekend, but I had to pass, just not ready for that again yet. I did ask Clay to tell Yona hello from me if he happened to see her, which he did. Being the proverbial hound dog that he was, he also came back with her phone number for me. Yona was a sweet lady indeed.

My cash that month for the condensate hauling was *high*. For the first time, I had broken $10,000, and maybe things were going to pick back up again. I went out one night to pull a couple of loads, and as usual, I always checked for tire tracks on the lease road just to see who has been in and out of the tanks. On the second tank of the night, I was messing around, and I noticed some new tracks—a big, wide Mudder-style tire with outside Z grooves. It was a unique pattern and the first time I had seen it. It was a very strange tire track, and I pondered it as I went to the tanker yard to drop my load.

In the tanker yard, I met the long, tall drink of water from Houston, Joe Reed. I was dumping my last pull-behind tank, and he was getting ready to drive a tanker truck down to one of the "stations." He opened a big cooler and invited me for a couple of beers, which I accepted. I asked him about the big Z-groove Mudder tire tracks, and he agreed they were strange and said that we should keep our eyes open. Again, I still did not get it that what we were doing was illegal as shit. We had a few more beers while he talked about his Special

Forces days in the military, his two tours in Vietnam, his kids, his wife, his girlfriends—Texas good ole boy to the core.

"You meet Brian from Pauls Valley yet? He's been hanging around up here for about four months now," Joe asked as he handed me another beer.

"I have seen him around, just don't really have time for him," I replied.

"That's best, Drew. He is going to be a problem," Joe said as he took a real long drink of ice-cold beer.

Before I could respond, he said, "OK, bro, I gotta go and do the show. Good catching up." Joe shook my hand, finished his beer in two gulps, and headed out.

"Thanks for the beers, Joe," I replied with nothing else clever to say.

This Brian Dugan cat must be something. Joe Reed is an ex–Green Beret from Vietnam, and if he says watch him, then I better watch him. That's like three out of three peeps have told me to watch him.

The next day, Tony called me into the west plant office and explained that, with the summer months coming on and the weather getting hotter, I would need to drop two loads from two of the company tanks every two weeks. "The heat causes the crude to evaporate and keep line pressure high. You don't move as much oil, can't produce as much, so we all have to take less. Just the way things are. However, in your case, you're staying out at Dave Raymond's place, and he has those two upgraded wells that are producing a lot of condensate, high-grade stuff. You could easily slide several loads out of there a month to make up the difference to you . . . and to me. I normally would not offer permission to bootleg from a rancher. I usually let them sort themselves out, but that's your territory, and those wells are like fat hogs just waiting for someone to make bacon."

"Roger that. Thanks, Tony," I replied absently, not really paying too much attention.

Later that night, I was hooking up the 1,000-gallon pull-behind to Dave's tanks, and my little trailer was halfway full when it hit me like a ton of bricks. *I am stealing, have been stealing. And now I am stealing from my friend, maybe one of my best friends. What the hell have I become?* That was the one and only load I ever pulled from Dave Raymond's tanks.

I kept up with my other loads, but my heart was not in it at the moment. Everyone seemed to notice something was amiss, but no one had all the details. I finally went out for beers with Clay and Mark, and I had to say, as always, I had an enjoyable evening. They were who they were, and it all started with being born-and-bred Oklahoma good ole boys.

A few days later, I was having beers with Dave down by the lake late one evening; and after we covered the usual topics of politics; blond, brunet, and redhead chicks; old dogs; and new tricks, he invited me to a special Oklahoma BBQ. "It's going to be a big bash, Drew, and chances are it will be one of the last big BBQs before the summer kicks in. There will be a lot of folks there, some you might even know. You might be surprised," Dave said with a twinkle in his eye.

"Where is the BBQ going to be?" I asked absently as I tightened up the line on my fishing pole. I had been playing with a catfish for ten minutes now, and he was about to get serious.

"It's going to be at Tom Moyer's place. It's real nice. The Moyers have been around here for a long time and are very well connected. Judge Macklemore from Stillwater will be there. It's a big to-do around here, and there will be loads of pretty little Oklahoma ladies running around. You can go with me, and you might be surprised who you see there," Dave said wryly for the second time.

"The judge from Stillwater? Dave, what kind of a BBQ is this going to be?" I asked, losing a bit of interest in the catfish in the lake, at least for the moment.

Dave laughed. "A very good one, Drew. Plan to be ready to go Saturday at four, OK?"

"Roger that, Dave," I replied. *I am going to a BBQ with a judge, and who knows what I will find there? Hoo-boy, what could I really say though?*

"And, Drew, wear your best. It may be a little warm for a sport jacket, but wear your best. The ladies will all be wearing theirs. It's that kind of party," Dave said, advising me.

"Copy. Thanks, Dave, for the invite. It sounds like a good time, if not just a bit out of my league, but I am looking forward to it."

"Good," Dave said, slapping my shoulder. "I am sure it will be something you will never forget."

Neither of us knew then just how true his statement would become.

31

I finished the month hauling my normal loads minus the four every two weeks that Tony had told me to drop. On Thursday, Tony met me in the shop with my cut of the monthly haul and a conversation. "You're light on bringing in loads this month, and your grade is down also. I would have thought, with adding a couple of loads of that high-grade condensate, you would have maintained your earning or, as smart as you are, even found a way to bring in more. I recommend you think about that, Drew. Maybe have a chat with Mark tonight as well. I like you, but you can go out of this thing just as easy as you came in. The only difference is if you go out, you go all the way out," Tony said dryly.

What did he just say? More importantly, what exactly does he mean? I stared at Tony for a moment, and he stared back at me with unblinking cold, dark eyes, like a Logan County great white shark. "Tony, you told me to expect production to drop when it starts warming up. What's the problem?" I said in what I thought was a questioning manner, but he took it as a straight-on challenge.

"I also gave you a solution. You need to recall the entire conversation, not just the convenient parts. It's your area. You run it however you want. Just don't drop your earnings too low, and I suggest you talk to Mark—today," Tony said quietly and eerily. Then he turned and left the shop, leaving me alone standing there holding my cut.

I opened the envelope up and slowly counted it all out—$7,800, not bad at all. Despite everything that had occurred, I had $20,000 cash stashed in the A frame and another $28,000 in my bank account—and lots of new toys and clothes. This sort of put things back in perspective, and I did the only prudent thing I could do at this point. I called Mark.

We agreed to meet at Randall's that night, and after playing a couple of games of pool, listening to Clay whine about Ann about to have his kid for nearly an hour, and then listening to Mark tell us how much Lori liked the new horse and how great everything was on his side, we finally got around to talking about my situation with Tony. I told them both the whole story going back three weeks from the beginning, including what happened today. "You lucky bastard, you mean Tony told you to haul loads from those new wells on the Raymond place? That's high-grade product, man. How cool is that?" Clay said excitedly.

I just nodded. "Yeah, that's what he said, all right."

"So the problem is you did not want to haul anything from those tanks on the Raymond place, and now Tony is pissed because he thinks your haul dropped lower than it should have. Drew, don't you get it? If you make less, then Tony makes less, and Tony does not like to make less. You need to keep your earnings up, buddy," Mark said emphatically.

"Man, I wish I could haul some loads off the Raymond lease. That would be some nice bank," Clay went on, again oblivious of the point.

I wanted to change the subject, so I said, "OK, so I obviously don't want to piss Tony off, and I will work on this. How bad could this get? I mean, what's he going to do? Beat the crap out of me?"

"Nah, he likes you. He will probably talk to you a couple of more times, but if he ever decides he needs to get physical, it will be much worse," Mark replied quietly as he looked at his beer. "See, he likes you, and you're an outsider. He took a chance on you, and it's been working out great so far. But it would kind of be like an embarrassment to him if it did not work out. Get it? So he might have to make an example of you or something worse. Best thing you can do now, Drew, is start hauling from the Raymond tanks and keep your earnings up."

"Remember, it's the same as Duster. The big difference between your old pal Dwayne Robinett, Bonnie's ex, and Tony is that Dwayne has only killed one guy. Tony, on the other hand . . ." Clay commented, now half drunk. "What is your problem with hauling from the Raymond lease tanks anyway? Jeez, man, I would love to have that option."

Says the guy who is three days away from having a newborn baby, little or no moral fortitude. I paused for a moment and then said thoughtfully, "Well, gents, I guess I draw the line at stealing from a friend."

32

The next day on Friday, I again declined Mark's invitation to go out. Ann had apparently gone into labor, and even Clay wasn't stupid enough to go prowling around while she was having his baby. I just stayed home to get ready for the big Moyer BBQ on Saturday.

I had bought a new brushpopper shirt from Linda at the warehouse the week before just for the BBQ. It was white with black stars falling down the back and over the shoulders, sort of the reverse Night Rider look, and it was called Southern Star. I added a John Cougar Mellencamp Western-style silver and black bolo necktie and was wearing the Lucchese ostrich boots. The weather was very nice, so I wore a very thin black sport coat. Dave had gone all out and was wearing a Texas tux, which was a long-tailed black tux, blue jeans, and boots with a bow tie. He topped this off with a black Stetson hat. We both looked pretty sharp indeed as we pulled out of the yard and headed over to the famous Moyer ranch for the BBQ.

Dave was in a good mood and chatted incessantly about the Moyers, the history of BBQ gatherings in Logan County, and how many pretty girls we would see today. As interesting as most of these subjects were, I was keener to get to the Moyer ranch and explore the last subject of the topic, my favorite—the Oklahoma girls. There were over a hundred vehicles in the parking lot when we pulled up, and traffic was being directed by two off-duty deputy sheriff officers. It looked like quite the "do" indeed.

We parked the truck, and immediately, I caught the eye of three lovelies heading onto the BBQ just in front of us. They were dressed to kill and looked very sweet as they waved at us. Dave elbowed me in the side, grinning like a schoolboy, and we followed them into the ranch area.

We were all met at the main entrance by Jay and Rhonda Mae, two employees of the ranch who welcomed us on the Moyers' behalf and sort of gave us the lay of the land. It was a grand place with a very large main house next to a nice full-size pool. They had two bars set up on opposite ends of the pool, so we headed for the north one and took a couple of cold beers from the open bar.

Dave introduced me to Tom Moyer and his wife, Susan, and we enjoyed the beers as the sun went down. They had two big BBQ pits cooking dead cow and dead pig; one was an underground, buried pit, but you could still smell the wonderful aroma of the cooking flesh. They had several tables full of great-smelling food, and I was impressed. The Oklahomans really did know how to BBQ.

I wandered around by myself for a while as Dave caught up with old friends and new acquaintances. The party was alive now, and there had to be over 200 people here spread out all over the main house grounds, BBQ area, and yards. The scenery was amazing; the landscape was not bad either. There were pretty Oklahoma women turning up everywhere I looked.

Then I saw her standing there like a long cool woman in a black dress—Myra the Tigra. She was drinking white wine and tossing her hair back as only she can do while she was chatting up an influential couple. I knew that conversation. She was turning it on, and they were spilling their life story to her.

She caught my eyes and smiled like a tigress. Gracefully, she finished her drink, ended her conversation with the couple, and—moving like the feline femme fatale that she was—began to walk slowly in my direction, pausing only long enough to get a new glass of wine. I could smell an amazing exotic perfume on the light breeze as she came in close to me. The very air around us began to pulse with energy. "Hello, Drew," Myra said, and she said it so much more than seductively, like she was queen of the jungle night, and she knew it.

"Hey, Myra," I blurted out while my eyes roamed every inch of her stunning long body in that short black dress.

"I did not realize you were so well connected. This is a pretty posh event." She purred.

"Er, uhm . . . neither did I," I stammered. "Nice to see you again. Did you come here with someone?"

"Yes. Bob is running around here somewhere, socializing," Myra responded. I noticed her eyes were also checking me out thoroughly, possibly in this manner for the first time.

"And you?" she asked, gently raising an eyebrow and staring into my eyes.

"Er, no, I mean, well, yes. I came with Dave Raymond but am here . . . alone." *You're sounding like an idiot.*

"Well, mister, I am here alone. Let's walk. I will introduce you to a few people, and we can . . . talk . . . while we walk," Myra said as she hooked my arm in hers. Her touch brought about that sparking electricity that only came with a very few women. With Myra, it was like 7,000 volts hitting me every time we touched.

She finished her wine, set the glass down, and held on to my arm with both of hers as we walked around the ranch grounds. She smiled, laughed, looked at me, tossed her hair, squeezed my arm, smiled some more. I would have done anything she asked me to at that moment—anything.

"Myra, do you mind if I ask you how you learned to shoot so well? Don't want to pry, just curious, is all. You were quite impressive on the gun range," I asked conversationally.

"Not at all. I can see why you would be curious. Bob has always been a shooter and hunter as you know. I guess I just tagged around with him in the beginning, learning to shoot pistols, rifles, shotguns. I enjoyed it. I went to the University of Connecticut for two years and realized that just wasn't for me, but I did get a BA in liberal arts and decided to try the Connecticut Police Academy in Wilcox Township. After four months in the academy, I decided that was *not* for me, so I went to modeling school and did a few other things for two years in New York. As it turns out, those things were for me, and I began to travel a lot. I just went from there to here in a roundabout fashion after a few years of doing them all."

If Bob was born and raised in Oklahoma, then why is she spending all this time in Connecticut and New York? Southern belle gone Yankee? And why doesn't she have a drop of an Okie accent?

We continued to walk and meet people, and she steered us toward a specific target person she saw standing off to one side. "Drew, this is

Assistant District Attorney Jim Dawson. He is an old friend," Myra said as she introduced me to a sharp-looking guy who had lawyer written all over him. "Jim, this is Drew Hall, a new . . . friend."

"Nice to meet you, Jim," I said, shaking his hand.

"Likewise, Drew," Jim replied. "Where are you from?" While he did not say the words, the implication was clear. *Not from around here, are you, boy?*

"Colorado, southwest corner mostly." Not to be outdone, I responded, "And you?"

"Accent that much of a giveaway, is it? From Chicago originally, but before coming here to Oklahoma City, I spent five years in Miami," Assistant District Attorney Dawson said with a smile.

Again with the Miami thing? "When did you arrive in Oklahoma?" I asked him.

"Six months ago," he replied, absently sipping his beer.

Then exactly how can he and Myra be "old" friends?

"Catch you later, Jim. As always, good to see you," Myra said as she began to stroll away.

"You also, Myra," ADA Dawson replied.

Myra introduced me to a few more people, and we said hello to Judge Macklemore and his wife. He never mentioned the Stillwater event, but his manner was gracious and appreciative, something which I did not miss and also enjoyed.

It was difficult to concentrate on anything other than Myra as I watched her body move at every chance while we walked and talked, but I found a way to do it. She was indeed the tigress right now. Every now and then, she would brush her breasts against my arm and smile sweetly, almost *innocently*—a word I would just not use to describe Ms. Myra Breittlinger in any context, not now, not ever.

An hour later, I found myself with her alone under the stars, off to one side in the back of the main house, just the two of us. She was silent, turned, and looked at me like the stunning woman she was. I knew what to do. As our tongues entwined, our bodies followed suit, and we melted together into each other's arms. I knew I would never be the exact same man again after this. Her black silk dress slid up easily over her firm hips and waist. I pulled her up and in. *Like I said, I knew what to do, and I did it, and she liked it. There are some things a woman just can't fake.*

"Hey, Drew, where have you been? Did you get a chance to try some of that pork? Wasn't that some of the sweetest meat you ever had?" Dave called out as he approached me later from the side of the house.

Oh, Davy Boy, if you only knew. He was apparently having a grand time. He had his black cowboy hat tipped back and was feeling no pain at all. "Just socializing, Dave. You said it would be a good time here, but I really had no idea how great it was going to turn out to be. Truly unforgettable," I answered dreamily.

Dave cocked his head and looked at me almost knowingly. He shrugged, and we both went to the north side of the pool and grabbed a couple of more beers. I saw Myra leaving a little while later with her brother, Bob. She smiled and gave me the slightest wave. Her eyes stayed on me until she walked out the gate; my eyes never left her. *Unforgettable. I knew this was probably a one-shot deal. She is just too classy, but man, what a shot!*

Dave and I left the BBQ around midnight, and I drove home as he had been at it all night and had several to many. I parked his truck at his place and got him inside. I looked up into the night sky as I walked to the A frame and just breathed in the experience. It had been a once-in-a-lifetime evening for sure. I seemed to be having these frequently in Oklahoma.

The moon was half full and bright, and I took a moment to appreciate it. I happened to glance at the soft ground about thirty yards from the A frame, and I saw two deep tire tracks. They had the same print—the same big, wide outside-Z-groove tires that Joe Reed and I had seen at the trailer yard. *Who is driving the truck with those tires, and why are the tracks outside my front door?*

I followed them away for about fifty yards and then lost the tracks as the ground got harder. They seemed to be heading toward Dave's two wells on the back of his property. *Is somebody sneaking back there and grabbing a load? What is going on with this?*

33

I spent the next couple of days drifting in and out of memories of Myra the Tigra's tongue in my mouth and sliding her black silk skirt up her thighs. Like I said, it was a once-in-a-lifetime experience; and like Yona and several others, these things just kept happening to me here.

I found it tough to concentrate on work more than once. We had a busy week at the west plant with a complete overhaul on one of the big clean-burn engines. I kept dropping wrenches and bolts, and Mark was laughing at me and teasing me about who had my head all wrapped up. Clay had taken the week off to be with Ann and their new baby girl, so we were shorthanded. With all the work we had going on, Tony had called a sort of all-hands-on-deck thing, and we had seven new guys in and out of the plant helping in one way or another for the whole week.

On the last day of the overhaul, I saw several new vehicles parked out in front of the west plant office. I noticed one rig that stood out. It was a big white 4 × 4 Ford pickup with a six-inch lift kit. It was parked right in front of the door to the plant office. It had big, wide tires with Z grooves on the sides.

We fired up the overhauled plant engine just fine, and everything went well during the plant restart. Tony had us all in the office drinking beers by four. There were a couple of guys I did not know well who were there that afternoon, so I watched each of them leave to see who was going to get into the big Ford. It did not take long.

One of the first guys out of the door after a beer or two was the same guy who always left early. I looked out the side window of the office and watched Brian Dugan climb into the driver's side of the big white pickup. *What the fuck? Why is he driving around the trailer yard? And I damn sure want to know why his truck was outside my A frame.*

I looked around to try to find Joe Reed to discuss this with him, but he must have left also. I decided not to say anything to Mark or Tony yet; I wanted to get with Joe first. I knew where to find him later that night, so I waited. I said goodbye to the crew and headed to the A frame. My head was full of the fact that it was Brian Dugan who drove the truck with the tires. I hardly thought of Myra the Tigra all the way home—well, only once, maybe twice.

I hit the super spa shower and drove back to get the 1,000-gallon pull-behind trailer. I took a load out of one of the tanks and headed to the trailer yard to wait for Joe. He showed up at about eight, and as usual, he had a cooler full of beer. After a brief catch-up, I told him about the tire tracks at my place and seeing Brian jump into the big white Ford rig. Joe took half his beer in one gulp and asked, "The tracks were headed for the wells on the Raymond lease? Those are your tanks, right? How much are you pulling from them each week, Drew?"

I kicked the dirt around a bit and had a drink myself before answering, "None. I don't pull from them." Joe stared at me blankly.

"Look, Dave is a friend of mine, and it doesn't seem right to me, so I don't pull any loads from them, even though its high-grade stuff and all that," I said in response to Joe's stare.

Joe grinned a big Texas grin. "That's OK by me. Not enough people in this game have any semblance of integrity. No problem here at all. You keeping your earnings up? Tony will not accept a drop in earnings," Joe asked, concerned.

I nodded. "Yeah, we had that discussion. I am holding my own, and he hasn't said anything else."

"You think Brian is trying to bootleg loads off those tanks? Maybe watching you guys for the right time when you're both gone?" asked Joe.

"It's possible. But we are seldom both gone at the same time. Besides, that would really piss me off if he is hanging around like that. If I catch him, I'll kick his stupid Okie ass," I said with plenty of venom. "Crazy or not, I'll shut him down if I see anything at all even remotely close to that."

"This is serious now, Drew," Joe said thoughtfully. "We all knew he was trouble. We just did not know where it was going to start. Have you told Tony?"

"Not yet. I wanted to talk with you first. But I need to tell him soon."

"Yes, you do. That's his job to sort Brian, not ours. If Tony knows Brian was nosing around on your leases, he will take care of it for sure. Keep in touch with me, Drew. If you're going to make a move, let me know, and I'll be your wingman. If you notice, Brian always has some lowlife hanging with him in case shit goes down," Joe said.

"Thanks, Joe, it means a lot. I won't be stupid, but if I catch him on Dave's place, I will deal with it right then and there. No other choice," I said firmly.

"Roger that, buddy. Roger that," Joe replied, handing me another cold one.

I pulled into the plant office early the next morning, hoping to catch Tony alone, and he came in right behind me. I told him the story slowly and carefully, from the beginning when I had found the Z-groove tire tracks at the trailer yard and then at my place going toward the wells to the time when I saw Brian's truck tires at the office yesterday. I could tell he was *not* happy at all. "Does anybody else know about this?" Tony growled.

"Yeah, Joe Reed and I have seen the same tracks before. Even though we have never actually seen him out on the leases, his tires are pretty damn unique, and we talked about it being a possible issue, so I told you this morning. Like I said, haven't seen him, just the tracks. Only telling you what I know, and you tell me what you want to do, and we will follow your lead," I said, exhaling.

"You're sure they are his tracks?" Tony inquired seriously.

"No, I am not sure they are his tracks. I am very sure he has the exact same tires as those tracks, and Joe believes it also. It makes sense, Tony," I replied.

Tony growled again, "I knew that shithead was going to be trouble."

"How do you want to play it?" I asked.

"You do nothing. Tell Joe to do nothing. I will deal with this dumbass," Tony answered clearly.

"Roger that, Tony."

34

I told Joe about my chat with Tony, and he just laughed. "I told you Tony would take care of it. Williams is as solid as they come. Just stay on his good side," he said.

We had the monthly area safety meeting three days later, and Brian showed up with a huge black eye and swollen jaw. He glared at me throughout the entire day. He looked at Joe and me a couple of times during the safety meeting, and I did one of the Alfred E. Neuman from *Mad* magazine's "what, me worry?" shrugs while Joe laughed. If we knew what Brian had planned, I would not have been laughing nearly as much.

On Saturday, I returned to Tumbleweeds with Clay and Mark for the first time in over a month. It was a great time. I danced with Yona during her break, and we both laughed at Clay and Melanie's shenanigans. Yona was breathtakingly beautiful again as usual, and it was a real pleasure to spend time with her that night. We talked about the realm of possibilities of us getting together and then made out a bit in the parking lot. Of course, I wanted more, but she drew the line at some heavy petting. She was a special lady indeed, and I did not mind waiting.

The cowboy band with Garth as lead singer was playing again, and they really were getting good now. A couple of the bouncers came over and said hi, which was cool. All in all, it was a good night.

The following week, I had operator-on-call duty, which meant I worked from 7 a.m. to 3 p.m. and was on call 24/7 for a ten-day period, and then we rotated. If anything went wrong in the plant at night, I would get called out by an ADAS II automatic dialing alarm system phone page and I would respond to the alarm and fix the problem or restart the plant. There were over a hundred alarms that could call you out. About 25 percent of these could cause the entire plant to shut down if you did not respond within an hour. I had been called out before on small things and also on entire plant shutdowns several times while working at both east and west plants. I had learned a lot and was a fairly solid operator. By this time, I knew what I was doing with the process plants and confident in my understanding and abilities.

There was maintenance going on of some kind almost each day, and the lead operator, plant foreman, or superintendent would log in the status of any open items in the daily logbook and the maintenance logbook. Most of the guys doing the maintenance were mechanics or support like Brian Dugan and several others. As the operator on call, I had a cushy week with only some minor tasks to perform. I would see Brian Dugan and the others almost daily, and he never failed to at least give me a thirty-second glare. He was, however, very knowledgeable about the plant systems, and he was often in charge of some sophisticated mechanical work. I had to give him that. He did know his way around the plant and was good with the start-up controls and operating panels as well.

There had not been any callouts in over two weeks now, and the plant was running well; it seemed to be in fine shape. I was having a couple of relaxing beers with Dave down by the catfish pond at about nine on Monday evening and was surprised when my pager went off with three plant fault alarms. I gave the pole to Dave and hauled ass to the plant. I reached it in twenty-five minutes.

We had seven big, eight-cylinder natural gas compressor units and one six-cylinder that ran the propane refrigeration process. The plant was on roughly ten acres of land and was surrounded by an eight-foot security fence. Immediately outside the fenced area was some open pasture, but just beyond that were all woodlands.

When I arrived at the west plant, I went straight to the control panel. The propane refrigeration compressor was down on a high-vibration alarm; however, the compression system was still pressurized. I had one high-liquid-level plant alarm and nothing else. *No big deal so far. This should be cake.*

I checked the refrigeration system, vessel, and three-phase chiller exchanger temperatures, and it appeared that all I would have to do was blow down the propane refrigeration compressor through the internal discharge system and restart the unit, and I would be back at the A frame in an hour, maybe even catch a catfish before bedtime.

I quickly checked the maintenance logs and plant daily logbook to make sure there was no maintenance under way or any other adjustment to the plant that I needed to be aware of before starting things back up and clearing the alarms. There was *nothing* written in *any* of the logbooks to suggest anything was out of order or under repair, so I reset all the alarms and began to open valves and blow down the pressurized propane to the discharge system and flare. Thus began one of the most significant, dangerous, and scenic nights of my life that would end up making a Fourth of July fireworks celebration look like a wayward kid's sparkler.

The discharge flare system was tied in with all eight compressors and was connected through a four-inch pipeline system. The propane refrigeration had 640 psi in the system, and normally, when you start to blow down a pressurized compressor with that level of pressure, you get a significant pipeline vibration, and you can hear the gas hissing rapidly through the piping. Good operators open the four-inch valves smoothly and slowly to ease the pipe vibration; if not, you risk causing an incident or can have one of the relief valves blow off. I had watched the idiot boy John yanking valves open like a moron when he would get all pissed off, and this would cause the pipes to jump, shake, groan, and shudder; going from 0 psi to 640 psi by slamming valves open was one hell of a rapid pressure shift.

So that was the scene. Everything was going smoothly until I opened the discharge valve to the flare line. Once I did this, I was in some real trouble. I heard a series of small explosions and saw 100-foot-high flames begin to shoot up the sides of three of the big eight-cylinder compressor units. I had no idea what was happening, but I realized the flames had started when I opened the propane discharge line into the flare system, so I quickly shut the valve and then ran over to hit the emergency shutdown (ESD) switch on the control panel to shut the entire plant down.

This action stopped the flow of propane straight into the engines. The flames dropped to about twenty feet high because I had turned the gas off, but the fan belts and other parts of the compressors were now burning. I hit the alarm to the fire department, which would also automatically send a page notification to Tony, the plant foreman, and the senior mechanic. I grabbed the largest wheeled fire extinguisher that we had and pulled it over to unit no. 1, where I sprayed the pressurized powder into the burning areas on the first compressor, dousing the fire. Then I moved to the second unit and sprayed it also, putting out this fire.

I was moving to the third unit when I noticed something near the edge of the woods about fifty yards outside the plant security fence. The extinguisher powder was blowing around from the first two compressors, and the flames on the third were still burning down, so it was smoky and chaotic all around. I sprayed the third compressor and glanced back to the movement outside the fence.

Just driving away slowly into the trees with its headlights off was a pickup. Even through the blowing powder, the smoking, burned compressors, and the darkness, I could clearly see the tailgate of a jacked-up white Ford truck with large, high tires drive away into the trees. I knew then, somehow, he had to be involved with whatever had happened, and I began to shake in anger.

35

We had the senior management from Oklahoma City arrive the next day, and an investigation into the fire and overall incident was conducted over the next four days. It was discovered that three of the relief valves for the flare line had been taken out of the discharge line, and the pipes had been left open ended. When I opened the discharge valve to blow down the propane compressor, the pressurized propane blew through the open pipe straight into the moving parts of three of the GTLA compressor engines, causing the wall of flames to shoot up into the air and catching the engines on fire. The removal of the valves was not logged in any logbook, nor did anyone admit to pulling the relief valves out.

There were only four flange bolts for each large relief valve, and they were of solid-state design, so all the parts were internal. It would have been a simple quick feat for almost anyone to pull the three valves out. The fact that they were removed without a permit or authorization, not logged down at all, and that there was no evidence to confirm who had done this was quite troubling to everyone. It was beginning to appear to be a form of oil field sabotage instead of some kind of operator error.

It was a harrowing experience for me. The four days of the management investigation were grueling and not something I wanted to repeat. Tony was unapproachable and started terminating people within the first day of the investigation. Two of the first guys he dumped right off just for spite were Brian Dugan and one of his cronies. This, of course, got Joe Dugan all pissed off, and it looked like a mini-war was going to erupt between him and Tony. As an attempt at a happy medium, Brian and his lowlife buddy went back to the Pauls Valley system to work for Joe again. Brian took off that afternoon, so I never had a chance to confront him directly about what I had seen the night of the fires.

Talking about it later with Joe Reed, we came up with the theory that Brian was the one who somehow pulled the relief valves out. He had a personal vendetta against me, which was no secret. We talked about how he possibly pulled the valves and triggered the alarms so I would get called out, and then he had been watching the whole thing from outside the fence like some psycho pyromaniac. We had no evidence, and it was a pretty wild theory, but I knew he was involved in the incident somehow, and Joe agreed.

With Brian's departure and all the shit that was going down right now in the plant, we soon forgot about him for the time being. I kept waiting for Tony's wrath to come my way since I was the catalyst who had started the whole event, but it never did. He was up several people's ass daily but hardly spoke privately to me during the entire investigation. We had county inspectors, civil defense and OSHA inspectors, and a variety of other agencies that he was dealing with daily, so I just figured he would take a chunk out of my ass after everything calmed down.

After seven days, the repairs on all the clean-burn GTLA engines were complete, new relief valves were installed, and we started the plant back up again. For all intents and purposes, the event was over without further drama; and other than a few additional corrective actions, everyone was ready to move past it.

One of those final action items was to pay an OSHA fine and to designate a plant safety representative from among the full-time staff. I was in the west plant compressor area one morning when Tony called me on the radio to meet him in his office. *Here it comes. He is going to rip me a new one. Doubt if he will fire me though. He would have done that earlier.*

I arrived at the office and met Tony at the coffee machine. He was in a better mood than I expected, so I grabbed a cup of joe and sat down in front of his desk. "Do you think you can finish out the week without burning anything down or blowing any more shit up?" Tony asked, his eyes twinkling a bit.

"If we can keep ghosts out of the plant," I replied. "It's a bit tough when someone sabotages the plant on us, Tony."

"Yeah, I get that. I think I took care of that problem though. The plant looks good, seems to be running OK. What do you think?" Tony asked.

That's an interesting question. "Yeah, it seems to be. The mechanic crews from Bixby and Tulsa did a great job of repairing the clean-burn engines," I answered.

"You read the final report on the incident along with the investigation findings, right? Including the OSHA findings and actions?" Tony inquired of me.

I nodded. "Yes. From what I understand of OSHA, a $7,500 fine for what happened really is not that bad."

Tony took a drink of coffee and stated, "Nobody got hurt, so they had nothing else to go with. I was talking with the third-party investigators, and they said you saved us a lot of money and time by putting the fires out and pulling the ESD on the plant. That whole thing could have been much worse. They said a trained firefighter could not have done better."

"The final report did not identify root causes or who was involved. It just said 'inconclusive.' Do you have an idea what happened? How it happened? Hell, why it happened?" I asked curiously.

"Yeah, I have a damn good idea. And like I said, I took care of it," Tony replied, almost growling at me over his desk.

I wonder where he is going with this.

"Did you see the part in the report where we have to designate a plant safety representative and send them to OSHA training in Norman?" Tony said without the growl this time.

I nodded again. "Yeah, I saw it. Who do you have in mind for this?" I asked.

"Management from the city want you. I agree with them. You have enough sense upstairs, and you proved you can take action in a crisis. You're always taking the lead in our safety meetings, and besides that, you're the one guy I can take out of the field 50 percent of the time to watch after the safety stuff, and it won't hurt production or plant performance. What do you think, Drew?" Tony asked, eyes twinkling for sure this time.

Gee thanks, Tony. You really know how to make a guy feel so good. Not sure if I am valued or not on this one.

While I was pausing to figure this development out, Tony said, "There is a 65¢ an hour raise that comes with it, and we send you to school and seminars."

Without further hesitation, I said, "I am in then." Thus began my illustrious career into the world of industrial safety.

36

Tony told me I would be going to the University of Oklahoma campus in Norman in one month's time to attend a weeklong safety seminar and certification, so I should start studying up. I received my first copies of the OSHA Codes of Federal Regulations Title 29 part 1910 (General Industry) and part 1926 (Construction) in the mail the following week. No stranger to research, I began to study the safety regulations and prepare for my upcoming certification seminar. As I studied the safety standards for the operating oil and gas industry, I began to realize our gas plant was full of safety violations that created some very hazardous conditions.

I started spending time in the Central State University Library down in Edmond as part of my research to find safety checklists, forms, and procedures that applied to my industry and the plant. I was developing a robust safety program which, before my feeble effort, had been nonexistent.

The coeds who frequented the library at Central State were always a plus. Attractive, intelligent, and helpful—what else could a guy ask for? *I do love the Oklahoma girls.*

I continued to haul my pull-behind trailer and get my weekly loads, but I was really quite focused on this new career challenge. *This is strange, like, Jim Morrison strange. I am driving around stealing condensate and low-grade crude, I have a gun in my truck, and I drink four to five beers easy most nights. I was the guy on call when the plant blew up, and yet they make me the safety guy? How weird is that?*

I caught up with Joe Reed at the tank yard on a Wednesday for our usual beers and a chat. "How much do you know about what goes on behind the scenes around here, Drew?" asked long, tall Joe.

"Not much really. I hear bits and pieces, but Clay and Mark are always telling me 'don't ask questions,' so I don't ask questions about things too much," I replied in between beer sips.

"You know about the territories? The crews? Duster?" Joe asked.

Now this is an interesting turn in the conversation. "I know they are there. I mean, I have heard people talk about the different areas, and I have heard the name Duster a few times. Do you know who he is?"

Tall Joe shook his head. "No. I know he is the big dog in Oklahoma, maybe other areas too, and he runs all the crews in this area, but I have no idea who he is," Joe replied.

"Could it be Tony?" I asked curiously, again not thinking about what killed the cat.

"Could be, I guess, but I doubt it. My understanding is that Duster has been around awhile and is connected in high circles. He is at least two tiers higher than Tony in the hierarchy of things and is some kind of big-shot player. Tony is good at what he does, but not sure he is sophisticated enough to be at the top. I get the feeling that Duster is more . . . national . . . more interstate, maybe even international, certainly more dangerous. I guess it is the best way to say it," said Joe.

More dangerous than .45-Colt-packing Tony? "Who's your source of information?" I asked absently.

"Sources." Joe chuckled. "I have several, some all the way back in Houston, all confidential, of course. If I tell you, I have to kill you. Anyway, the reason I bring it up is that there may be some shit going down soon, and I want you to have an idea about what you might run into."

"What kind of shit exactly? I have heard several rumors and seen a few things but nothing concrete. What's up, buddy?" I asked.

"It's Pauls Valley for one thing. Joe Dugan has gone over the top finally. After his feud with Tony began heating up, he started stealing Caterpillar D8s, small planes, and other heavy equipment from local construction companies. Brian is involved. They are drawing too much attention to themselves, and the word is traveling fast. There is talk this might get the feds involved. Now Joe is also pushing to expand his territory. I hear that Brian stole a tanker truck from over by Elk City, which is way out of his jurisdiction. You don't want to mess with the Elk City boys. If the PV idiots cross into our territory looking to score, even one foot, Tony will go to war, and all hell is going to break loose," Joe stated solemnly. "Elk City may already be on the war path, and they won't care who they shoot—us, PV, even out-of-staters. When they decide to go, they are like African soldier ants and just wipe out everything in their path."

Jeez, is he serious? Is this even possible? "Are you serious?" I asked incredulously.

"As death," tall Joe replied. "So be aware and watchful all the time. If you think it's going down, it probably is, so shoot first, and ask questions later, OK?"

Shoot first? I thought this was 1986, not 1886. "Roger that, Joe. Roger that. You think this could really happen?"

"Bet on it, Drew. Shit is going down—and soon," Joe stated.

I finished the night pondering the conversation with Joe. I thought about calling Clay or Mark, but something was bothering me in the back of my head that I could not quite get a handle on, and I wanted to sort this first. I ran the past year of my life here in Oklahoma over and over again in my head as I headed home.

It was early—well, by our standards anyway—only ten o'clock, when I returned to the A frame. I had a frantic message from Clay to meet him at Jack's Bar ASAP. I hit the super spa shower quick, changed clothes, and headed out to Jack's Bar to see what Clay had his panties all in a wad about. I joined Mark and Clay at a back table, ordered a beer and a bourbon shot, and was about to ask what was up when both of them started yammering away at the same time like errant schoolboys. "Brian Dugan stole a tanker from Elk City territory," Clay burst out.

"Yeah, and two Elk City crew went over to talk with Joe Dugan about it, and they never came back," Mark added quickly.

"This is bad, Drew. Shit might start going down here quick," Clay said.

"Yeah, it looks like Joe Dugan is running crazy, stealing small planes and shit. It's out of control down there," said Mark.

"I hear Brian stole another tanker on the eastern side, out by Shawnee. This is getting crazy," Clay said.

"If they come up here, Tony will go ballistic," Mark added.

Are they reading from a script? This sounds like a rewind of my conversation with long, tall Joe.

"Drew, are you listening to what we are telling you?" Clay said, exasperated.

I took my bourbon shot and said, "Yes, I am."

"So why haven't you said anything?" Mark asked excitedly.

"Because I can't get a word in edgewise with you two morons carrying on like crazy geese," I replied. "So there is some shit coming down. It must be serious shit because it has all you guys in a hell of an uproar. I guess my question to you two gentlemen now is, what are we going to do about it?"

37

Tension and a lingering sense of dread along with near panic were in the wind for the coming days. You couldn't go into the west plant office for a cup of java without listening to John rant and rave about how we were on the verge of "Armageddon."

I was thirteen days away from my week at the University of Oklahoma campus, and after listening to Clay tell everyone how hot the Sooner girls on campus were, I was ready to begin my seminar right away. I was doing a fair amount of studying and wasn't sure, at this point, how much I believed about this whole imminent turf-war thing anyway, and I was rapidly losing interest.

I met the boys for afternoon beers and BBQ at Randall's on Saturday, and no one mentioned the possible "war"—Pauls Valley, Elk City, or the Dugans. Clay was on about his young daughter, and Mark was winging that Lori wanted a new horse.

I drove back to the west plant and was surprised to find Tony, John, and half the crew there drinking beers and talking. It was the first of many surprises in store for me that day. Tony asked all of us to join him at the strip club Wellingtons Way, but I declined. I was in the mood for studying, so I left at around six in the late afternoon, thoughts running like a freight train through the middle of my brain as I drove.

War, huh? What is it good for? Absolutely nothing. Say it again? Who sings that? Edwin Starr?

Girls of Oklahoma University.

Who is Duster?

I wonder how Myra the Tigra is doing these days. Still a long cool woman in a black dress? I would have my answer to this last question and the status of Ms. Myra much sooner than I expected.

I made the final turn up the slight grade to the A frame, and my daydreaming came to a screeching halt. I slowed the Chevy truck down and stared at the scene in the yard of my little house. There were two dark brown sedans parked outside my A frame when I pulled up and an obvious employee of some government agency standing outside my door. *FBI? Here now? Why?*

I slowly came out of the truck with my hands clearly visible. I had just left the west plant with all the "crew," so if the FBI was going to make a play on this oil-racket thing, surely, there were bigger fish there to catch than me. I was not nervous yet, more curious at this point. After all, it was Oklahoma. *Half the ranchers and farmers in Logan County have pull-behind trailers, right?*

"Drew Hall? FBI Agent Phillips here," said the guy at the door, and he motioned for me to stand near the side of the house. "Larson, he's here." He called into the A-frame house.

My curiosity turned to outright shock when "Larson" and two other suit-wearing, gun-packing agent types came out of the house. When Agent Larson came into view, I was stunned. He had not changed much in two years, and I recognized him easily. He was the AIC guy from the shoot-out in Green River, Wyoming. While I was trying to keep all this straight in my head, one of the other suits approached Agent Larson. He had a small piece of wood in his hand that had the words "Union Carbide" burned into the side, and he handed it over to the AIC. *That's the piece of wood I took from the dynamite box in Utah. Why does that excite him?*

I was still only curious, until I saw one of the other agents carrying my $20,000 in cash out in his hands and then the gut wrenching hit me like a thunderbolt. I noticed their firearms—SIG Arms, just like the one I shot at the Rifleman. Agent Larson was a stereotypical, arrogant FBI ass, but he had the power behind him, and I knew it was better to just go along with it all for now—no matter what "it all "was.

"It's been a long time, Hall. Do you remember me?" Agent Larson asked, getting all up in my face.

"Vaguely," I said with far more attitude than I intended. "Green River, couple of years back? The raid on Rattlesnakes? Absaroka deputy sheriff got killed, along with a few others."

Larson smiled a greasy, gritty grin and nodded. "Not a bad recollection. Maybe you're smarter than you look."

He pointed out my $20,000, now placed in an evidence bag. "I am sure the IRS will be interested in that cash, unless you have detailed receipts and a ledger of where it all came from."

He spun the thin piece of decorated wood I took from Utah between his fingers. "Now this little piece of wood here is what I really like. It is from a stolen shipment of dynamite from the Union Carbide Corporation out of Uravan, Colorado. We tracked the shipment from the company supply stores. It was supposed to be delivered to the uranium mines in Dolores County but never arrived. Six cases in total went missing, and it was suspected that a couple of small oil field construction outfits were involved in the 'acquiring' of the TNT. One of them, a company you worked with for some time, had four explosive-related deaths in just over a year. I find that kind of interesting, don't you? That can get you ten years inside for manslaughter if you were in any way connected. This little piece of radioactive wood is strong evidence that you were involved somehow . . . don't you think?" Larson ranted on as he turned the wood again with his fingers.

Wood? Radioactive? What? How is that possible? It's just a freaking souvenir.

"Looks like you have been busy down here as well getting into who knows what kind of trouble. It should be a very interesting tale. Why don't we head down to the city office, and you can tell us all about it there?"

This is crazy. Why did they come after me though? I can't be this important, not compared with what else is going on around here. The funny thing was that I was really not too concerned about things yet. The piece of Union Carbide wood with the burned letters was easy enough to alibi. The radioactive comment was curious though. It was the $20,000 in cash that I was worried about. That would be a bitch to explain.

The drive to the city was longer than ever before as I spun the recent events around in my head. When we arrived at the Oklahoma

City FBI main office, they placed me in an "interview" room with the mirrored glass, cameras, the whole bit. I waited there for nearly two hours before anyone came in to interview me, but I was not in handcuffs. Finally, Agent Larson and Agent Phillips entered the room with a couple of files and a coffee for me. Larson asked me several token questions, but he seemed to be distracted, almost disinterested—a far cry from the greasy-weasel approach he had taken when he picked me up at the A frame. I was ready to ask for a lawyer at any time but held back because I still could not figure out what was going on.

"Tell me about the rock blast event in Monticello County, Utah, when you worked for Recco," Agent Larson asked dryly.

"Not much to tell. We drilled the rock. We loaded the holes. The licensed blast officer set off the charges. We cleaned up the rock, packed our kit in the trucks, and headed to the hotel and a cold beer," I replied almost as dryly.

"Not much to tell," Larson said with a small sneer. "The Division of Wildlife boys and girls might argue that point."

DOW? The game wardens? What the hell do they have to do with anything?

AIC Larson continued. "Add poaching to your list of crimes. The farmer whose field you blew huge chunks of rock into was walking in the wooded and sagebrush areas next to the blast area with his wife the following day when she discovered a gruesome sight, so gruesome she called the DOW officers out to investigate. They found a variety of dead animals within 150 yards of the blast's ground zero, including five mule deer, nineteen rabbits, twenty-one turtledoves, six squirrels, two coyotes, and one red fox. It takes quite a shock wave to take out wildlife like that."

Jeez, I knew we had created a little Hiroshima but did not realize we left a Mother Nature body count behind us.

"Were you involved in the Shiprock, New Mexico, blast that killed two men last May?" Agent Philips asked, deciding to jump in with his two cents' worth. Before I could answer, he threw out several more interrogatories. "Do you know Ray Stuart? Were you part of the crew that robbed the Bozeman Bank in '81? How many men have you killed in Oklahoma? How many in Colorado?"

What the fuck is this idiot on about now? I was again just about to holler "lawyer" when I heard a hard tap-tap-tap from behind the mirrored glass. Agent Larson and Agent Phillips exchanged looks, closed their files, and exited the interview room.

I finished off the cold coffee to the disagreement of my churning gut and waited another hour before the door opened again. A very different sort of FBI agent walked in. He had several files under his arm, was impeccable dressed, and seemed to be a courteous enough chap. He stuck out his hand and said, "Mr. Hall, my name is Jonathan Hargrove. I work for FBI recruitment, and we have a proposition for you."

Jonathan? Not Agent Hargrove? That's an interesting introduction. OK, you have my full and undivided attention.

"The presumption of guilt that Agent Larson presented to you is an archaic threat interview technique that is becoming antiquated. He, of course, has plenty of circumstantial evidence to cause a lot of grief in your life if he was left unchained or to his own devices. A couple of pieces of information for you before we go on. We have closed the statutory rape warrant on you from Dolores County, Colorado, and expunged all your trips to the local county jails around the Western US. For this proposal to work properly, you need to have a clean record," said Jonathan.

Clean record? Hell, I did not know I even had a record.

I was now very curious. "Why? I mean, why would you do this?" I asked.

"Your width of experience in, shall we say, a certain arena is impressive, and you possess certain abilities that will help us achieve success in an ongoing eight-year operation. You are also in a unique position to pull off a deep cover operative role and infiltrate a national racketeering crime ring. This is why, Mr. Hall," Jonathan said, almost beaming.

"You want me . . . to be . . . an informant?" I asked incredulously.

"Informant? Heavens, no, Mr. Hall. We have several informants already in place. We want you to be an asset. Are you interested?" Jonathan asked cheerily.

What exactly is the difference between an asset and an informant.

"And if I am not interested?" I asked.

"Oh, once you see the entire proposal, I am sure you will be, er, quite interested. We have been watching you for some time, and you are the selected choice asset for this operation. Shall I show you the proposal?"

Do I really have a choice here? I guess I should at least take a look at it. I nodded affirmative, and Jonathan pulled out a fresh, crisp folder from the pile. He opened it up and passed it over to me. It was a six-page agreement. I began to read it slowly and carefully as Jonathan went to get us more coffee. It took me about twenty minutes to get through it all, and Jonathan waited patiently while I read the contract. I had to admit, even though my head was spinning about the concept, it was an intriguing agreement.

"Do I have to sign it now? Can I have a couple of days to kick this around? It is an intriguing offer, but the way I read it, I am under total control and direction of my supervisor slash handler slash whoever you put in charge whenever I am on an assignment. I mean, who is my handler? I honestly just can't see myself working for a Larson type," I stated.

Jonathan smiled a bit wickedly as if he had knowledge of some deep, dark secret. "A two-part question? OK, part one, yes, you can have a couple of days to think it over." He shuffled around some files and brought out a nondisclosure agreement (NDA). "Just sign the NDA confirming if you discuss any aspect of this agreement or our discussion in any shape or form, you will spend a minimum of five years in prison. The second part, your handler is not Agent Larson. You will be working with other field agents but primarily solo undercover on your own. Your handler, also your supervisor, happens to be here in the building right now. Care for an introduction? I can arrange this promptly, if you wish."

Why not? I never saw any of this coming, so I may as well see what kind of character this handler is. "OK," I said sheepishly.

"Outstanding," Jonathan said with real enthusiasm. "I'll take care of this right now." He walked spryly out the door, and I watched him turn right and head down the hall.

A few minutes later, I saw the door open, and in walked my handler. The surprise I first had when I saw Agent Larson at the A frame was miniscule compared with the eye-opening shock I was currently feeling while looking at my new handler. "Hello, Drew," a sultry voice said. There standing in front of me, holding two folders, dressed to kill, and looking like a million bucks was Myra "the Tigra" Breittlinger.

38

She was wearing a dark blue pantsuit that accentuated her long legs and firm body. Her blond hair was slightly feathered back, and she looked amazing. I was totally confused about this new turn of events, but I could still appreciate how good Myra looked. *Is she my FBI supervisor? How is that even possible?* "Myra? I . . . uhm," I stammered, "I don't understand."

"You do look surprised, Drew," she said, eyes sparkling.

"*Surprised* is the understatement of the year, Myra. I am downright shocked and, well, basically freaked out. I mean, it's great to see you, and you look as, always, amazing. But I am confused for sure," I replied, now finally getting my bearings a bit.

Myra slid into the chair opposite me with her usual feline grace, never taking her eyes off me. "That's understandable, although I gave you enough clues. I did everything but write it down for you."

"How long have you been working with the FBI?" I asked, still not quite believing everything that was going on.

"First, the NDA and then your contract," she said, now all business as she opened one of the folders and pulled out the documents for me to read and sign. Without really thinking it through, I signed both documents and handed them back to her. She put them back in the folder and returned to looking at me.

"I started with the FBI ten years ago. I took a sabbatical year to work at the US Marshals Training Academy in Glynco, Georgia, which is where I fine-tuned my shooting. This was also my introduction to several prototype firearms, something I have stayed with. I am a part of AWTT, Advanced Weapons Testing Team. This is a select group of FBI agents and other federal groups who field-test new firearms and body armor. We provide the field data back to AWTT, who then provides future weapon selection recommendations to the bureau department heads and DC," Myra said.

"That explains the prototype SIG and the S&W .40-caliber automatic," I stated.

She nodded. "Yes, that explains my SIG. I have been stationed here in Oklahoma for the last three years as part of a multistate task force. The mission is identification, asset recovery, and closure of a large oil theft ring. This same ring is heavy into racketeering, selling stolen property, even dances around the occasional bank robbery and human trafficking in certain areas south of the border. There are three entities that form a core triad of illegal management for this group. We have identified two, but we want to take them all down at once. The other one of these three runs a major portion of the Oklahoma territory from West Texas all the way down into Mexico. It's very possible his influence is even bigger than that. That's all we know for sure now."

"OK, so what do you want me to do? I mean, I don't know very much about the FBI at all," I asked.

"First, you will process in today here at the main FBI office. That will take you another two hours or so. Then I will meet you at Jameson's Bar out on I-35 for lunch, and I will show you some things you will need to know about other operatives in the field, how you report, and some other rookie pointers. You're in the unique spot where we already know each other, uhm, quite well, maybe a little too well if truth be told, so we can meet as often as needed, and no one will make anything of it."

Did she just blush a tiny bit?

Myra looked at me looking at her for a moment, and then she continued. "The point is, since we do know each other that well and people know we know each other that well, we can meet anytime, and it won't raise suspicion. For now, don't change anything you are doing. FBI undercover agents go through months of training. They are trained on how to make it look like they are breaking the law without breaking the law. You're not an agent. You have not been trained. You are an asset. There is a big difference. So since we already know you're involved in some low-level, petty oil thievery, to keep you in a position so we can use you as an asset, you can't stop doing the things you're already doing. It would rouse suspicion, and you might not be able to continue to infiltrate and provide us information."

Makes sense, I guess.

Shifting her legs ever so subtly, Myra continued. "One key point is that you try not to fall any deeper into the abyss of illegal activity than you already are, and if you discharge your weapon at another person for any reason, contact me immediately, whether you hit them or not. Here is my emergency pager number." She wrote down her pager number and passed it over to me, letting her hands graze across mine ever so lightly, igniting the electric flame of passion once again.

Yes, I do believe I would do just about anything for Myra the Tigra. I suppose that is why she has the role of handler. I am sure I am not the first "asset" she has handled. "OK, so what do I do exactly?" I asked, now a bit frustrated.

Her eyes cut into me as only hers can. "What do you do exactly? Well, just about anything I want you to do. You will have weekly tasks, but our primary mission will never change—to identify and collect evidence on this entity or person who runs the eastern Oklahoma oil theft ring," Myra said, her eyes flashing now.

"Duster?" I asked questioningly.

"Yes, Duster," she replied firmly, moving her body just so again.

"Do you have any idea who he is?" I asked.

"No, all we know is he comes through this area occasionally or possibly even lives in Oklahoma but could be much bigger than that. We are tracking bank accounts, shell corporations, anything that might help identify him. So far, nothing solid."

My mind drifted back to the night I heard the gunshots on the Ghoul Bridge, the 100-foot-high flames, the fire from the sabotage at the west plant, and the gunfire that left a body at Trips. She must have seen something in my face that caused her compassion or at least concern. She reached over and grabbed my hand in hers. "Drew, for now, just listen and watch. I will meet you almost every day or at least every three days and will talk to you about what is going on, and I will give you instructions each time, OK?" she said, smiling supportively. "This is going to be a challenge, but you don't want to stop doing anything you have been doing. Go for beers with the guys. Keep doing the same things so there is no reason for the people watching you to be suspicious."

"What if they ask me about why I was brought down here? How do I respond to that?" I asked sheepishly.

"That's easy. Tell them about the Union Carbide wood, the blast in Utah, the robbery in Bozeman, and Agent Larson. Then tell them that he thought you were the one who stole the dynamite but that they could not hold you on anything. Might even get you some street creds. We will do the rest from here," Myra said as confident as a coyote after a cottontail.

Then with a slight smile and another body shift, she leaned in close and whispered, "You will soon become a master in the art of subterfuge under my . . . tutelage."

Yeah, that's every cowboy's dream, to learn how to become a deceiver. At least I will be . . . under you.

Myra escorted me to the administration section and gave them my signed documents. She squeezed my arm and said, "Jameson's Bar for lunch, OK? At one." Then she turned and walked away. Her body was exquisite.

Have I been in here all night? I guess I had. "Time flies," as the adage says, but was this really all that much fun?

I finished the processing at eleven thirty and wanted to get to the A frame and hit the super spa shower. I had called Tony, telling him that I was taking a day off, and he said fine. He figured I was hung over or hung up with some pretty thing in bed.

Agent Spearman took me home and tried to make some small talk on the way. He was a younger agent and wante to make the situation easier somehow with small talk. "Long night, eh?" he asked.

"Pretty long, yeah," I replied, not exactly interested.

Agent Spearman pulled out a case of cassette tapes and asked me, "So what kind of music do you like? I mean, what do you feel like?"

What are we, on a date? Guess he is just trying to pass the time. He doesn't look too harmful. "I feel like I am totally on empty, my friend, just drained," I replied as I closed my eyes.

"Got it," he said excitedly as he pulled out a worn cassette tape and plugged it into the stereo.

A very familiar song began to play, and I was struck by the irony of the lyrics from the song he picked. It was "Running on Empty" by

Jackson Browne. "Gotta do what you can just to keep your love alive. Trying not to confuse it all with what you do to survive. In sixty-nine, I was 21, and I called the road my own. I don't know when that road turned into the road I'm on. Running on, running on empty."

Agent Spearman dropped me off at my place, and as I headed for the super spa shower, I realized I was bone tired but still had to meet Myra again in less than an hour. About mid-shower, I began to feel the exhaustion and overall impact of what had happened. *If Tony finds out, he will literally kill me. Am I going to have to turn on Clay and Mark now? Shit, shit, shit!*

I finished showering, and for the first time since I had arrived in Oklahoma, I did not even notice what clothes I was putting on.

39

I met Myra at 1 p.m. at Jameson's. I had never been in the place before. It was on the east side of I-35, close to Oklahoma City and farther southeast than where I usually hung out. Plus, it was an upscale place, very well decorated with an upper-level clientele, almost chic by Oklahoma standards. *I hope they serve food here. I am famished. Becoming an FBI asset apparently makes a guy very hungry.*

Myra had also changed into jeans, boots, and a tight blouse. She waved me over to a booth, and I joined her. "Hungry, cowboy?" she asked with the slightest of smiles.

"Famished. I could eat a horse," I replied.

Myra ordered a Chardonnay and said sweetly, "Well, I don't see horse on the menu, but they have some great steaks and ribs. The catfish here is also very good, if you're in that sort of mood."

I ordered the biggest rib eye in the house with fried okra, sausage, garlic bread, and beer. Myra ordered a surf and turf with a filet, jumbo prawns, and a second glass of Chardonnay. *That answers that one. I guess it is OK to drink when you are an FBI ass–et.*

I was tearing into my steak like a rabid wolf when Myra asked me, "How much do you know about the activities of the Pauls Valley crew? Mainly Joe Dugan, Brian Dugan, and Ronnie Moore?"

"Not in too much detail. Other than the fire and sabotage at the west plant that Brian Dugan caused, most of what I know about him is hear say, rumors," I said in between bites.

"Fire? Sabotage?" Myra asked with a raised eyebrow.

I told her the whole story, including the tire tracks in the tanker yard and the tracks outside the A frame. After a few more questions, dealing with her batting eyelashes and shifting body, I told her about seeing Brian at Trips, the guy getting shot, and anything else that came into my head. My mind was spinning as I talked and watched her. It was like she held some magic power over me, and I was on the verge of losing control—again.

"When he walks in the room, he feels confused like he's walked into a play. And the music's so loud it spins him around, till his soul has lost its way." What was that old song by Helen Reddy? "Angie Baby"? Yeah, that's it. Witch words, I was under her spell.

"Well, Drew, it appears you're earning your keep already. This is great information. We are going to have to do these lunches more often," Myra said sweetly as she looked at her watch.

"How about the occasional dinner as well?" I asked boldly.

This caught her off guard just a bit, and then she smiled. "We shall see, cowboy. For now, concentrate on quietly and unassumingly gathering intel. Talk to you later, Drew." She eased out of the booth as only she could do and left me there to finish my last bit of food.

As I watched her walk away, my pulse rate increased considerably. Something I would always enjoy doing was to watch her walk. *Love to watch her strut? Yeah, song by Bob Seger, that's Myra the Tigra, all right.*

The spring weather was slowly warming up, but it was still pleasant enough outside when I left Jameson's. I played Bad Company's "How about That" on the stereo and did not spare the volume. My mind reeled with the recent turn of events as many of the pieces began to fall into place. *Will I get to keep my money, or will it be confiscated in a closeout deal when this is all over? What about long, tall Joe, Clay, Mark? Are they going to simply wind up as some kind of crazy collateral damage deal? These guys don't deserve to go down for anything. And what about Tony? Hoo-boy, this could get real ugly really quick.*

These and a few other pleasant thoughts were running through my head when I parked at the A frame. I was so distracted that I almost missed Dave walking up from his place. "You must have had a big night. Who brought you home this morning?" Dave said with a grin. "Anyone I know?"

"Big night, yeah. It was big, all right," I said softly, "life changing, if truth be told."

Dave studied me for a bit, put his arm on my shoulder and said, "A life changer, eh? Well, that sounds like a tale to be told over one of your beers. Don't mind if I do." Dave rambled on a bit as he grabbed a couple of frosty Coors Lights from my fridge.

I sat down at the table and had a long drink of ice-cold beer. That helped settle the edge, so I had another. Dave seemed to be waiting for me to start the conversation, and I obliged. "I guess you could say while Jupiter was not exactly aligned with Mars, I still had several shooting stars blast by. I did get to have lunch with Myra Breittlinger today. That was nice."

"Myra is always nice. She has that way of getting you to just ramble on and making you feel important," Dave added. "She is very easy on the eyes also. Where did you guys eat at?"

"Jameson's, down by the city. Do you know the place?" I asked.

"Yes, I do. I don't go around there much. It's a nice place for sure and upscale. A bit pricey from me, but they have some great food. What in the world were you doing down that way?" Dave responded.

Meeting my handler after spending a night in the hoosegow with the FBI. Isn't it obvious? "Uh, I was picking up some parts in the city for the west plant," I mumbled.

Dave gave me one of these uh-huh looks like he didn't buy a word I was saying, but he changed the subject just the same. "Had a beer with Leon Spencer the other day. He mentioned a rumor that some of those Pauls Valley boys that work for your company are starting to really get in deep. You know anything about that, Drew?"

"Same as you, rumors, but that bunch is bad news, that's for sure," I said, sipping my beer.

"That's what I was thinking. After you told me about what happened over at the west plant with that fire, maybe we ought to load up a couple of hundred rounds of ammo—you know, just in case," Dave suggested semi-seriously.

"You know what, maybe we might have to do that," I said as I downed my beer and headed for the reloading setup. Dave organized the bullets and the IMR 4320 powder while I pulled the polished brass cases from the tumbler and checked the dies. We were a precision-reloading team, and by now, it was just natural. He set the scales up to weigh each powder charge while I lubricated the Rock Chucker bullet press.

I grabbed two more cold Coors Lights from the fridge, and we went to work making the 9 mm rounds. Dave opened his beer and started measuring the powder charges in the scale. "Your silver female looks huge. She has to be carrying a lot of pups and could pop any day. Your amber lady is also obviously prego but not like the silver. She is gonna have several. Are you making preparations for the birth of the fox pups? I don't see any soft grass hay, alfalfa, or even straw in their hutches. You seem to be a bit busy lately. What have you been doing, Drew?"

What have I been doing? Davy Boy, if you only knew. "You're right, Dave, I have been a bit . . . distant from the fox. Thanks for pointing that out. I will . . . sort it," I said quietly.

"Drew, if you're overloaded, I got thirty bales of sweet, soft Oklahoma grass hay in the barn. It would make great bedding for the birthing. Want me to lend a hand? I enjoy the time with them," Dave asked as he measured powder charges, never missing a beat.

Shit, I am going to be going to Norman for the safety seminar soon. Shit, I may not even be here when the fox pups are born. What the hell is wrong with me? How could I miss this?

Before I could answer, Dave placed a firm grip on my shoulder and said, "And aren't you also heading to Oklahoma University in the near future?"

"Dave, yeah, I really may be in a bit of a bind, sir. And yeah, I have been distracted and did not realize the females were so close to birthing. I would really appreciate any help you can give me, buddy. The animals deserve good care. This seminar is a big deal but not a big enough deal to hurt my ladies."

His grip tightened on my shoulder and then softened with an affection that almost brought me to tears. "After we load these rounds, why don't we have another beer and then go out and grab a couple of bales of that sweet grass hay and organize the hutches so the mothers can get their nest set up and do what mother animals do?"

I love this guy. How lucky am I to have a solid friend like this? I am really glad I did not steal his oil.

"Sounds really great, Dave, and thanks. You're a class act, and I appreciate you watching out for the fox . . . and for me."

"Don't get stupid on me now while we are reloading rounds. I know . . . you would do the same for me," he said semi-serious.

You know damn straight I would, sir. I hugged him, and we loaded up the 200 rounds of precision 9 mm ammo, grabbed a couple of beers, and headed out to his barn.

On the way, Dave explained to me the qualities and types of hay and why long sweet grass hay was the best for female animals to make nests with when preparing to have their young. He had raised eleven foals on this prime piece of Oklahoma real estate and was pretty good at animal husbandry. We set the hutches up with twice as much hay as I thought they needed, but Dave explained this is the best way so the females can organize the birthing nest, and it brings out their maternal instinct even though they are in a cage.

In between, I managed to find time to grab another six beers or so, and by the time night fell, we were both pretty much three sheets to the wind. Dave placed his hand on my shoulder again and said, "Wherever your biorhythms are in relation to the universe today, son, nothing will set them straight like a couple of more beers and a trip down to the catfish pond. You up for it?"

"Yeah, it sounds great, but I am afraid we drank all my beers. I can run down to the 7-Eleven and grab a twelve-pack," I semi-slurred.

"Ha ha ha! Drew, I got an ice-cold twelve-pack of Budweiser in my fridge. If you can choke down some Anheuser-Busch products, then you go grab the poles and dig the night crawlers while I take a racehorse piss and load the cooler. Meet you at the pond in fifteen minutes."

"Sounds great to me, Davy Boy." I sorted all the fishing gear, and even in my near drunken stupor, I managed to wrangle up eight fat night crawlers and staggered my way down to the pond.

Dave had the lawn chairs set out as the spring moon was rising above the Oklahoma hardwoods, and we started a deep philosophical discussion about Venus versus the North Star, the Seven Sisters, the Black Eye Galaxy, Triangulum, and Orion's belt. I always enjoyed talking with Dave about the history of the world and his comments on all things celestial, but tonight he was especially brilliant. "This is your time now, Drew," he said profoundly from out of nowhere.

Time for what exactly? "How long will my time last, Dave?" I responded with as much anxious innocence as I could pull off.

"As long as you wish. Each crossroad you come to has a turn, and most of them are not really wrong or right. They just are. It's all up to you where and how far you go."

40

The silver fox female had eight pups a week later, and it was a very cool thing. Just like Dave had predicted, the sweet grass hay made a perfect bed for the pups, and the females were great mothers.

I was nervous as a cat on a hot tin roof during my first few of days returning to work after becoming an asset for the FBI. After a couple of the five o'clock beer gatherings at the west plant, I settled back into a semi-normal routine. I hauled a couple of my tank loads and shared some beers with long, tall Joe Reed at the trailer yard. I met up with Clay and Mark at one of our hangouts, just like normal. I was getting all set up to head to Norman the following Monday, and I was focused on that. Add to that the new fox pups, and I had plenty of distractions from my new job as an FBI asset.

Myra called me for a lunch at Randall's on Friday. She said she had a lead on Duster and needed to pass some assignments on to me. *Myra the Tigra, I guess a guy could have it worse.*

When I walked in, she was sitting at the bar looking like, well, Myra. She was wearing that same black dress she wore at the Moyers BBQ when we had our intimate encounter, and my mind began to spin with the memory. She crossed her legs as she waved me over to join her, and I was sure I stumbled at least once as my eyes were riveted on her nether region. "Hey, Drew, you're right on time. That's key in this business," she said with her sultry smile.

I am on fire here, and you're telling me it's good to be on time? "Uh, yeah, try my best. Jeez, Myra, you look great," I stammered.

"Business, Drew, let's start with that. Have you ever heard anyone in your wanderings mention the name Louis Cypher?"

"No, never. Who is that?" I replied curiously.

"It's the first solid lead we have had on who Duster might be. That's who it is. We found three different offshore accounts and a shell company coming out of Mexico that are all linked to him. They connect here in Oklahoma, Montana, and Wyoming. That's what we have so far, but it could be the break in the case we need. See what you can find out about the name Louis Cypher, but don't get yourself shot in the process." Her breathing was elevated, and she was obviously excited about this development. I was, of course, simply excited, and I could not help staring at her.

She looked across the table at me with those eyes, and I melted. "Are you hungry? Let's order some lunch, shall we?"

Oh yes, lady, I am quite hungry, but I will settle for some food—at least for now.

The food was great as always, but the company was better. Myra chattered away during the lunch, and she gave me a few asset-related "tasks" I could do while I was attending my safety seminar in Norman.

From out of nowhere, she asked, "What about Jay Randall? Have you heard of him before?"

My face turned pale as the memories of that first night at Tumbleweeds came flooding back. Yona, Lori Ann, Turned-Up-Collar Ted, Chipper, me almost killing the two jerks, and my ride back to Guthrie that night with Mr. Jay Randall. My memory went back to the moment Jay pulled up in his blue Chevy like it was yesterday.

I could see it in my mind like it was just happening all over again right in front of me and I let my thoughts drift back to that night.

Suddenly, a souped-up older-model blue Chevy truck pull alongside me and revved the engine. I looked inside and saw a familiar face telling me to climb inside. The police cars were starting to pull into the parking lot, and without a whole lot of options at this point, I quickly opened the door and jumped inside. The blue Chevy drove nice and easy right by the cops and out onto the road. The driver never said a word. He accelerated to five miles over the speed limit, and we headed toward Guthrie. I looked over at the man next to me and realized it would be a slow and possibly quite interesting drive home . . . with Mr. Jay Randall.

We had driven about ten miles when he said, "You seemed to handle yourself pretty well back there. With something like that, though, it's better to get out of Dodge first and then let things settle down in case you need to move on out of state."

I stared out the window, not sure at all where this was going or even if I wanted to talk to him.

"It took me a while to place you. I finally got it that night at Trips when you were with Tony." He went on.

Tony? Wait a minute, that's BS. I was already there with Clay by the time Jay, Brian Dugan, and Hawk Nose came in. "Tony who?" I asked semi-convincingly.

Jay snorted. "That's funny. There is only one Tony around these parts, and I got you sorted out now. You're one of his crew, but you're new, not from around here."

I wasn't in a real social mood; I was worn out from the adrenaline rush and fisticuffs. I wanted to keep the debate going that I did not know any Tony and shove it up Mr. Randall's ass; however, I considered Jay's eyes, and they oozed dark intelligence, so I figured it was a fruitless effort.

We drove another ten miles before he spoke again. "You remember me?"

"Rattlesnakes, Green River poker game. You're one of the guys who lived," I replied dryly.

"You took over $1,000 from me right before the feds broke in, and it all went to shit," he said, a bit miffed. "I never got a chance to win my money back."

I smiled, remembering Brandi, my fine girl; what a great month it was; and the cash pot I won from Jay. "Yeah, I believe it was closer to $1,500, but who was counting?"

Another ten miles passed by. "What does Tony have you doing? Making drug drops? Hauling cheap crude? Protection? You're in the minor leagues here, Drew."

How did he know my name? Well, I knew his, so I guess it made sense that he would know mine, kind of made us even. "Why did you pick me up at Tumbleweeds if you know who I am? Last I heard, you and Tony were sort of competitors," I mumbled.

"Competitors? Ha! That's a good one. I have territory from Montana down to Mexico and just stop off to take a piss now and again here in Oklahoma," he said arrogantly.

"Well, you have been here about as long as I have, so you must have one small dick if it takes you over a year to take a piss," I said, equally arrogant.

It was nearly fifteen miles of silence this time before he spoke, and just when I figured I had gotten to him and he was going to be quiet, he opened up again. "Like I said, you are in the minor leagues, but you play well. I need some new men who know Tony and his crew to help me with this area up here."

I said nothing, but my face was turning red, and I suddenly had a hell of a lot more energy as my blood began to boil.

"What's he paying you, Drew?"

I said nothing, just began to clench my fists and seethe at the seams.

"Whatever he is paying you, I will double it, plus a big bonus and plenty of babes hanging around," he said boastfully.

"I can get my own babes. What about this guy Brian Dugan and his idiot hawk-nosed friend? Where do they fit into all this on your side?" I asked beneath my breath.

"Oh, you will get along fine with Brian. He knows the ropes, and he and his brother Joe are going to start playing a much bigger part in all this very soon. So what do you say, Drew? You want to join the big leagues and play with the winning team?"

I was about to go full on berserker rage when I saw the lights for Jacks Bar coming up on the right side of the road so I took a deep breath, exhaled and looked Jay Randall dead in the eyes. "I say you can stop the truck and let me out right here. I also say if you ever approach me again, it will be the last time you approach anybody. I'll be sure and send Tony your best regards tomorrow."

I came back to the moment when I realized Myra was staring at me. "Drew, are you daydreaming? Did I hit a nerve with Jay or something?"

Better come clean. She is your handler. Besides, she will know if you're not telling the truth anyway. "Yeah, I know who Jay is. I ran into him a couple of times. Do you remember that poker game up in Green River, Wyoming, that I told you about? The one Larson jumped me over before I signed up?" She nodded. "Jay was there. Word is that he is trying to make a move into a piece of territory around here. Half the guys on Tony's crew are getting ready to go to what they call a war of some kind or another, just in case."

She sipped her Chardonnay and said rather cheerfully, "It may come to that, Drew. The idea is that we take them all down before a territorial war breaks out that could run from Mexico to Montana. You're going to be a big part of that, Drew, but it will get real dangerous real quick."

She talked about a couple of encounters she had in Miami and one in Georgia when she was with the US Marshals. She seemed to be in her element, which only made her that much more exciting to me. She told me about a couple of new things the bureau had in operational play at the moment and what to be aware of while I was working in the field.

What she did not tell me was that the feds had been using my 1,000-gallon pull-behind trailer to set up what would become the biggest evidence collector for this entire eight-year undercover sting operation. They had been putting ultraviolet dye in my pull-behind trailer unbeknownst to me. This ultraviolet dye was winding its way through the oil field transmission pipelines and terminal systems like a thousand-mile-long cobra just waiting to strike every time I dumped a load into a big tanker.

Monday arrived, and I made the "just over an hour" trip to Norman and the University of Oklahoma campus. It was everything that Clay had said it would be. The coeds were just unbelievable, and the nightlife was equal to Tumbleweeds, except without Yona. I hit the seminar hard the first day, totally focused on the material and studying up in the books at night. I was dedicated to learning all I could from this weeklong seminar and momentarily forgetting I was an FBI asset. I had visions of grandeur to make this a prestigious career move.

That lasted for the first two nights until I met a long-legged blond volleyball player named Jenny who invited me for a "drink" at the Garage Bar. The place was a sports-type bar with pool tables, TVs, great burgers, and wall-to-wall coeds. Jenny seemed to know everyone, and within a couple of hours, I had met a dozen ladies and finished five beers and several shots to go along with them. I closed the Garage Bar down with the rest of them, and Jenny and I staggered home—together. I would have seen the sun come up if

I had not been so focused on watching Jenny's body move on top of mine. *Man, I do so love Oklahoma.*

Jenny was still asleep in my bed when I hauled ass out the door, over an hour late for class. I grabbed coffee on the way, quietly opened the classroom door, and found my seat. Nobody paid much attention to me, so I just joined in the session like I had been there the whole time as I ignored my pounding head. I noticed that one of the girls in the class was wearing sunglasses, and I wondered if her night had been anything like mine.

So it went for the rest of the week. I hung out with Jenny, who showed me all the cool college hangouts, and she also showed me that University of Oklahoma girls volleyball players were not only, sexy and in incredible shape but also surprisingly flexible. I got an average of about two hours' sleep a night for the duration of the week but somehow made it through the course with an 88, which was respectable. I stayed over at Jenny's place on Friday instead of going back to Guthrie. We knew it was just crazy college sex, but it was real damn good crazy college sex, and it worked well for us both.

I left Norman at ten the next morning with a big Oklahoma smile on my face from the whole experience. It was a smile that would fade within a few weeks and never would I truly return to that level of young man's innocence again.

41

Dave welcomed me home with a couple of cold beers, and even though I had only been gone a week, the fox pups had doubled in size. They were getting their fur in now and starting to take on a nice shade of color. They were wandering around the hutch in their little-blind-eyed-fox-puppy way, mewling like kittens when they were hungry and falling down around themselves as newborns in a litter would do.

Dave was like a first-time parent, always checking the straw, cleaning out from under the cages, making sure that none of the wee ones had come to any harm, and generally coddling them. I believe the old boy had pretty much adopted those pups by this time, and I felt a warmth for the man that was overwhelming. It was a feeling I would carry with me until the end of my days, and while mine were still innumerable, the days of my good friend Sir David Raymond were in question, and neither of us had a clue about what was coming.

A few days after I had returned to the A frame, we were down by the catfish ponds with cold beers in our hands and profound thoughts in our conversation. We were on the east pond, feeding the catfish, reflecting on life, and not so much interested in catching but more interested in experiencing the Okie leviathans as they were often spectacular behemoths to behold.

"You sure there is a galaxy called Black Eye, Drew? I consider myself semi-well-read and have an engineering degree from Texas A&M, but I have never heard of that one," Dave stated.

"Yes, Dave. Gospel, mate. Heck, I can even click off fifteen or sixteen of the fifty-three named galaxies right now," I responded with bold arrogance.

"Oh really? I'll buy all the beer this week if you can even name ten in sixty seconds. Go."

Hell, I can do this in my sleep. "Uhm, yeah sure, easy peasy. Uhm, Milky Way, Andromeda, Alpha Centauri, Black Eye, Whirlpool, Sombrero, Messier 87, Triangulum, Fornax Dwarf, Pinwheel, Virgo Stellar Stream, Tadpole, Leo I, Sunflower, Ursa Minor Dwarf, Starburst, Dwarf Star 5 . . . Segue 2 . . . uhm, let's see . . . I believe that's more than ten," I said with extreme confidence.

"Time's up. You rattled off eighteen names like an auctioneer, but I have to call bullshit, Drew. C'mon, Tadpole Galaxy? Sunflower? Pinwheel? You're just pulling words out of your ass. There ain't no galaxy named Tadpole or Sunflower, is there?" Dave scoffed.

"Would you care to bet next week's beer on it also?" I said with an opossum-shit-eating grin.

Dave looked at me hard in the eyes and then broke out with a shit-eating grin of his own. "Nope, I guess those names are just too silly not to be real. I believe you have me on this one, Drew. I stand corrected."

Dave made a small bow and reached for some of the dog food in the pail to toss to his catfish. He watched them come up to feed with somber and searching eyes, something which I did not immediately understand. Then he asked the question. "When was the last time you saw Joshua?" he asked me.

I looked at all the mighty catfish that were feeding on the floating dog food. *Come to think of it, when was the last time I had seen the giant fish?* "Not sure, Dave, I haven't seen him in a while now. It's getting warmer. I imagine he is just sleeping down in the cooler, deeper water where it's more comfortable for him."

Dave stared at the pond and said, "Not sleeping, Drew. He is resting peacefully in eternal comfort now, I believe. He never misses a bite of pounders, and I haven't seen him in the last seven days."

Seven days? He counts how many times he sees and feeds the fish? Well, it makes sense. After all, he has names for all of them, and his family started the tradition.

Dave continued on. "Death is a part of life and the inevitable end of the trip. It's not about how we reach the end of the journey, Drew. It's about how we travel along the way. Doesn't matter what others do to us so much. What matters is what we do to others."

"Dave, he was just a catfish, mate. What harm could he have possibly done to others?"

Dave looked at me through the eyes of the wisest man I had ever met or would meet again, and for a brief moment, I thought he was going to smack me in the face. Then he shook his head slowly and chuckled. "Hell, Drew, he ate his children, probably was eating his grandchildren and great-grandchildren right up until the time he passed. All of God's natural creatures do what they do by design. In human terms, we would call it murder. In God's nature, it's just who they are. We think everything is on our terms and nothing could be farther from the truth. Get back to nature's terms, and you might realize a thing or two. You ever hear the story of Jonah and the whale?"

"Well, yeah, every kid hears that story in Bible school," I replied curiously.

"Yeah, that is what most of the Baptist Bible schools teach. The story of Jonah and the 'whale.' If you take the direct translation from Latin to Greek to the King James Version, it says, 'And Jonah found himself in the belly of a big fish,' not a whale, which is a mammal, the belly of a big fish. Do you know, Drew, there are huge catfish in the oceans? What if Jonah was swallowed by a big catfish or something similar and not a whale?"

"Uhm, well, I never really thought about that." *This is an abstract path he is going down, but it seems to be important to him, so let him walk it.*

Dave's voice took on the pitch of a preacher at the pulpit, almost booming as he carried on. "And that is exactly my point. *You* never really thought about it. There is a hell of a lot of things you never think about, Drew, that you damn sure better start because life is fleeting like a comet through time's sky, and like time, if you don't start thinking about what you need to think about, you will soon become comfortable traveling the wrong roads, and it becomes accepted in your mind. Then one day you realize all the different choices you could have made. I am not saying bad choices, Drew, just different ones that will one day no longer be options."

Life, like a comet through the sky of time. What exactly is he trying to say to me? Ah shit, does he even know?

Dave continued. "So now do you still say Joshua was just a catfish? What if he was so much more than that? We can all be so much more than people believe. Don't you think?" he said almost knowingly.

"Dave, honestly, sir, each time we have a chat . . . you open up possibilities that leave me reeling, and I often don't really know what I think. I do know this. I am sure I am a better man for meeting you."

The older man looked at me again in that way that he did, placed that hardworking, strong gripping hand on my shoulder, and said, "You're going to do fine, son, just fine. Once you pull your head out of your ass, you will be fine."

42

The next week was all work at the west plant with a turbo going out on one of the GTLAs, so it was workhorse days for most of the week. I was driving everyone crazy with all the safety rules and regulations I was imposing on them after returning from the seminar. The guys did not like being told what to do, but once I explained the risk involved with working the way they had been and why the regulations were in place, they all simmered down a bit. I even found a video of the famous Piper Alpha offshore production platform explosion and fire that killed twenty-nine people to show at the next safety meeting. That got everyone's attention.

Later that week, I was grabbing lunch with Clay at a new BBQ place and swapping war stories about the University of Oklahoma and about all the things I did in Norman. "We need a night at Tumbleweeds now just so you can compare again," Clay said with a gleam in his eye. "Have you talked to Yona recently? It might be good for you to check in with her. She likes you, ya know."

"Not since the seminar. Yeah, I like her too. I think I really do. I need to give her a call and see how she is doing," I mumbled in between bites of pulled pork and beef brisket. "I'll ring her later tonight."

I talked with Yona that night, and she was in a good mood. We chatted about my seminar in Norman and how things were going up in Stillwater. I told her I was thinking of coming up to Tumbleweeds on Friday, and to my absolute delight, she said she would work an early shift that day and get off by nine on Friday night. "So let's just make it a date." I agreed so fast that I tripped over the coffee table, nearly falling down, and she started laughing.

"Easy, Drew, I'll be here when you get here. Just relax, cowboy," Yona said sweetly. So there it was; I had a date with Yona at Weeds on the Friday, and I was sure Clay would be riding shotgun. New baby or not, he was also ready for a night out.

I had fallen behind a bit on my tank loads while I was in Norman, so I decided to spend the next few days doing double time to catch back up. I had eight days left in the month, and I could just get caught up if I hoofed it hard. I promised long, tall Joe that I would meet him in the trailer yard on Thursday for a couple of cold beers if I was back on schedule and damned if I didn't make it. I ran into him at around ten on Thursday night at the tanker park area. I noticed that a few small drops of purple liquid ran out of the end of my hose when I dumped the load into the big tanker but thought nothing else of it.

"Hey, Joe, how's the week treating you?" I asked as I pulled a beer from his cooler.

"Mighty fine actually, all good on my side," Joe replied as he drank half the can in two quick swallows. "My girlfriend is not pregnant, my daughter just got straight As on her report card, she's not pregnant either by the way, and my wife is planning a cruise for us down to Cabba Wabba, Mexico, next year. Doesn't get much better than that." He gave a sarcastic wink.

I laughed. "Jupiter is indeed aligned with Mars, and the planet slipstream is flowing deep and smooth for you then, Joe."

He looked at me like I was an absolute idiot and then pulled out his .45 Colt 1911. "I have been practicing while you were down in Norman schooling, and I believe tonight is the night I will outshoot you. Do you feel up to it? Let's say thirty-five yards?"

"Paper or cans?" I asked confidently. Joe and I had taken to doing some target practice in between drinking beer and hauling stolen crude and condensate. We were both getting to be real fair shots, but as of now, I had always come out in the lead in our contests.

"Paper, smallest group from outside corner edge to corner edge?" Joe replied eagerly.

"Roger that." I pulled two fresh 12" paper targets with 8" bull's-eye centers from behind my pickup seat and handed them to Joe, who tacked them to trees thirty-five yards away. I noticed the trees had severe evidence that someone had indeed been practicing shooting there and began to feel like long, tall ole Joe was about to take me for a ride.

"Flip to see who shoots first?" Joe asked, reaching for a coin.

"Nah, I would just have to shoot the spinning quarter in the air and ruin your whole night," I said, grinning at him. "You go ahead first, Joe."

The long, tall Texan from Houston lined up and fired three booming shots from his .45 Colt. It was a nice group. It looked to be about four to five inches across. Very nice shooting. I lined up on my target and squeezed off three shots that appeared to be about the same spread. Joe fired three more, and I did likewise. As we walked up to the targets, a small breeze began to blow and tore them both ever so slightly.

We retrieved them from the trees and went back to the trucks, the beer, and the tape measure. While Joe had three shots touching, my target originally looked to be just a slightly tighter overall group. Since the wind had torn on both targets, however, we could not get a precise measurement, so we just downed a cold beer and agreed to call it a draw.

We continued shooting at miscellaneous targets for a while and then put the firearms away. As we sat down to finish off his last two beers, I got an inspirational thought. Just on a hunch, I asked, "Have you ever heard of a guy named Louis Cypher?"

"Uhm, nope. Should I have? Why do you need to know?" Joe replied.

"Curiosity, I guess, mainly, like we talked about a while back. There is some wild stuff going down with the Pauls Valley bunch, and who knows how that's going to turn out or who is involved in it? I heard that name somewhere. Can't rightly place where I heard the name, but it seemed to be in way that the name meant something."

"I'll keep my ears open and let you know, but the name does not sound familiar to me." Joe gulped his last swallow of beer, tossed the can on the refuse heap, and stretched up to his full 6'7" height. "You ever been to Houston? I am heading down that way this weekend. You're more than welcome to join me. It's your kind of place for sure."

Better than Oklahoma? I am not sure I could take it. "Thanks, Joe, I appreciate it, but I have several things going this weekend, so I am going to stick around. I am going to Tumbleweeds on Friday with

Clay. I have a date with a girl up there and don't want to miss that. Enjoy Houston and tell me all about it next week."

"Roger that, amigo. Hasta la vista. Cuidado."

"Tambien, amigo, Tambien," I replied and bid Joe good night.

I was in a rather good mood when I hit my last tank spot of the evening. The big lease tank was over half full, so I had good head pressure and was done loading in just over half the normal time. I was thinking of Yona and heading to Weeds in two days. I unhooked the hoses; little purple drops again dripped out of my hose. I loaded everything and was walking around to the driver's side door when I looked at the ground, and my blood literally froze.

There on the ground in front of me was the imprint of two big outside-Z-groove tire tracks right up next to one of my leases and less than a half a mile from our tanker yard. It had rained two days before, so these were fresh tracks.

43

I followed the tracks back toward the main road but lost them when the ground turned to hard gravel. *What the hell was Brian Dugan doing back up here again?* I drove back to the tanker yard to unload and to try to catch Joe and tell him about the tracks, but like the Eagles song, he was "already gone." I parked the pull-behind trailer and headed to the A frame. I thought about calling Tony to tell him I had seen the tire tracks, but it was late, and I could do it in the morning.

I hit the super spa shower and checked my messages. My thoughts refocused when I heard a sweet message from Yona on my machine asking me to call her no matter how late it was. I called her, we talked about the coming weekend, and Yona told me to plan to stay with her for the two days. Being the aspiring southern gentleman, how could I refuse? I put my head down, dreaming of Yona and forgetting all about the big Z-groove tires and the psycho from Pauls Valley.

It was John's week to be on call, and I saw his truck parked at a crooked angle when I pulled into the west plant office the next day. He was passed out asleep with his boots on the operator's desk when I opened the door. It was shades of déjà vu, reminding me of the first time I opened the door to the west plant over eighteen months ago and saw him in the same shit state he was now in. I checked the operator's log to see what had ruined John Boy's beauty sleep, and it was a low-engine oil supply shutdown on compressor number 3. The moron probably forgot to check the oil level in the storage tank before he left the plant yesterday. I slammed the operator's log shut with a bang, startling John out of his semi-drunken state.

"What the hell did you do that for? Damn, a guy works all day and half the night you would think he would get a little respect," John mumbled as he straightened up his Coke-bottle glasses.

"Yeah, John, that's what I have for you, a little respect, damn little," I replied as I poured a cup of java.

"What's up your ass this morning?" John asked as he stumbled over to the coffeepot. "You know what a workhorse this sumbitch plant is. I figured you would understand."

As John continued whining, I noticed the Logan County paper on the operator's desk with the headline CRUDE OIL TANKER STOLEN. I reached for the paper and began to read the article. Anadarko Oil Company reported that a large crude oil tanker with a full load was stolen from their east Guthrie terminal, the fourth crude oil tanker stolen in the tri-county area in the last month. *That terminal is three miles from our east tanker yard . . . and about two and a half miles from where I saw the Z grip tire tracks.*

Tony came in a few minutes later, and I asked to have a word in his office. "Got something on your mind, Drew?" Tony asked.

"Yeah, wide Z grip 4 × 4 tires to be exact. I saw them last night at tank E22. They are fresh, Tony. It rained on Tuesday," I told him.

"Brian Dugan? You sure they are his tracks?" Tony asked, raising one eyebrow.

"I track and shoot coyotes for piss' sake, Tony. I am pretty sure I can read truck tire tracks," I responded dryly and way more sarcastically than I intended.

While Tony was trying to decide what to say next, I grabbed the Logan County news and tossed it on his desk. "Check out the headline." Tony read the story, raised his head slowly, and looked at me.

"We know he was involved in stealing those two tankers from Elk City. He was supposed to be out of this area. The tracks say he is not. It adds up he could be involved. You mentioned territorial issues coming down with Joe Dugan. Maybe it's all part of it," I said firmly.

Tony slammed his fist hard on the desk. "We don't need this shit, not now, not ever. Joe Reed is in Houston this weekend, and Mark is at a rodeo in Tulsa. Are you in town? What about Clay?" Tony asked.

"Er, I had planned to be in Stillwater for the weekend," I replied. "What do you need?"

"OK, fine, don't worry about it. Get the word out that we will all meet here a week from this on Monday at five. This shit has to be dealt with," Tony said commandingly. "Will you see Joe Reed tonight?"

"Yes, I should. I will pull a load and catch him at the tank yard. I'll pass it on to him."

"You do that, Drew. You do that," Tony said, staring at me." And, Drew, you might want to reload some 9 mm rounds next week."

Myra paged me and said she had some news, so we met for lunch at the Wagon Wheel, a new BBQ place near Crescent. I brought her up to speed on the tire tracks and the stolen Anadarko oil tanker. Normally, Myra took in the food on her plate like I did; but as I spoke, she slowed down and sort of spun her fork around, listening to me.

Myra looked at me with deep concern. "You're in it, Drew, and you're right, Brian Dugan and others from Pauls Valley are in the area, and they are planning some kind of a coup against Tony Williams and Jack Lambert. I think they are hooking up with Jay Randall and making a move to take over the area, maybe Elk City too. We have spotted several guys from out of state with a history of being where trouble starts, probably hired guns for one side or the other. This is going to be a rough couple of weeks, and you're going to be in the middle of it, like it or not."

"Tony says the same thing. He is calling a meeting for all of us a week from Monday. He is serious, Myra, not messing around," I added.

"This is serious, Drew. We are bringing in five additional agents as backup. Plus, if we move on an op to stop this takeover, we plan to notify the ATF as well. The coup is going to happen soon somewhere, somehow. You need to call me after the meeting with Tony and his crew and give me a briefing, OK?"

Even when she was serious, Myra was still something incredible to behold, and my mind drifted a bit as I stared at her. Sensing this, she changed the tempo of the conversation. "So any plans for the weekend?"

"Yeah, I am going to Stillwater both days," I replied with a bit of a gleam in my eye.

"Tumbleweeds again, Drew?" she asked, rolling her eyes. "I would have thought you learned your lesson by now."

"You said to keep doing what I have been doing," I replied with a slight grin. "Well, that's what I have been doing."

"Is anybody going with you?" she asked.

"Clay Haynes is coming up on Friday, but I don't think he is staying the weekend."

"Watch yourself up there. Just because we have information something is going down soon doesn't mean they won't start hitting you guys one at a time, OK? Keep your guard up," Myra said with sincerity.

"My guard has been up for a few weeks now, Myra. I got it." I finished my sliced pork and fried okra and said goodbye to Myra the Tigra.

I ended the day at the west plant and hooked up the pull-behind trailer number 6 to pull some loads. There was a puddle of water near the pull-behind, and for the second time, I noticed a small amount of blue incandescent liquid in the water. *That's a sort of pretty color. I have never noticed it around the plant before. I did see it drip from my tank hose last night. Interesting.*

The sun was going down when I stopped by the A frame, and I noticed Dave was cooking on the grill outside. I filled the cooler with beer and took a look at what he was grilling up. He had a full coon cut up and marinated, and it smelled great. We started a chat, and a bit later, I had some BBQ raccoon with Dave. It was almost as good as Bob Breittlinger's.

"So you're going back to Stillwater for the weekend, eh, Drew?" Dave said as he sliced off some more grilled coon. "A girl, or you just a sucker for punishment?"

I laughed. "Yeah, a girl, Yona, the bartender there."

"The pretty Cherokee?" Dave asked, suddenly interested.

"The drop-dead gorgeous Cherokee. And she is a class act also. I like her Dave. I really do," I responded.

Dave went to the cooler and grabbed a couple of beers, shaking his head. He looked at me with a smile. "Do you know how many times you have told me that since you moved here?"

"Well, I am assuming more than once?" I said, returning the smile. Dave laughed, and we talked about politics; blond, brunet, and redhead chicks; and old habits we ain't kicking, like two old boys would do and we had done. I really enjoyed those times with the man.

I thanked Dave for the dinner and company and drove away to finish my loads before the weekend. I caught up with Joe right on schedule and told him about seeing the tire tracks again. I also passed on the message about the all-hands meeting scheduled for Monday next week. "He will have to be dealt with as Tony says. Hell, they will all have to be dealt with. I've seen this before. It seems to happen about every five to six years, and it's been quiet for a long time now," Joe said, slamming his beer. "What kind of war strategy do you think Tony has planned for all this?"

"No idea really, Joe. It's new to me. I guess it will be a sort of 'do unto them before they do unto us,'" I said dryly.

Joe choked on his beer and started laughing. "Never figured you for a Bible thumper, Drew, but I like your style, and that was funny."

"The Bible is loaded with wisdom and anecdotes, buddy. Give it a read now and again. Might do you some good," I replied. "You know, the closer we get to this thing, the better reading a bit of the Bible sounds." I winked at him.

"You know, the closer we get to this thing, the better getting the hell out of Dodge sounds. If I didn't have the wife, daughter, and girlfriend here, I might just stay in Houston for a few weeks and let this whole damn thing blow over." Joe sighed as he finished his beer. "You take care, Drew. Take good care, buddy."

Jeez, is he going to hug me now? Never saw the big guy like this.

He tossed his beer can and reached his long, lanky arm out to shake my hand with that grip of steel. "I'll see you when I get back." And with that, long, tall Joe Reed turned, walked away, and was gone.

44

Finally, on Friday, I had the cooler packed with ice-cold beer in the pickup and jumped in the super spa shower to start the evening. From my wardrobe, I selected my Tequila Sunrise brushpopper button-down, black Levi's jeans that fit just right, and a new pair of dark gray Tony Lama El Rey alligators I had bought a couple of weeks back. They looked black in the bar light, but you could still see the gator cuts in the skin, and they were a very sharp-looking pair of boots. I took a spare outfit along in case Yona wanted to go out on Saturday as well. I checked in with Myra, and she just said to keep my pager on and let her know if I saw anything out of line or if too many of the Pauls Valley gang showed up in Stillwater, so everything seemed to be set for the weekend.

Dave was outside feeding the wee fox pups tiny bits of soaked opossum jerky through the cage wires when I got ready to leave. They had been crawling around on the wires now for a few days and were yipping and yapping as Dave fed them. I waved at him as I pulled out of the driveway, and he bid me adios. I plugged in Molly Hatchet's "Hide Your Heart" and pointed the truck toward Stillwater America.

I rolled into the Tumbleweeds parking lot at around eight. Yona was off work at nine, so I wanted to be there plenty early. I saw Clay's truck parked off to the side and remembered that he had been a little pissed the last time I talked with him. I was not sure if that was because he had to drive up alone or because I was staying the weekend with Yona or what. Either way, I didn't give much of a damn and figured he would get over it.

Yona was working at one of the side bars when I came in. She saw me coming and had a beer and a shot of Jack Daniel's ready by the time I walked over to her station. "Hey, Drew, you're looking nice in that shirt. You have a date or something?" She flirted.

"Yeah, matter of fact, I do," I replied. "Real cute one too. Reminds me of you a little bit, only taller." *That is the best you can come up with? What a dork!*

Yona rolled her eyes and grabbed my hand as we talked. "Have you seen Clay?" I asked her.

She nodded toward a bar at the other end of the big dance floor. "At Dark Lady's bar station," she said. "He has been parked there for over an hour."

I glanced that way and, again, was struck by how amazingly attractive Melanie was on the first impression. Yona must have sensed something in my look as she smacked my hand and laughed. *Is it me? Am I that obvious? Or do most girls just get it when you're looking at another girl?*

"Dark Lady plays black magic. Maybe tonight he will get lucky," I said, sipping my shot. "If he did, it would probably shock him so bad he wouldn't know what to do with her. I think that's half the allure for him, to obtain the unobtainable."

Yona laughed, leaned in close to me, and said most coyly, "What would your date say if she saw you drooling at Dark Lady like that?"

I looked at her striking face with those cheekbones and sultry eyes, and I said smugly, "Uhm, you mean after she smacked me? Well, Melanie is always worth a drool or two, but I think my date would make very sure that she did . . . whatever it took to keep my attention for the rest of the evening."

"Are you serious?" She rolled her eyes. "In your dreams. I always knew you were a flake, but at least for tonight, cowboy, I guess you're my flake." She winked. Another bartender came over to chat with Yona, and they talked about work. "Caroline is cutting me a break and taking over now. I am going to go change and meet you back here in about thirty minutes, OK?" she said sweetly as she brought me another beer.

"You look great to me, Yona, but yeah, that's cool if you want to change. I'll just go hang out with Clay . . . and Dark Lady," I said with a wink. I ducked just in time to miss the roll of beer coasters she tossed at me, but she was smiling when she left the bar station.

I strolled over toward Clay and noticed Dark Melanie had picked me out with her eyes when I was about twenty feet away. She turned on that smoldering stare, and I stared back. She was stunning; I had to give her that. She dropped her brown hair down over one eye with an "I'm going to be in *Playboy* magazine" look that she did so well and gave me a slight smile.

Clay turned and also saw me approaching. He gave me a slobbering big bear hug. "It's about time you made it. I figured you got lost without me to guide you in here," he said with that Robert Redford smile.

"If you weren't with the Dark Lady, I would think you missed me," I said a bit too loud. Melanie's eyes flashed fire when she heard this, and if looks could kill, I would have had two daggers through the heart. *With her looking at me with that "go to hell" stare, she is still attractive. Damn near makes me want to take the hot trip down there to see what she looks like in leather. She is all black ice inside though. I can feel it.*

"Nah, I am about like you now. I just turn the truck loose, and it finds its way here," I said with a grin. Dark Lady Melanie moved away down the bar to other customers with a huff, so Clay and I began to compare notes from the week.

Clay was eager to go first, so I sipped my beer and let him run. "Word is that Duster is in town finally. Have you heard anything about that?" he asked anxiously.

Which town would that be exactly? Guthrie, Kingfisher, Crescent, Oklahoma City? Los Angeles? "Clay, do you even know who Duster is? I mean, really?" I answered his question with a question—well, two questions.

"Well, no, not by name or sight. I mean, I have heard a lot of things, seen a lot of things but mostly just talk. Hell, there is even one rumor he is some big honcho from south of the border. I only go by what Tony says and a few other guys. Getting crazy around here, though, and the point is whoever he is, he is one bad mutha, and he is in town." Clay leaned in close to me and said, "I also heard there are a ton of feds around. They are supposed to have two or three guys on the inside of some of the crews, so keep your eyes open."

At least he didn't mention the word "asset." And he is right. It's starting to get real crazy around here. I could feel the blood start to drain from

217

my face as the guilt set in, so I drank quickly from my waning beer and asked, "You think there are any feds in our group? I can't imagine who they would be, but I don't know all the players like you do."

"Nah, not in our crew. Tony would make sure of that." Clay finished his beer and suggested to the Dark Lady he was ready for another. She ignored him indicating that she had lost all interest in us and moved on down the bar. Not bothered, Clay waved Linda over, who brought us two more. He continued to chat but changed the conversation. "Yona looks good tonight. How did you wind up staying at her place for the weekend?" he asked.

"Was her idea. She invited me, and I accepted," I said, tipping my glass to him for the beer.

"You're a lucky bastard, Drew," Clay said, returning the beer salute.

Apparently, the Dark Lady had decided that whatever we were discussing, we were now having too much fun to be left alone, so she sashayed back over to our end of the bar to see what was going on. I said hello to her, and she started doing her *Playboy* thing. Before she hit second gear, I noticed Yona coming up from the back, so I grabbed my beer and returned to Caroline's bar, leaving the Dark Lady hovering in full-on smoldering centerfold mode with only Clay for an audience. Melanie's face turned scarlet, and her jaw dropped when I walked away, but she never said anything.

Yona joined me at the bar looking great. She was wearing the same thin fringed white doeskin vest she had worn the first time we met and looked amazing. She had on tight white Levi's and teal roper boots with a custom-made dark brown Indian weave leather belt with turquoise stones around her sweet waist. Caroline brought her a beer and tequila, and I quickly ponied up the cash plus tip to pay Caroline for the beverages for my Indian princess. "Are you two going to enter the dance contest?" Caroline asked, nodding toward the growing line of two-step contestants signing up over in the corner.

"Up to you." I shrugged to Yona. "I am happy to just sit here and stare at you, but I am game if you are. You already know I am seriously lacking on the dance floor but always up for a challenge."

She rolled her eyes at me again. "Cornball. Why not? It might be fun." She exclaimed, "Let's go!" She grabbed my hand, and we headed over to the sign-up line. I noticed Melanie was now gone from the bar, and Clay had moved on to his next potential conquest, a new girl with blond hair in faded jeans and boots. Yona signed us up, and we pinned the numbers to the back of our shirts and hit the floor for a couple of warm-up runs. Yona was a great dancer and really moved nice. Like most pretty Oklahoma girls, she made me look good on the dance floor.

The first song we danced to was Sweethearts of the Rodeo's "Since I Found You," and it went great. There were twenty-eight couples who had entered in the contest, and the songs alternated between country swing and two-step. We were the eighth couple sent off the main floor once the contest started, but we had a blast for the rest of the night watching the dance competition and enjoying each other's company. Tumbleweeds really was a one-of-a-kind-dance hall.

We headed for her place at around 2 a.m. and had a fantastic night. It was everything I could have imagined and so much more. Yona was magical and caring to an incredible depth of spirit, which infatuated me. Saturday was more relaxing, and we went out for a nice dinner at the Saltgrass Steak House and then a few drinks at the Crystal Palace Cow Town Saloon. We saw the sun come up on Sunday morning, something I was keen to do whenever I was with a lady in Oklahoma, and as sweet as this sunrise was, it would be the sunset of the day that I would never forget.

45

Yona had to work the early evening shift on Sunday, so I kissed her goodbye at around two thirty and headed toward Guthrie and the A frame. The sun beat down on my windshield with the last dying breath of spring and spoke of the imminent hot summer months ahead. The drive home was drowsy in the warm sun, and my mind drifted over hill and dale of the previous three days. *Yona, lovely, way smarter than me, and tough, tall, sexy. What was that song? "Infatuation"? I wonder if Clay made it out of Tumbleweeds alive. I guess I would have heard something by now if not. Dave knew where I was and where Clay was.*

I stopped at the Crossroads Country Store to buy some beer and talk with Linda for a bit. I arrived at the A frame as the sun had begun to descend in its afternoon parochial arc and parked the Chevy out in front. I could not remember ever really being so tired yet so happy. The feeling was going to be short lived.

I jumped in the super spa shower just because and then checked my phone messages. I had three. The first one was from Clay. He was fine, nursing a hangover, and wanting to meet up with Mark and me at Jack's Bar for a beer later tonight.

The second message was from Joe Reed and nothing at all to do with refreshments or being fine. The message said, "Drew, it's Joe. Been a helluva a weekend in Houston. It's Sunday morning, and I will be heading back to Oklahoma soon. I saw two of the Pauls Valley gang at a beer ice house out by the Miller Bridge. One was Larry Crowley. Not sure who the other was, but they saw me and tried like hell to act like they didn't see me, which tells me they were there to, well, watch me. Keep your eyes peeled. If they are watching me, they may be watching all of us. Oh yeah, this Louis guy you mentioned, I checked with some old crew down here from El Paso about the name. And if he is the same guy they are talking about, he is one really bad hombre. They said he hangs out south of the border, Juarez or Chihuahua mostly but can be anywhere. He's a real mystery though. Lots of stories. You got to tell me more about what's going on with this guy and why you asked about him when I see you tomorrow." The call ended with a click of the receiver on his end.

I listened to Joe's message again. *Pauls Valley guys following him down to Houston? And he has some inside on Louis Cypher? I guess it had been an interesting weekend.*

I played the last message on the machine. It was Joe again, this time with a more excited tone in his voice. "Drew, Joe here. It's four thirty Sunday afternoon. I am calling from a gas station about twenty miles north of the Texas-Oklahoma border. Larry Crowley snuck up on me on I-35 about thirty minutes ago and fired some shots at my truck. I swerved and fired back. I took an east side frontage road to get away. I don't see them now, but no telling where they are. I am staying off the interstate and going to lie low for a day to make sure I lost them before I come back. Tell Tony I won't be in until Tuesday. Damn Pauls Valley sons o' bitches."

I heard Joe muttering this last part as he hung up the phone, and I felt a cold chill on the back of my neck. *This whole situation had now just gone way past interesting.*

I looked out the window and noticed Dave's truck was in front of his place, so I decided to go down and have a chat with him about some of the things the weekend had wrought. I couldn't be totally forthcoming, but I could toss out the stuff about what happened to Joe and see where Dave took the trail. I headed out the door and turned to go check on the fox before stopping by Dave's.

It was strangely quiet at the pen area. Normally, the wee pups were yipping it up around sundown, and all kinds of activity was going on. I looked for the adults as I approached. Nothing.

Then I saw them in the first pen. The big silver male and female had been blasted nearly in two by a shotgun. I went around to the back of the hutch and saw more shotgun blasts through the wood. I opened the lid slowly and heard the flies buzzing around the eight dead silver fox pups, and my stomach twisted with knots. I ran to the other pens and found the same thing—the adults torn apart by gunshots and the pups all killed in the hutches.

I could feel the bile building in the back of my throat, one thought filled my head, and I began to run. *Jeez, I got to tell Dave. He is going to go nuts. Who could have done this? Who would want to do this? Why? And why hadn't Dave noticed?*

I stopped cold when I saw the front door open. *Dave always has his screen latched. He hates it when opossums or coons get inside. How . . . could this have happened . . . if Dave was home?*

Fear crept in as the bile in my throat was pushing up hard now and my saliva glands began the liquid lubrication reflex that always ended in a one-way regurgitation of my stomach contents. I was shaking as I entered the silent house and was thinking I should go back for my Glock, but I kept moving forward . . . until I saw him. There on the floor in his kitchen, with a shotgun blast directly in his back, was the body of my friend Dave Raymond.

The pooled blood on the floor was clotting and nearly dry, which meant he had been dead for at least twelve hours, maybe longer. My head began to spin as I stumbled to Dave's phone. I dialed Leon Spencer with a shaking hand, even though Dave had the number of the sheriff's office written down right next to his phone. I gasped out the details of the scene to Leon as the bile in my throat hit that point of no return. I left the phone hanging off the hook and stumbled outside, retching with a torrential outburst that made my whole body shake as if I were trying to make the entire experience somehow surreal. It seemed as if I could not stop vomiting for over a minute, but then slowly, it subsided into a session of slow, emotional dry heaves.

My face was flush from the warmth of the day and the recent retching of my guts out. I wanted cool water on my face, but I could not will myself to go back into Dave's house, yet I could not leave to return to the A frame either. I settled for the outside water pump about fifty feet from the front door. I opened the spicket and let the cool water flow across my head and face. I drank deep and felt the knots in my stomach loosen a bit.

I could hear the police sirens in the distance, and I tried to compose myself and started walking out toward the road to meet them.

There on the edge of the road to Dave's place, pushed deep into the soft ground outside, were two sets of wide Z-groove heavy tire tracks.

46

I stared at the Z-groove tracks as Leon's police cruiser screamed in, followed by a deputy sheriff's car and an ambulance. The EMS team had been briefed on their way in, and the deputy escorted them inside the house to his body. EMS confirmed the death of Dave Raymond, and the deputy called the coroner per procedure. The detectives came in to investigate the crime scene as Leon took my statement.

I already knew who had killed Dave; there were just a few details I still needed to work out, so I stayed around the place all hangdog while they investigated to see what I could pick up. I doubted if Brian had acted alone, and I was still overwhelmed with his motive. I mean, if he wanted to kill me, I would understand. But why kill Dave, and for piss' sake, why shoot all the fox? *Could he just be that much of a psycho?*

I showed Leon the Z-groove tire tracks but did not share my thoughts about who they belonged to. The lead detective working the scene was a young guy who had just moved down from Tulsa, and he was very thorough. They took boot casts and tire track casts and found several shotgun shells and pistol casings, and I thought they might actually stumble onto who did this.

I called Clay and told him what had happened, including the part about Joe Reed being shot at and hiding out for a day before returning to Oklahoma. He came down later with Mark and a full cooler of beer, something that never hurt to have around. They arrived as the last police car pulled out, and Clay parked in front of the A frame. In a way, I was in no real mood to talk, yet I knew they both suspected Dave's death was part of the storm that was coming and would have questions. *They are good old boys and just helping out a friend while we figure out what our next move is going to be.*

I told them about Joe Reed's phone calls again, and they told me about one of the guys from another crew found dead off Highway 59. It was starting; that much we knew. The storm was coming, and who knew how strong the winds would blow or how hard the lightning would strike?

"Did you call Tony? About Dave?" I asked Clay as I closed my eyes and opened a beer.

"Yeah, I told him about Joe also. He was quiet, strangely quiet, but told us to be sure and stop by to check on you," Clay answered somberly. "We all knew you and Dave were pretty close. Everybody liked him."

That was when it hit me. The tears started coming, and it was a good ten minutes before they stopped. When they did stop, the emotional sense of loss was replaced with a ragged-edge need for retribution. I was not really interested in justice; I wanted vengeance and was determined to get it.

I showed them the tracks out front, and Mark picked up the trail like a bloodhound. We grabbed our firearms, jumped in my Chevy, and started to follow the big Z-groove tracks. They were headed back toward Dave's two big lease tanks. Sure enough, it was pretty clear that Brian's truck had been used to pull at least a couple of loads from Dave's tanks, possibly more.

"He had to know I was in Stillwater. That's the only way they would have tried this shit," I said with venom.

"How the fuck did they figure out I was gone?" I shouted with fury.

"Drew," Mark said, trying to calm me, "it would not have been hard. He was probably watching the place or had someone watching the place. A lot of people knew about the lease tanks and the fact that you would not let anybody pull from them. Shit's going down all over, buddy."

"The same bunch probably killed that guy Lanny and will be moving in on all of us now. Tony wants to move the meeting up to Wednesday as soon as Joe gets back from Houston. I think he is planning to kick this war into high gear now, my brothers. There will be blood," Mark added, nearly white as a ghost.

The boys pulled out around eleven, and I finally drifted off to sleep at about two. I awoke the next morning at around ten when I heard a car pull up over at Dave's place. It was Dave's son, Rory, and his girlfriend. I threw some jeans on and went outside to meet them, not having any clear idea at all about what I was going to say. I explained what I had found when I arrived and what had happened to Dave to the best of my ability, skipping over the part that Brian Dugan was the killer or at least one of them.

The detectives had placed the yellow-and-black crime scene tape up on the front door, but the back door had not been affected, and Rory asked if he could go inside. *I am not exactly the legal representation here.*

I shrugged and said, "Back door is not labeled 'no access' with the crime scene tape, and even if it was, this is Logan County. You're the next of kin, so I doubt anybody is going to make an issue unless we tell them. Still, I suggest you don't stay inside long."

Rory went through the house and collected some of the important documents to set things in order, but he was obviously shaken up. He said there was no plan at all to sell the place, and I was welcome to stay at the A frame as long as I wanted. I thanked him and, of course, offered to help out in any way that I could.

When I asked him how I should pay the monthly rent, where to send the check to, he said, "Dave enjoyed having you around and seemed to get on well with you. For the next couple of months at least, if you can just keep this place together while I am finishing this semester at school, make sure nobody vandalizes the place, that will be more than enough." I assured him I would take great care of the place and that he need not concern himself with anything of that nature right now. They spent some more time in the house, and then just after one, they drove away.

I went back to mine and made maximum use of the super spa shower as I rolled the previous days' events over again in my mind. *Brian Dugan, Pauls Valley crew, Joe getting shot at, Dave getting . . . shot dead. Jeez, what a mess. Where is Brian hiding? What else are they planning?*

When I finished, I returned to the A frame, and I had a message on my phone from Myra. She had been informed about the murder and was checking in, so I called her back. "How are you doing, Drew?" she asked in that Myra voice.

"As good as I can. Jeez, this is some shit. Why kill Dave? He is not even involved," I mumbled.

"Since we started this task force up nearly five years ago, we have suspected the Pauls Valley group of more than twenty killings. Most of them involve Brian Dugan. We just never had enough evidence or a solid case. He is most likely a psychopath, and there is no rhyme or reason to many of the things that he does. His file is loaded with strange fires and linked killings statewide."

"He went after Dave because of me, Myra. That's plain enough," I said through gritted teeth. "That's the only explanation."

"Well, you're most likely right on that. However, eventually, someone was going to go after the condensate in his tanks. The only reason no one bothered them was you . . . and Tony. With the Pauls Valley group and Jay Randall making their move now, it was only a matter of time before damage was done. Let me know how it goes at the meeting with Tony today, OK?" Myra asked.

I told her the meeting was changed to Wednesday and what had happened with Joe Reed down south. "That's across state lines. I can bring in additional support now if they made a move into Texas. Stay close to your pager, Drew, and let me know of any—I mean, any—new developments," she demanded.

"Roger that. Any idea what the next move is, Myra?" I asked solemnly.

"Yeah, we have an idea. Let's see what Tony tells you, and then we can go from there."

47

I stopped by the west plant that afternoon and filled Tony in on most of the details, and we talked about the meeting coming up on Wednesday. He briefed me on a couple of possible options he was looking at, and none of them sounded like a diplomatic approach. He was in a mood worse than a grizzly bear that had just been castrated, and this I could appreciate. He was planning to take it to them and take it to them hard. I left his office and did a few things out in the field, but my head was around Dave's death and the possible scenarios that could be coming in the next few days.

Tuesday, I hit the field early and then onto the west plant, anxious to get through the day. I tried to take my mind off Dave and get more focused on what can be done about the Dugans and Jay Randall's takeover attempt. At about noon, I sent Joe a page for him to call me. I sent him another page at four. By six on Tuesday night, it was not looking very good on hearing from Joe. I called Tony, and a dozen of us took off southward to see if we could get any information about where the hell Joe was at. We covered miles of ground all the way to the Texas border in search of the tall drink of water but to no avail. We rolled back to Guthrie at around midnight empty handed and without a clue where he was or if anything had happened to him.

It was tough getting to sleep, and when I finally did drift off, I dreamed that I was on a dusty Oklahoma back road with a crude oil tanker heading straight toward me at high speed. The tanker was on fire, with flames shooting everywhere, and I could see the driver. He was like some roughneck version of the Ghost Rider—all skull, hair on fire with a burning pistol in his hand. I woke up in a sheen of sweat and shivering. It was a restless long night.

Wednesday morning, I woke up starving, and I realized I had hardly eaten anything in the past two days. I cooked a big breakfast of steak, eggs, fried okra, toast, and grits. I slammed a cup of coffee and felt like a new man. I checked my Glock and the three loaded clips I always carried. All were in order. I had also started bringing along an extra fifty rounds in the Chevy glove box, just in case.

I met Mark at one of the east field tanks, and we chatted about some of the possible "battlegrounds" that we might find ourselves on in the coming days. "I heard Tony's got some big-shit news to announce at the meeting," Mark said absently as he unhooked a gas meter.

"About?" I asked curiously.

"Don't know what about for sure, but it's big. He is irritated as shit. I saw him at Jack's Bar last night, and he damn near tore my head off over nothing. Hell, John would hardly sit at the operator's desk yesterday. Tony was such a rag ass. I don't think I have ever seen him like this," Mark added.

"Oh, you mean there's never been two rival factions of thugs ganging up on him, trying to steal his territory, and running around killing people? Ya think maybe that has anything to do with it?" I said sharply, way too sharply. Mark did not deserve that. He just gave me a blank look.

"You don't have any idea?" I asked, my voice softening. "What it is?"

"Best guess I have is he is bringing in some heavy muscle from out of the area to help kick Joe Dugan's ass out of the territory. But the bigger threat is Jay Randall. He covers a lot of the out-of-state stuff. Nobody knows how deep it really goes," Mark said with a shrug.

I helped him load his measuring equipment up and headed over to the eastern compressor station to change some valves and filters out. I noticed two pickups pull in behind me on the road and started easing up on my rear end a bit too close for my comfort. I started to sweat and pulled off to the right at a well station while reaching for my Glock. They drove on by, paying me no attention. *Probably just Billy Bob farmer doing his own thing. I am getting paranoid. Still never hurts to be aware though. They killed Dave. They can go after any of us, damn near at any time they want.*

I grabbed a pork poor boy sandwich at the Crossroads Country Store. I had not seen Linda in two days, and she gave me a big hug, took a break, and had lunch with me. "I heard about what happened to Dave Raymond. That's a real shame. I loved Dave," Linda said emotionally.

"We all did, Linda. Real shit situation, that one for sure," I said dryly.

"You found him, right? Was he . . . was he really shot?" she asked, her voice shaky. I nodded with a lump building up in my own throat again at the memory.

"Bastard! Who would do that to him?" she asked emphatically. I knew she was just upset and did not mean to get me going, but I started feeling a wild rage building up inside me. The more she talked, the wilder my rage got. We finished lunch, and I promised to stop by more often, and it was my turn to give her a hug.

As I drove off in the Chevy, the song "San Francisco" by Scott McKenzie came on the radio, and I began to calm down a bit. *Funny, I think that was the first time I had talked with Crossroads Linda that we never mentioned Bonnie. Those days seemed like light-years away. I wonder what she is doing now.*

I made a final pass through the field and pulled up to the west plant office just a little before five. There were plenty of vehicles parked out front, and I could not help being a bit edgy knowing everyone inside was packing firearms, and only about half of them knew what the hell they were doing or how to use them.

Clay gave me a beer when I walked in, and I could hear John Lordell running his dumbass mouth, obviously half pissed already. It looked like Tony was in his back office with Mark. Most everybody had a beer and was talking among themselves. Mark came out of Tony's office and walked over to join Clay and me. His face was white as a sheet. He started to say something, but Tony kicked the door open with a loud bang, shifting the mood of the meeting from mild tension to cable-snapping tautness.

Tony's mood was grim, and he got straight to the point. "You should all have an idea about what's been happening. Joe Dugan and those Pauls Valley sumbitches have tied up together with that lily fag Jay Randall and are trying to move into our territory. We know they killed Lanny from Jack Lambert's crew, and Jersey Joe Reed has not made it back from Houston yet. They have caused all kinds of shit with the Elk City crews, and they are taking product from every territory out there. Other people are missing as well. Looks like they even gunned down Dave Raymond," Tony said in a deathly tone, which was greeted by murmurs and cursers around the room. A few of the guys looked my way and tipped their beers in salute to Dave. I acknowledged them.

"It's pretty obvious they are not going to stop, so we are damn sure going to start. Pair up, all of you, or stay in threes when you're out in the field, and don't get caught out alone. If you see any of them from either of those crews in your area before Saturday, gun 'em down. Don't piss around. Just blast 'em. If they are in our area, they will damn sure be looking to blast you all."

John interrupted Tony in a drunken slur. "Before Saturday . . . what the . . . fuck that, shoot 'em all, just whack 'em . . . hell, we don't need a date. Just kill 'em all dead . . . sumbitches."

Mark shut John up as Tony gave him the glare of death with his eyes. "Before Saturday . . . after daybreak on Saturday, you don't shoot unless you're shot at or until I say otherwise. There is a meeting at Six-Mile Saturday at four. Five crews will be represented, including Elk City, and it will all end then and there. It's not my call. I would rather just shoot it out. But this is the way he wants it, and that is the way it's going to damn well be. Whatever is decided on Saturday is the way forward, and that is fucking that." Tony walked to the fridge and grabbed a beer, nearly draining it in the first drink before he continued.

He? He who?

"Chris, you have three kids. We don't know how this thing is going to go yet. It's going to be his call. You stay home on Saturday, OK? Jim, Miles, and John, you guys stay home also," Tony ordered.

"What the fuck?" John slurred drunkenly. "I ain't got no damn kids. I ain't staying home. I'll kill them sumbitches. I'll . . . I'll . . ."

"You'll shut the fuck up, you damn idiot, and you will stay home. You would be the first one shot if anything went down. Hell, the way you're acting now, I would shoot you myself," Tony said decisively, glaring at John again. He stared at John now, but he was speaking to all of us. "If any one of you says a word about any of this outside this room until we meet on Saturday, you will fucking deal with me.

It will be way worse if he finds out, so keep your damn mouths shut and your eyes open."

Tony slammed his beer and left the office. The others all started to drift out also until it was just Clay, Mark, and myself, so I felt inclined to ask, "Who is *he*? Who is Tony talking about?"

That ashen look returned to Mark's face as he spoke again "Duster. He is coming to take care of the problem. Too many people dead, and too much revenue has been lost. He is coming to deal with it personally. Shit, shit, shit."

"Duster. Jeez, no shit, man, this is going to be so fucked. Nothing good will come out of this, nothing at all, no way, no how," Clay said as the color also began to leave his face.

I looked at them both, the gravity of the situation not quite fully on me yet. "Well, at least we will all get to finally find out who he is."

48

I called Myra and told her we had finished the meeting at the west plant, and she wanted to catch up with me for a debriefing, like, now and not at a bar. She said to meet out in the boondocks on an old oil lease road just off Highway 59. We parked side by side in the early moonlight, and as usual, I was captivated with her. "What happened with Tony and your guys at your meeting?" she asked, tossing her hair slightly.

"There is a 'come to Jesus' meeting this Saturday at the Six-Mile Bar with the five crews. Duster is rumored to be coming personally to broker a peace, resolve the issues, kick some ass, or shed blood as needed among Tony, Jay Randall, Joe Dugan, Jack Lambert, Elk City mainly, but I get the feeling he will take out anybody who gets in the way. No idea how that's going to go. Too many dead bodies are showing up and cutting into profits. Apparently, he is pissed about it. Tony wants me there, wants most of us there. Do I go?" I asked Myra.

"Yes, you go, and stay sharp. We knew this meeting was coming, just not when or where. Good work, Drew. Now that we know where the meeting is, I will also be inside talking with an agent we have placed at Six-Mile, just blending in. She looks like a rough ex-stripper turned biker turned thug, but she is a damn good undercover agent, one of the best. You won't miss her. She is the brunet bartender there," Myra said. "Are you sure Duster is coming?"

Brunet bartender from the Six-Mile Bar, Mandy? The one that Tony has been banging? She's an agent? Never saw that coming. "Pretty sure. You have suspected he is in the area, Tony is as nervous as I have ever seen him, and everyone is really wound up about it. The locals are sending the women and children to higher ground," I said with a feeble attempt at humor that she did not appreciate in the least.

"I would say it's the best chance you will ever have of finding him," I replied quickly, trying to recover. "Does anybody even know what this guy looks like?"

"Not certain, but we are close. I think we might have a photo or a very good lead on him before the meeting on Saturday," Myra replied. "I will inform the district attorney's office and take it from here."

Myra reached into her purse and pulled out a small unit that looked like a tiny hearing aid. "Wear this inside Six-Mile Bar. No one will be paying attention in this redneck hellhole, so it should not be a problem. You can hear what the agent in charge and the ADA will be saying. You will know when they are coming in and how they will play it. They can't hear you. It's only one-way coms, but you can hear them. Plus, watch me. And when it all happens, just get out of the way and under some cover."

"What about Brian Dugan? If he shows up, I am taking him out. I swear it," I said, my voice shaking angrily.

Myra's eyes softened a bit. "If you do go after him, you better make sure he has a gun in his hand and you don't get killed doing it."

"I thought, as an asset, I was licensed to engage when threatened," I reminded her.

Myra gave me one of those looks that both excite and castrate at the same time. "Get out of the way, Drew, and you won't *be* threatened." And then with that, looking like a midnight angel, she drove away into the night, leaving me to ponder my thoughts alone.

After a brief minute, I did the same. My thoughts turned to what was coming. *Louis Cypher, Myra has the intel. Do we even know who he is yet? Was that his real name? Might as well be Robinson Crusoe for all we know.*

The next two days really dragged on, and it was tough to concentrate on work. There was still no word from Joe Reed, although one of the Pauls Valley guys, a Keith somebody, was talking some drunk shit at a bar down in Caddo County and said that they took him out. *Damn it, Joe, where are you?*

Tension hung in the air everywhere, and it was a stressful time. I reloaded a new batch of fifty rounds of ammo, but it just was not the same without Dave there. Clay and Mark stopped by late on Friday.

We had a couple of beers and discussed some possible scenarios about how tomorrow might play out, none of which left us feeling warm and fuzzy. I had a restless night dreaming of the Dark Lady Melanie from Tumbleweeds riding a red horse and Yona riding a white stallion, with long cool Myra in her black dress on a black stallion across an endless Oklahoma prairie as lightning flashed in the sky and between them. I woke up on Saturday at daybreak, drenched in sweat. My stomach was tied in knots, but I was ready to face whatever I had to do today.

I met Clay and Mark at the Wagon Wheel BBQ for lunch, but none of us really ate much or said much. I brooded over Dave, now possibly also Joe, and my mood was dark and sullen. Mark had met with Tony earlier, and he passed some information on to us about how the setup might look at Six-Mile later today. We finished lunch and agreed on a plan to meet at the Six-Mile Bar at about three thirty, driving separate vehicles.

The parking lot was crowded with cars when I pulled in at three thirty, most of which I did not recognize. I walked in quietly, slid over to an open spot at the bar, and began to check out who was in the place. I caught Tony right away, with Clay and Jack Lambert next to him. Mark was opposite of me with a couple of guys I had seen before, but I could not recall their names. He saw me and gave a brief nod. I responded and scanned the rest of the room. Jay Randall had a sizable and ugly bunch around him who were sitting directly opposite Tony, and Joe Dugan was to his left with several of the Pauls Valley crew. Jay's big gun, Ronnie Moore, was with him. I recognized two guys from Elk City, but there may have been more. There must have been over thirty men in the place, and surprisingly, I saw several women. *"Girls with Guns," that old song by Tommy Shaw.*

I saw Brian Dugan and Hawk Nose sucked up tight behind Joe like weasels, and the rage returned full on. I noticed two guys who I was pretty sure were FBI agents trying hard not to look like they were FBI hanging out by the side door. Myra was at the end of the bar talking to the brunet bartender slash agent slash Tony's side babe.

I could hear the agent in charge talking to several feds outside on my coms piece and knew they were in position and waiting. Then I heard the voice of ADA Jim Dawson. If he was here, this was going to be bigger than I thought. It appeared that the agent in charge was waiting for the assistant district attorney to approve something or other. I wondered if Tony or Jay had any lookouts outside. It would have made sense. They probably had lookouts watching the lookouts.

I checked the crowd over again, focusing on the ones I did not know, and tried to figure out which one was Duster. I assumed he would have an entourage, and while there were some mean-looking dudes around whom I had not seen before, none of them had a lot of backup and just did not seem to be a fit for the El Patron badass I had been hearing about.

I caught Myra's eye, and she seemed to tense up as if she had just picked up a lead on Duster. The brunette next to her tensed also, looking into the crowd. I could feel the nervous bile start to build up in the back of my throat. I followed Myra's eyes toward the crowd on the floor but still could not pick out anyone who fit the bill as "the man."

The agents outside were getting anxious, and the tension inside the bar suddenly rose a couple of octaves. Myra was moving toward the back wall, and she was about to pull the SIG out. *Shit, it's going down. The Tigra is on the prowl.* Tony and Jay's crews were all antsy now, and their hands moved close to their guns, concentrating on one another, not realizing the feds were about to make a move. There were four doors at the Six-Mile Bar, and the feds were now stacking up behind three of them.

I heard Assistant District Attorney Jimmy in my earpiece. "Duster has to be inside. Take them all down now. Move in. We have confirmation that Louis Cypher is here somewhere." He gave the go signal, and the entire force of the US federal agents assembled outside the bar came to life.

Fifteen agents drew their guns as a loudspeaker blasted out the words "FBI, all inside, drop your weapons, and hands over your heads," said an authoritative voice.

Yeah, like that's going to work.

The first guy through the back door was Agent Larson. The rest followed. Jay's crew opened fire when they saw them enter, and bullets started flying everywhere. Myra shot two of Joe Dugan's crew, and Tony was blazing away with his .45 at anyone he did not recognize. I saw Ronnie Moore draw a bead on Myra, and I pulled my Glock quickly and put two bullets in his throat before he could fire a shot.

ADA Jimmy had joined the fray, wearing a flak jacket and firing his own Glock. He was searching for Louis Cypher when he saw me take Ronnie out with the throat shots. He was stunned and shocked, what with me being an untrained agent and all. I guess they expected me to be a waste with a weapon, but he also seemed to appreciate the action. I caught Myra's eye, and I knew she did not expect that level of involvement from me either.

The feds appeared to be getting the upper hand, and the Oklahoma crews were dropping slowly back to a defensive position. I looked around hard for Brian Dugan or Hawk Nose but could not see either of them. They must have slipped out or been hiding. Clay had taken a bullet in the shoulder and was down on the floor, wide eyed but alive. He looked at me with my gun out and thought I was part of the Okie crew. It never registered with him I could have been anything else. I saw Mark lying on the floor, and with the amount of dark blood pouring out of him, I knew he was gone or going.

Tony took three bullets in the chest, but all that did was seem to piss him off. He had already unloaded his first clip on the feds, putting two of them down, and he dove behind the bar as he slid a second clip into his Colt. Jay was firing wide eyed and wild but missing everything he shot at. Two feds tackled him down to the ground with ease, taking him out of play.

Then just like that, it appeared to be over. The Okies started dropping their guns and putting their hands in the air. The feds thought they were in complete control, and the local crews continued to raise their arms and drop their weapons as instructed.

Suddenly, the main door of the bar was kicked open, and the room went black from something shadowy blocking out the late afternoon sun. I never saw his face, just a silhouette of the biggest man I had ever seen, just a black shape against the blazing Oklahoma sun backdrop in the doorway. He was wearing a long duster coat despite the heat and had a flat-brimmed cowboy hat on his head like what Clint Eastwood wore in his old Westerns. He was an ominous figure as he pulled out two 9 mm Heckler & Koch (H&K) automatic machine pistols. He blocked the entire door with his massive frame as he stood there, making Tony look like a schoolboy in comparison.

As long as I live, I would never forget the words he said as he pointed the assault pistols at the feds and anyone who was standing. "El Diablo ya ha llegado ahora. Prepárate para morir en tu mundo y ven a vivir en el mío." (The devil has now arrived. Prepare to die in your world, and come live in mine.) He opened fire with both machine pistols and took out five agents in a six-second blast. The first one, bloody and dying, was Agent Larson, followed by agent Miller. The silhouetted demon shot four more dead in another six seconds. Myra took a bullet to the leg, and ADA Jimmy had three hit his chest that knocked him down hard, but his flak jacket saved him from sure death.

Bodies were strewn all around the bar floor by now, and my gut began to wrench as I once again smelled that acrid odor of gun smoke in the air and the metallic copper rankness of fresh blood. The huge man kept firing, and people kept dying.

I moved to Myra and quickly checked her leg. The bullet had passed all the way through, but she was bleeding pretty bad, so I put her arm around my shoulder and started looking for a way out. Even in the midst of the firefight, I could not help but think about how beautiful she was. I was so pumped with adrenaline that I literally picked her up off the ground and headed to the side door. I grabbed ADA Jimmy with my right arm and dragged them both to the nearest door as Duster blew the hell out of the rest of the room. He was shooting indiscriminately and just killing everyone he could find—feds, crews, and locals alike.

Duster dropped the clips from his H&Ks and slammed two new ones in the assault pistols, but nobody was returning fire in his direction now. Anyone left alive was trying like hell to take cover or get out of there. He saw me with Myra and ADA Jimmy trying to make it to the side doors, and my heart nearly burst from my chest as he took aim at us. There was no way in hell he could miss us at that range, and I had my hands full of ADA Jimmy and Myra and could not even take a shot. I looked directly into his eyes under that flat-brimmed black hat—blazing, hollow, fiery red eyes like demon pits. It scared the living shit out of me. I knew all was lost and that it was over. Then he suddenly lowered the pistols, and just like that, he was gone, vanished like a shadow demon out of the door into the early night.

ADA Jimmy was solid, even with most of his men dead, he radioed out for backup and medical support. Myra was holding my left hand; the future district attorney was pumping my right. I could barely hear what he was saying as my mind was flooded with the fact that I was still alive, but it was something like "Outstanding work, everyone. Drew, you're going to Quantico. That was amazing baptism under fire." I felt strangely dizzy.

Why didn't he finish us off? It made no sense. He had us dead to rights, and he just walked away. Maybe he needed somebody alive as a herald to spread the message of the day.

Then it hit me. *The blazing red eyes, the demon look, Louis Cypher... LouisCypher... Lucifer? Is that even possible?*

I was suddenly very dizzy, felt warm blood trickle down the side of my temple, and wasn't sure if I was shot, stunned, dazed, or what. My legs buckled, and I could feel unconsciousness drift in and reality fade away.

49

I woke up in a hospital bed with a pounding headache and hungry as heck. I looked over, and Myra was in the bed next to me with her leg bandaged up. "What? How did I get here?" I stammered as I sat up.

Myra was amped up on Demerol for the pain in her leg, and her eyes were a bit glazed, but she was still stunningly attractive with that Myra the Tigra movement. "You got grazed in the temple by a wild shot and went unconscious after all the excitement was over. You did a hell of job, Drew. Jim wants to send you to Quantico for a six-week training program and is pushing to get you accelerated agent status."

Accelerated agent status? Do I even want that? You would think they would have asked me first. "What happened? I mean, it looked like the body count was pretty high," I said groggily, holding my head.

"Twenty-seven dead in total. Ten federal agents and seventeen local boys and girls, it was a blood bath, the worst I have ever seen in my time with the bureau. Made the Miami incident look like some kid's playground," Myra said quietly.

"Tony? Clay? Did they make it?" I knew better than to ask about Mark.

"Tony is alive in the County General Hospital under heavy security. He took five bullets and is one tough SOB. He has been indicted and will be facing some serious charges. Clay is fine and should be discharged along with you today or tomorrow. Neither of you have been implicated or called to testify yet. You can thank Jim for that. He said his fast-track push to make you an agent might be compromised if you had to testify. If they call Clay, then they call you, so it was a pretty easy choice. We are still chasing down several people who are heavily involved in the procurement and distribution of the stolen oil. That ultraviolet dye we put in your little trailer has been tied into over twenty oil-receiving terminals across five states, including Mexico. None of the crews saw that coming. I knew this was big, just had no idea it was really this big . . . international. Jeez, Drew, what a story."

She paused to take a sip of water and then continued. "Joe Dugan was shot several times, and he died on the scene. Jay Randall, well, he is a real piece of work. He is in custody and will be turning state evidence on three major players that we were not even tracking. He is going into WITSEC [Security Program] during the rest of the investigation and prosecution."

"Duster? What happened to him? Jesus, did you see his face, his eyes? That guy was a monster, a damn real live demon," I said, recalling the moment. "Did you catch him?"

Myra chuckled softly. "He was a bad man, Drew, but I seriously doubt if he is a demon. You took a glancing shot to the head, remember? And you were probably just fading out. No, he is still out there. We have an APB out for him, and Interpol is chasing him through Mexico should he surface there, but he seems to have vanished. Every federal agency within five states is looking for him on our side of the border, and we will get him when he turns up again."

She sipped more water again and looked back at me. "There are several stragglers still out here, Brian Dugan for one, so the task force has started a roundup-and-closeout-type mission that you will be a part of once your released from the hospital. We need to clean this up as best we can, Drew," she said sweetly.

"Any news on Joe Reed? Did he turn up anywhere?" I asked hopefully.

"Not yet. It doesn't look good at all for Joe, I am sorry. They found his truck on a back road close to the Texas border but no Joe," she replied with emotion. "Drew, we still have a lot to do here. This roundup mission is high risk, and I need you to get ready as soon as you can. You're the best asset we have in the field in this area, and your cover has not been blown as far as we can tell. All our intelligence suggests no one has made you, so once we finish cleaning up around here, you just close out with Clay and the west plant crews, and you can fade away to your next assignment at Quantico."

Close out with Clay? Close what out? Fade away? Just wait a damn minute. I still have a job and some cash here, right? Er, don't I? "What about my job, Myra? The west plant and all?" I asked emotionally. "Look, I am just not sure that being a fast-track agent is where I want to go." I slumped back on my pillows as frustration began to seep into my thoughts.

Myra's eyes took on an understanding look, and she said, "Well, we know that Brian Dugan and John Ballick are still in the area as they can't get through the APB net. Lyle Crowley and Keith High, the two suspected of taking out Joe Reed, are also in the area. Whether you want to be an agent and go to Quantico may not be the most pressing issue."

"Who is John Ballick?" I asked, interrupting her.

"The guy you call Hawk Nose, the one who has been hanging around with Brian Dugan for the last year. So I guess my question for you is, do you want to be part of this roundup-and-closeout task team?" she asked, all business.

Damn straight, lady, no way in hell I would miss out on this. "Yes, Myra, I want in. I want to catch those assholes and finish this up. Who is in charge?" I replied with fortitude and dedication.

"I will still be your handler for now. But FBI Special Agent Frank London from Chicago is overall in charge. Any more questions?" she said dreamily now as another shot of Demerol kicked into her system.

"Yeah, how soon can I get out of here?"

50

I returned to the west plant two days before Clay, and things were surprisingly, well, normal considering five days earlier twenty-seven people had been killed, and Tony was in jail, indicted on eleven federal charges. John was wandering around like a lost puppy on quaaludes, but for the most part, the operation was running smooth.

A new superintendent named Bob Orsini had moved up from the Oklahoma City office to run things, and he seemed like an iron-fist kind of guy with zero personality. One of the key things I noticed when I walked in that first morning back to work was that the beer fridge was gone from the office. *The ending of an era. Makes sense. Management needs to put on the persona of above reproach from now on if they are going to survive.*

He had also brought in a foreman from Shawnee, a local guy with twenty years of experience named Ralph Waits. Ralph seemed like an Oklahoma good old boy who took no bullshit but was also fair if you did your job.

The two of them called me into the office and read me the riot act that I was on probation for the next three months and that they had a letter of reprimand placed in my file for "conduct unbecoming an employee" concerning the fact that I had been in the Six-Mile Bar the day when the feds raided the place. *"Conduct unbecoming an employee"? What the hell is that? This is not the military, and if the FBI gave me a green light . . .*

Discretion being the better part, I just nodded, signed it, and headed out to the compressor area, where I ran into John. He was a broken man, and I almost felt bad for him, almost. He told me he had received four disciplinary letters in his file, including one for mandatory alcohol rehabilitation, and I had to stifle a chuckle. Apparently, John had one of his beer-sodden callout encounters the night before Orsini and Waits came to the office for their first day, so they saw him in all his glory. I was able to get him focused on some work tasks, which seemed to help, and we made it through the day.

Clay called that night, and we decided to meet for a beer at Jack's Bar. I had been cleaning up the fox cage area, taking them apart, and taking care of Rory's place a bit each day, but it was too damn depressing to hang around there.

We grabbed some beers at the bar, and I brought him up to speed about the west plant situation, Orsini, Waits, and John's predicament. Clay was doing pretty good, way better than John, but like all of us, the event had affected him, and his shoulder was still pretty sore. "I wonder how many of these damn letters they put in my file. Bastards," Clay said as he slammed his beer and ordered a shot.

"Clay, where do we go from here with the condensate loads? I mean, do we all just stop? I don't see how we can keep hauling loads now that the feds are crawling around like maggots everywhere," I asked.

"I don't know. Really, I just don't know, but yeah, you're right. We need to lie low, and sure as hell, somebody will be watching what's going on now," he replied dryly.

From my conversations with Myra, I knew they had identified many of the terminals where the oil was being sold at but did not really know much more than that. "Has anybody been out to the tanks or leases to see what's been going on?" I asked Clay as I ordered a shot of my own.

He shrugged. "I doubt it, but it might be a good idea to just take a look."

"When are you back to work, amigo?" I asked him, concerned.

"Monday. Jeez, how did we wind up in this mess?" he said as he placed his hands over his face.

Do you really have to ask? The better question is, how could we not have seen this coming with all the shit we had been pulling for so long? "It's day by day from here on out, Clay. I'll see you around," I said more sternly than I meant to, but my mind was on other things.

We finished the night at Jack's, so I headed back to the A frame. I had a message from Myra on my machine, and I returned her call.

She wanted to brief me on some developments but not on the phone. We agreed to meet for lunch the next day at Randall's.

To my surprise, she showed up in tight faded blue jeans and a T-shirt that was equally tight and faded. With her blond hair drawn back in a ponytail and that Myra-the-Tigra look, it was almost exactly the way she was the day I saw her at the Rifleman. It was an intoxicatingly sexy look, and I was floored.

I asked how her leg was, and she said it was sore and throbbing a little, but she could walk now and had started some therapy. We ordered lunch while she briefed me on all the activities still going on in the area that the feds had been keeping tabs on. I was surprised the area was still so active with thugs.

Myra handed me an FBI Nextel radiophone and said, "Do you know how to use a Nextel?"

"Sure, we use them in operations all the time," I replied as I took the Nextel from her and looked it over. Something about it was different. Then it struck me. The mic key was blocked. I looked at Myra, puzzled.

"It's like the earpiece I gave you. It's one-way communications. You can receive but can't send. You can hear what the agents are saying in the field, but you can't communicate anything back. You will have to find a payphone and call or page me if you hear or see anything of significance." I nodded and checked out the phone again. "Most of the chatter for this area and the roundup mission will be on channels 10, 11, and 12. You can play around all day if you're bored though. I think we have seventeen active channels on this network here in Oklahoma," Myra added as our food arrived at the table.

Maybe if I make fast-track agent, I will get a Nextel that has a mic.

"What's going on with your old crew? Is anyone still pulling tank loads or the crude trailers?" Myra asked as she ate her Caesar salad.

"Not sure. I was thinking about making a run out in the field later today or tonight and see if anyone has been working the leases. I can also check the tank levels and see if they have increased since the 'Six-Mile Bar battle,' which will be an indicator that anyone's been taking loads from the tanks," I said like a veteran agent and then added, "What is the latest word on the location of Brian Dugan, Hawk Nose, Lyle Crowley, or the other guy you mentioned that we are looking for?"

"Brian was sighted near Pauls Valley two days ago, but that doesn't mean much. He could still easily be anywhere. With his psych profile, Drew, he will do as much damage as he can before he goes down, so be vigilant. You're pretty high on his hate list, you know."

Likewise, Myra, likewise. "Copy that, Myra, I am on it," I said.

"They picked up Keith High in Tulsa on Friday. No word on John Ballick or Lyle Crowley so far." She continued.

We finished lunch, and I walked her out to her LTD Crown Victoria, and as usual, I could not keep my eyes off her. "Make sure you check in with me after you make your run through the field tonight. I don't want to have to come looking for you," Myra said seriously.

I leaned in as close as I dared, and I said in a seductive effort to try to release some of the tension, "Well, perhaps I would like it if you came looking for me."

Her eyes blazed in fury. "Don't screw around now, Drew. I don't want either one of us dead. You got it? I need you to have it together on this." She opened the car door and climbed into the driver's seat, still fuming. She slammed the door hard, clearly suggesting she was not pleased with my comment. Then she rolled the window down and said in a gentler manner, "Just check in with me, OK? We are getting intel from almost every area except this one, and we need to see what's going on over here. You don't know what you're going to find out there, OK? And I really need your head in this game."

"Roger that, Myra, I'll let you know," I said humbly.

"And for piss' sake, Drew, *don't* go after any of those guys alone. If you do and they don't kill you, then I swear I will."

51

When I arrived at the A frame, I saw Rory Raymond and his girlfriend parked at Dave's place. The police crime scene barriers were gone, so it was now pretty much Rory's place. I walked over to say hello and see if they needed a hand with anything. It was after 9 p.m. before I finished talking with Rory, and I realized I still needed to make a field trip.

I loaded my beer cooler, more out of habit than anything else, and checked the three 9 mm clips to make sure they were full. I slammed one into the Glock and put a fresh box of fifty rounds in the glove box out of habit. I also plugged in Don Felder's "Heavy Metal" in my cassette deck as I headed out to make a tour of "our" field area. I saw the normal number of farmers and pumpers with their pull-behind trailers, even though it was late, and waved at them. Some waved back; some did not as had always been the case.

After my second beer, I stopped at one of the tanks that were on my normal run. It was nearly full, an indicator that no one had been pulling condensate from it since my last load. My second tank was the same way, and as I drove around listening to music and checking things out, a strange feeling came over me like an eerie déjà vu. Mark was dead, Dave was dead, Tony was indicted and in jail, Joe Reed was MIA but pretty much considered dead, Clay had been shot, Myra had been shot, ADA Jimmy had been shot, hell even I had taken a glancing round off the side of my head. My guts tightened a bit, and I drank a long swallow of beer to settle it. I reached over and turned on the FBI Nextel radio for a distraction.

It was relatively quiet on the radio. There was a tandem stakeout with two cars under way at an oil terminal south of Edmond. They were tracking the movement of crude oil tankers coming and going from the terminal. There were also three other agents interfacing with local LEOs on some stolen oil field property, but not much else was going on at the moment other than that.

I'll take a cruise over to the east plant leases and check out our tanker yard. It was the stakeout chatter that gave me the thought, but I thought it was a good idea from a prospective agent's perspective, and I went with it.

I parked at the tank yard, and the memories of my last visit there and the shooting contest with long, tall Joe came flooding back. I picked up the Glock and a target and walked out to his tree, placing the target at thirty-five feet, just like the last time we had practiced. *This is for you, Joe, wherever you are.*

I drew a bead on the bull's-eye and was about to squeeze off my pattern of three shots when something struck me as very odd. I looked around the trailer yard, the gate was closed, and the two crude oil tankers inside seemed fine. There were several tracks up and down the lease road when I drove in, but that was normal. I shrugged it off as emotional paranoia, set my sights back on the target again and eased into the trigger on the Glock.

Two trailers? What the piss? Last time I was here, there were three full trailers. No one should have been here since Joe went to Houston, and he hasn't come back. Nothing has gone on since the raid on Six-Mile. Where the hell is the other trailer?

I moved quickly to the tank yard gate to check it out. It was closed and locked. Just inside the gate, there were fresh tanker truck tire tracks running over week-old tracks, suggesting someone had driven a loaded tanker out of the yard recently. I opened the gate and scouted the yard. Long, tall Joe wore a size 14 boot, which you could not miss. I saw some of his older tracks, but I also noticed two sets of boot prints that were about size 9 to 10—and they were fresh.

I decided to contact Myra about this, and as I headed out the gate, I stopped as if hit by lightning. There on the ground right in the center of the fresh new tanker tire tracks, I saw two large drops of oil. I touched them both, and they were warmer than the night air. The trailer had left the yard within the last hour or close to it. As I was locking the gate, I got a second shock. On the inside edge of the road corner, just barely visible, was a wide Z grip pickup tire track. *Psycho Brian, the bastard.*

I locked the gate and headed to Queen's Gas Station, which was the closet pay phone, and tried to call Myra. No answer at hers, so I left a detailed message: "Myra, one of our crude oil tankers is missing from the east plant tank yard. Only Joe has authorization to move those tankers, and as you know, he has been missing for over ten days. I think it was stolen. And there are fresh oil drops in the tracks, suggesting it was stolen recently. This could be a hot one. And, Myra, I saw a clear wide Z grip tire track at the gate corner just like the ones Brian Dugan has."

I paged her the number of the pay phone and waited. While I was waiting, I decided to turn on the FBI Nextel again. It was basically the same chatter as before. I was about to grab another beer from the cooler when I heard the payphone ring. "Drew here," I said quietly when I answered.

"Hey, Drew, it's Myra. That's some message you left. Are you sure the oil drops you found are fresh?" she asked with mild exhilaration in her voice.

"Yeah, I am sure. The oil temperature was warmer than the night air, Myra," I said with confidence. "That tells me it recently came from a running engine."

"And the Z grip tire, are they for sure Brian Dugan's?" she asked a bit more anxiously.

Why does everyone always ask me if I am sure about those tracks? "Yeah, they are his tracks," I growled between my teeth.

Myra exhaled deeply and asked, "Do you happen to know the license plate number of the tanker by any chance?"

"Yeah, sure, it's Oklahoma plate OTC-011. The other two are 012 and 013. They are company tankers," I replied.

"OK, I am going to call it in now as a stolen vehicle. What are you doing now? What is your plan?" Myra asked again questioningly.

"No plan. It's already 1 a.m. I will probably check out a couple of more lease tanks and then call it a night."

"Drew, you're not going after that tanker, are you?" Myra asked with concern.

"Well, not that I am opposed to that at all. I want his ass, you know that, but hell, Myra, I wouldn't even know where to start looking. At best, it's been gone one to two hours, and it could be in Texas by now for all I know. I am just going to see what else I can find out here. I am to wound up to sleep right now anyway." That was what I said, and at the time, I meant it and was 100 percent truthful.

"Just be careful, and don't be stupid. Check back with me after you get to your place for the night. Great work, Drew," Myra said almost admiringly.

"Roger that. Copy."

I grabbed a beer from the cooler and opened the door to the Chevy. I had left the FBI radio on and could hear the droll banter of the two cars on the stakeout teams, obviously bored out of their minds. I steered the Chevy back out into the oil field area and drove a few of the lease roads while I thought about the stolen tanker.

It was now 3 a.m., and I was about to head home when I heard a local LEO announcement on the Nextel. "All units, be on the lookout for a crude oil tanker Oklahoma plate Ocean Tango Charlie 011. It's been reported stolen by an FBI agent and is suspected to be part of the oil theft ring crowd we have been dealing with lately, possibly connected to the Six-Mile raid. The vehicle is a priority, and consider any persons associated with it armed and extremely dangerous."

The radio suddenly came alive with several roger-thats and numerous conversations about all units checking in, FBI and ATF agents jumping online, and the Oklahoma State Patrol dispatch dedicating channel 12 just for the search of the stolen oil tanker.

That really got them going. Looks Like Myra has some stroke in this game.

I switched the radio to channel 12 and followed the chatter about the units checking in, stating which areas had been searched and which areas were confirmed clear with no tanker sighting. Without really realizing it, I had traveled another eight miles into the woods of the oil lease area, and I was about twenty miles from a main road when an excited state trooper's voice came on channel 12. "All units, oil tanker Ocean Tango Charlie 011 was located and refused to pull over. It is northbound on I-35 at a high rate of speed. The vehicle contains one driver and one passenger. We have two units in pursuit and expect the FBI to join in the chase at any moment. Pursuit just passed mile marker 157."

Well, psycho Brian, your stupid ass might be in for it now.

I kept driving along slowly, following the chatter and wondering if I should head to I-35. However, I had told Myra I would not chase them down.

"The tanker has taken Exit 40 and is now heading east on Sloan Road" came the update from state patrol dispatch.

Then five minutes later, an anxious voice announced, "Medical response needed at the corner of Sloan and Pine Needle Roads. Shots fired, officer down. Repeat, officer down. Tanker is now on oil lease road 17, heading north."

Officer down? Ah shit. I wonder if Leon Spencer is involved in this chase. Lease road 17, jeez, that's south of here about ten miles. Where is the truck going? Where is he going?

The chase continued as the tanker drove through the oil field back roads, getting farther into the hardwoods and away from the main highway. I did not know how much time had passed, but I could see the first gray light of the false dawn begin to appear on the horizon, signaling that a new day was coming. I saw the familiar outline of Skeleton Creek Bridge about a mile away, and the memories of Mark and Clay flooded in.

"Tanker is turning east on another lease road, smaller one. It's an unnamed gravel road but will eventually intersect Skeleton Creek Road, close to the bridge," said the voice from dispatch. "Any available units in that area, coordinate with FBI Agent Reardon if you're able to support the pursuit."

Intersect with Skeleton Creek Bridge? I know where he is, and I know right where he will come out to hit the bridge road. I told Myra I would not chase the tanker down, but *what if they come to me?*

I drove the mile to the bridge and parked my Chevy at the road pullout near the south end of the bridge. The false dawn gray had given way to a definitive orange glow now as sunrise was imminent in about thirty minutes. I grabbed my 8 × 32 binoculars and my Glock and put the two extra clips in my vest. I could hear the police sirens very faintly in the distance as I approached the intersection where the tanker would be connecting to the Skeleton Bridge Road. I walked up the road about fifty yards as the sirens became louder. I could hear the roar of the tanker's engine now and see a billowing dust trail in the distance moving rapidly in my direction.

The tanker came into view at about 200 yards away, and I checked out the driver with my binos. *Brian Dugan. Looks like Hawk Nose is riding shotgun.*

I moved the binos to my vest and pulled my Glock out and up into a shooting position. I could feel the warm rays from the rising morning sun at my back as I stepped in front of the oil tanker that was rolling hard straight at me, traveling at forty miles plus an hour. I pulled a target bead directly on his head. He saw me and recognized me, and even with the tanker moving that fast, I could see his face twist in a psychotic grimace of loathing and hate. He accelerated, thinking he was going to take me down and out with the full force of the big truck.

I waited.

The sun's brilliant rays flashed from behind me straight into the windshield of the oncoming truck. Then when he realized what was about to happen, when I saw his eyes open wide and wild with fear, it was then that I put two bullets straight through the windshield and into his sick brain. I saw the gray matter explode all over the rear window as his head slammed back against the seat like a gelatinous mass. He bounced forward with his arms flaying outward, causing the tanker to veer wildly out of control, turning over and sliding straight toward me, barely slowing down at all.

I leaped to one side but was hit hard in my right shoulder by the tanker side mirror, and it knocked me sprawling into the brush. I heard my shoulder crack and felt excruciating pain on my right side. I saw sparks spinning inside my head and could hear the sirens close now, almost on top of me. I thought I saw a state trooper's car skid to a stop just behind the tanker as I began to fade in and out of consciousness.

The passenger door of the tanker opened, and I saw Hawk Nose climb out of the cab. His face was bloody from several cuts, and he held an automatic pistol in his hand. He staggered over to me, his eyes wide in shock and fear. He saw me on the ground, and the fear was replaced with hatefulness and a desire to kill. He slowly raised his gun and took aim on me at point-blank range.

Isn't this ironic, don't you think? After all this, all that's happened, it's Hawk Nose that does me in.

I heard a gun fire three times but never felt the impact of a bullet. Instead, I saw Hawk Nose blown backward as he took three rounds in the chest. I was starting to fade to black from the pain, but I was able to turn my head just enough to see State Trooper Leon Spencer with his gun drawn and smoking. He was pointing it at the dying John Ballick.

I always liked you, Leon. I really did.

Now it was done. Dave Raymond and somehow long, tall Joe had been avenged, Dave at least by my hand.

I could see other state patrol troopers and FBI agents moving around now to support Leon, and I even heard Myra's voice approaching. I saw her dressed in a black T-shirt, flak jacket, and black jeans looking like, well, Myra. Just as the final blanket of unconsciousness covered me and before I faded completely to black, my final thoughts were about how good she looked.

52

I awoke sore as hell. I was ragged, way beyond torn up, hurting bad, and going to be no man's friend today, but it was done; that much I knew.

I saw an empty coffee cup near the chair sitting next to my bed. Next to the cup was a copy of the *Oklahoma City Herald*. I leaned over just enough to pick up the paper, ignoring the pangs of agony shooting through my shoulder. I noticed the lingering smell of perfume on the air near the chair as I rolled onto my back with the paper. It was hers and I knew she had been there.

The headline in the Oklahoma City Herald read Two KILLED IN SOUTH LOGAN COUNTY AS THEY FLEE FROM FEDERAL AGENTS. The story line read:

> Early Friday morning two Oklahoma men were killed by State Police and FBI agents after a lengthy vehicle chase leading through multiple counties. The men were wanted for questioning in the hijacking of several crude oil tankers in the Chickasaw oil fields East of Cimarron and the Elk City area. The chase began when State Troopers attempted to pull over a crude oil Tanker that had been reported as stolen. The men sped away in an effort to escape and were pursued by law enforcement for over an hour. The chase ended when the driver of the stolen tanker was shot dead causing the truck to tip over on an oil field lease road in South Logan County near Skeleton Creek Bridge. The passenger tried to continue on foot and fired at the police repeatedly. The Police then returned fire also killing the

second man. The men are believed to be part of a large crude oil theft organization that has been operating in Oklahoma, Texas, & Mexico for the past several years . . . names not yet released . . . ongoing investigation . . . FBI involved . . . local officials . . . potential cases worth over $18 million . . . Several indictments have already been served . . . connected to the recent FBI Raid leaving twenty-seven dead.

I closed my eyes as I let the story sink in and was daydreaming about all that had happened when my nurse came in. Her name was Donna. She was from Oklahoma City and a real cutie. She gave me a shot of Demerol and showed me how to work the morphine pump for the pain. She saw the paper on my lap, and we talked about the front-page story for a while.

After a few minutes, my shoulder pain had subsided substantially, and I was chatting quite comfortably with Ms. Donna when I noticed Myra standing at the door. She was wearing a very nice black pantsuit that fit her exquisite feline form perfectly. I could also see she had a shoulder holster with a concealed weapon under her jacket, which I found interesting. Donna excused herself and promised to check on me later as she left the room.

"How do you feel?" Myra asked.

I raised the morphine pump with the red button up and said with a sheepish grin, "Much better now. How's your leg coming along?"

"Good. I am back up to running about three miles at a stretch now, and most of the pain is gone," she replied.

"I'd love to see the scar sometime," I said devilishly as the morphine had fully kicked in now.

Myra laughed and pulled out a folder. "Can you move your fingers enough to sign some stuff? I have about a week's worth of paperwork to get done, and I need your John Hancock on several things."

"Yeah, no real problem from the elbow down. I should be able to sign stuff. Shoulder hurts like a bitch though. What do you need me to sign?" I asked.

"First, we need to start processing you for Glynco, which will take some time, and the marshals are not always thrilled to get an FBI agent shoved at them, so that may also slow some things down,"

Myra said and handed me a form and pen. I scratched out my name on the line as a stared at her leg and waist area. She did not seem to mind.

"Then we need to start your FBI fast-track-agent level clearance documents. Thanks to Jim, you're going to sail through without any issues. You will have three months of courses at Quantico starting in September or just about as soon as you can function and then a month of physical training. That should give you enough time for any needed physical therapy to get your shoulder 100 percent again, and then you're off to Glynco. After you're done there, you will be placed on assignment."

Is this really happening? Quantico? In September? Through my morphine-addled brain, something about that sounded vaguely familiar, but I could not quite place it. "What about you, Myra? If I am going to Quantico, where are you going? And where the hell will I be assigned to?" I asked, suddenly realizing I might not see Myra for a while, if ever again.

"Well, I am really not sure where I go next, Drew. Your background is the oil field and plant operations, and after your time at Glynco, you will be properly trained in firearms and shooting techniques, so I guess I would expect them to put you in an operation of that nature somewhere. Look, Drew, you're only 21, and you have already had one hell of a run. You'll be an FBI agent by the age of 22, which is pretty incredible, and best of all, you won't be going to federal prison. I don't think that's too bad of a deal all in all, do you?" she said with that Tigra smile as she handed me another document to sign.

We talked for a while longer about some of the case details until finally she gave me a hug and stood up to go. As she got to the door, she said, "I am sure I will see you around, Drew. It's been . . . real," she said.

"Thanks, Myra, you know where I will be at least for the next year or so any way," I replied. She stared at me for a moment and then winked and walked away.

Quantico, FBI, September—where had I heard that before? Then it hit me. *I needed to clear this Popsicle stand of a hospital, head down to the Rifleman, and catch up with Amy. Maybe we could ride to Virginia together. What was that song Leon Spencer always liked so well, an old Hoyt Axton song. What was that line? "I'd rather be a lover than a fighter of wars, to be from Oklahoma than the Nebular stars..."*

EPILOGUE

"Squeeze the trigger, yes, but don't take eons while squeezing it, or the perps are going to blow your ass away while you're practicing SEAL team slow-shooting sniper techniques," the big man in the US Marshals jacket told a class of trainees.

"The key is to get your trigger pull and travel at a minimum, so you can squeeze firm and fast but maintain accuracy. Hall, demonstrate the technique," Chief Instructor Art Savage barked at me.

I had completed my Glynco marksmanship training five weeks earlier but had been wrangled into sticking around for a while. Chief Instructor Savage was from Wyoming, and we had got on really well during the course. He had requested that I stay at the academy for two months to help train the next class of recruits. They were two instructors short, and I had scored high during the training. Since the FBI did not have an immediate assignment for me and the academy was going to pay for my expenses, the bureau agreed to let me instruct there temporarily in the interest of strengthening the relationship with the Marshals Service.

I had been able to catch up with Rifleman Amy at Quantico, which was a real pleasant surprise for both of us. We went through the initial phases of training together, and she performed excellently. I was on a fast track, though, so I was only there for four months, and she had to stay the entire six. We hung out together a lot and became good friends. As much as I would like to say we were friends with benefits and we saw many a sun come up, that was not the case. Amy was all business, and that was that.

"Hall, target slot 2. Demonstrate," Chief Art barked again.

257

There were three man-size waist-up targets lying down flat at distances of twenty-five, thirty-five, and forty-five yards respectively. All three popped up at once, and I drew my Glock and fired—three shots in the heart at the first target, three in a six-inch body group on the next, and then three in a ten-inch group on the last target. My time was 7.22 seconds. I had changed my shooting position three times.

I moved along the target slots to help the recruits with their shooting techniques and provide assistance as needed. Art was doing the same. I enjoyed being a shooting instructor, even if it was only temporary, and I was starting to settle in well.

We finished the session, and as I headed to the lockers, one of the academy administrators met me on the field. "Hey, Drew, you have a message," she said, handing me a note. It was from Myra. It had been almost a year since I had heard from her. "Meet me at the South Side Bar and Grill at seven tonight. I'll buy you dinner, and I have your next assignment."

Always nice to see Myra, but isn't that a bit strange that she should be the one telling me about my next, well, I guess my first real assignment as an agent? And what is she doing in Georgia?

I passed the information on to Art that I was meeting Myra and that she would be giving me an assignment. He said to meet him at the Fifth Street Bar afterward if it was not too late and let him know how things went.

I toyed with the idea of wearing a suit to dinner with Myra and then just grabbed my Night Rider brushpopper and my dark gray alligator El Rey boots and called it good. My blue back-cut boa El Reys had not seen much action since Oklahoma and the memories of Tumbleweeds and the Six-Mile Bar.

I saw Myra standing at the bar when I walked into South Side. She was wearing a short black dress and, as always, looked amazing. It was not the same black dress that I remembered the long cool woman from Oklahoma wearing, but she was smoking it, and she looked incredible. Her hair was feathered back very nicely in a different cut, and she was still a stunningly attractive woman.

I walked up to the bar, and she gave me a nice hug, which I over-returned in a clumsy effort to hold on to her as long as I could. She just rolled her eyes at me and smiled, and we ordered some drinks at the bar. "How have you been, Drew? It looks like things are going well here at Glynco. It's a rare occasion when an FBI agent is called on to assist the marshals. How did you pull that off?" she asked with a wink as her Chardonnay arrived.

"Chief Instructor Art Savage is from Wyoming, and we found a lot of common ground. We get on pretty good. They had an unexpected class of recruits and trainees coming in and were short of instructors. He asked. I agreed," I said matter-of-factly.

Myra raised her eyebrow at me as if the confidence of my answer surprised her, and then she sipped her drink and continued. "You scored well on most of your courses at Quantico. You blew your language aptitude exam, but we can work on that. You also need to focus on your global political scenario awareness education, but all in all, you did pretty good for a Rocky Mountain cowboy. At 22, you're one of the youngest agents ever to get into the bureau, and you did it without a college degree. Not bad, Drew, not bad at all." She raised her drink in salute, and I responded in kind as I stared at her. She was once again drawing me into that mysterious realm of Myra's magic web, where I would do just about anything for her.

"Do you have a passport by any chance?" she asked.

Oh, come on, you have all my files, birth certificates, educational documents and even know who I lost my virginity to. You know everything about me, including the fact that I don't have a passport. She must be going somewhere with this.

"No, I don't. But you already knew that," I said, now my turn to wink.

She opened a folder and handed me a passport application form already filled out, including the two required photos. "Sign here. You're going to need a passport for your next assignment," Myra said, handing me a pen.

"Passport? I thought the FBI only operated in the United States? The CIA covers the rest of the world," I stated questioningly.

Myra responded, moving her hair in that way that drove me wild, "Not entirely true. The CIA can't operate on US soil unless sanctioned by the FBI and has agents on the case. However, the FBI is invited, basically hired by several countries, to help gather intelligence and train their local agencies. We have agents in Mexico,

Dominican Republic, Argentina, Colombia, Chile. We even have 2,000 agents on support missions in the Middle East."

I finished signing the passport application, handed it back to her, and ordered another drink. "Interesting. Is that why you were on about the language aptitude thing? You want me to learn Spanish and head down south?" I asked with more cockiness than I intended.

She smiled and asked for some menus. "The marshals have a language division here at Glynco, and as you are here for two more weeks, I have enrolled you in a night crash course, so learn quick, and practice often. You're going to need to have a basic understanding of the language where you're going."

"Roger that. *Hablar Española un poco.* I used to play around with Spanish a bit with Joe Reed and some of the guys in Oklahoma. So where is my assignment? Is it Colombia? Maybe Argentina?" I asked curiously as visions of lovely Latina girls in bikinis began to dance in my head.

I always did have a thing for the Latinas. Maybe this won't be such a bad gig.

Myra looked at me with her Tigra eyes boldly and said, "Neither. You will be taking the Arabic course at the academy, and you're going to be assigned to Abu Dhabi, the capital city of the United Arab Emirates, in the Gulf."

I stared blankly back at her, waiting for the punch line that never came. She glanced at her menu and then looked at me again. She was serious. I was going to the UAE.

I think I am going to need a few more drinks before tonight is over and this all sinks in. At least the view is nice. Always great to see Myra.

THE END

Bonus Short Story

To the real Ad Five: Mike Bradley, Gerd Ortloff, Nick Cooper, Wild Will Kelly, and Andrew Howell

THE AD FIVE

Throughout the history of the known world and the unknown worlds (does anybody really know how long that is for certain?), definitely for the last 10,000 years anyway, there has always been one conspiracy theory that has maintained a semblance of consistency—the theory that a very powerful elite group of individuals runs the world for as long as civilized man has been recording its history. I have said individuals, not necessarily people or humans as we perceive them. The rise and fall of great civilizations, historical occurrences that effect global change, certainly all significant wars, technological developments that exceed our understanding yet continue to flood the world annually—all of these have been influenced somehow. A person is smart. Humanity, as a whole, tends to use far less than the average 5% of their Brain.

So there has to be more. If you review history in a rapid intelligence-gathering session, it only makes sense. There is more at work here than is written in our history books.

This theory that the world is being controlled by this select group will answer so many questions, explain the deepest mysteries of humanity's existence, and solve our most fascinating puzzles. Imagine the possibilities. Shall we step into this realm?

261

The knight was badly wounded, cut several times by the swords of the soldiers of Saladin before he slew them. He knew where he had to go, and he knew what he had to do, but this was his first venture into Portugal, and after being attacked twice, he was struggling to reach his goal.

The year was 1327. Fourteen years after the Templars' failed coup on the island of Cyprus. Their global mission to hide and protect their legendary treasures of gold jewels, untold wealth, and historical artifacts was now complete, but nothing in the secret, hidden vaults of these soon-to-be Free Masons could compare in value with what the soldier carried.

He could see the Rock of Gibraltar in the distance, and he knew his destination was close. He walked for another hour until he saw a narrow crevice winding its way back into a small cliff bank. *Could this be the place? It is in the correct location. I shall ask the all-knowing.*

He found a large cedar tree and sat down to rest in the shade. The smell of the cedar was pleasant, and a light, cool breeze had started to blow in from the Mediterranean. The knight drank the last of his water and reflected on the week.

He was a strong knight, much stronger than most men of the era, and he had lived for 145 years in a day and time when the average life span was about 45 years. This, in itself, gave rise to the fact that there was something very different about this knight—something universal.

He was exhausted from fatigue and loss of blood and began to drift off to sleep. He would have to wait for the moon to rise to its apex before he could confirm if this was, indeed, his final destination.

The knight awoke, his body stiff and sore from the recent fighting, and his head was pounding from dehydration and loss of blood. The moon was high in the night sky as he made his way slowly into the narrow crevice. He entered walking slowly backward, looking out toward the Mediterranean at the edge where the cliff sides met the starlit sky. Five steps and then turn, five steps and then turn. The crevice wound around and changed course often. In his physical condition, it was a difficult walk.

After thirty minutes, the knight saw the first sign, a two-feet-high ledge of what appeared to be natural rock blocking the pathway. He stepped deftly over the small wall, turned back to face the direction of the entrance to the crevice, and was continuing to walk backward when he saw the next sign—a moonlit white crucifix shining on the cliff wall about chest high. He traced the source of the moonlight back to a very small angular cross cut into the rock overhead. He returned to the white cross on the wall and examined the stone cliff.

There it was, a small stone lever just above ground level, directly below the cross. He pressed the lever, and a section of the rock slid open, revealing a one-foot-square chamber about two feet in length. The knight reached into his leather satchel and pulled out an object bound all in leather. He slowly unwrapped the leather to reveal a golden square that was warm to the touch. If you listened closely, you could hear a small humming noise from the object. It had several symbols on each side in a language the knight did not recognize.

He wrapped the golden square tightly in the leather again and placed it inside the chamber. He then filled the chamber with sand and small stones. He pressed the lever again, sliding the rock section back into place, and retreated from the crevice, erasing all evidence of his passage.

The knight stared at the stars for a brief moment and then walked for three hours before he began to get dizzy. He took his white Templar field shirt with the red cross, his king's sword, his daggers, and his light chain mail and buried them under a large rock. He walked for another hour until he found a second Cedar Tree. He lay down in the cool sand and rested until his life passed from him. It was the year 1327, and it would be 685 years before the square golden object left the chamber in the crevice to return to the world again.

Six hundred ninety years after the knight died underneath a cedar tree within sight of the Rock of Gibraltar, two men were in the Mood Indigo Bar at a hotel in Abu Dhabi having a pint and chatting as men would do in a pub. There were three pints at the table but only two men at the moment.

"The thing with solar power here in the UAE is that the sand eats away the protective film on the panels too quick and then starts damaging the conductors," said Nolan an international American who had been in the UAE for the last ten years. He was a bit of a mystery, and he seemed to know a little about everything and a whole lot about some things. He was from Oregon, and every now and then, he would let it slip that he had been either a bit of a renegade or at least somehow involved in some very interesting situations. He had also done a ten-year stint with the FBI and certainly knew the North American intelligence system and industrial processes very well.

"Those nuke plants west of Ruwais they are building will change the Middle East and the world forever if they ever get them licensed and up and running." Nolan continued, "I remember when they put the first nuke plants in Washington State, caused one hell of an uproar, but the entire Northwest never had any more power issues."

His colleague at the table was named Miles and was from the UK. It was no real secret what Miles did. He had recently retired after thirty-five years with MI5, although you would never know it. He was a big guy and was always the last man standing in a night out no matter how many pints he had. He was kind of quiet for a big guy but never seemed to miss a thing. "Same thing in the UK," Miles said. "Nuclear power changed Europe, and it's still changing."

The third man walked up and took a sip from his pint as he joined the table. He was another American from Colorado, a bit younger than the other two but no less experienced. He was a charismatic guy who claimed to work in oil and gas and was an aspiring writer. To most people, that was probably all they saw. To the experienced operator, however, he was something . . . much . . . different. He claimed to have a Navy background, and he sure talked a good game even if he had never served. If you were a student of history and in the know with intel, you might realize he was the spitting image of the Knight Templar who died under a cedar tree in Portugal in 1327, but most of you are not, and this is why so many missed the connection.

"What's Trump up to today, Drew?" Miles asked him chidingly. "Is he handing out shovels at the border to get the wall built?"

"You been chatting with Nolan for an hour. Why ask me how Trump is doing? Nolan probably knows more about the US political machine than I do. Why haven't you asked him?" Drew responded, semi-irritated.

"Because you're so much more fun to wind up." Nolan chuckled. "I don't get excited about it anymore."

The three men laughed and brushed the moment off as a fourth member arrived. He was German and a solid member of whatever this troupe was that was gathering at the bar. "Guinness?" Drew asked him with utmost respect. The German nodded and smiled as they all shook hands.

Nolan continued with his conversation about the developments of nuclear power in the UAE, but it was as if he were talking to a ghost audience. His eyes were moving quickly, and he was catching the side conversation between his fellow "American" and the German. "The submarine passed through two checkpoints this week and surfaced yesterday for a final battery recharge in the far western Pacific, north of Taiwan as planned. It should be ready to receive our signal in three hours," the German said quietly.

The younger American nodded, dropped his head for a moment, and then responded just as quietly, "My friend, I like this world. It intrigues me. Yes, I know the score, more than most about the regime, and I support them, but is this the right move? Is this the right time? Why now?"

"It has to happen. The Chinese are moving quietly behind the scenes to a strong position of amazing power. The Americans control everything but understand nothing. The Russians are forming for a big undersea move, and they don't even know what they are doing. They are just positioning for possibilities and will take full advantage of anything that comes. They are very dangerous. The Indians, the Australians are also very active under the sea. Even the Thais are developing submarine technology. It will happen very quickly. The Japanese, even now as we speak, are circling Ice Station Zebra in the Arctic. One of their new submarines in a fleet of three HDW 220s has two ICBMs that Dark Star cannot detect. They are nonnuclear. I do not know what their payload is or their mission, but I do know these boats. I helped build them all four years ago. One of them has the same technology as our boat. We must follow the plan and take out North Korea to balance this world again."

The German paused and sipped his beer. "Their leaders are not human. As you know, it is a Gargan stronghold. And well, my friend, frankly, how many times do you want this world to live through that again? You know what the Gargans can do. Caligula? Ivan the Terrible? Lyndon Baines Johnson? Wasn't Hitler enough? It's time we remove the Gargans from this world," said the German somberly.

"And you know I chose the newly renovated submarine from Venezuela for this critical mission because no one can track it. With the off-world technological upgrades from your people and the new DuPont coating, it is now untraceable. It is as it was, as it is now, and as it always shall be—the plan of the regime," the German added profoundly.

The young American hung his head again for a brief moment and then caught the eyes of Miles and Nolan. "I guess our options are indeed limited then. Shall we drink, amigos?" Drew said, raising his glass. Well, for whatever changing global events that were about to occur, the group certainly seemed to be united on one thing, and that was always another drink.

The Ad Five had been together for a while. Ah, but wait, it seemed we only had four gathered at the moment. Another member was destined to arrive.

Thirty minutes later, a boisterous young English lad arrived at the Mood Indigo Bar. He waved at the four gathered in their spot, clearly suggesting that he was one of the troupe, but before he joined them, he sat down with two prepaid Ethiopian girls and began to chat them up. He was a sex fiend with English manners, and he bought them drinks with sincere promises of a romantic rendezvous later. He was always sincere, just seldom serious.

He then made a round through the bar, saying hello to everyone, those he knew and those he did not. He seemed to be quite a social lad with nothing really unusual about him, until you looked closely. He was obviously of a high intellect that he tried to hide through juvenile antics. If you watched him close enough and often enough, you would see his eyes blink quite strangely—not so much alien or reptilian or psychopathic strange but more of a cosmic-aura, electrical-beam-passing-through-them strange.

As happy hour was drawing to a close, he joined the other four at the bar and said to the local bartender, "Can I have sixteen pints, five jaeger bombs, and seven shots of tequila on happy-hour price?" The proprietor and bar staff were somewhat stunned, but as this was not really all that unusual for the young English lad, they agreed and placed the order.

His name on the planet Earth was Wesley Kelly. In the galaxy of Andromeda, his family was called Entropies. Wesley William Kelly Entropies hugged and chatted with his four mates as men would do in a pub.

To all outward appearances, it was just another night in Abu Dhabi with mates having a bit of a drink. To the Israeli intelligence network, the Mossad, however, the gathering was a hugely significant event, and they were preparing accordingly. They had been watching the Ad Five for over a year and had their own contacts inside the regime. Also, the young American was not the only one connected to the Knights Templars from the 1300s. The Mossad had their own plans for tonight.

"So what's the Donald tweeting today, Drew?" Wesley asked.

"Well, he's not handing out shovels at the border yet?" Drew replied dryly, to which the other three laughed.

"Ah, he's just like you at darts, mate. Always changing the rules," Wesley said, laughing.

"If you hadn't been sniffing glue and paint thinners as a kid, maybe you could remember the dart rules, and I would not have to repeat them every five minutes," Drew replied. The conversation moved through a variation of subjects covering dart cheating, sheep shagging, which alien race introduced Velcro to the planet, strippers from Seattle in black Cadillacs, the best way to park an alien sky cruiser before uncloaking, and rats and vipers on submarines and then just expanded into normal bar banter.

Since Wesley seemed to be set up for the evening, the other four members ordered their pints for the night at happy-hour prices as well, and the alcohol flowed. To the astute observer who might possibly catch the significance of what was occurring, they might ask themselves, "Why? Why do these guys give a good god damn about how much you're paying for drinks when you have control of the world's destiny in your hands? And will this night's decision turn everything to shit again, or for once, will something work out right?"

The answer was simple. It was the one thing they all had in common—an enjoyment for socializing with colleagues and an appreciation for beers in a bar. That and the fact that they shared this brief, fleeting moment in their lives that was going to change a world. And with this global change, they may also be affecting the galaxy and possibly contributing to the beginning of the next intergalactic war. This was always the intent of the regime: to defeat the Gargans on all fronts, all galaxies. Earth was just a stepping stone.

Wesley was on his stage, chatting up his mates, the Ethiopian girls, the two lovely Ukrainian ladies who had just walked in, and any other ladies in the vicinity. He even found time to sit with the attractive, psychotic dark Nigerian girls, just chatting his mouth off as a deference technique to the uninitiated or anyone who would listen.

"And have you ever tried to park a Star Chaser 515 over your roof when the cloaking device is out?" Miles overheard Nolan asking Drew.

Nolan and Miles smiled at each other, and Miles reached for his cell phone. To the world, it appeared to be a cheap-ass 150-dirham local cell, which was exactly what Miles intended. In reality, it was one of the most sophisticated intergalactic communication devices on the planet. Nolan had a similar one, with just one key difference.

As mentioned, Miles was quite a big guy but quiet, only saying what needed to be said. He only joined the conversations sporadically and seemed quite content to listen, for you see, Miles was a skilled galactic communicator, and the skill of listening is often a lost art—something that, in MI5, Miles excelled at.

Miles watched the German and Nolan begin to reminisce about aviation aircraft, and the young American, Drew, joined in the discussion. He seemed to be totally in tune with military jets and naval aviation, all the *Top Gun* shit, while Nolan and the German obviously had a much better technical grasp on aviation overall, with Nolan having the edge on off-world fliers and fighters who would often be seen on Earth.

Miles smiled to himself. He was, for the moment, content. This last year had been surprising and rewarding, revealing much of the truth about the universe and this tiny planet's effect on it. Plus, he liked the Heineken pints. They were very good lager, better than the New Canaan mead of the lost world—well, in his opinion anyway.

His phone buzzed. It was the premiere commander of the regime. *Bloody hell*, he thought, *with everything going on in the universe tonight, he needs to check up on this punk-ass wee operation?*

He read the message from the regime commander, and he typed in his response: "The Ad Five are gathered, and the plan is moving FW. Final decision in two hours, terra firma time."

The response from the regime commander came clear and quick. "Good, but remember, the final decision has to be theirs. So it has always been, and so it shall always be. Influence it to our means if possible, but the future of terra firma is in the hands of the Ad Five."

"Roger that," Miles responded promptly as he knew the commander did not accept delay.

He sipped his pint and watched the other members of the Ad Five enjoy their night. He chuckled to himself.

Isn't this quite comical? In the end, with all the alien influence of the past 12,000 years, real or perceived, isn't it a bit ironic that it will be a colonial terra firma who sends the final approval?

Shutting his ego down, Miles accepted the fact that he would simply be communicating the final decision of the Ad Five to the regime and not making it. In the overall scheme of things, it may matter little; but to MI5 Miles, it was the culmination of a lifetime's work.

"The Columbia River has six full-length dams to control water flow and provide hydroelectric power to the Northwest. If you think about it, this really is quite a feat for the king and silver salmon to navigate through these spillways for 120 miles back up to the tributaries where they were first spawned," Nolan commented. "The electricity provided by the dams is a bonus. The real reason they are there is for the salmon and flood control."

"Not that much different than the southern natives of Sherra from Black Eye Galaxy on a pilgrimage," Drew said to no one in particular, and as he was speaking to no one in particular, no one paid any attention to the comment.

Nolan seemed to be rambling abstract to the bar crowd, as was his nature, but his eyes were keen, always watching the entire bar, never missing anything. Late in the evening, he would sometimes let his guard down just a bit because everyone was drunk or near drunk. On a rare occasion, if you watched closely, you would see his eyes blink sideways now and again like a reptile's, instead of up and down like a human.

MI5 Miles had tried to kill Nolan six years earlier when he recognized the reptilian features and behavior and incorrectly classified him as a Gargan. He could not have been more wrong. While Nolan had been born on Earth, he was not of Earth. While they may call him Nolan in the bar, in his ancestral home world in the Triangulum Galaxy, his family had been the sworn enemy of the Gargans for uncountable millennia. They were the Raz'ak Kar, and Nolan was their prince with an Oregon accent and deep-seated reptilian features.

On the other side of the world, a newly refitted submarine prepared to breach the surface at the same time the Ad Five were sharing spirits and conversations in the UAE. There was no real mission need to surface the boat; it was simply the desire of the Venezuelan captain to take a look at the skyline of Niigata, Japan. The skyline was quite beautiful, and the lights were brilliant. He checked out the shoreline with his 26 × 100 digital binoculars as he stood on the conning tower platform. He saw a news helicopter circling the city. He saw the lights from the Niigata University complex shining like diamonds.

As he watched the city, he wondered, *Will these lights go out soon, or will they be safe? Does the regime really know what it is doing? North Korea might be the target, but what if something goes wrong?*

The boat was a modified HDW class 212 A built in Kiel by Thyssenkrupp five years earlier. Its normal advanced systems, the air-independent propulsion, and the fuel cell plant had been enhanced with off-world technology at a secret underwater submarine development center near the coast of Caracas, Venezuela. The Guinness-drinking German member of the Ad Five had been in charge of the refit operation in coordination with a race from the Black Eye Galaxy, the Sherra. Yes, it was the same Sherra that Drew had mumbled about in the bar five minutes before.

The German reflected on the high-tech submarine and pondered the future. He had spent his lifetime working on submarines, and few others in the world could match his experience and capability. This was not his first high-tech sub refit using off-world technology by any stretch. He had supervised six others as well, but if everything did not go exactly as planned, it might be his last.

Wesley's eyes began to flash in white-and-red blips like a Zylon robot, and he realized he was badly in need of a discharge. He politely excused himself from the two lovely Ukrainian ladies he was sitting with and headed to the men's room for a much-needed discharge. *Good, no one is in here. I hate it when I have to mesmerize people in the toilet, and I sure can't make it back to the room in time to let this out.*

He closed the bathroom stall door just as Simon, one of the local patrons, staggered in to relieve himself at the single urinal. As Simon was doing his thing, Wesley began his discharge in the stall. Suddenly, bright lights of white, blue, red, and amber began to flash from within the bathroom stall and dominate the walls of the toilet. A low, humming sound emanated from Wesley's stall as sparks and the smell of electrical burning poured out of the stall.

Simon pissed all over himself in shock and turned to see what was happening. The lights flashed brighter and faster, spinning. The sparks crackled like seeping electrical power and then just stopped. Simon suddenly decided that he may have had enough to drink for this night, and pissy hands or not, he quickly left the toilet and headed for his room.

Wesley washed up and doused himself with some eau de parfum to clear any burned smell before returning to the bar. This time, he joined the rest of the Ad Five. He was animated and appeared to be happy. The conversation flowed as the men enjoyed their drink for another hour.

As if from some unspoken signal, the men gathered closely, and MI5 Miles began to speak. As mentioned, he did not speak often, so the other members of the Ad Five listened closely. "Gents, it is time to decide. Is there anything we need to discuss before taking the vote?"

"Do I have time for a quick shag?" Wesley said, only half joking as he glanced back at the Ukrainian ladies.

Each of the men met the eyes of the others for a full minute, but no more words were exchanged. "It must be done as planned," the German said softly. The American with the blood of Sherra nodded. Wesley's eyes turned a bright white for just an instant, and the reptilian Raz'ak Kar prince with the Oregon accent also nodded.

"So we are all in agreement then?" MI5 Miles sought to confirm.

"What happens if the signal goes too far outside Korea? The golden box has never been opened. Do we trust the regime that its range is limited to that region as they say?" Wesley burst out suddenly.

"The research is sound, my friend. The Golden Square contains limited energy, and it is exhaustible. It will have a limit. We may not know the exact range, but you would need multiple power sources of this nature to extend the signal or triangulate it for mass effect," the German said quietly, trying to reassure.

After another moment of silence, MI5 Miles asked for a second time, "So are we in agreement then?" The men nodded in unison.

MI5 Miles reached for his phone and sent the text to the regime commander. "The Ad Five are in agreement. It is affirmative. I repeat, it is affirmative."

From a galaxy light-years away, the regime commander received the message and barked an order. "Bring up visual on screen 7. Target 1T1 on Terra 601 stat."

The HDW 212 submarine sitting off the coast of japan carried the small Golden Square that the Knight Templar from the planet Sherra had given his life to hide 690 years ago. The Golden Square contained a powerful alien energy source that would create a massive and sustainable electromagnetic pulse (EMP). This was something the Ad Five were quite familiar with, and they had worked for years to coordinate this EMP attack on North Korea to make the remaining Gargans on Earth vulnerable to the regime.

The Venezuelan captain received his orders from the stars and set things in motion to carry them out. He would release the EMP into North Korea in the next sixty seconds, forever changing the world. He had been involved in making the plan and was an ardent enemy of the Gargans. However, neither he nor the Ad Five had any idea of the extent that this world was about to change.

The HDW 212 submarine and the previously mentioned Japanese HDW 220 were not the only high-tech submarines on a global mission this evening. A smaller but no less deadly Israeli HDW was approaching the French coastline on the same route as the US Marines did on D-day in 1944. In fact, the sub was just now within two kilometers of the historic Omaha Beach site.

The Israeli boat captain intercepted the message to the stars from MI5 Miles and set his own plan in motion. He signaled his crew, and they carefully loaded a small triangular blue object into the payload section of a medium-range ICBM. The object had strange symbols on all four sides and was vibrating slightly and glowing. You could hear it humming if you were close enough.

"Arm the missile to explode at an altitude of 6,200 meters," the Captain ordered.

His crew complied and then closed the inner doors, opened the outer deck tubes, and looked at their captain. "Send the message to the world," the captain said solemnly. The smaller HDW submarine vibrated as the missile went skyward.

The HDW 220 might have been classified as Japanese, but its crew was multinational; actually, multigalactic would be more accurate. The boat had traveled around the Arctic Circle, as the German had suspected, and was parked in the Laptev Sea off the coast of northeastern Russia. The captain had surfaced the boat and was watching the lights of the Russian city Tiksi through his digital binoculars. He did not need to intercept any message or make any assumptions. He knew he would be receiving his orders directly from the highest authority.

He retreated down the conning tower and went to the deck missile tube area. He watched a small circular glowing green object with strange symbols on all sides being placed into the payload section of a medium-range ICBM. If you stood close enough, you could feel it vibrating and hear it humming. "Arm the warhead to activate at 7,700 meters altitude," he ordered.

The missile was sealed up, and the captain returned to the control room. "Sir, I have received the launch codes from the Galactic Command and direction to launch in thirty seconds," a crew member who was managing the telecoms informed the captain.

"Load the codes, and launch on my mark," the captain said as his eyes flashed with eerie bright white-and-red Zylon robot lights that reflected off the steel walls in the control room.

The Ad Five all had fresh beers and seemed relieved that the decision had been made. They asked the bartender to turn on the world news while they continued their conversations. They were in mid-chat when MI5 Miles got a text on his superpowered, low-profile telecom device. Suddenly turning to the German, he asked anxiously, "Did you know the HDW 220 boat the *Midnight Sun* was making the turn around the Arctic Circle?"

The German's face paled. "I knew there was a boat from Japan up there. But I had no idea it was the *Midnight Sun*," he replied firmly. "That boat is *not* under the control of the Japanese. My friends, I think something is amiss, and our plan may not work as we expect."

"Or we were just part of a bigger plan, pawns used to set something else in motion. I had a very strange interstellar message this morning from an old friend telling me to leave the Earth today. He was drunk. I ignored it. Damn it," Nolan said as he slammed his fist into his palm. "It's always the same, plans within plans, deals within deals."

The German's cell phone buzzed from an incoming text. He read the message, and he turned to Drew solemnly. "It seems the Golden Square your ancestor hid in Portugal is not the only object of its kind on Earth. Missile launch codes have been initiated from the *Midnight Sun* HDW 220 submarine, which is under intergalactic control. The warhead is a small medium-range nonnuclear set to detonate at 7,700 feet, according to the codes. If its payload also has an EMP, then the elevated signal at that altitude could hit the Western world, possibly severing all power, all communications, all technology," said the German as his voice drifted off.

MI5 Miles got another incoming text on his cell phone, and he looked at the rest of the Ad Five. "Communication from an Israeli sub, same thing, confirmation of the launch of a midrange, non-nuke ICBM set to detonate at 6,200 meters over Europe. Could there be a third EMP?" MI5 Miles said.

"If there are three, then they will now be triangulated, and this is the worst possible scenario. It could cover 75 to 90 percent of the globe with an EMP," the German replied.

"Damn, I knew I should have went for that shag," said Wesley as small flecks of white light began to flash back and forth across his eyes.

"Is this a Gargan counterattack or some kind of defense response?" Drew said quietly. "This makes no sense. Who is behind this? Who would want to take out the entire globe?"

The German chuckled dryly. "It is as it was, as it is now, and as it always shall be—the plan of the regime."

The electrical power in the bar suddenly went out, causing the girls to scream, and minor chaos ensued in the near-pitch-black environment. The only thing visible was Wesley's eyes flashing like Zylon robots.

Nolan pulled out his cell phone, which was fully functioning to the surprise of the other Ad Five members. "What?" Nolan shrugged to his colleagues matter-of-factly as he dialed. "It's EMP protected." He spoke quickly into the phone in a language none of them recognized. He completed the call and said, "C'mon to the pool on the fifth floor—now."

The Ad Five scrambled up the stairs, counterflowing against the screaming surge of panicking people headed downstairs, until they broke out on the open-air fifth floor. They watched the events in the streets from their perch on that level. The chaos became elevated as people realized their cell phones were out, and they began to rush from the bar and scramble for the hotel exit. The chaos in the hotel, however, was nothing compared with what was going on outside as people poured into the streets by the thousands, screaming, pushing, and fighting.

An ambient airship suddenly appeared uncloaked and hovering above the fifth-floor pool. It was a Raz'ak Kar ship which had an organic, living power source, so it was not affected by the EMP. The Ad Five climbed on board, and the little ship jetted off to a Raz'ak Kar stronghold in the foothills of southeastern Turkmenistan.

It was less than ten minutes after the ship flew out of sight that the first large store window in Abu Dhabi was smashed, and it was only ten minutes after that groups of men began to drag women and children into the backstreets. The screams from the women were horrific, the cries of the children bloodcurdling.

How fragile is the human mental condition? Are we barely held in check by a fleeting semblance of civilization? If the restraints of civilization are removed, will this always be the result? If it can happen in twenty minutes . . .

Thus began the global anarchy of 2017, which eventually led to Intergalactic Conflict III.

The regime commander stood near screen 7 watching all this unfold. He turned his attention to screens 8, 9, and 10 also and watched the power go out around the world. There seemed to be one little section of about 500 square miles in northern Canada, Ontario possibly, that had not been affected for some reason. The commander seemed deeply concerned about the turn of events on Earth and was lost in thought.

"Sir, is there anything wrong, sir?" his top aide asked him.

He turned and headed toward the command center exit.

"Sir, is anything wrong? Can I get you anything, sir?" the aide tried again.

The commander paused at the doorway and turned to face the aide. "I am going to my quarters," he said firmly.

"Quarters, sir? Are you sure there is nothing wrong?" the aide inquired for a third time.

"I am going to celebrate with some Targillian brandy. Everything is perfect and according to plan."

About The Author

Andrew was born in the mountains of Colorado, where much of his family still lives. While spending his early years traveling the globe as a Navy brat, he eventually returned to the Western United States and began a career in oil field construction, where he had spent over thirty years as a health and safety manager. This life experience once again took him around the world to exotic work locations like Colombia, Chile, Peru, Turkmenistan, Dubai, Saudi Arabia, Iraq, and Egypt.

He had a background rooted firmly in the gun-smoke-and-roughneck-style oil culture of the mid-1980s, which he was able to shape into a well-written fictional tale of the wild life in the oil field towns that was often led by the men and women who worked in this rugged industry. Add the FBI, the mysterious El Patron, and the long cool woman in a black dress, and the story takes off into a highly entertaining read.

Andrew currently lives in Monteria Colombia and has been writing for most of his life. In addition to *Duster*, he has published three books in the fiction genre. He is a founding member of the Inner Circle of Creative Writers (ICOCW) in Abu Dhabi, UAE, while working full time in the engineering and construction field. He has also added a teaser short story from another genre as a bonus at the book's end.

Preview

My first introduction to the Federal Bureau of Investigation was outside Green River, Wyoming. I was working for an outfit named Sundown Construction, and the boys on the crew and I became quite fond of the Gordon Lightfoot song of the same name ("Sundown"). In the bars at night, you would often see us chatting with one another, eyeing up local ladies or rowdies, and we would wink and sing softly to the words of old Gordon. "Sundown, you better take care if I find you been creeping round my back stairs."

The card game was fairly high stakes, with invitation-only players in attendance. There were about $10,000 showing round the table, and I was getting good cards. I had caught the eye of a sweet brunette called Brandi (and yes, she was a fine girl), and I knew it was going to be a good night.

What I did not know was that three of the other six people sitting at the table were high on the FBI's Wyoming most wanted list. I mean, seriously, how would I know this? I never went to the post office and never saw the wanted posters. FBI's most wanted? C'mon, really? That was Hollywood crap.

In those days, I never thought about carrying a gun. I always wore boots, and I had a pristine double-edged Arkansas toothpick with a six-inch blade tucked very nicely in a slight sheath attached to my right boot. It was mainly for show, but the ladies liked it.

It was rare that I was involved in one-on-one disputes or fisticuffs. I was just a popular guy and usually talked my way around issues. Most of my troubles came in big chunks when ten to twenty guys would go at it, and I just happened to be in the vicinity. In these cases, I would usually grab the drunkest guy I could find and swing him around in front of me until the cops came, or the fight otherwise broke up. I learned that this was not an uncommon way to get a solid reputation as a brawling badass without ever really having to brawl or be a badass.

Had I known how my attendance at this card game with the FBI's most wanted gents would eventually affect my life, I truly believe I might have just walked away. However, if I did that, I would have missed out on Ms. Brandi; and even knowing what I knew now, she was worth it.

Just after midnight, the mood at the table became a bit serious as the game drew to a close. I had just won a pot of about $1,800 and really pissed off a guy with a ponytail who was wearing John Lennon specs, boots, and a bright blue button-up shirt. He was giving me the bad eye when the place suddenly exploded. Two doors were kicked open, and the place was raided by half a dozen feds. The agent-in-charge (AIC) lead guy was wearing shades, even though it was midnight, when he busted in. They were joined by some Bureau of Alcohol, Tobacco, and Firearms (ATF) guys and some local LEOs.

As the chaos ensued around the room, the AIC shades man started grabbing guys and slamming them around. I was able to grab most of my cash and shove it over to Brandi, who had suddenly materialized next to me. She stuffed it in her shirt and was gone like a ghost. Several fights broke out, and I grabbed a really drunk guy from Cheyenne and started my brawler dance, keeping him between me and the feds.

Then all hell broke loose. The drunk Cheyenne guy pulled out a .45 Colt automatic from his waistband and slammed me upside the head, gashing my temple something fierce. Then he leveled his piece at one of the players from the table and pumped three rounds into him. The FBI AIC shot the Cheyenne guy, and I heard reports from at least three other guns, including one booming blast from the firearm of Randall Pederson, a big lean Wyoming state trooper who was blazing away with a .44 Mag.

I dropped to the ground and tried to find some kind of cover. I was in good company as there were several guys and gals trying to do the same thing. There must have been over a dozen shots fired, and it was, without question, the most intense life scene I had ever been involved in. When the shooting stopped, I saw at least six bodies on the ground oozing blood and not moving.

One of the bodies wore an Absaroka County deputy sheriff's uniform. A second body was of the guy sitting across from me at the table, and then there was the drunk Cheyenne guy, also dead as a road-killed cat. I could smell the acrid copper odor of blood and see pools of red mixed up in the sawdust on the floor. Gun smoke hung heavily in the air, and my ears were ringing like a brass band from all the shooting.

After the ER teams hauled away the dead and wounded, the feds carted about ten of us off to the local jail for sorting. I was given the third degree by the AIC shades guy and a couple of his cronies, but I could tell their hearts just weren't in it. I didn't have a clue what was going on and no idea what they were after, and they knew it. They did their best, though, to try not to show me that they knew I did not know. I was beginning to think I was being used as some kind of interrogation training tactical dummy for some junior agents to practice on. After an hour, I was taken back into the holding cell with the rest of them.

After three hours, I was bailed out by my soon-to-be favorite Wyoming cowgirl, Ms. Brandi.

CPSIA information can be obtained
at www.ICGtesting.com
Printed in the USA
BVHW03*1423060718
520865BV00012B/25/P